REAPER AND RUIN

SAINT VIEW MURDER SQUAD
BOOK 3

ELLE THORPE

WWW.ELLETHORPE.COM

VI

For Trystin Reed Melville, who fought bravely, outwitted the masses, and emerged victorious in the battle for this dedication.

Legends will speak her name (probably)...or maybe it'll just be X outside her window.

1

WHIP

I fucking hated heights.

Not in the way Levi hated small spaces; he had a real reason for being claustrophobic after being locked in a prison cell for six years.

I just hated them because staring over the edge of the Saint View bluffs churned my stomach and tightened my chest.

So jumping off them wasn't exactly on my bucket list.

Then again, watching X plummet off the edge, into the inky blackness of the swirling sea below, hadn't been on my to-do either.

The explosion that had disintegrated the edge of the cliff face still rang painfully in my ears. The rain from the storm pelted my face in sharp, stinging bites, drenching my skin and clothes.

But it was Violet's screams that X couldn't swim that drowned out all of it.

And the entire reason I threw myself off the edge after him.

I hit water as hard as concrete, the force slamming up through my feet and legs, vibrating through the rest of my body in a bone-jarring thud I would be feeling for days.

But then the waves rushed over my head.

Freezing cold.

Pitch-black.

Utterly terrifying.

Panic threatened to rush in but was quickly shoved away by the thought X was down here somewhere too, and unlike me, he couldn't fucking swim.

So instead of succumbing to the cold shock and sinking deeper, I kicked out hard, and then again, over and over until I broke the surface.

I gasped, sucking in air, fighting the choppy waves threatening to smack me in the face.

"X!" Levi shouted from somewhere beside me.

I hadn't even realized he'd jumped as well.

"Levi!" I shouted. "Violet—"

"She didn't jump!"

Relief flooded me, but it was short-lived.

Because even if Violet wasn't down here, X was. "X!"

My clothes weighed me down, the pull of the sea threatening with every wave.

But no way was I giving in to it.

I kicked off my shoes, instantly losing them to the bottom of the ocean, and pushed myself in circles, scanning the water for any sight of him.

Guilt clutched at me. I'd been so fucking mad at him. He'd left Levi and me stranded out in the middle of nowhere, with a pile of dead bodies, when Violet had needed us.

But now it was his stupid ass that needed saving.

If the idiot drowned and broke Violet's heart, I would seriously kill him all over again. She'd already lost enough people.

I ignored the voice in my head that whispered if he drowned, it wouldn't just be Violet's grief I'd be dealing with.

It would be my own too.

For all X pissed me off and drove me mad, I apparently loved the idiot.

Or at least liked him enough to not want to see him dead. "X!"

"Whip!"

I closed my eyes for the briefest of seconds, because X's gasping voice had never sounded so good. He was nearby, and I squinted through the darkness, Levi at my side doing the same.

"There!" I caught sight of X's flailing hand before he sank under the waves. Not waiting for Levi, I swam with sure, strong strokes, gaze fixed on the spot I'd last seen X, mentally praying for his head to pop back up and assure me I was on the right track.

The waves came from all directions, whipped up by the wind and the rain. The dark storm clouds blocked most of the moonlight, making it impossible to see much, but I held my breath, waiting and silently urging for him to pop back up. "X!"

All that surfaced were his fingers.

But it was enough.

I desperately dove for him, plunging beneath the water, frantically feeling around, my heart pounding when I couldn't get a grip on anything but the freezing water. The seconds ticked by, a roar in my head, each one screaming he'd been under too long, and that if he died, it would be on me.

My hand hit something solid, and on instinct more than thought, my fingers clenched around it.

His head broke the surface, and he gasped for air. "Took you long enough!"

I blinked, kicking hard to keep both of us afloat. "What?"

I was fully sure I was hallucinating. Hell, maybe I'd swallowed too much seawater and it was me who was drowning.

"Took you long enough!" He grasped at me, yanking me in closer with his panicked, clawing fingers. He pushed me beneath the swirling water, trying to keep himself afloat.

I kicked away from him, enough that I could get up and get another breath while still keeping my grip on his arm. I broke the surface only for him to shove me beneath the water again in his panic.

When I got back up, I spluttered, heaving in water-laced breaths. "X! You idiot! You're drowning me! Just chill the fuck out!"

But he thrashed about in the water, dragging me under, over and over again. He held on to my shoulders like I was his damn island while I fought uselessly to keep us both afloat.

"I am a land-dwelling creature, Whip! I am not made for the sea!"

We were both going to be made for a watery fucking grave if he didn't stop drowning me.

"I'm Rose, not Jack! Let me on the door!"

I took in another mouthful of water and mentally planned all the ways I would kill him and his *Titanic* references once I saved him.

"Levi!" I bellowed the next time I managed to get my head above water.

As if I'd summoned him from the depths of Hell, Levi appeared out of the darkness. "X! Stop! You're not fucking drowning anymore, you're killing him!"

He wasn't wrong. I was struggling. My energy rapidly depleted in the cold water. I coughed and spluttered, trying to untangle myself from X's grip.

If I didn't get away from him, Levi was going to be saving us both.

But X couldn't stop. He flailed and fought to keep hold of me, his survival instinct outweighing everything else. He gulped air wide-eyed, like he'd never see the sky again.

I went under once more, my curses turning to silence beneath the water.

Fuck this.

The next time I managed to break the surface was just in time to see Levi grappling with X. They wrestled, Levi swinging punches at X in an attempt to get him to let go of me, but none of them landing well because he couldn't get any momentum while treading water. His shouts rang in my ears, but I was too waterlogged to make sense of them while I fought to save my own damn life.

I was *so* fucking glad I'd jumped off that cliff. Drowning was *such* a pleasant way to go out.

Water poured into my mouth again as Levi fisted X's shirt and slammed his forehead into X's face.

There was a groan of pain, and X finally went limp.

"Holy shit," I gasped, finally able to kick away enough that X couldn't try drowning me again. "Did you just headbutt him?"

"Yeah."

X floated between us now, heavy and limp, water lapping at his slack jaw.

I squinted at him, wary. "Did you knock him out?"

Levi shook his head, hooking his arm around X's and keeping his head out of the water. "I don't know. But that was my intention."

I grabbed X's other arm.

We both kicked for the shore, dragging a limp and bleeding X along with us.

"Next time," Levi muttered, "he's wearing floaties."

"Next time"—I shook my head, straining my way through the water, coughing up lungs full of liquid—"we let the fish have him."

2

VIOLET

*I*n the darkness, the rocky path that led down to the beach was treacherous.

I slipped and stumbled on loose, wet rocks, praying the entire time the explosion hadn't weakened this part of the cliff face as well. I knew hikers used this path, but I never had, preferring to take in the beach by hopping off the bus in the parking lot and setting up my towel by the lifeguard's tower. Getting a drink from the café. Applying some sunscreen and lying out on the sand to read my smutty book...

Like a normal freaking person.

This path from the bluffs felt like a surefire way to fall and break my neck. I'd watched people walk it from my vantage point on the sand, a cold drink in hand, and wondered why on earth they picked that option when they could have just...not.

Because this hiking business was not fun. Not in the least.

But I supposed most people didn't try it in the dark.

In a storm. And most people weren't running down the barely visible track as fast as they could because the three men they loved were drowning in the ocean at the bottom of it.

The physical act of keeping myself from tripping and snowballing down the cliff face was the only thing stopping me from screaming. The terror inside me built with every step, only eased by the sharp breaths my lungs forced me to take.

My ankles twisted.

I fell more than once but hauled myself back up and kept going, knowing that whatever pain I was in, those three men were in a lot more.

Tears streamed down my face and I silently begged them all to live.

It felt like a lifetime before the ground beneath my feet changed from rocky dirt and gravel to sand.

I dragged myself along it, hair and clothes soaked and plastered to my face and body. Hot and sweaty, despite the rain that still came down in sheets.

I ran to the edge of the water, scanning it desperately for any sign of life.

"X!" The dark waves smashed against the edge of the sand, black and inky as the night. "Levi! Whip!"

"Here, sweetheart," Whip's voice came back through the darkness.

I burst into tears at the sight of the shadowed figures crawling out of the ocean. I rushed forward into the frigid water to meet them, my gaze running over first Whip and then Levi, looking them over, making sure they were okay.

They were both on their feet, drenched and shivering but whole and well.

X's feet trailed along the sand between them, his head hanging limp.

"Oh my God! Is he okay? X!"

They hauled him up onto the beach, lying him out on his back. I dropped to the wet sand at his side and pressed my fingers frantically against his neck, checking for a pulse. I found one easily then bent down, lowering my ear toward his chest to make sure he was still breathing.

Relief crashed over me at the rise and fall of his chest, and I rolled him over onto his side, in case he had water in his lungs that needed to come up.

Levi and Whip had both crashed to the sand, the two of them exhausted from swimming in clothes and shoes and tugging a fully grown man back to shore. I wanted to check on them too, but X was in much worse shape.

"I don't understand. Why isn't he responding? He's got a pulse and he's breathing..."

"Levi knocked him out."

I widened my eyes. "You what? Why?" And then a second later I added, "How?"

Levi shook his head, then winced, like the movement caused him pain. "Just know it was a lifesaving measure."

I didn't really know what that meant, but at the same time, X's body convulsed violently, and he coughed up a spout of ocean water.

I thumped him on the back, even though I wasn't at all sure that's what you were supposed to do for someone whose lungs might be full of water. But I didn't know how else to help.

Eventually he groaned, and I helped him roll onto his back again. I hovered over him, taking out my phone and switching on the flashlight so I could see better.

He was vaguely gray, his lips a bluish purple that concerned me.

"I'm calling an ambulance."

But X shook his head and reached up, stroking a hand down the side of my face adoringly. "I'm already dead. Too late for that."

I couldn't help the flicker of a laugh that crossed my lips. "You aren't dead."

He blinked. "But this is Heaven."

Whip snorted from a few yards down the beach. "If this is Heaven then I'm pretty glad I'm going to Hell. Because this sucks."

Levi pulled a piece of seaweed out of his hair as if to prove the point.

X struggled to lift himself up onto his elbows and I helped him. He moved his arms and legs and got himself up to sit, testing they all still worked. Apart from one side of his face swelling and some bleeding cuts and grazes, he seemed to be in one piece.

He really was staring at me like I was an angel who'd fallen from Heaven though.

"Omelet," he whispered, though a whisper with X was never really all that soft. "I'm alive."

The laugh I let out was tinged with a sob of relief. "Yes, you are. Thanks to Whip and Levi."

X held his hands up in front of his face, wriggling his fingers and staring at them in amazement like he'd never seen them before. He scrambled up onto his feet, and Levi stood just as quickly, catching him by the arm when he stumbled. But the off-balance wobble didn't deter X any. He flipped his middle finger up and shouted into the dark night, his words all aimed at the whirling ocean. "Stop trying to kill me, already!"

"Technically a pool tried to kill you the first time," I murmured.

He frowned at me. "Omelet! Whose side are you on? Mine or the water's?"

"Definitely yours," I assured him.

He nodded, satisfied with that answer.

Whip pushed up to his feet wearily. "Well, as fun as this has been, can we get the hell out of here before the cops show up? That explosion might have been written off as thunder, but it's only a matter of time before the sun comes up and people start noticing there's a whole chunk missing from the side of the cliff face. And I don't think we need any more attention coming our way."

I agreed and got myself beneath X's arm, even though he was supporting his weight just fine by himself. I just needed to be near him, to have the reassurance of his arm around me.

Whip coughed pathetically, and I reached my free arm out to him, but he just squeezed my fingers as he passed, leading the way back up the path I'd come down. Levi fell into step beside him, his arm jerking every time Whip stumbled, like Levi was just waiting to catch him.

I eyed the two of them from behind, worry for and gratitude to both of them filling me all at once. But X's mouth clearly hadn't been damaged in his fall, and it was running at a million miles an hour.

"Isn't this beautiful?" he asked. "What a wonderful night."

I squinted through the rain. "It's pouring. It's freezing. We're all soaking wet, and you nearly drowned."

"But I didn't! Twice now I have been brought back from the dead! I'm like Jesus, Violet."

"Maybe those bobblehead Jesuses they sell at the gas station for your car dashboard," Levi muttered from a few steps ahead of us.

X ignored him. "I have risen from the dead!"

"More like lugged from the ocean with sand in your ass crack," Whip countered. "And the only thing rising is my blood pressure."

X acted like they hadn't even spoken. "Look at the stars. They're so bright! Feel the wind on your skin!"

"I feel it," I agreed. "It's freezing and miserable. Can we just get back to your van?"

X turned on me, clutching my upper arms tight in his fingers. "It's a miracle."

Levi sighed. "The only miracle is that Whip hasn't killed you yet."

But nobody was putting a dampener on X's apparent new lease on life. "I was saved tonight, you guys. Saved!"

Whip trudged on, his grump mode resurfacing. "If you thank the Lord for his divine intervention after you nearly fucking drowned me, I swear, I'm going to cut you."

I glanced at Whip sharply. "He nearly drowned you?"

Whip waved his hand dismissively. "I'm fine."

I wasn't so sure. He coughed violently, and I knew I was right to be concerned.

X pointed at the dark shadowy trees. "Look at that tree. Isn't it just beautiful?" He glanced back down at me. "I've been given a second chance at life. I'm going to use it so well. I'm turning over a new leaf. Being a better person."

Levi glanced over at him, vague amusement in his tone. "So you're saying your life flashed before your eyes and now you're a changed man?"

"Yes! Exactly that! You see me, Levi! Thank you!"

Levi squinted at him. "I see you being crazy. You think you're going to stop killing and live on the straight and narrow just because you swallowed some seawater?"

X made a face at him. "What?" He snorted on a laugh. "I'm not giving up killing. Are you crazy?"

All three of us stared at him.

He grinned back. "I'm going to get a nose ring!"

3

LEVI

The bluffs swarmed with Slayers by the time we reached the top of the long, winding path that snaked its way up the side of the cliff face from the beach below.

Fang strode right past me, beelining for his sister. "Violet!"

She lifted her head at his voice. "What are you doing here?"

He stopped a few inches short, not hugging her, even though I knew him well enough to notice his fingers twitching like he wanted to but wasn't sure if that sort of contact between the two of them was okay. But his gaze ran all over her with big-brother concern. Satisfied she was in one piece, he answered her question. "Chirp called me after Levi stole his bike."

Violet looked at me with questions in her expression.

I caught Whip's arm, steadying him and making sure he wasn't going to pass out. "I didn't steal his bike. X left us out..." I was going to say at the Murder Squad dump site, but after what we'd found there, the bodies of a dozen mutilated and abused women, I didn't want to scare Violet. So instead I just said, "In the middle of nowhere. We hiked out on foot until we had phone reception, and then I called the club for a pickup. We got your message while we were waiting."

Violet's mouth twisted into a line. "Oh."

Truth was, Whip and I had both been wild with fear over Violet and anger over X by the time the prospect had shown up on his bike, like a bloody dumbass. I didn't know how he'd thought he was going to get both Whip and me anywhere with only one bike, and with Violet's message burning a hole in my brain, we'd left him there and taken the bike for ourselves.

I glanced over at Chirp now and cringed at him. "Sorry."

At least the kid had been smart enough to make sense of the tumbled mess of words we'd shouted at him as we'd stolen his bike and had gotten the rest of the club out here, even if it had been too late to help.

Everyone was in one piece, and that was the main thing.

Well, except for the cliff face.

Whip coughed again, spitting up water.

I eyed him but said nothing.

Hawk studied all of us. "If you aren't going to the hospital, you all need to come back to the clubhouse so we can assess you. I'll get Grayson and Kara up to help."

But X shook his head and moved toward his van. "I don't need a doctor. I've never felt better in my life! Look at the grass, blowing in the breeze! Isn't it magical? Hear that owl? What a magnificent creature!"

Violet frowned at him. "I really think you should let Hawk check you over... You might have a concussion..."

I was more concerned his brain might have been starved of oxygen while he'd been underwater, but then again, X acting crazy wasn't actually all that unusual. To his credit, X did not seem to be in any sort of physical distress. He pulled himself up into his van and waved at everyone.

"Enjoy this splendid night, friends! Live every moment to its fullest!"

Everyone stared at him like he'd lost his mind.

Because he probably had.

Hawk twitched. "He shouldn't be alone right now. None of you should. You all need to be monitored." I'd seen Hawk studying for his paramedic's degree at the table in the Slayers' compound and knew he worked shifts at the hospital too, so his warning wasn't taken lightly.

But X was too high on his second chance at life to listen.

"I'll go with him," Violet offered. "Can someone take Bliss's car? Keys are in the ignition."

I wanted to argue, or at the very least, go with them, but there weren't enough seats for all four of us in X's van, and he clearly wasn't going to be talked out of anything tonight.

My bigger concern was Whip and the way he kept fucking coughing.

Was nobody else noticing that?

"We're all on our bikes," War said to me. "Can you drive Bliss's car? Just take it back to the clubhouse, we can get it back to her in the morning."

I gave my prez a curt nod. "Yeah, of course."

He eyed me. "You're good to drive?"

If X was, I was. "I'll be fine."

"Does anybody think I could be a pro hockey player?" X called through the open window of his van.

Whip raised an eyebrow in his direction. "Uh, no?"

X pointed at him. "Wrong! I'm going to try out. I think it's my destiny."

"Do you even skate?"

X shrugged and flapped his hand around. "Details, details, Whip. I survived! I can do anything!"

Violet rolled her window down. "I'll try to get him to rest. I'm sure he'll calm down once he's had a hot shower and some sleep."

I doubted it. But I strode to the side of the van and pressed my lips against hers. "Watch him. I don't know how long he was underwater for, and his behavior is erratic."

She glanced over at X, who was flipping through radio stations and singing a few lines of the song on each before moving on again. "His behavior is always kind of erratic though."

She had a point.

"Call me if you need me."

She nodded, kissing me back. "I love you."

I couldn't help but grin. "Love you too."

"Get Whip home safely."

I promised I would, though my words were probably lost to her in the spin of the ice cream truck's tires. X had clearly grown tired of waiting and decided our conversation was over.

Or he'd heard her say she loved me and was deliberately trying to kick mud up into my face.

Both could have been true.

I wiped the flecks of dirt from my cheeks, thanked my brothers from the club for coming, even though it had all been over by the time they'd gotten here, and made my way to Bliss's car.

Whip already sat in the passenger seat waiting for me, his arms wrapped around himself. A violent shiver racked his body.

I turned on the engine and then the car heater, cold to the bone as well after being in that freezing ocean for who knew how long.

The bluffs weren't far from the club grounds, and it was less than ten minutes before we were following the convoy of bikes down the dirt road that led to the Slayers' gates.

It was only then Whip seemed to notice where we were. "I need to go home."

I shook my head. "You need to see a fucking doctor."

"I'm fine. Just take me home."

I eyed the stubborn prick. "Why? So you can dry drown in the privacy of your own bedroom with no one watching?"

"What the hell is dry drowning?"

I huffed out an impatient sigh. "Something you're not going to die from because you're coming back to the clubhouse where it just so happens a doctor lives. And so I can keep an eye on you."

Whip went back to staring out the window. "Fine."

I gripped the steering wheel and nodded. "Fine."

The warm air from the heater hadn't helped much by

the time I was parking Bliss's car within the Slayers compound. If anything, it just burned my cold, wind-chapped skin painfully.

Grayson stood at the door, nodding at each of the guys as they walked through into the bar and communal area. Whip and I were the last to get there. I eagerly anticipated a bourbon with my name on it.

Gray stepped in front of us before we could enter. "What the hell happened out there tonight?"

I sighed. "Can we talk about this when we aren't soaking wet and half drowned?"

Grayson eyed me, but his gaze quickly turned to Whip and hovered there, visually checking him out with his doctor's eye, even though his words were for me. "Or you can give me the CliffsNotes now because I won't sleep a fucking wink until I know what the hell happened with all of you tonight."

I sighed, palming the back of my neck and trying to pick which piece of information to feed him first. "There's a pile of bodies out at Trigger's favorite dump spot."

Grayson shrugged. "So?"

"Female bodies," Whip filled in wearily. "Mutilated, tortured, abused bodies, who, without checking their ID, I'm sure are not on the list."

Gray recoiled. "You think Trig and Ace and Torch..."

I shook my head. "No. Shit, I dunno. Maybe. It could be this fucker messing with us, trying to set us up."

"Or yeah," Whip practically drawled. "Or we've been looking outside the group the whole time when maybe we should have been paying attention to those in it."

The thought left a sour taste in my mouth, and clearly one in Grayson's too. None of us wanted to believe Trigger or Ace or Torch were responsible for that pile of bodies we'd found. And yet, the possibility couldn't be ruled out either.

Whip coughed again and leaned heavily on the brick wall, looking like he was ready to pass out on his feet at any minute.

I moved in, making sure I was close enough to catch him if he decided to go and faint or something.

Gray noticed too, and ran his hands through his already messed-up hair, his brain clearly working overtime. "Nobody says a word about this until we can properly debrief with X and Violet. Where are they anyway?"

"Pretty sure they're off celebrating life by running with the bulls or swimming with sharks," I said dryly.

Whip coughed. "Please don't even joke about swimming right now. I don't think I'm ever getting in the water again. Why does he get to feel like a million bucks while I feel like death?"

"Because he's fifteen years younger than you maybe?"

Whip shot me a dirty look.

Grayson nodded. "Go on. We'll talk more tomorrow. Whip, if that cough gets out of hand or you start having chest pain or breathing difficulties—"

"Yeah, yeah. I'll call you."

Grayson crossed his arms over his chest and nodded, clearly not one-hundred-percent happy with the fact not much could be done tonight. "He doesn't go out of your sight, Levi. Not even for ten minutes. Someone needs to watch him, and if he's not going to go up to the hospital, then it needs to be you."

I nodded, taking the responsibility seriously because I knew Grayson wasn't just blowing smoke up my ass. Even

I could see Whip was exhausted, and he had to have taken in a lot of water when X had been holding on to him for dear life.

"I've got him," I assured Doc, while Whip muttered complaints over us talking about him like he wasn't even in the room.

Doc disappeared into the darkness of the night, his footsteps crunching over dead leaves as he made his way back through the darkness to the house he and his family shared within the Slayers' compound.

Whip could barely peel himself off the wall. He stumbled, and I caught him, getting myself beneath his arm and helping him inside.

"Bourbon," Whip requested passing the bar.

"Not a fucking chance." Though I really wanted one as well, I was too scared to let him drink when he looked as rough as he did. "Shower and bed. You can drink if you're still alive in the morning."

Whip raised an eyebrow and trudged along the hallway. "Some lovely, positively uplifting words of encouragement. Thank you, Levi."

Whatever.

I half dragged him to my room, locking the door behind us.

Whip moved to sit on the bed, his legs giving up the fight now that the adrenaline had worn off and his body knew he was somewhere safe.

"Nope, not going to bed in wet clothes." I hauled him toward the bathroom. "Shower."

"Sleep," Whip argued back.

Worry coursed through me. If he was so exhausted he was willing to sleep in wet clothes, that couldn't be good.

Though his cough had eased up a bit, each one sounding drier than the last, so I was less worried he still had lungs full of water.

I hauled him into the shower, both of us still fully clothed. though he was missing his shoes. I hadn't even noticed until I'd kicked mine off and turned on the water.

A cold stream ran over us, and we both winced until the hot water kicked in and warmed it up.

His gaze caught mine.

"Take your clothes off." The words came out gruffer and more demanding than I'd meant them to.

Whip raised his head slowly. "I don't think I can," he said honestly, though it was clearly killing him to admit it.

I didn't make a big deal of it. Just grasped the bottom hem of his shirt for him and lifted it up his body.

That's when I knew exactly how exhausted he was. Because he just let me. He allowed himself to be vulnerable and accepted my help.

I unbuckled his belt and then the fly on his jeans and pulled them down his trembling body until there was a pile of wet clothes on the floor.

He groaned, leaning back against the tiles, his knees buckling.

I caught him. "Stay on your feet. If you end up on the floor, I don't know if I'll be able to get you back up."

But a full-body tremor racked him, and I used my body weight to press him into the wall, keeping him upright.

I angled the spray so it was covering us both, but my wet clothes weren't helping any. I got my shirt off without letting go of him. Then reached between us, undoing my pants, and managed to get them halfway down my legs before he wobbled again.

I pushed him up against the tiles, my chest and stomach to his, a surge of heat passing between our bodies.

He closed his eyes, leaning against me heavily, and I found myself wrapping my arms around him, not just to keep him up, but because I wanted him there.

"You fucking scared me tonight," I whispered, water falling down around us. "You jumped off that fucking cliff like you didn't matter."

"I don't."

I shook my head. "You do."

We fell silent, the words too honest, too raw, too fucking traumatizing to even process.

We just breathed in time with each other, letting the water warm through aching muscles and joints until he could lift a little of his weight off me.

I reached for the simple bar of soap I kept in my shower and dragged it across his chest.

He watched me. "You wash your balls with that?"

I snorted, glad to see some of his dry sense of humor returning. "Yeah, and my ass crack. Be thankful I started with washing your chest and not your face."

Whip let out a noise that was probably supposed to be of annoyance but sounded more like a half laugh. He closed his eyes again, letting me glide soaped-up fingers over his chest in much the same way I had done to Violet a few nights earlier.

But where Violet was soft, Whip was hard. His chest had none of the gentle curves that Violet's had. He was all defined lines and coarse hair and strong muscle. I couldn't stop touching him, even when the soap fell from my fingers, leaving behind only its scent on his skin.

"I smell like you now," he said quietly with a deep exhale.

I pulled back to look at him. The instinct to make some sort of joke, to tell him he could smell like me every day if he got rid of his fancy bodywash and just bought the cheap dollar bars of soap like I did. And yet the words that came out were, "I thought he was going to drown you tonight."

Whip's breath stuttered. But then he answered honestly as well, "So did I."

I squeezed my eyes shut tight, trying to keep out the memories of X fighting for his life, his base instinct to survive in full gear. I couldn't be angry at him for what clearly hadn't been conscious thought.

But it hadn't changed the outcome. That I'd had to watch Whip's head go under the water over and over while I fought against the waves to get to him.

It had taken too long. He'd gone under so many times it made me feel sick to think about.

I was sure it was going to be his dead body I dragged from the ocean.

This time, the full-body shudder was mine.

And it was Whip who was there to catch me.

I clutched him, my fingernails digging into the tawny muscles of his back, holding him tight like if I let go the ocean might take him from me.

I kissed his shoulder, and then his neck, working my way along his jaw until my lips hovered over his.

Our gazes met, and this time, it wasn't just heat and attraction between us.

It was something so much more.

Something I didn't have it in me to label so I just kissed him instead.

He kissed me back softly, the touch assuring both of us we were still here and not resting in some watery grave.

Words I couldn't say to him burned my tongue. His lips were soft, our tongues meeting in the middle and finding a natural movement together that only emphasized the feeling inside me.

Fucking hell.

I could have lost him tonight.

I couldn't tell him how that made me feel.

But I could show him.

4

WHIP

*L*evi and I stood in that shower kissing until the hot water ran out. I probably would have stood there longer, not caring about the icy water droplets that splattered my skin, but it was all too reminiscent of that ocean.

I wasn't sure I would ever be able to swim in it again.

I switched off the water and blindly groped around the shower curtain for a towel, not wanting to remove my lips from his. My fingers found purchase on one hanging from a rail, and I clutched it, drying him off the best I could just by feel.

Levi practically growled into my mouth and walked me backward, out of the shower and through the bathroom, water still sluicing down my body in a river from my hair.

Puddles formed at our feet on the tiles, and Levi's tongue ran down my neck, chasing the water droplets. I clutched him to me, head tipping to one side to give him better access, my dick so fucking hard between us because his mouth felt so damn good.

"Levi," I groaned.

But I didn't know what else I wanted to say because he was taking the towel from me and dragging it down my body as he got on his knees. I'd been so exhausted I had barely been able to stand, and yet lust had me forgetting everything except him. His hot mouth was around my cock in seconds, a welcome change from the cold water my brain seemed so fixated on. He sucked and licked me, and I let myself have that for a few minutes, staring down at the tattoo just beneath his eye that had become so familiar. My cock pushed in and out of his lips, his tongue working the veined underside of my erection so perfectly I could have come right there, buried deep in his mouth.

But we both knew that whatever crackled in the space between us was more than just a quick BJ on the bathroom floor. We'd been there, done this, and there was an urgency in our movements tonight that hadn't been present before.

Something had changed in that ocean. Something neither of us could walk away from.

On the verge of coming, I urged him up onto his feet. "Not this."

His gaze connected with mine, and even though the words didn't really make sense, he knew exactly what I meant. His mouth slammed down on mine again, his lips tasting of salty precum that reminded me too much of the ocean, but beyond it was the taste of him. One I'd come to crave, especially when the entire world felt like it was falling down around me like it had tonight.

He felt like a lifeline. One I needed so fucking bad it was killing me.

I kissed him back, trying to take control of the situation because I knew it was me with more experience, but to my surprise it was Levi who guided me to the bed. Levi who splayed me out on my back then covered my body with his.

He kissed me hard and deep, an urgency to his kisses that hadn't been there before we'd both gone over that cliff. His cock rubbed against mine, and I widened my legs, allowing him a gap for his body to rest. He fumbled for the bedside drawer, taking out the bottle of lube we'd used on Violet earlier in the week.

But this time there was no woman between us. No hiding from the connection that had formed between him and me, not just tonight, but over the past few weeks of constantly being around each other.

"Need you," he murmured into my neck, alternating words between kisses. "Fuck."

I rocked my hips up, opening myself up to him because his raw and vulnerable words were ones I'd thought I'd never hear him say.

If I'd thought about what a relationship with him would be like, I would have assumed it would be nothing more than quick BJs in bar bathrooms and maybe the odd 'accidental' touch when Violet was between us.

But this...the way he moved in time with my body, the way he grasped at me, held me tight, breathed in time with the rise and fall of my chest, told me this was something so much more.

I dug my fingers into his back, holding him close,

encouraging him with guttural groans of pleasure, his dick pressing against my entrance. "Need you too."

It came out like a promise.

I'd fucked other men before. Let them fuck me.

But it had never had feeling behind it. This was entirely new. Suddenly, I felt about as experienced as a virgin on his wedding night.

But I knew I wanted him.

He was rough, all hands and tongue and unforgiving cock, knowing where it needed to be and impatient to get there. He held back long enough to swipe the tip of him between my cheeks, lubing me up just enough for him to thrust hard and fast inside me.

We both cried out.

He went deathly still, his body trembling over the top of mine, shuddering with the effort of keeping his weight from crushing me. "Are you okay?"

"Just give me a second."

His gaze connected with mine, and something inside his eyes softened. He lowered his mouth and touched his lips to mine.

My entire body relaxed, and I shifted beneath him, encouraging him to keep going.

He groaned, still holding himself taut, but my actions grew bigger, bolder, until even though he was barely moving, we were fucking hard and fast, his cock bottoming out inside me as I ground up to get what I needed.

I saw the moment his reserve snapped. His mouth slammed down on mine, and his hips jerked, meeting my upward thrusts with downward motion that had me groaning out in pleasure.

"Fuck," I moaned into his ear. "Harder."

His hips pistoned, our bodies slapping together as he drove into me. My dick was so fucking hard between us, precum spread across my belly and probably his too.

He got an arm beneath my knee, tilting me back into the mattress, changing the angle so it was deeper, both of us shouting into the little room in the middle of the clubhouse, not giving a flying fuck who heard.

Because I wasn't pretending anymore. Wasn't pretending I didn't want him as much as I wanted Violet.

And neither was he.

"Need to fucking come," he groaned. "Need you to come first."

He drew back just an inch, maybe checking my expression to see how close I was, but it gave me space to get my hand between us. I grasped my fingers around my cock and gripped it hard, stroking it fast, quickly finding the same rhythm Levi had.

He glanced down between us, watching me jerk my cock, another moan on his mouth.

I was so fucking close. So full of him. My balls clenched, an orgasm threatening to explode if we didn't stop.

Neither of us wanted to.

I closed my eyes, cock pulsing hot cum over my fingers and belly. I thrust into my grip, jerking myself in just the way I liked.

But this time I had the added pleasure of him inside me, filling me, taking his pleasure too.

Our moans mingled, his name on my lips, mine on his, our bodies connected so deep the pleasure spiraled and pulsed, the room spinning until he shouted my name, then collapsed down on top of me, not caring about the sticky mess between us.

He was still inside me, but softer now, and not moving. Just connected.

"Are you okay?" he asked quietly, his voice muffled by the pillow behind my head.

"Could use a cigarette."

He lifted his head. "You smoke?"

I grinned. "Only after a good fuck."

Levi's cheeks went vaguely pink, and he rolled off me, lying on his back beside me, both of us staring at the ceiling.

He cleared his throat. "So that was good?"

I glanced over at him. "It wasn't for you?"

He snorted, like it was the most ridiculous thing he'd ever heard. "No, it was good. Really fucking good."

I wanted that smoke so bad, if only so there was something to do with my hands. "You're surprised by that?"

"No."

"Then what?"

He shifted onto his side. "This just a fuck to you?"

I paused, then countered with a question of my own. "Is that what it is to you?"

Levi shook his head slowly. "I don't think so."

I grinned at him. "You want to be my boyfriend, Levi?"

He grinned and elbowed me. "Fuck off." But then he added, "I'll buy some cigarettes."

I sniggered into the room. Because I was pretty sure that despite his words, Levi had just declared that we were going to have sex again.

5

X

"Saint View Tattoo will still be open, so it makes the most sense to do the nose ring first. Second," I grinned at Violet, "sunrise bungee jumping."

She peered over at me from the passenger seat of my van. "Haven't you had enough falling off cliffs for one night?"

I screwed up my face. "Good point. Sunrise hot air ballooning then! Bungee optional!"

She reached out and squeezed my thigh. "Or, and this is just an idea, we go home, have hot showers, put on dry clothes, and go to bed."

I blinked. "I can't go to bed, Violet! I cheated death! Again! I can't just waste my second chance sleeping!"

I didn't mention that if I closed my eyes, even for a second longer than it took to blink, I knew I would be right back there, water filling my mouth and nose and ears and eyes, the crushing pressure of it caving in my chest as I gasped to breathe.

If I closed my eyes, or stopped for even a second, I knew I would start thinking about the way I'd clung to Whip, drowning us both because my body had never gotten the memo on how to keep itself afloat, no matter how many times I'd tried to learn.

I was scared if I closed my eyes, when I woke up, Violet might have realized all of that and would have left me alone.

I didn't want to be alone with my thoughts. My head was a storm of them, and the only way they quieted was when I was constantly doing something.

But Violet was shivering in the passenger seat. I pointed all the heating vents in her direction, and she smiled at me gratefully, but I knew I needed to get her some new clothes.

Saint View Tattoo, despite the late hour, was still open as we cruised through town, just as I'd predicted it would be. I had skulked around these streets in the dark enough times to know that at this time of night, the two things you could rely on were a hot, cheap meal at the Dead End Diner or a tattoo in Dax's shop.

I'd spent many nights doing both. She'd be safe inside, with me, and Dax, and the other guys there, working on pieces. No creepy killers in vans were going to follow us into a brightly lit tattoo shop.

I would be the only creepy killer driving a van around Saint View, thank you very much.

I parked it beneath the neon-pink sign of the strip club and offered Violet a hand getting out. She took it, wrapping her fingers around mine.

They were ice-cold.

I was such a fucking asshole.

But I could fix it. I hurried her into the tattoo shop, and a couple of the guys glanced up from various pieces they were working on. The space was warm and cozy, and my gaze landed on the rack of hoodies and sweatpants embroidered with the store's logo.

I pounced on them like they were precious treasures, and threw two sets of sweats on the counter.

Dax eyed me. "You know those are horrifically over-priced, right? Nobody buys them."

I gawked at him. "Well, sir, that is their loss. Violet and I are going to be your walking, talking billboards. Just charge them to my card."

His glance moved between the two of us, taking in our soaked clothes and the bedraggled state of Violet's hair. "You two get caught out in that storm?"

That was putting it mildly.

"Something like that," Violet told him.

Dax rang up our items and winced at the total. "That's two hundred and fifty dollars."

I handed over my card. "I just fell off a goddamn cliff, Dax. Charge me whatever you want. Hell, throw in a face tattoo while you're at it."

Violet widened her eyes at me in alarm.

I shrugged. "What? Levi has one!"

Dax frowned at me. "You don't really strike me as a face tattoo sorta guy, X."

"Because I'm too pretty?"

Dax snorted. "Because the last time I tattooed you, you howled like a wolf during a full moon. And your face is going to hurt a whole lot more than your chest or your biceps."

I mulled that over. "You have a point." I shot him a dirty look. "You said you were going to keep the girlish screams a secret, bro. Be cool."

Dax mimed zippering his mouth closed, though it was really a little late for that. I didn't want another tattoo anyway. Especially not one on my face. "Just one nose ring, please..." I turned to Violet. "Unless you want one too? My treat?"

She picked up the gray tracksuit I'd already bought for her. "I think the clothes are enough for tonight."

I nodded. "Just the one nose ring then, please. I promise I won't scream."

He glanced at Violet. "Did he really fall off a cliff tonight?"

"Unfortunately, yes."

Dax's eyes widened. "Shit." He squinted at me. "I'm really not supposed to do tattoos or piercings when someone may be under the influence of drugs or alcohol."

"I'm clean as a whistle. Want me to pee in your cup?"

Dax subtly moved his hand to cover his coffee mug. "I'm good. But if you hit your head, maybe you'd be better off at the hospital tonight?"

The mention of the hospital had every muscle in my body seizing.

I wasn't going there. The first night I'd met Doc, he'd practically stared straight into my soul and known exactly what I was on the inside. Doctors were too perceptive. They could do too many tests. Someone would realize my brain didn't work right, that I enjoyed things no sane person should.

And then they'd lock me up.

I didn't care if I'd hit my head and was bleeding internally.

I'd rather die than go to a hospital.

Plus, my head was fine.

At least physically. The desires inside it, probably not so much, but hey, you win some, you lose some.

"Just the nose ring, please."

Dax looked at Violet, and she nodded.

"He's okay."

I slung my arm around her neck and kissed her wet hair. "So are you."

Dax pointed to a sign on the wall that indicated there was a bathroom at the back of the shop. "Go get changed out of those wet clothes first, and I'll set up for it."

Satisfied with that answer, I ushered Violet into the bathroom and followed her in, locking the door behind us.

I dumped my clothes on the closed toilet lid and set to work undressing her.

I cringed at the soggy wet clothes I peeled off her and the way her skin was so pale it was vaguely blue. "Shit, Violet. You're freezing."

She shook her head. "Not as cold as you are." She rubbed her hands up and down my arms. "God, X. Your skin is like ice."

It was? I hadn't even noticed.

But the worried expression creasing her pretty face said she knew what she was talking about. I stripped her off quickly and got her into dry clothes, grinning at her wickedly. "Violet in sweats with no panties underneath. Why is that so hot?"

She laughed a little but did the same for me. My fingers trembled, and I shoved them into the warm, fleece-lined pockets of the hoodie with the Saint View Tattoo logo on the front before she could notice.

I couldn't feel anything. I was numb, inside and out.

Which seemed like the best time ever to get a piercing. I doubted I'd even feel it.

Despite the fact Violet had no panties on, and that was a very tempting thing in itself, I dragged us both out of the bathroom before I could do anything about it. One of Dax's guys, who I knew I'd been introduced to but could not for the life of me remember his name, pointed to a black slip of plastic on the counter. "Dax left a garbage bag there for your wet clothes. He's waiting in room two for you."

"Thank ye, kind sir." I saluted him and tossed the pile of soaking clothes inside it. Leaving it there at the desk for us to collect on our way out, I threaded my fingers through Violet's and tugged her toward the door marked with a graffiti style number 2 on it. "Come in and hold my hand?"

"Of course." She lowered her voice. "But, X, we need to talk about what happened on that cliff tonight."

I nodded seriously. "We should also probably discuss the pile of mutilated bodies we found."

She jerked to a stop. "What?"

"Oh. No one told you about that yet?"

"No! When would anyone have had time?"

I shrugged. "My free fall off the cliff took a few seconds. You, Whip, and Levi could have had a cup of tea and a catch-up."

She sighed and nudged me toward the piercing room. "Go get your nose ring. Maybe the pain will focus you."

"Can't feel anything right now," I countered. "So I doubt it."

"What do you mean you can't feel anything?"

I shrugged. "Might be the cold. Might be a psychopath thing. I don't know. I feel...detached from my body."

She bit her lip. "You need a hospital."

I pulled her into my arms and held her tight. "I just need you."

She sighed and laid her head against my chest. "Okay."

I was grateful she wasn't pushing it.

Dax lifted his gaze from the tray of sterilized tools as we walked in. "So, just confirming, you definitely want this nose ring?"

I flopped into the chair like a rag doll. "And maybe a sticker for bravery."

Violet stayed standing until I tugged her closer and caught her hand in mine. She squeezed it gently, grounding me in a way that made my chest ache.

Dax snapped on gloves and picked up the clamp. "A nose ring it is, then. Left nostril, right, or septum bullring special?"

"Dealer's choice. I trust your artistic vision."

Dax shook his head. "That sort of decision is way above my pay grade. I'm not the one who has to see your face every day."

We both looked at Violet.

She considered me for a second. "Right. It's your better angle."

My mouth dropped open in mock outrage. "I have no bad angles, Violet!"

Dax snorted and dabbed antiseptic along the side of my nose. "Okay, hold still. One deep breath."

I sucked in air, puffed out my chest. "Hit me with your best shot."

Dax counted off. "One, two—"

"AAAAGHHHHH!" I screamed like he'd stabbed me with a flaming sword.

Violet jumped, wide-eyed.

Dax recoiled, nearly dropping the needle. "X! You *promised* you weren't going to scream this time!"

"I lied!" I howled, clutching at the chair dramatically. "I am but a fragile vessel of pain!"

Violet blinked at me. "You said you couldn't feel anything."

I sat back and gave them both a sheepish smile. "I can't. I just thought it'd be funnier if I screamed."

Dax groaned and tossed a bloody wipe in the bin. "You're the worst kind of client."

"I aim to entertain."

Violet shook her head, her lips twitching. "You scared the hell out of me."

"I scared *myself*. Did you hear that scream? Oscar-worthy."

Dax leaned in, inspected his work, then stepped back. "Well, congrats, you're officially pierced and insufferable."

I touched the ring, admiring the cool metal. "How's it look?"

"Hot," Violet said softly. "Dangerous. Slightly unhinged."

I grinned. "Just my vibe."

Dax peeled off his gloves and gestured toward the front. "We like to keep an eye on you for ten or fifteen minutes so we can make sure it doesn't bleed too much, or in case you have any adverse reactions, so go take a seat on the couch, yeah? Try not to traumatize anyone else on your way out."

"Got it," I promised, though I could make no such promises about not traumatizing anyone. If this thing started bleeding, I would most definitely pass out.

Victim blood was one thing. My own? Different story.

We wandered back into the main shop area, where the couch near the window was empty. I collapsed onto it with a dramatic sigh, tipping my head back like I'd just survived war. Violet curled up beside me, our thighs brushing.

She watched me for a long second, then said, "You really didn't feel it?"

I shook my head. "Not a thing. My body's here, but I'm...not."

Her fingers brushed the side of my face, tracing the edge of the new ring, then dropped to rest lightly over my heart. "Well, I feel you. You're in there somewhere."

"You always say the nicest things to emotionally unstable psychopaths."

"Only the cute ones."

I rummaged on the counter behind me and snagged a purple lollipop from the display. I peeled off the wrapper and held it out to her.

She blinked. "A grape lollipop? How romantic."

"Only the best for you."

She took it, popped it into her mouth, and gave me a

soft smile that made my ribs feel like they were finally starting to expand again.

And just like that, the noise in my head got a bit quieter.

Maybe I *was* in my body again.

Just a little.

6

VIOLET

I finally convinced X to come back to my apartment with me somewhere around dawn. He'd flat-out refused to go to his place, and I couldn't take him to Fang's because I didn't trust he wouldn't do something completely unhinged, like try to swing from the staircase railing while yelling about how he could be the next Tarzan, if only someone would give him a loincloth.

I chuckled at the idea and wondered if his odd sense of humor was rubbing off on me, or if I was as weird as he was for even considering it.

He practiced his running man in the hallway while I got the door unlocked, the dead bolt still nicely shiny with newness. The door opened easily, but I wrinkled my nose at the smell on the other side.

X caught sight of the face I'd made. "Uh-oh. I know that look. Food that was left out on the counter too long, or dead body?"

I glanced at him. "They smell the same to you?"

"Pretty much."

I flicked on a light, illuminating the open-plan living area of my apartment. "No dead bodies in sight." I spotted the open bottle of milk on the counter and winced. I hadn't been here since the night of Toby's murder, or rather the morning after I'd had a foursome with Whip, X, and Levi in my bedroom, and Whip had made us pancakes afterward. The rest of the kitchen was clean, but he'd clearly missed the milk.

I pinched my nose and turned the bottle upside down, emptying the congealed contents down the drain. The smell was foul.

X made overdramatized retching sounds. "If I die from dairy-related gas inhalation, tell my story."

I ran the hot water, trying to clear out the obnoxious stench, and then lit a candle.

It didn't do much to help, but it was better than nothing.

X clapped his hands. "So, you go sleep. I'll do a YouTube workout, clean your bathroom, and maybe bake a batch of brownies because me and my new nose ring could definitely use some sugar."

I raised an eyebrow. "Or you could come sleep with me."

He grinned. "And by sleep, you mean sex, right?"

"By sleep, I mean sleep."

"Sleep sex?"

I squinted at him. "How does that work?"

"You go to sleep but give me permission to do wicked, wicked things to your body while you're out."

Why the hell did my body come alive at the very

thought of that? I was dead on my feet. I'd been awake for almost twenty-four hours straight, and a pretty traumatic event had happened in the middle of it. And yet one mention of him touching me and I was ready to go.

My breath came out sort of wheezy. "I think I would like that. You have my consent to do whatever you want to me while I'm asleep." I clenched my thighs together, the anticipation of waking up with him between them, stirring up desire and maybe a kink I hadn't known I was into.

"BZZZZ!" he shouted, making something that maybe could have passed for an incorrect answer buzzer on a gameshow.

I flinched but I don't think he noticed.

"That is the wrong answer, Violet Garrisen! You do not pass go. You do not collect two hundred dollars."

I had no idea what kind of game show-Monopoly mash-up was going on in his head, but as with all things X, it was easier to just go along with it. Even still, I squinted at him. "Can I dispute that ruling? What exactly about it was wrong?"

He sighed. "You can't let me do things like that to you, Violet."

That tingle between my thighs and the daydream of him playing my body while I was out of it refreshed inside me, a new heat curling around low in my belly.

"You can't put something like that on the table then take it off," I complained.

"It was a test! You were supposed to be scared and say no!"

"Well, instead I got kinda hot and sweaty and am now eagerly awaiting it happening. So tough luck."

He sighed. "I shouldn't even be here alone with you."

"And yet, we've been together for hours. You've had all the opportunity in the world to kill me. And I'm not dead yet."

He gave me a look that said it wasn't funny to joke about things like that. Which was kind of rich, coming from him, who had built his entire personality on inappropriate humor.

"Just come to bed, X. You aren't going to kill me." I wrapped my arms around his waist and lifted my face just a few inches so I could kiss his mouth. "I trust you."

His eyes darkened. "You shouldn't."

But he could protest all he wanted. It wouldn't change the fact this was the man who'd been willing to sacrifice his life for mine. This was a man who had eagerly replied to every text. Who had shown up every time I asked him to. Who had gone out of his way to introduce me to his family.

Maybe he was scared of himself.

But I wasn't.

I tucked my hand into his, trying not to notice Toby's closed bedroom door as I passed it, and pulled X down the hallway.

Even though there was no need to, I closed the door out of habit and then drew back the covers on the neatly made bed. I wondered if it had been Levi or Whip who'd made it up with fresh sheets after our group sexy times on it.

I went to slip into it, when X cleared his throat from the other side of the bed. "Take those sweats off first."

I nodded. "You're right. I should find some pajamas. It's gross to sleep in clothes I've been wearing for hours."

But he shook his head. "Not asking you to put on pajamas, Violet. Asking you to wear nothing."

My breath hitched at the gleam in his eyes. "Are you saying..."

"Am I saying I don't want any barriers to me fucking you in the middle of the night while you're sleeping? Yeah. That's exactly what I'm saying." His gaze drifted over my body, like he could already see what was beneath my clothes.

I took off my hoodie and then my sweats. Everything else was soggy and wet in the garbage bag we'd brought back from Dax's shop.

I stood in front of him, completely naked, the overhead light on, showing off every dimple and curve and fat roll on my body.

Yet he gazed at me like I was only going to be asleep for a minute before he pounced. He stripped off his clothes as well, and both of us got into bed. He pulled up the covers and fit himself in behind me, his dick hard, but him ignoring it between us. "Go to sleep, Violet."

I snuggled into him, enjoying the feel of his arms around me and his warmth radiating through my back. Despite the anticipation of waking up with him inside me, I was suddenly exhausted, my body registering a safe space to finally rest, and the adrenaline high of the last twelve hours finally ebbing away enough that I could fully relax.

My eyelashes fluttered involuntarily, my blinks becoming slow.

"You haven't been calling me Omelet," I said sleepily.

"It's hard to call you Omelet when I just want to call

you mine." He shifted behind me, pressing a gentle kiss to my shoulder. "I love you. Violet."

A soft smile spread across my lips. But I was asleep, dragged under by exhaustion and emotions too big for my body before I could respond.

7

X

I didn't sleep. Just held her while her breathing evened out into slower, deeper breaths that misted her plump lips. I held her as her body slowly warmed mine. My brain whirred, trying to process the last twelve hours and the numbness that followed.

At some point, I realized the hole I'd pierced in my nose throbbed. It was more of a minor irritation than a true pain, but it was pain my brain registered, nonetheless. The heat of Violet's body became more and more noticeable, until she was too warm and I had to throw the covers off us.

But I didn't let her go.

She was mine.

I could be okay with sharing her with Whip and Levi. I saw the way they loved her. Saw the way she needed that sort of love from them. Saw they could give her something I couldn't, and I wanted her to have everything she needed.

She deserved that.

They weren't trying to take her from me.

But last night, up on the bluffs, somebody had.

It could have been her who had gone down with that cliff face. I didn't know how I'd walked away from that with nothing more than lungs full of water, but I had.

And now I was here in bed with a woman I didn't deserve but wasn't willing to give up.

She'd given me full rights to her body.

I'd wanted to let her sleep. She needed the rest. But fuck, I needed to be inside her. I needed to be selfish.

I brushed her hair away from her neck and kissed her there.

She didn't move. Her breathing didn't change.

I kissed her skin again, my fingers roaming over all the bare inches of it I was somehow lucky enough to be given full access to. Her tits rested heavy in my hands, overspilling fingers that stroked her nipples, slowly and gently testing each one to see if she'd wake.

Her breathing changed slightly, and she shifted, but I was still fairly sure she wasn't mentally aware of what I was doing to her.

But physically, her body responded. I dragged my hand down her belly, finding her little nub of pleasure between the lips of her pussy. I nudged it with my fingertip, testing it to see her reaction.

She didn't move, but when I slid my finger lower, searching for her entrance, I found the hot, wet center of her, slick and ready for me.

"Fuck, Violet," I whispered into the stillness of the room. "I could take you right now, couldn't I?"

She didn't respond, and her breathing settled back into that familiar pattern of sleep.

Heat rushed through me, my dick kicking at the knowledge this wasn't right.

And yet, she'd given me permission. Not just that, she'd practically begged me to do it.

She wanted to wake up with me inside her.

Her tits didn't sit perky on her chest. They lolled to the sides, natural and heavy and so fucking soft I wanted to use them as pillows every night for the rest of my life. Her nipples were beaded and taut, needy for my mouth, but my tongue wanted to taste her.

With the blankets somewhere on the floor, I gently nudged her legs apart and slid down the bed until my face hovered over her glistening core. I couldn't resist the urge to tongue her there, to slide it through the silky arousal at her opening and spread it to her clit. I played with the bundle of nerves, flicking at it with my tongue, my gaze firmly pinned on her face, backing off when her eyelashes fluttered too much, signaling she might be waking.

I wanted her body so needy it welcomed me inside without an ounce of resistance. She'd put so much trust in me tonight, and I was desperate to show her I deserved it.

I needed to show her I didn't have to listen to that voice in my head that demanded I put my fingers around her perfect throat and squeeze.

There was nobody here to stop me.

I could do whatever I wanted to her, and no one would be the wiser.

Yet the urge to squeeze her throat, normally so loud in my head whenever I was alone with a woman, was quiet, satiated by licking her sweet pussy instead and making a game out of not waking her.

Her eyes stayed shut, her body completely relaxed beneath me. My dick ached so hard I couldn't ignore it anymore. Careful to keep a gap between our bodies, I hovered over her, palms pressing into the mattress, no longer focused on the pulsing point in her throat that would have normally begged for my fingers.

I notched my cock at her entrance, slicking up the head of it, and then inched inside her so slowly it was like dripping molasses. Bottoming out, her pussy swallowing me whole, I stared down at her, waiting for her eyes to open.

It didn't come.

There was no way she would have still been asleep normally, but neither of us had slept in over twenty-four hours. Add in the trauma and physical exertion of running up and down rocky cliff faces and fighting angry seas, as well as the emotional impact of being sure we were going to die, it was hardly surprising her body had shut down as heavily as it had.

I fucked her slow. So damn slow it was torture, when all I wanted to do was slam into her hard and fast and wake her up so she could fuck me back.

The urge for her to respond increased as her body reacted to mine, and her breaths grew into something that sounded more like pants. A moan slipped from her lips twice, and I was driving in and out of her, fucking her for real before her eyes finally fluttered open and she registered me above her.

I waited for the fear to show in her eyes. For her to tell me to get off her.

But she just gasped.

And then her hands were in my hair, drawing me down, and she was kissing my mouth, our hips pistoning together.

The last of the numbness inside me melted away.

I sank down onto her, crushing her beneath me, but she didn't complain. If anything, she drew me in tighter, wrapping her legs around my waist and anchoring me to her so I couldn't pull out more than a few inches. We moved together, my pubic bone against her clit, her hips driving up to take every thrust.

With my weight resting on one forearm, I slid my hand up the side of her body, needing to touch her, needing to ground myself in her and remind myself she was still here. That she was warm and real and she wanted this as much as I did. That she was choosing my weirdness that had done nothing but terrify women in the past.

I skimmed my palm up her side and over her breast. My fingers splayed across her chest and inched higher until they were around her throat.

"Fuck," I groaned, staring down at her, her pulse thumping beneath my fingertips.

Her hand came up to cover mine. "You aren't going to hurt me, X."

My heart squeezed at the sincerity and surety in her voice.

Nobody had ever trusted me the way she did. Nobody had ever believed in me like she did.

I'd never wanted to change for anyone. Had been sure I couldn't.

She made me want to try.

Her pussy fluttered around my cock, drawing me deep inside her, strangling my erection as her orgasm drew closer. She stared up at me, her eyes at half-mast with desire and need, her body writhing beneath mine.

I tightened my grip on her throat.

She sucked in a breath and moaned loudly.

The sound sent reassurance through me.

She could still breathe.

I played with the strength of my grip, watching her face intently for the second I went too far and cut her off completely.

But it didn't come. For once in my life, I was fully in control of not only her and her pleasure, but also myself.

That was a heady feeling.

I let out an animalistic growl and fucked her faster, harder, slamming into her body with my fingers around her neck, cutting off her air just enough to make her a tiny bit breathless but never enough to scare her.

Or me.

She moaned beneath me, our bodies moving, her hand gripped around my wrist, holding the pressure on her throat.

Giving me what I needed.

She fell off the cliff with me buried deep inside her. Her body pulsed and spasmed around mine, throwing me over the edge with her.

Unlike the night before, where I'd landed in cold water and had to fight for my life, this time I landed in the softness of her arms, her trembling body beneath me, her whispered words in my ear, saying my name over and over like a prayer.

"Fuck, I love you," I whispered on her lips. "I love you so much, Violet."

She smiled softly. "Not the first time you've told me that."

She was referring to the days after we'd met, where I had told her I loved her in a million different ways.

Today, I didn't laugh or make a joke like I normally would have. "It's the first time I've truly meant it."

She kissed me gently. "I know. I love you too."

The whoosh of relief hit me hard and was instantly followed by my more regular insanity, my body getting hyped up on the excitement of feeling it too. "Marry me."

She laughed and shook her head. "I love you. But no."

"We'll have a ceremony in the park so Reginald can attend! I'll get him a little ducky tux!"

She snorted on her laughter. "We aren't getting married by the pond so your duck friend can be your best man."

I nodded seriously. "Scythe would probably be mad at being upstaged by a bird. How about on the beach then? The mountains? The city?"

Amusement played out all over her mouth. "I'm getting the impression the location actually doesn't matter to you."

"I'd marry you in a dumpster if that was your lifelong dream."

She raised an eyebrow. "Even that one out behind my place that always smells like piss?"

I cringed. But nodded.

"You hate piss."

"I also hate vomit and shit, but maybe you haven't been paying attention for the last few weeks. So if that's the case, hear me now." I stared at her, all the laughter fading away. "I'd do anything for you."

She wrapped her arms around me and pulled me down on the mattress beside her. "Loving me is enough."

I drew her in tight, so her head rested on my chest.

For maybe the first time in my life, I slept without demons in my head, or in my heart.

8

———

VIOLET

oices in the hallway outside my apartment woke me, and for a long moment, I was confused as to why it was so dark in my room at this time of morning.

Only to realize I had slept the day away and night had fallen again.

The front door to my apartment jiggled, the voices muffled, but someone was clearly trying to get inside.

My heart rate picked up, and before I'd even properly woken up, I reached beneath my bed for the baseball bat Toby had put there years ago, just for situations exactly like this.

I'd asked why the hell he was giving it to me? I wasn't going to be any use against an intruder. Then we'd both realized the alternative had been him being the one with the bat, which was laughable considering the man had screamed and run around like a headless chicken at the sight of a spider. So I'd taken the bat, stashing it beneath my bed, praying like hell I'd never be in the situation where I'd need it.

So far, I hadn't.

But apparently, my luck had run out.

Because someone was definitely trying to break into my apartment.

"Don't worry, Omelet. I'm armed and dangerous."

I jumped at the voice next to me in the darkness, my brain taking too long to remember it was X. I breathed out slowly, reassured by his presence.

And then curious. I had the baseball bat. I knew he didn't carry a gun. What the hell was he armed with? Had he brought another freaking knife into my apartment?

I flicked on the light.

He was sitting upright in the bed, his attention focused on the door, his body primed for action.

My vibrator clutched in his hands like a bat.

"Oh for God's sake, X." I threw the actual baseball bat at him. "Would you go already!"

He dropped the vibrator and took it from me, leaning in to steal a quick kiss. "In my defense, if I'd known you had that under your mattress, we could have gotten a whole lot kinkier last night."

I shoved him. "X! There is no point being in love with a psychopath if you can't even take care of a couple of street thug home invaders!"

He gave me a look like I was being incredibly insulting and then launched himself out of bed.

I followed tight behind him, creeping along the hallway and then through the living room to where the doorknob twisted and turned uselessly, thanks to the deadbolt Levi and Whip had installed.

It was only as we reached the door that I realized he was still completely naked. "X! You have no clothes on!"

"Well, that's their punishment, isn't it?"

Seeing X naked wasn't much of a punishment if you asked me. But that was kind of beside the point.

X cleared the sleepy gravel from his throat. "You can just be on your merry way now! We're awake, we've called the police, and we are naked!"

I rolled my eyes.

He was the only naked one. At some point during the night, I'd put on the shirt he'd given me the day we'd met, snuggling up in it with him wrapped around me so it would smell like him again.

"Who are you?" a voice called from the other side. "This apartment isn't yours! Now I'm the one calling the police!"

X snorted, but I recognized the voice and lunged for the door, twisting the deadbolt and flinging it open. "Judy!"

The small dark-haired woman on the other side blinked at me in surprise, her slightly taller, though still-not-as-tall-as-me husband standing behind her. I threw my arms around Toby's mom, and she quickly relaxed in my embrace, hugging me back.

I grinned at Toby's dad over her shoulder, and he smiled back affectionately.

But his eyes held a sadness I'd never seen in them before.

Mine probably did too.

"I'm so sorry," was all I could get out. It didn't even begin to cover the vast, gaping hole inside me that opened up any time I was reminded of my best friend.

Judy patted my back. "Violet, are you aware there is a naked man in your apartment with nothing but a frying pan to cover himself?"

I cringed and glanced back at X, who had indeed grabbed the frying pan Whip had used the other morning to make us breakfast. He'd left it on the countertop to dry after he'd washed it.

And now X was defiling it with his junk.

I was going to have to buy a new one.

I gave Judy a strained smile. "Uh, yes. I am aware. X, meet Judy and Warren, Toby's parents."

He grinned sheepishly. "I normally wear less frying pans when meeting parents."

They both gave him a disapproving look.

He grimaced and jerked one thumb toward my bedroom. "Maybe I'll just go down here now."

He spun on his heel, and I tried to hold in a laugh at his naked ass leaving the room.

I turned back to Judy and Warren, ready to explain, but Judy gave me a disappointed frown. "Must be nice for you, having a lovely time while our son is dead."

I froze to the spot, her sharp, biting words cutting right through me. I was so shocked I couldn't even speak, let alone defend myself. Guilt roared in my ears, screaming that she had a point. I'd spent the last couple of weeks bed-hopping with gorgeous men.

While Toby lay in a morgue somewhere, waiting on a coroner to release his body for burial.

"I'm sorry," I whispered.

Judy passed me by, beelining for Toby's bedroom that I hadn't touched since that night.

She didn't make eye contact though.

Tears pricked the backs of my eyes. Toby's parents had never had a problem with me when he'd been alive. We might not have been close exactly, but we'd definitely been friendly. They'd been warm and welcoming when he'd taken me back to their place for Thanksgivings and Christmas dinners because I had no family of my own to go home to.

It had always just been me and Toby. They'd accepted me because I was an extension of him.

Now, by the way his mother was acting, that was over.

It just felt like another part of me had been ripped away.

Warren squeezed my hand after his wife disappeared into their son's room. "It's not you. She's just struggling with her grief. We just need to get some clothes from his room. His body has been released, so we've organized the funeral."

"Oh," I said quietly.

He let my hand go and followed his wife into Toby's room.

I leaned heavily against the wall, staring numbly at the closed bedroom door. The sounds of their grief echoed back, her sobs, his comforting words with a voice so broken it brought tears to my eyes.

X found me there but said nothing, just wrapped his arms around me from behind. We stood there like that until the door opened again and Toby's parents emerged, Judy's arms full of her son's clothes.

"We'll let you know when the funeral is." She sniffed, her gaze not meeting mine, but her voice a little less harsh than before.

"I'm so sorry for your loss," I said pathetically, knowing it wouldn't help.

They'd lost their only child. There was no consoling them.

She gave a curt nod. "And I for yours."

Those few simple words went a long way to easing the guilt building inside me. I saw them to the door and locked it behind them.

I'd thought I'd been doing okay with my grief, but seeing them made me realize I'd just been keeping myself too busy, too distracted, to feel it.

It all rushed in like a freight train of destruction.

X moved to Toby's door. "I'll close this."

But I shook my head, striding across the room. "No. I need to face it. I can't keep ignoring he's gone." I swallowed hard. "I can't afford this place by myself. I need to box up his things so I can get a roommate."

Just saying those words out loud crumpled the last tether I had on my grief. I choked out a sob but pushed on anyway, stepping into Toby's bedroom.

X followed close behind me, not giving me any personal space, and I was grateful for it.

Toby's room looked like it did most days. The bed a tangled mess of sheets and pillows and blankets because he didn't believe in making it just to get back in a few hours later. Brightly colored clothes were flung around, like he'd tried them on, dismissed them, and then sent them flying. Various posters hung on the wall, advertising his varied interests, from LGBTQ support to the urban photography he'd come to love in the past few years since he'd found a decent camera at a pawnshop and come home claiming he was going to be the next Andreas Gursky.

It had surprised us both when he'd actually been good at it.

I picked up his camera from his bedside table, accidentally knocking off a pile of black-and-white printed photos beneath it. X knelt and picked them up for me, his attention catching on them.

He sat back on his heels and flicked through the images. "Damn. These are really good." Then he shrugged. "At least they look good to me. I don't know anything about photography."

I didn't really either, other than what I'd learned from Toby. I took the images as he passed them to me, studying each one, taking my time on the details he'd somehow managed to bring out. I smiled at the places around Saint View I recognized. "The Dead End should have this printed on their wall. Place looks better in this photo than it does in real life."

The greasy diner on the main strip of Saint View was a cheap, run-down place but popular with the locals nonetheless, mostly because of the prices. But Toby's image, taken at night, with the lights on behind the grubby glass windows, and shadowed silhouettes of people moving around inside had captured something beautiful about it.

I shifted through the other photos, taking in the familiar sights, all taken at night. The strip club. Dax's tattoo shop. Psychos. Even Clean Sweep, nestled in between other stores in the worst part of town.

X paused, staring down at one photo.

I waited for him to pass it in my direction, but he bit his lip.

"What?"

"I don't think you'll want to see this one."

Of course, that only made me want to see it more. I reached over and plucked it from his fingers.

My stomach sank.

It was the warehouse where Toby had been killed.

A lump rose in my throat, and just as quickly, I was ripping the image up, tearing the paper into tiny slivers, destroying the horrific image over and over again until the pieces were confetti-sized.

X said nothing, just let me do it, until it was out of my system.

"I guess that explains why he had maps of that part of Saint View downloaded onto his phone," I said quietly, my brain fixating on that memory of the night he'd died, rather than any of the other horrific events that had happened after. "I'd kind of thought maybe he was dealing drugs or something in this area. He always had extra money. More than anyone makes working as a nail technician. He said it came from photography, but I helped him print and frame the only photo he ever sold to a collector. That wasn't an everyday occurrence. When I saw those maps on his phone, I definitely thought they were of his drug-dealing territory."

X shrugged. "Did you ever see him with drugs?"

I shook my head. "No. Never. I didn't even really consider it until that night."

"So maybe he was telling the truth? Maybe he was selling digital downloads?"

"I guess so. It doesn't matter now anyway." But it was a

relief to no longer have the idea lurking in the back of my mind. Whatever money Toby had earned would go to his parents. "Do you think they'll want all these photos?"

X kept flipping through them, his brow crinkling as he took each one in.

"X?" I asked again when he didn't respond.

He glanced up. "These aren't all landscapes."

I peered over his shoulder and stared down at the image clutched in his fingers. Two men in an alleyway, deep in conversation about something, their expressions pinched and angry.

I frowned at the intense photo in grainy black and white. X passed me a few more, all of the people seemingly unaware they were being watched through a lens. One man featured in a lot of images, but there were probably a dozen different faces, in various places around the backstreets of Saint View.

A sinking ball of dread filled my stomach. "What are these?"

X's lips pressed together in a tight line. "Nothing good."

"They're drug deals, aren't they?"

X squinted at me. "Could be weapons deals. Could be women." His upper lip curled. "Or children."

The photo slipped from my fingers. I shook my head and whispered, "Is this what you meant when you said you were sorry? What the hell were you doing, Toby?"

9

LEVI

aking up with Whip in my bed was fucking weird. Not unpleasant, because for a guy in his forties, his body didn't look it. Even in sleep, the muscles across his back were noticeable, his ass right there, perfectly sculpted and just begging for me to fuck it.

My dick flickered at the idea of getting on top of him again.

Eyes still closed, his hand snaked across the mattress, searching for me. His warm fingers found my skin, and his palm wandered down my body, finding my morning erection waiting for him.

I groaned when he wrapped his fingers around it, pumping my shaft.

He raised his head sleepily, eyeing me without bothering to say good morning. He shifted on the mattress, spinning himself around so he could take my cock in his mouth.

"Fuck," I bit out at the feel of his wet mouth enclosing my dick. Shit, why the fuck did that have to feel so good?

Half on his side, half on his stomach, his weight propped up on one arm, his other hand gripping my base, he tongued the tip of my dick. His lips encased me, and he bobbed his head, taking as much of me as he could.

I closed my eyes, accepting the pleasure he was handing out so freely, until I couldn't lie still for a second longer.

I twisted to my side so we were facing each other, his head level with my junk, my head level with his. I grabbed his hip, fingers sliding around and digging into the muscled globe of his ass and dragging us together so I could get my mouth on him too.

I wrapped my lips around him, tasting the precum leaking from his tip. His hips jerked, thrusting himself into the wet warmth of my mouth, unforgiving, taking exactly what he wanted.

It only turned me on more. My hips moved in an identical fashion, the two of us writhing on the bed together, sucking each other off, grabbing at each other's balls, and squeezing them just enough to increase the need to come.

He rolled us, taking up the position on the bottom so he was on his back, my knees either side of his head. I braced my weight on my forearms, still sucking his dick, while vaguely attempting not to choke him with mine.

The urge to thrust down his throat was there though, and I took him deeper with every pass of my lips.

He stopped sucking me just long enough to shove his

fingers into his mouth, but then his mouth was back and his fingers drifted from my balls to find my asshole.

I tensed, and he slowed down until my body relaxed again. The next time he touched me there I was more prepared for it and let him.

It took less than three rubs for me to realize what I'd been missing. I groaned around his cock; glad it was deep in my mouth to muffle the indecent sound. I didn't need the whole fucking club knowing what we were doing, and yet I wasn't going to stop either.

Rubbing turned into penetration, just the tip at first, but when I got used to that, he gradually gave me more, until I was taking his whole finger and fireworks were going off in my brain.

There was no fucking way I was going to hold on. My balls clenched, and I let out a moan as my cock kicked, spurting cum from the tip.

He let go at the same time, his erection hard in my mouth, the salty taste of his orgasm spreading across my tongue. I didn't stop, didn't lift away. I took every ounce he gave me and gave him just as much in return. My brain spun, my entire body went taut with release, and then eventually relaxed.

I fell over onto my side, his finished-off erection slowly fading, me just as done at the other end of the bed.

Our heavy breaths filled the room, both of us on our backs, heads at opposite ends of the mattress, chests rising and falling from the effort.

I peeled open an eye and peered at my phone on its charger, the time displayed on the lock screen. I sat bolt upright. "Shit! I have to go to work!" I scrambled onto my knees and vaulted over him, rushing into the bathroom and turning on the shower.

I was out in under a minute, smelling of the cheap bar of soap I'd done nothing more with than run over the most vital areas: dick, ass, pits. It would have to do for now. At least I wouldn't smell of the sex Whip and I had been having for half the damn night and now the morning as well.

I barely dried myself, dropping the towel on the bathroom floor and striding through my room naked, pulling clean clothes out of the tiny wooden free-standing closet that I had barely half filled with my meagre belongings. I'd been living in the same pair of jeans and my club jacket, but I found an old flannel that had been packed up in a box of my things and stored in the basement until I'd returned. It was a little tighter than I remembered it being, six years of working out daily in prison would do that to your biceps, but at least it was clean.

Feet shoved in boots, laces not bothered to be tied, I lunged for the door.

At the last second, I turned back, eyeing Whip in my bed.

He flicked his hand at me with a gruff laugh. "Go, dickhead. I'm a big boy. I can see myself out."

It wasn't that.

It was that I wanted to kiss him goodbye.

Like a fucking needy loser who had feelings he didn't know what to do with instead of just being satisfied with having good sex.

My feet felt glued to the floor, my brain saying just walk out the door. My entire body and something deeper inside me drawing me back toward him like a magnet, demanding I stay.

My fucking heart won. I crossed the room to the bed and leaned over it, pressing my mouth to his.

His surprise was there in the pause where my lips hit his, but it fell away fast, and he kissed me back.

It wasn't a long kiss, there were no demanding tongues seeking entrance, no moaning and groaning or turning it into more.

"Have a good day," I murmured.

His blue eyes were barely focused before I was slamming my way out of the door and running for my bike.

War looked up from the table in the common room, a mug of steaming coffee clutched in his fingers. His eyebrow quirked, and I knew if he'd been sitting there long enough, he would have heard everything Whip and I had been doing.

"Shut up," I grumped at him.

He smiled smugly. "Wasn't going to say a word."

I hoped he didn't see the half-smile that crept across my face as I turned away and jogged out the door.

My bike waited for me in the lot and made quick work of getting me into town. I got to the tattoo shop five whole minutes before the time Dax had texted me to start.

Five minutes I could have spent with Whip was my first instinct, but my second was if I wasn't in bed with him and Violet, then the shop was definitely the next best place to be.

I couldn't stop the grin that emerged just from knowing this was where I was supposed to be. I wasn't much into all that woo-woo bullshit, but Lynx, my old cellmate, had been. I suspected he would have said my soul had a connection here. At least that's what it felt like each time I walked in and saw the art covering every available surface.

Dax stopped wiping down a table, and leaned over it, offering me his hand. "First day. You scared?"

I squinted at him as I shook his hand. "Should I be? Is there a hazing ritual I need to pass first?"

A blond guy, with the most piercing blue eyes I'd ever seen, paused from where he was drawing on an iPad. "Dax didn't tell you about that?"

I glanced at Dax. "No?"

He stifled a laugh and shrugged.

I turned back to the blond guy, pulling back my shoulders. "I'm up for it, whatever it is."

"Good, because I'm just about done designing your new tattoo." He grinned and turned the iPad around to show me.

It was a bright-yellow rubber ducky.

It was hideous and ridiculous and didn't match with any of the other ink I had covering my skin. It would stick out like dogs' balls.

Both men laughed at my expression.

Dax slapped me on the back. "He's joking. There's no initiation. We aren't that Neanderthal."

The blond guy stood and offered me a fist bump. "Couldn't resist messing with you. I'm Roarke."

"Not to be confused with me," another voice called from a storeroom off to the side.

I jumped a little, not realizing there was anyone else there, and then an identical face to Roarke's popped out around the doorjamb. "Hey. I'm King. Well, Tim King, if you want to be specific, but since our parents gave Roarke the bad-boy tattooist name and me a name only fit for an accountant, I go by King."

Roarke sniggered and flashed the iPad at his brother. "Like my ducky?"

King recoiled. "That's fucking hideous. What dumb asshole wants that?"

Dax laughed, peering over Roarke's shoulder at it, and then over at me. "Friend of yours, actually."

I groaned. "Let me guess, X wants Reginald written in a banner underneath it too?"

Roarke sniggered. "How did you know?"

"Don't ask."

Dax chuckled, but then a customer walked in, and then another, and pretty soon the place was a busy hum of consistent activity. I didn't do much, with it being my first day, and there was a lot of me cleaning off tables between clients, running to the storeroom and blindly searching it, hoping I would be able to find whatever it was the guys had asked for. But there was also a lot of time watching them work. Marveling at the way they moved the tattoo gun across skin to bring together designs I could only dream of creating. They all had different styles, and I didn't know where mine would fit in here, but an excitement pulsed inside me, a desperate need for knowledge.

I wanted to learn everything they knew until I could sit where they were.

It was fucking humbling, starting at the bottom, knowing nothing other than this is where I wanted to be.

It was late afternoon when the bell above the shop door rang. I paused, broom in my hand, mid floor sweep, and a slow grin spread across my face at Violet in the doorway, Nyah by her side.

Nyah squealed at the sight of Dax and ran across the small space to throw herself at him. But Violet just smiled at me sweetly, respecting the fact I was at work.

I appreciated that, even though all I wanted to do was storm over and wrap her in my arms. I did a full visual sweep of her, checking her over, making sure she was okay after everything that had gone down.

But she seemed perfectly well, her oversized purse tucked beneath her arm, a "Clean Sweep Cleaning Services" shirt tight across her tits, identical to the one Nyah wore.

Nyah wrapped herself around Dax, and he lifted her into his arms, kissing her like there wasn't a roomful of his employees, plus Violet, all watching.

Roarke and King both groaned and made jokes about getting a room, but Violet took the opportunity to wander over to me.

"Hey, you."

I grinned down at her. "Just so you know, if it wasn't my first day and if I wasn't trying to pretend I was all professional and making a good impression, I'd be kissing you like that right now too."

She grinned up at me and winked. "Just something to look forward to later then."

I swallowed down a groan at the very thought. A night with Whip hadn't changed my feelings for her one iota. And some part of me knew that when I'd suggested Violet didn't have to choose between me and him, I'd also meant that I didn't have to choose between the two of them. It would have been her. I'd been in love with her since her fifth letter. She'd been the only bright star I saw in a place that was full of darkness and misery.

But there was something between me and Whip too. Something that had felt fucking right. Something that had felt good only because of how he felt about her too.

"I need you tonight," I whispered to her. Being apart for over twenty-four hours, after the things we'd experienced up on the bluff, had been too long.

She pushed up on her toes, so her mouth was close to my ear. "So you can tattoo my pussy?"

I groaned.

She leaned back and grinned at me. "That's twice I've asked now, days apart. You said I had to ask three times, and you'd do it."

"Keep looking at me like that and I might change my mind, get you naked, spread your legs, and do it right now while I've got all the equipment at hand."

Desire lit up her expression. "I'd like that. But just so you know, Nyah—"

"Levi!" she interrupted, like she'd heard Violet mention her name. "Dinner tonight. You, Violet, me, and Dax. Capiche?"

I blinked and glanced at Violet. She nodded.

"Uh, capiche," I called back.

Nyah clapped her hands. "Excellent! It's a double date!"

Violet stared up at me. "Are you sure? We don't have to if you don't want to."

There were a million other things we should have been doing. Trying to track down the psychopaths who'd nearly killed Violet and X being top of the list. But I didn't think I'd ever been on a date. Pre-prison, the idea of them had always seemed kind of stupid and a waste of time. I hadn't ever been interested in anyone enough to want to put on clothes, take them out, and actually have a conversation. I might have done it a couple of times pre-club days, but the aim had always been just getting them home and getting them naked. Then I'd joined the club where there had never been a shortage of club bunnies willing to bounce naked on my cock for as long as I could keep it hard.

But I'd had a year of getting to know Violet without any opportunity to see her in person, and it had been the biggest blessing of my life. As much as I loved seeing her naked, I loved finding out every little detail about her more. I already knew a lot, but I had no idea what dating her in person felt like. I had no real idea what doing anything normal with her felt like. But I wanted to know. I wanted to go grocery shopping with her, to cook meals together, to do the world's most boring shit like paying bills and filing taxes. Fuck, I'd actually have to do that now that I had an honest-to-God, legitimate job.

Mostly, I wanted her to forget that we were in the middle of a shitstorm. That had been her life for so long now, I needed her to know there could be good, even when everything felt like it was falling apart.

I brushed a lock of hair out of her face. "I can't wait."

10

VIOLET

I got ready for our double date in Nyah's run-down little house, not all that far from my apartment in the shittiest part of Saint View. It was an odd space that didn't really feel like it fit her vibrant personality. It took me thirty minutes of trying on outfits and another fifteen of debating makeup colors with her for me to put my finger on what felt wrong.

There was nothing personal to be seen. Other than her clothes, that overspilled a rickety-looking chest of drawers, and her purse she'd slung over one of the mismatched kitchen chairs, there was nothing of her in the space. It might as well have been a hotel room. There were no knickknacks collected on the flat surfaces from travels or shopping trips. There were no family photos on the walls, no favorite pieces of art, no calendar reminding her of family birthdays.

She was new to town, so it stood to reason she hadn't decorated, but it also gave me the vibe that the life she'd left, she didn't want to remember.

Knowing your father was going to use you as a pawn to further his underworld business dealings or marry you off to the highest bidder would do that to you, I guessed.

I understood. I'd been lucky enough to walk away from my past. At least I had, until Travis had shown up again like a bad smell no one wanted hanging around.

The roar of Levi's bike outside cut through my curiosity over Nyah's house, and I shoved the outfit choices Nyah had given the thumbs-down to back into my oversized purse. The file full of Toby's black-and-white prints stuck out of the top, a reminder I needed to show them to Whip and Levi, so we were all on the same page.

But tonight wasn't the night. Tonight, Levi and I were just going to be a regular couple, doing regular couple things.

I was going to pretend some psychopath hadn't tried to murder us all, and try to forget someone was leaving piles of dead bodies around Saint View.

You know, just the typical problems a girl liked to avoid by going out for cocktails with new friends.

That black cloud could have lingered over me if I'd let it. But instead, I let Nyah's infectious excitement fill me.

She ran to the window, all fairylike on her tippy toes, and squealed. "Dax is here too. Let's go!"

I gave myself one final once-over in the mirror and nodded at my reflection. The outfit wasn't anything particularly special, just a maxi dress that managed to cover up my cleavage enough that it was respectable, and a cropped jacket, matched with a pair of white sneakers. It was casual but cute. At least I hoped it was.

Though not terribly practical for riding on a bike, I

realized, as Nyah towed me out her front door and kicked it shut behind her.

Despite the fact she'd only seen him a few hours ago when we'd ducked into the shop, she ran across the dead leaf-littered lawn to Dax and threw herself at him, zero concerns about whether he'd catch her or not.

He did, of course, and spun her around, her laughter tinkling through the air like glitter dust.

Levi and I weren't exactly the 'run to each other like we were the lead characters in a romantic movie' sorta people.

He leaned on his bike, arms crossed over his chest, jacket pulled tight across his broad shoulders like he didn't give a shit about anything.

But I saw his gaze snap straight to me, and the way it rolled over every inch of my body. I crossed the lawn to him, my skin tingling with a growing blaze.

I stopped in front of him. "Hi—"

That was all I could get out before he was grabbing the back of my neck and hauling me in, claiming my lips, kissing me stupid.

My knees went weak. Those traitorous bitches just gave right on out like a I was a damsel in distress and needed him to catch me. His arms tightened around me, pulling me into his chest, his mouth never leaving mine, deepening the kiss.

I lost track of the time. Of my surroundings. Of everything but him.

Nyah cleared her throat behind me. "Uh, just wondering how long you two are planning to make out for? Our reservation is only held for another fifteen minutes."

I dragged myself away from Levi with a giggle, rubbing my lips together as they lifted into a smile. "Sorry. He nearly died earlier this week."

Nyah grabbed my hand. "Yeah, yeah. We know."

"We do?" Dax asked, his eyebrows pulling together in a frown. He glanced at Levi for confirmation.

Levi just shrugged.

Nyah let out an exasperated sigh. "You two were together all day. You didn't once talk about it?"

Levi shrugged. "No."

Nyah looked at me, and I just rolled my eyes. It was pretty much all Nyah and I had talked about during the jobs we'd had together. I'd word vomited the entire thing at her the moment I'd realized we were scheduled on together for a couple of big jobs Francine had picked up at a local office building.

She tugged me toward Dax's beat-up four-wheel drive that had dried mud splashed up its sides. "Come with us, since you're wearing a dress and we're all headed to the same place anyway. We can fill Dax in on the way."

I glanced at Levi, and he nodded, following us. But he stopped Nyah when she went to sit in the back seat. "Violet and I will sit in the back."

"Your legs are twice as long as mine. You literally will not fit. Take the front, it's fine." She climbed up into the back seat and settled on the driver's side.

Levi didn't seem terribly happy, but he got into the front passenger seat.

Nyah was right. My knees touched the back of his seat, and he was a good five inches taller than me so he would have had no chance.

But I was a little disappointed. It would have been nice to curl up with him.

Nyah's motormouth filled Dax in on the whole bluff ordeal as soon as he started driving. His jaw dropped open by the end of her first sentence and stayed like that until he connected the dots. Finally he had the full picture, it hadn't just been the rain that had me and X turning up soaking wet at his store.

Levi said nothing. Without twisting back to look at me, he reached his hand behind him, between the gap in his and Dax's seats.

I stared at his hand for a moment, not understanding what he was doing.

He wriggled his fingers at me.

A rush of happiness filled me when I realized he was asking to hold my hand. I was lucky I was sitting because those knees of mine were definitely weak again.

I threaded my fingers between his, staring down at the ink across his knuckles and how it contrasted with my undecorated skin.

Nyah paused in her long-winded story when she noticed us and mouthed, "Cute!" in my direction.

We were freaking cute.

This was what I'd dreamed of for all the months we'd written each other letters. Just a normal life, doing normal people things like going on a date with friends. In that daydream, we'd lived in a house not unlike the one Nyah rented, though I would have filled it with pink and all my trinkets.

I still had that dream. Only now Whip and X lingered around the edges of it, my brain not quite able to work out how it all fit together.

Dax was fully caught up on all the drama, or at least the version I'd given Nyah, which was ninety-percent truth with just a little held back to protect Murder Squad secrets, by the time we reached the restaurant. Levi untangled his fingers from mine so he could get out of the car, and I waited for him to open my door because I knew he would.

I wasn't disappointed. I picked up my purse and let him help me out and guide me inside the pretty Providence restaurant.

"Geez, I forgot how fancy this place is," Levi muttered. "I feel underdressed."

I squeezed his hand reassuringly. "You're overdressed if you ask me."

His gaze turned instantly hot. "Don't say things like that if you want to actually make it through the meal without me dragging you into the bathroom and bending you over the sink."

My breath caught.

He raised an eyebrow at my silence. That quickly became more of a smolder when I didn't complain.

A low grumble rolled through his chest, and I was pretty sure I heard him utter a deep, "Fuck" Geralt of Rivia style, but Nyah was also excitedly exclaiming over how pretty the restaurant was, so I might have heard wrong.

We followed the hostess to a table in the back corner, and I pulled my chair close to Levi's.

Nyah stared around the darkened room lit with table candles and twinkling lights. "Have you guys been here before?"

Levi nodded. "This is Hayden's place."

Dax's eyes widened. "This is Chaos's place? Shit, I didn't even realize when I booked it. I heard through the grapevine he had his own joint. 'Bout fucking time. His talent was wasted at the shitty holes-in-the-walls he was working at in Saint View."

Levi grinned at him. "Did you know about the sex maze in the back?"

I hid a laugh at the expressions on Dax's and Nyah's faces.

"The what?" she managed to squeak.

Levi went to answer her, but his gaze caught on something across the room, and his words died on his tongue instantly. He shoved to his feet so suddenly the table rocked and then, despite the classy atmosphere around us, Levi forgot himself entirely.

"Lynx?"

A man across the room turned in our direction.

My heart stopped.

Neither Levi nor the man noticed me going into cardiac arrest and clutching my purse beneath the table.

Levi moved to get around me, but the other guy was quicker and made his way over to our table before Levi could get very far. Their smiles were wide and genuine, and the two of them embraced hard, colliding like two mountains and slapping each other on the back like they were long-lost friends who'd just been reunited. They were a bundle of smiles and laughter and tumbled words as each spoke over the top of the other.

All I could do was dig my fingernails into the straps of my bag.

Levi eventually turned to me, his arm around the man. "Violet, I want you to meet Lynx." He lowered his voice so the entire room wouldn't hear. "He was my cell-mate when I was inside."

Lynx turned pretty blue eyes in my direction.

I instantly felt like I was being sized up. His gaze ran up and down over my body, but unlike when Levi had done it, there was no warming buzz that started up inside me.

When Lynx did it, I wanted to cross my arms over my chest and sink beneath the table. It wasn't so much that there was anything sexual in the way he looked at me. More that his gaze made me feel like a living specimen, being studied under a microscope.

His gaze felt calculating and scientific. Like he didn't see you as a person, but more as a weapon in his arsenal that he was deciding how best to use to his advantage.

He held a hand out to me, and for a long second, I considered not taking it.

But one quick glimpse of Levi's face and the hopeful expression on it told me I couldn't.

This man meant something to him, and that alone filled me with fear.

But it wasn't smart to play my cards too soon, so I stood and took Lynx's hand, making my grip as firm as possible so he didn't notice the tremble in it.

"It's nice to finally put a face to the name." Lynx's fingers wrapped around mine, holding on longer than I wanted him to. "I think your letters were all that kept my boy here going in that last year."

All I could do was offer a stiff smile. I tried to pull my hand away, my heartbeat spiking when, for a second, instead of letting go, Lynx only gripped them tighter.

I was sure he could feel my palm sweating.

Levi squeezed his shoulder to catch his attention. "You're out! When? Why didn't you tell me?"

Lynx gave me one long last look before letting go of my hand and turning back to Levi. "Not long after you, actually. They had a busload of new inmates and nowhere to put 'em. A few of us got brought up early for parole to make room."

Levi shook his head like he'd never heard anything so miraculous. "Unbelievable. That's so good. You should have called me!"

Lynx laughed. "On what? Not like you left me a number."

"Could have found me at the clubhouse."

Lynx frowned. "You said you weren't going back to them." His gaze dipped to Levi's jacket then raised to his face again. "Guess plans change, huh?"

Levi shrugged. "Things are different."

There was a moment of silence then Lynx elbowed him. "Listen, I should get back to my group, but don't be a stranger, yeah? I'll see you around."

Levi nodded. "I'm working at the tattoo shop."

Lynx grinned. "Of course you are. I'll come in for some new ink."

"See you then."

Lynx glanced at me and nodded, and then moved back through the room to his table.

I didn't miss the way his gaze trailed back to me and Levi though. Levi sat back down happily, shaking his head like he couldn't believe his luck.

I felt sick to my stomach over the fact I was going to burst his bubble.

I probably should have waited until we were in

private, but secrets had never done me any favors, and I wasn't keeping another one from him even for a minute. I twisted my seat so my back was to Lynx and pulled the folder of Toby's photos from my purse. "Levi. You need to see these."

He was still grinning and shaking his head in wonder, clearly surprised but thrilled by the fact his old cellmate was out and walking around the streets of Saint View.

I was a whole lot less thrilled about it.

Because I'd recognized Lynx's face the moment I'd seen him.

He was the same man who appeared in almost all of Toby's photos. The one lurking in shadows, making deals with strangers, money passing hands in dark corners of Saint View's seediest locations.

Levi stared at the photographs I'd found in Toby's room. Dax and Nyah watched on without saying a word, clearly realizing that something was wrong and not wanting to get in the middle of it.

Levi's smile fell off his handsome face, and I hated I was robbing him of this one small happiness so quickly.

He shifted through the photos. "What are these?"

"I don't know for sure, honestly. But I found them hidden in Toby's room."

Levi's gaze snapped to mine. "When?"

"Earlier today."

He swore under his breath and darted a look across the room at Lynx.

"Uh, not to sound naïve, but why does it matter if Toby had some photos of a guy in a dark street?" Nyah winced at one of the images and stabbed a pretty pink fingernail in its direction. "I did a cleaning job at that building last week. Place is a hole. I probably passed three drug deals in the process of lugging my mop from Francine's van. Not exactly an uncommon occurrence in Saint View, from what I've noticed."

Levi sighed heavily. "Maybe it's not connected. But Toby had photo evidence of crimes taking place. Crimes that Lynx is clearly a part of." He glanced over at him again. "And now Toby is dead."

His words hung in the stillness between us.

I didn't know about the others, but it suddenly felt like Lynx's gaze was burning a hole in my back. I didn't dare turn around.

"What do we do?" Nyah echoed the questions rattling around in my head.

Levi tucked the papers back into the folder and handed them back to me. "Nothing for right now. We're in a restaurant full of people, and I need time to think."

I put the photos back in my purse and tried to be level-headed. I hated that this was hurting him. "We don't know for sure Lynx had anything to do with Toby's death. Even if he is doing something shady in these photos, he didn't necessarily know someone was watching him." I bit my lip, knowing that coincidences in a situation like this were probably rare. And that where there was smoke, there was probably fire. "Should I have not shown you?"

Levi shook his head and met my gaze again. "Of course you should have. I don't want secrets between us."

His voice was so strong and firm I was instantly reassured I'd done the right thing. But my heart ached for him anyway. He'd been so excited by the idea of having his friend back, and I'd just thrown a bucket of cold water on it by accusing him of having something to do with Toby's death.

I could see that same idea playing over in Levi's head as we ordered our meals, and again when our food came. He was quiet, staring into space, not participating in the stilted conversation Dax, Nyah, and I tried to maintain. The whole thing felt awkward and weird, but I forced myself to make idle chitchat since we couldn't just leave mid-meal.

Dax and Nyah carried the conversation, but the tension was getting to me. I wasn't even sure he was looking in my direction, but I could feel Lynx's presence looming over me. All my brain could think about was if he had something to do with Toby's murder, then he was the man whose heart I needed to stop. He was the man who'd taken my best friend and who needed to be put in the ground.

I had no solid proof, nothing but circumstantial evidence that would have been laughed out of a court, and yet my brain screamed there was something off about this man. That he knew me even though I didn't know him. That his polite words hid a snake coiled within.

I pushed back from the table, even though the waitress had just put a steaming plate of juicy steak in front of me. "Excuse me, please. Bathroom."

I threaded my way through the room, my footsteps faster and faster, Lynx's sharp-eyed gaze following me until it was all I could feel. Anxiety wrapped itself around my chest, forcing breathless gasps, my brain screaming I couldn't just sit there and eat steak in the same room as the man who could be responsible for Toby's death.

I'd thought this whole thing had been about me. The things I'd seen. The things I'd done. The men I knew.

What if I was right, but it wasn't Levi, Whip, and X who were the problem? What if it had been Toby who'd set this entire thing in motion by sticking his camera lens where it didn't belong? What if it was him who'd dragged me in, and me who'd dragged in the others?

My brain was a whirlwind of thoughts and theories, none of them quite fitting, but unable to think clearly enough to dismiss any of them either.

I slammed my way into the bathroom, finding it a blissfully empty space to have a mental breakdown.

I gripped the bathroom sink, hunching my shoulders, heaving in shuddering breaths, panic seizing my body.

The door opened.

I snapped my head up, a sudden realization that I was alone and if Lynx followed me in here, I'd be trapped.

But it was Levi's green eyes that met mine.

Relief flooded me as he locked the door and stood behind me, wrapping his arms around me.

I couldn't stop my brain shouting of dangers lurking just outside the door. "What if—"

His hand lifted from where it was tight against my chest and shoulders to press a finger against my lips. "I know. I know all the what-ifs. They're running on a screaming loop inside my head too."

But my heart rate wouldn't slow. My breaths wouldn't calm. I forced his fingers away. "All this shit happened after you got out of jail. If Lynx got out not long after...It feels like all the pieces are there, but I just can't work out how they fit together. Dickson was there that night. He was in prison with you too." I shook my head. "I don't understand. I thought this was all about me, but what if it's not? What if it's Toby? What if it's you?"

"What if it's all of us?"

"I can't keep doing this," I said miserably. "The stress is too much. The constant not knowing. The constant edge of fear that never goes away. All I wanted for tonight was to go on a date like a normal couple and not worry about any of this shit, but it follows us everywhere. When is it going to stop?"

My chest heaved, trying to suck in breaths that it couldn't seem to hold.

I knew what a panic attack felt like, and this one had me in its grips.

"Breathe, Vi. Nobody is going to hurt you. Not in here."

My brain latched on to that. The safety in his words. The promise in his voice that I believed without question.

I couldn't go back out there like this. Palms sweating, eyes wild.

Levi kissed my neck.

I nudged him with my elbow. "Stop it."

"You wanted a proper date, right? That was all you wanted tonight. To just be normal?"

A tiny smile tugged at my lips. "Yes."

He kissed my neck again. "Fucking you in the bathroom mid-date is normal, right?"

I couldn't help but laugh. "I don't think so."

His tongue slid up my neck until his lips brushed my ears. "I disagree. I think you wore that dress tonight, knowing I was going to find it irresistible to take off you."

"I wore it because it makes me feel pretty."

"Let me make you feel pretty with it rucked up around your waist."

He'd asked for permission, but he hadn't waited for me to give it. He'd lifted my dress with one quick bunch of his fingers in the fabric. His hands roamed the globes of my ass in the panties I'd picked out, knowing he'd see me in them. They were sexy, half my ass cheeks showing.

He hummed his approval, palms skating over my skin, tugging the panties into the crease of my ass to expose more of each cheek.

The tight pull of the fabric had the added bonus of putting pressure on my clit and asshole, the silky fabric wrapping tight around his fingers.

"We shouldn't," I whispered, only because I knew it was the words I was expected to say.

But no part of me wanted to go back out into that dining room. No part of me wanted to see Lynx's face while I tried to choke down a meal, the entire time wondering if everything we'd gone through was because of him.

I just wanted to stay here with Levi. Here, where all I had to think about was his hands on my body and how that made me feel. I gripped the sink tighter.

His hand switched from caressing my behind to dragging across my hip to my front, and sliding down beneath my dress and panties to cup my mound. His other hand found the untucked hem of my top and groped beneath it, taking a handful of my breast, tweaking my nipple through the soft fabric of my bra.

A man smaller than him wouldn't have been able to wrap himself around a woman of my size, but Levi had always made me feel small. His broad shoulders and long limbs gave him the reach he needed to fully enclose me in his embrace, slowly working my pleasure points until one finger slipped inside me, and then another.

I gasped at the intrusion, my eyes closing.

He bit down on my shoulder. "Eyes up, watching me, Violet. I want you to see how beautiful you are when I make you come."

The reflection showed his hands molding and tweaking my breasts, big, groping handfuls that sent pleasure roaring through my system. The sight of what he did between my legs was cut off by the sink, but I didn't need to see it. I felt every movement, every thrust of his fingers inside me, each one building me up until I was begging for him to go faster, to give me more.

I ground my ass back against him, rocking on my heels, needing his cock inside me, needing us joined. The stress I'd been carrying around for weeks had all culminated in the last twenty-four hours, and my body demanded a release.

Letting him fuck me into oblivion was better than having a full-blown mental breakdown in a restaurant bathroom.

He dropped his hand from my tits to undo his fly, his lips at my ear the entire time. "You know what's through the doors at the back of this club? It's Psychos on steroids. Do you have any idea how much I want to take you out there and tie you up, just to watch every other man choke on his desire for you while they watch what I'd do to your body? Do you have any idea how much I want to watch you ride one of the dildos they have imbedded in the walls and the benches? I want to put you on your knees in front of one of those glory holes and fuck that pretty mouth. You won't be able to see, but you'll know it's me anyway."

I gasped at the darker, more dominant tone in his voice, one I hadn't really heard from him before, but one that did things deep inside my core so I just wanted him to say it more. "Yes," I moaned, knowing he was distracting me from all the other dark thoughts inside my head, also realizing it was exactly what I needed.

"You want me to fuck you like that, Violet? Publicly make you mine like X did in that cam room?"

I ground back on him, my arousal soaking his fingers. "Yes," I groaned, sure in that moment, with him edging me toward an orgasm and whispering the dirtiest things I'd ever heard in my life, that I would have agreed to anything he wanted to do to me.

I trusted this man with everything I had. Everything I was.

I loved him.

I wanted everyone to know how much. I didn't care who saw. It only turned me on more.

My gaze met his in the mirror.

There was a challenge there. Like he knew he was pushing me, testing me to see how far I would go.

"I could reach over and unlock this door right now."

I met his challenge. "Or you could stop wasting time, fuck me hard, and let me unlock it."

It was apparently exactly the right thing to say. His answering growl was feral. He jerked me from the sink and pushed me up against the bathroom door instead.

I braced myself with my hands, fingers inching toward the lock, fully intending that my words hadn't been an idle threat but more of a promise.

If someone walked in her right now and caught us fucking, then so be it. I needed this.

Needed him.

If he wanted to walk on the wild side, then I would walk with him.

I was pretty sure I would walk anywhere with this man.

His hands covered mine on the lock, and before I could protest, he slammed into me from behind.

I forgot all about whatever distraction game we were playing with our dirty talk and promises of public claiming.

I fell into the pounding of his body against mine, the stretch of his cock inside me, filling me so perfectly I could weep. I ground back on him, taking as much of him as I could, deepening the angle so he could bottom out.

All games were forgotten in the swirling desire that filled me.

He pulled my hand from the lock on the door and guided it between my legs, both of us working my clit together, until I was gasping and moaning, begging him to let me fall over the edge.

He gave it to me exactly how I wanted it. No fucking around, no holding back. He pushed me right to the brink and then broke through it, sending me spiraling into pleasure.

He went with me, my name a groan on his lips, his cock jerking inside me, one final slam of his body against mine ending his orgasm while he was buried deep inside.

He leaned on me, both of us resting on the door, our breaths heavy, any stress I'd been feeling now totally evaporated.

"Our food is going to be cold," he eventually murmured, still deep inside me, neither of us willing to move.

"And there's probably a long line of women about to pee themselves." I giggled.

I could feel his smile as his lips pressed to the back of my neck. I was sure it was vaguely sweaty from having him all over me.

"You good to go back out there?" he asked.

"Your cum is dripping from me."

He groaned and put my panties back into place. "Exactly how I like it."

I couldn't deny that I liked it too. I was going to end up with a UTI if I didn't clean up a bit, but it could wait a few more minutes.

I liked having part of him inside me, even when he wasn't.

He pulled out, and we washed our hands, grinning at each other in the mirror like naughty kids who'd most definitely done the wrong thing but didn't care.

And by the time we walked out of the bathroom, Lynx and his party had left.

But the memory of the encounter hadn't.

No amount of quick, hard, fast, and dirty sex could erase that something was very wrong in this town, and that until we worked out what it was, none of us were safe.

11

WHIP

I'd been ignoring my personal phone for over a week. Every time a call from an unknown number flashed up on the screen, I sent it straight to voicemail then conveniently didn't listen to the message.

But that was getting ridiculous. I wasn't going to have a business if I never answered my phone. I couldn't just continue not working. I had savings but I wasn't made of money.

Besides that, what the fuck else was I supposed to do with my time? I couldn't just chase Violet around and keep X and Levi out of trouble as my full-time job. That wasn't exactly going to pay the bills.

Except the idea of having sex with anyone other than them was about as appealing as going to the dentist.

I needed to get my shit together. It was a job. Nothing more. I'd always been able to detach myself from it, so why the hell couldn't I do that now?

I'd thought more than once about getting a regular

job. A nine-to-five, like I'd had once upon a time, but the thought immediately sent fear through me.

I'd had a normal life once. A regular job. A woman to sleep next to. Beautiful kids who had run outside every night when I'd gotten home from my office job in the city.

And all of that had been taken away in a heartbeat. In one stupid moment, my entire life had been wiped out because the three of them no longer existed.

Now all I had left of them was this house I could barely stand to sleep in and a photo in a frame that reminded me I was no longer the man I'd once been, and I couldn't go back, no matter how much I might want to.

Because losing it had nearly killed me once.

I couldn't afford to do it again.

There was no going back to a normal job. Sex work paid the bills, and it reminded me to never get too close to anyone because everything was transactional.

I needed to go back to work.

I rolled onto my side on my couch and forced myself to pick up my phone and play the voice messages.

"Hi! Uh, is this Wyatt De Leon? A friend of mine gave me your number—"

I hit delete.

Her voice was too high-pitched. There was no way I was going to listen to that for an entire hour.

"Hey, man. I'm looking for someone to fuck my wife while I watch. A guy I know said you do that sorta shit. Hit me up if you're interested."

My finger hovered over the delete button, mentally searching for a reason to press it.

But the truth was, I didn't have one.

Other than the fact the only person I wanted to have sex with while another man watched was Violet.

My fingers shook as my heart screamed to press down on the delete button.

But my brain reminded me I needed to actually pay for this roof over my head and the too-fancy car I had a loan on and couldn't really afford but needed because it went with the whole schtick. The guy I hired as my driver had been messaging me all week, asking if I had work for him. I felt like an asshole ignoring his messages as well, when I knew he needed my gigs to make ends meet.

I sighed and hit a different button, returning the call of the guy who wanted to watch and setting up a meeting for the next night.

Even before I hung up, guilt swamped me.

I tossed my phone across the room. "Get yourself together, you idiot. It's a job. And you aren't in a relationship. They'll understand."

But a terrified part of me was sure they wouldn't.

A knock at the door was a welcome relief. I pulled my head outta my ass and rolled off the couch.

The knocking kept coming, in varying patterns that sounded somewhat familiar.

By the time I opened the door, I wasn't even surprised that it was X on my steps.

I squinted at him. "Was that 'Greensleeves' you were playing on my door?"

X grinned and pushed past me like he owned the joint. "I play it in my van sometimes. Got stuck in my head."

"You're so fucking weird."

"I know. Where's your hockey stick?"

I blinked, following him through my house while he opened cupboards and rummaged around in them.

"My hockey stick?" I asked.

"Yeah, you know, that thing you whack little black discs around with on the ice? I know you have one 'cause you locked me in the house with it that one time when Violet came over."

I took a pile of freshly folded towels out of his arms. "It's not in my linen cupboard, I can tell you that much. It's out back, I think. Stop touching everything." I put the towels back on the shelf.

X happily trotted after me as I led the way to the back door.

"What do you want a hockey stick for anyway?" I asked.

"I'm trying out for the team."

I glanced back over my shoulder at him. "What team?"

"The CHL team."

I stopped with my hand resting on the lock. "You're trying out for the Coastal Hockey League team?" I snorted on a laugh. "X, you know they're one step away from the pro league, don't you?"

He nodded. "Yep."

I squinted at him. "Do you skate?"

He scoffed at my skepticism. "I'll have you know I won several figure skating competitions. You're breathing the same air as the Under Nine's state champion."

I raised an eyebrow. "Is that true?"

"No, of course not. I did one month of lessons when I was about twelve and then got bored and took up karate."

"How long did that last?"

"Six weeks, I think."

"You get bored easily."

"I'm already bored with this conversation. The stick, old man. Or did you already forget that's why I'm here?"

I led the way out to the little shed in my badly tended backyard and twisted the dial on the padlock until it sprang open.

My rarely used lawnmower sat inside, along with a variety of other gardening tools I didn't use as often as I should. Cobwebs clung to the corners of the tin structure, and the one window was grimy but let in enough light that I couldn't ignore the two kid-size bicycles and the sealed plastic containers that held all the belongings from a life I couldn't bear to throw away. I knew exactly what was in each of them without even opening one. Their clothes. Their stuffed toys. Photos. Memories.

A lump rose in my throat. "Get the stick and let's go."

X's eyes lit up. "You're coming with me?"

I grabbed the stick and thrust it at him. "Coming with you where?"

"To the tryouts." He shook the stick at me like it was a pom-pom. "I need someone to be my cheer squad. You got one of those little skirts you can wear?"

I shoved him out the shed door and locked it behind me again, along with the memories it stirred up. "Your tryout is today? Seriously? You haven't even trained!"

He shrugged. "Gotta seize the day, Whip. I nearly died. What if that ocean had taken my life? I would have never found out if I was destined for the pros. I can't let that opportunity go!"

I squinted at him. "Aren't you scared of the ice melting and drowning in it?"

He stopped abruptly and spun back to face me. His mouth dropped open. "Do you think that's actually a possibility? I have a thing about drowning, Whip!"

"I heard it happened to a guy in Australia. It's hot there, you know. So the ice just melted and down he went."

"No!"

I eyed him. "You're too gullible for your own good, you know that?"

He pointed a finger at me. "When you buy a jersey with my name on the back, I'm not going to sign it for you. I hope you know that."

I snorted on a laugh. "Come on, Wayne Gretzky. Let's go see what you're made of."

In the grandstand of the Saint View Ice Rink, I rubbed my arms briskly, warding off the chill that floated off the ice. The bleachers around me were mostly empty, save for a dozen or so small groups of family and friends, waiting to watch their loved ones take to the ice.

I raised my hand when Levi and Violet pushed through the glass doors, and they both waved back, making their way along the rubber-matted floors and then climbing the stairs to where I sat. Violet settled next to me, immediately putting her hand on my leg and sliding in close, Levi on the other side of her, rubbing his hands together.

"Wasn't sure I read your message right. You did say X is trying out for the team, right? Is that even possible?

Don't they just scout talent from people who are already, you know, playing?"

I shrugged. "Probably. But have you ever tried to tell X no? I'm fully convinced he could talk his way into becoming president if that's what he really wanted. I have no doubt in my mind he smiled at them, bamboozled them with some sort of word vomit story, and they said yes just to shut him up."

Down on the ice, players were starting to warm up. They glided out, their movements sleek despite their bulky protective padding. Little black pucks whizzed across the ice at speeds my eyes could barely keep up with.

Violet's leg bounced nervously. "I don't want him to get hurt. I'm really thinking that maybe we should have forced him to go to the hospital after the other night. He's been acting even crazier than normal. What if all of this is because he has a brain bleed?"

I shook my head. "He's just had a brush with death and is in the afterglow period where you're just glad to be alive."

Violet gazed up at me. "Did you have that...after the accident."

I stared out at the ice, but all I saw was the mangled wreck of the car accident I'd walked away from. The one that had taken the lives of my entire family.

All I remembered of the days and weeks and months afterward was the darkness. A deep, aching loneliness and depression where every minute had been a battle not to take my own life so I could join them.

The only thing that had stopped me was the knowledge that their murderer still walked the streets, out on bail thanks to his fancy-ass lawyer who'd delayed the tests that would have confirmed the guy was drunk off his ass when he'd hit us.

I'd smelled the booze on his breath when we'd both stumbled out of the wreck. I'd seen the unfocused eyes. My entire family had been wiped out because he'd been too fucking selfish to get a cab home from whatever bar he'd been drowning his sorrows in.

His had been the first life I'd taken. I'd hunted him down and made him swallow a bullet, zero fucks given because I had nothing left to lose.

And then I'd kept on doing it, lurking in the shadows, taking out men who didn't deserve the families they had. Taking out men who were a danger to society. Abusers who hurt their wives or kids. My actions escalating until I couldn't stop myself, each kill a blatant fuck you to my own life, the one I didn't want.

I'd just been waiting to get caught. Waiting to pick the wrong target, the one who would actually fight back. Waiting to go down in a hail of police fire when they finally caught up with me.

Grayson finding me had slowed me down, focused me, gave me some sort of direction, but I had never really stopped wanting to die.

Until now.

Because suddenly I had something to live for again. And they were sitting right next to me.

"Sort of," I told Violet, finally answering her question about whether I'd been glad to be alive after the accident. "Not in the same way he is, but nearly dying changes everything, and he's just trying to work out how to handle it. Trying out for the CHL team is probably the least destructive way to process what he went through."

"He got a nose ring too," she said with a smile.

Levi leaned forward, resting his elbows on his knees. "No shit? It look good?"

I glanced at Violet too because I hadn't even noticed it when he'd come to my house.

A little pink flushed her cheeks. "It's pretty hot actually. Suits him."

Levi squinted at the crowd of players still registering at the end of the rink and then clapped as X, in borrowed gear, waddled his way toward the gate that led onto the ice. He cupped his hands around his mouth and shouted, "Let's go, X!"

Violet took her cue from him and stamped her feet, waving her arms at him. "You got this!"

All three of them turned to me. I pretended I was half-heartedly waving a miniature flag. In my best "I'm bored" voice, I said, "Go, X."

Violet elbowed me, but it was playful.

I think we all knew by now my disdain for X was mostly for show. I actually cared about the idiot. I wouldn't have been sitting here on my ass in the cold rink silently supporting his ridiculous quest if I didn't. I wouldn't have called the other two in, and I wouldn't have been secretly hoping he did well.

I didn't have any hope in hell of him making the team, of course, but I had a silent respect for the way he never hesitated to give something a go.

Violet grabbed both my and Levi's hands as X stepped out onto the ice.

All three of us froze, waiting for his skates to slip right on out from under him.

I think we released a combined breath when he skated straight and smooth across the ice, not at all out of place amongst the other skaters. He glided around the ring, as gracefully as was possible in that much gear, my old stick clutched in his fingers.

"Wait." Violet squeezed my fingers. "Can he actually skate?"

X rounded the corner closest to us and lifted his arm to wave. "Hi, Omelet!"

That was all it took for him to lose his balance. His feet slipped from beneath him, spraying up ice, his arms windmilling wildly. The expression of pure joy at seeing us in the stands turned to sheer terror as he tried to save himself from hitting the ice.

He went down hard on his ass. All three of us cringed.

"Shit, that had to be painful," Levi muttered, half out of his seat like X might need him to go scoop him back up. But louder he called, "You're good! Nobody saw that!"

X waved back that he was okay, then tried to get back up on his feet. Which proved difficult with all the pads on. He rolled from his back to his front, then tried to get up onto all fours, but his feet slipped out from him each time.

Violet covered her mouth with her hand.

"Don't laugh!" I said to her, unable to hide my own laughter.

X slid himself along the ice on his stomach, narrowly missing the blades of other skaters, all of them staring at him and shaking their heads as they zoomed past.

"I'm not!" she protested, but her snort of amusement

couldn't be contained. "He's like one of those penguins sliding on their bellies."

X finally got himself back up on his feet, but only because one of the guys was nice enough to stop and help him to the railing.

"Thanks, MacIntosh!" X called, waving off the guy as he skated away, his last name printed across the back of his local league jersey. X glared back up at us. "That's my new friend. Who I'm going to replace all of you with since he's the only one not laughing right now."

We all sobered.

"Sorry," I called back, making sure the laughter was fully removed from my voice. "You're doing great. You've got this."

X gave us a thumbs-up, then attempted to strike what I think was supposed to be a confident, athletic pose, one hand on his hip and the hockey stick slung across his shoulders like a sword.

He immediately lost his footing again and crashed into the boards with a thud that echoed around the rink.

Violet winced. "He's going to need a chiropractor after this."

"Or a priest," Levi added. "He might actually die this time. Do you know one who can administer last rites quickly?"

A whistle blew, and one of the coaches leaned over the bench, flipping through paperwork on a clipboard. "Number Thirty-Four! You're not on my list."

X stood, finally, and shouted back cheerfully. "I know! I'm a late addition! I emailed the manager's intern's second cousin's roommate!"

The assistant coach squinted at him. "This isn't an open tryout. You can't just be here if you weren't invited."

X skated up to him, managing not to fall this time. "But the ice is my soul. The puck my chaotic joy. I skate toward greatness."

"Jesus Christ," I muttered. "Was that a haiku? I think it's time to go before they call security."

Levi was already on his feet, clearly in agreement. We hurried down the steps to stop behind the bench where the coaches sat.

I tapped the guy on the shoulder. "We're sorry about him. He's been hit in the head with a puck a few too many times. We'll just go."

But X gave the guy his most charming smile. "I really want to be on the team. I could be an assistant coach."

The assistant coach raised an eyebrow. "We already have one of those."

"The waterboy then!"

The coach cleared his throat. He was an older guy, with thinning white hair and a pot belly stuffed beneath a thick warm jacket with Saint View Vipers Hockey printed on the back, a deadly black snake wrapped around a hockey stick as the logo. "Son, this is the CHL. We aren't the pros; we don't have a waterboy."

X's face fell. "Oh. Okay. I understand. Thanks anyway."

He looked so defeated it stirred up something inside me. He tried so fucking hard, all the damn time. Seeing him get knocked back was like watching someone kick a puppy. An overgrown, yappy, completely insane puppy, but a puppy nonetheless.

"What about a mascot?" I asked the coach. "Do you have one of those?"

The coach sighed. "Again, this is coastal league. There's no budget for any of that."

"He'll do it for free," Levi butted in.

The coach raised an eyebrow and turned back to X. "Son—"

X grabbed his hand. "I'll supply my own costume." He glanced over at me. "You can sew, right? I'm thinking a black snake. With giant fangs. And sequins!"

I rolled my eyes, but X didn't notice. He'd already turned his attention back to the coach. "I'll be the best damn mascot this team has ever seen."

"You'd be the only mascot this team has ever seen," the coach countered dryly.

"What do you have to lose?" I asked. "You aren't paying him. He'll supply everything. And I think you've already seen, he can be quite entertaining."

"What's funnier than a hockey mascot who can't skate?" Levi backed up my argument.

The coach blinked fast, glancing between me, Levi, and X, and then shook his head and threw his hands up, clearly bamboozled. "Okay, okay. If I say yes, will you get off my ice so I can actually start the tryouts?"

I clapped the coach on the back. "You got it. Just pretend we were never here."

"I don't think that's possible." He wiped sweat off his brow.

X was already shakily skating away. "MacIntosh! Guess what! I made the team! But I'm all out of best friend spots." He glanced over at me and Levi. "I've already got a couple of those."

12

VIOLET

*S*equins littered my living room floor. They were down the cracks of couches, sprinkled across the countertop, and I'd even found a couple floating in my bath. I stared at the sparkly black blob as it floated along between the bubbles, and flicked it out, kinda hoping to never see a sequin again in my life.

We'd taken a crash course in sewing, aided by Queenie who'd heard about our plight to make X the biggest and best costume we possibly could. And thank God, because without her, the thing would still be in pieces. She'd whipped the four of us into a production line and somehow turned huge bits of foam and fabric and mesh into a giant snake's head that X had been wearing proudly for the past two days, claiming he was a method actor who needed to be in character at all times.

I'd drawn the line at him wearing it, and nothing else, to bed. If I'd ever even thought of having some sort of snake kink, it had been well and truly satisfied.

But it had all been a good distraction from

psychopaths who lingered out of sight, watching us in the darkness, and it had kept me from counting down the days and hours to Toby's funeral. I'd had a stilted phone call from his cousin, a woman I'd never even heard him speak of, telling me the date and time and place.

It hurt me his parents hadn't called me themselves, but they were mourning, and I understood.

I smoothed out my long black dress, flicking off another damn sequin that seemed intent on hitchhiking. When X knocked on the door to pick me up, I half expected he would still be wearing his mascot headpiece, but he wasn't. He just stood there, all six feet something of him in a suit that was slightly too short.

"Did you wear your brother's suit again?"

He tugged at the sleeves that didn't cover his wrists. "He really needs to grow."

"Or you need to buy your own."

He grinned at me. "I have one. It's snake shaped."

I shook my head and tucked my arm into his. Levi and Whip both waited downstairs, leaning on the side of Whip's car. I sucked in a breath at the sight of them. Whip in a suit wasn't anything I hadn't seen before, but I'd barely seen Levi in anything other than ratty jeans and his club jacket.

"Wipe your drool, Omelet."

I elbowed X but let him go so I could greet Whip and Levi. Whip put his hand to the small of my back to draw me in for a kiss that was so featherlight across my lips it did nothing but leave me wanting more.

Levi brought the more. He waited until Whip had his turn and then grasped the side of my face. He tilted it up so he could bring his lips down over mine. "You look beautiful, Vi."

He kissed me before I could respond, stealing any words that might have been lingering on my tongue, and then opened the back door for me. He helped me in, and I slid over so he could get in behind me.

Whip and X took the front seats. We drove silently to the only church in Saint View. I couldn't remember ever going there before, but I'd seen it in passing, from the back seat of the bus I took into Providence when a job had me out that way. It was surrounded by neatly cared for green grass, the graves of the deceased stretching far behind the little church and its surrounding buildings and parking lot.

Whip found a spot to leave the car, and the four of us got out, the men flanking me as we walked toward the doors.

Nyah and Dax waited just to the left of them, in dark-colored clothes that matched ours. She stepped forward and squeezed my hand.

I smiled at her gratefully. "You didn't need to come. You didn't know him."

She shook her head. "Funerals aren't for the dead. They're for those left behind. And you need your friends around you today."

I swallowed down the lump building in my throat and half laughed. "I'm going to be a blubbering mess before this even starts if you keep saying things like that. But thank you. It means a lot to me that you're here."

She linked her arm through mine, and we led the way inside the church, the guys falling into step behind us. We found a pew, and I waited for Dax and Nyah to squeeze in first, so I could sit next to her with my three guys to my right.

Toby's parents sat in the front row, talking quietly with the priest. I glanced around, searching for Devin, but couldn't see him anywhere. I'd sent him a text when Toby's cousin had called me, but he hadn't replied. I really hoped he'd come. He and Toby might not have been together all that long, but I knew he'd made Toby happy. He should be here.

I ignored the waves of a couple of people we'd gone to high school with, who sat in the back. I had no idea why they'd turned up. They hadn't had any time for Toby and me back then, why act like we were friends now? They were just here for the tea. The entire town buzzed with speculation about how Toby had died, and I wasn't about to fuel it by discussing it with any of the people who still hadn't learned to mind their own business.

My phone vibrated in my bag, and since we still had a little time before the service started, I pulled it out and checked my messages.

There was one from Rebel, and another from Bliss, both of them apologizing for not being here today but they had their kids to take care of. Fang was away on a club run with War and Hawk, but he'd called while I'd been getting dressed, and in his gruff way, with barely any words spoken, checked to make sure I was doing okay and that I knew he was thinking about me.

It warmed my heart to know these people who had never even met Toby cared about me enough to reach out.

I smiled at the most recent message.

Nyah glanced over my shoulder at it. "That was nice of her."

I nodded. Francine's message read:

FRANCINE:

Sorry about your friend. Nyah said you
were both going to a funeral.

I chuckled again when a second later another message came through:

FRANCINE:

Did you take an extra bottle of bleach
from the storeroom yesterday?

Nyah just rolled her eyes at Francine's cheapness, and I put the phone away.

The priest left Toby's parents and stood in front of the altar, a little microphone pinned to the collar of his robes. "Friends and family. We're gathered here today to celebrate the too-short life of Tobias Warren Horton."

His words washed over me. A numbness crept in, but I didn't fight the feeling of grief. I let it in, knowing I had to feel it so I could let him go. Minutes ticked by that felt like hours. Cold air kissed my skin, the old church drafty as hell. Nyah's fingers wrapped around mine, and Whip's hand squeezed my leg every few minutes, helping to keep me warm.

The priest spread his arms wide. "Would anyone here like to come to the front and say a few words about the departed?"

I waited for his parents to stand, but they didn't. His

mother sobbed uncontrollably in the front row, his father's arm around her. The people filling the second row all gazed around at each other, as if they knew someone should get up and say something but nobody actually wanted to.

I knew for a fact the assholes from high school behind me weren't going to say a word.

I hadn't prepared a speech. Nobody had asked me to make one, but I sure as hell wasn't going to allow this funeral to end without someone getting up and telling the world how amazing my best friend had been.

I pushed to my feet, and all three of my guys stood with me. They moved out into the aisle to let me pass, each of them touching me just a tiny bit as I passed, letting me know they were there for me.

But this was something I needed to do alone. I moved slowly to the front of the room, my fingers shaking because public speaking had never been my thing. I hated attention focused on me.

At the altar, the priest offered me a microphone, but I shook my head.

I turned to face the room.

"For anyone who doesn't know me, I'm Violet Garrisen. Toby was my roommate and my best friend. And I'd really like the opportunity to tell you how great he was."

The words tumbled out surprisingly easily after that. Each memory flowed from me like he'd put them right in my head. I could practically hear his voice reminding me to make him look good and to not tell them about the times we'd gotten blackout drunk on cheap wine while wailing about our lack of love lives.

My eye caught on Devin, sitting just a couple of rows behind the pew I'd vacated. "Toby found love recently, and I couldn't have been happier for him. He and Devin didn't get long enough together, and that will always break my heart." I connected my gaze with his. "But thank you. Thank you for giving him that, even for the short time he had it."

Devin nodded at me, his eyes shiny.

I knew mine were too. I blinked hard, trying to keep the tears at bay until I'd said everything I needed to say.

I couldn't keep looking at Devin's devastated face if I was going to hold it together, so I let my gaze slip past him to the next row.

My fingers clenched into the fabric of my dress.

Travis stared at me smugly, like he knew exactly how unsettling his presence would be. My lips parted, words on the tip of my tongue demanding to know why he was here.

He'd known Toby. Travis and I had lived in the same foster home, so he'd been around for many of the years Toby and I had scraped through school together.

In theory, he had every right to be here. Just as much right as the other assholes in the back with their crocodile tears and fake memories of a man they'd never truly known. But unlike the others, Travis didn't pretend. There was nothing in his expression that said he was here for Toby.

It was all about me.

Slowly, he mouthed, "You. Owe. Me."

I stumbled on my words and turned away, focusing instead on Whip and Levi and X.

One glimpse at their faces, and it was clear they knew

something was wrong. Levi glanced over his shoulder, following my line of sight, but I wasn't sure whether he saw Travis sitting behind them like I did from my higher-up vantage point on the altar steps.

My fingers trembled, but I managed to keep the shake out of my voice. I wanted to say the truth. That he'd died protecting me. But nobody knew I had been there that night. Nobody knew the horrors of what had gone down in that empty warehouse.

They were secrets I'd have to keep until I met him again one day.

All I could do was brokenly whisper that I loved him and missed him.

And then set him free.

I slunk back to my seat, and Nyah gripped my hand once more. "That was perfect. Well done."

I didn't feel like I deserved praise. I stared blankly at the wall for the rest of the ceremony, Travis's gaze burning a hole in my back. I leaned in and whispered to Whip that he was there.

He nodded and whispered back that they'd take care of it after the service.

But by the time the priest invited everyone to attend a celebration of life and people began to file out, Travis was nowhere to be seen.

I didn't even have a chance to be relieved about that. Devin walked away toward the parking lot, and I chased after him, not wanting him to go until we'd had a chance to speak.

I caught up with him at the edge of the lot. "Devin."

He turned around and gave me a sad smile and a half shrug. "Violet. Hey. Sorry, I just can't hang around and do this. Your words were beautiful, but I don't want to mourn him like this. This wasn't him."

I knew what he meant. Toby didn't do stuffy, formal events. He would have wanted glitter and music and laughing.

But as Nyah had said, funerals weren't for the dead. They were for those left behind. And if this is what Toby's parents needed, then that was okay.

I grabbed Devin's hand so he couldn't leave. "I know. This wasn't him. They didn't know him like we did." I let out a shaky breath. "But I think even I didn't know the real him." I watched his expression carefully. "Did you?"

I saw the flash in Devin's eyes. Something that looked a whole lot like guilt.

My breath caught. "What do you know?"

Devin glanced over my shoulder, making sure no one was listening. "You found his photos, then?"

I nodded.

He mirrored the action. "I figured you would. I should have taken them all. I was going to that night you let me into your apartment. But in the end I just sat there, surrounded by them, and couldn't do it. His whole room just felt like something I didn't have the right to touch. And I convinced myself it didn't matter now anyway."

"Why did he have those photos? You knew enough to know you should get them from him, even though you didn't."

He ran his hand through his closely cropped hair. "I'm a cop."

I was pretty sure my heart stopped. At the very least, it skipped several beats, finally picking up again in a speeding rhythm that echoed horses' hooves thundering down a racetrack.

"What do you mean?" I whispered, even though I'd heard his words perfectly and there had been no room for misinterpretation.

"It's how Toby and I met. He brought his photos to the department, and I was the one assigned to go over them. I'm a low-level nothing. I get all the grunt jobs, and the sergeants assumed Toby's photos weren't important."

"But they were, weren't they?"

He nodded. "It was an accident the first time. He said he'd been out night shooting, practicing something to do with the lights. But he brought us the photos because he thought he'd inadvertently caught a drug deal on camera.

"Had he?" I whispered.

Devin nodded. "I suspected so, but the people above me didn't care. They dismissed it, citing that minor drug deals weren't of interest to them. I told Toby to keep it confidential in case the gangs found out they'd been photographed. I didn't want anyone to be able to tie anything back to an innocent guy, who'd just been out taking photos in the wrong place at the wrong time. But my sister died from a drug overdose, and I couldn't just let it go. It's the salt in the wound, you know? That one thing I got into policing to protect others from, and it fucking grated that they didn't care."

He sighed heavily. "So I took my own camera out to the streets, trying to get proof of more." He smiled ruefully. "And found Toby hiding out, doing exactly the same thing."

I shook my head. "Sounds like my stubborn best

friend. Tell him not to do something, and he'll do it just to spite you."

Devin smiled fondly. "Yeah, I learned that lesson the hard way. I tried to keep him out of it for longer than I should have." He sniffed. "I tried to keep him out of my bed for longer than I should have too." He lifted a watery gaze to meet mine. "I regret that so much now. If I'd known I would only get such a short amount of time with him, I would have kissed him that first night I found him in the shadows. The chemistry was there from the get-go. If I'd known..."

I stepped in and hugged him. "No one could have known."

He squeezed me back but stepped away, clearly needing to finish the conversation. "He was just trying to help. He knew where the gangs hung out. He had the equipment to watch them from afar. But I owe you an apology. I owe all of his family and friends an apology. I lied to you all about what I did for a living, and I shouldn't have let him get so close. I should have locked him up or something, but I was selfish. I liked that I kept running into him out on the streets. I'd only just moved here, and I was lonely, and sitting in the dark with steaming cups of coffee and whispered conversations while we waited for something to go down was the highlight of my days. I should have pushed him away, but instead I drew him in. Made him a part of it. Made him lie to you all about who I was." His voice cracked. "And I got him killed."

I folded the man into my arms, and he sank in against me, holding me tight as grief poured out of him in guilt-racked waves I knew all too well.

I tried to make my mouth move. Tried to tell him it wasn't his fault. That everything had happened because of me, not because of Toby.

But I didn't know that either.

I couldn't forget Lynx's snakelike eyes, staring at me from that black-and-white photo. He wasn't the only man in them. The photos dated back to before he'd been released, but it was clear to me he was deeply involved. That as soon as he'd been released, he'd taken up the position he'd left behind.

And he'd been staring right at the camera.

I'd been so convinced this entire thing was about me, but I just didn't know anymore.

I wanted to pour out every thought in my head, every theory, every worry.

But my eye caught on the three men I loved standing to my left, watching on from a distance.

And I pressed my lips together, knowing that my only job now was protecting them, the way I hadn't protected Toby.

13

___

X

I hated seeing Violet sad. It ate away at me like a buck-toothed rabbit with chlamydia.

Or maybe that was koalas who had STDs. I didn't know. But I didn't like it.

We gave her and Devin space to talk, but it was killing me not to go over there. My fingers twitched to pull her into my arms and tell her stupid jokes until she laughed.

It was a relief when Devin finally hugged her and walked away.

She came back over to us, her cheeks tearstained. We surrounded her, the three of us enclosing her like the rest of the world would hurt her and we weren't having it.

"He's a cop," she whispered.

I was pretty sure my mouth couldn't have dropped open any farther. "Are you serious? Skinny Devin?"

She nodded and filled us in on their conversation.

Whip let out a long breath. "Does he know anything...more? Did you say anything about us?"

She shook her head quickly. "No. But there's something else. Travis was here. He's still saying I owe him."

I rolled my eyes. "That little fuck? I'll get rid of him."

I waited for Violet to tell me not to again. But she didn't.

Excitement lit up inside me at the very thought of taking that fucker out. It had to happen eventually anyway. The guy was on the list. But I hated the way Violet shrank in on herself every time he was around.

I would take great delight in ending him.

Maybe I'd get some of that koala chlamydia from somewhere and give him a good dose of that so he suffered first.

I found that idea oddly delightful.

She didn't exactly seem happy by the idea though, and that brought me right back to being sad. I clapped my hands together, startling the three of them.

"Okay, so how about I cook dinner tonight? I think we deserve a nice meal after all of this."

"You cook?" Levi asked, skepticism rich in his voice.

I didn't miss a beat. "I also vacuum in heels and throw dinner parties for my imaginary friends. Try to keep up."

Violet covered her mouth to hide her smile.

And my job was done. I'd pat myself on the back later.

"So, you in?" I asked Levi.

He shrugged. "I'm never going to say no to someone who wants to feed me."

"Violet? You trust my cooking abilities?"

"Of course. I can't wait."

We reached Whip's car and took up the seats we'd had on the way here, me in the front with Whip. I pulled my seat belt on and waited for him to say something, but he didn't.

I snapped my fingers in front of his face. "X to Whip. X to Whip. Do you read me? Are you coming to dinner?"

His gaze fell to his hands on the steering wheel. "I can't, not tonight."

Levi poked the back of Whip's seat with his knee. "Come on. What else do you have to do?"

I snorted. "Maybe he has a hot date."

Whip said nothing.

I narrowed my eyes at him. "Wait, do you have a hot date?"

He started the car without looking at me. "It's not a date. But I have a client, yeah."

"You're going to get naked with someone other than us?" I moved my mouth around, silently repeating the words. "Well, that was a sentence I never thought I'd say." I pinched my jaw and opened and closed it a few times, distracting myself from why I suddenly felt weird about the very thought of Whip rolling around in the sheets with some random woman.

Unlike Levi, who was probably well acquainted with Whip's naked form by now, I had no desire to do the same. I was a one person sorta man, and Violet was the only one I wanted to be naked with.

But despite popular belief, I wasn't stupid. I knew she was in love with Levi. And I knew Whip was her safe place. I wasn't even entirely sure how I fit in, but maybe I was a bit of both. She'd made room for me, and I wasn't going anywhere for as long as she let me occupy that space. If that meant sharing her with the two of them, then I would.

I would give her whatever the hell she wanted. If she wanted me to build her a bed big enough for ten men, then I would.

I didn't know how I would afford the wood, 'cause that shit was expensive, but hopefully one of those other guys was a builder and had a trade discount.

Whip backed out of the parking lot. "I have to work. It just is what it is."

He'd said it matter-of-factly, but his gaze kept flicking to the rearview mirror, and I knew he was trying to get a glimpse of how Violet was reacting.

I folded my arms across my chest. "I don't like it. On behalf of the people in this car who have sucked your dick, I vote you quit."

Levi punched my arm, a lot harder than a playful slug. "You've sucked his dick? When the fuck did that happen?"

I flinched, rubbing the spot and twisted so I could see him. "I never said that! I said on behalf of the people who had. Meaning you two!"

Levi crossed his arms over his chest and stared out the window.

I hid a laugh. "Oh, look at jealous little Levi. All mad because for a split second he thought I'd had Whip's anaconda in my moist cave of wonders."

Whip groaned and shoved me with one arm without taking his eyes off the road. "Please shut up before I run us into a tree. And never say moist again. Especially not in conjunction with cave of wonders."

I gagged. "Okay, I'm sorry. I heard it. It was bad." I glanced back at Levi. "You gag like this when his steel pole is tapping out Morse code on your tonsils?"

Levi rolled his eyes. "It's such a shame your mother didn't drown you at birth."

The banter continued the entire way back to my apartment, mostly courtesy of me trying to keep it light after an afternoon that had felt all too heavy. I kept glancing at Violet, waiting to see if she reacted to any of our antics, but by the time we were all piling out of the car outside my building, it was clear she was very quiet.

She got out of the car quicker than the rest of us and walked ahead. I trotted to keep up with her, leaving Levi and Whip to lock the car.

"Hey," I said quietly. "You okay?"

She lifted her head, but her smile was forced. "I'm fine."

"You're allowed to not want him to go."

She sighed heavily. "It's his job. And we've made no promises to each other. I can't ask him not to leave just because the idea of him with another woman makes me crazy."

I pushed open the door to the lobby and waited for her to walk through.

Then let it swing shut in Levi's and Whip's faces.

I slung an arm around Violet's neck and pulled her in close, so my lips were to her ear. "Tell him not to leave."

She shook her head. "I can't. And don't you say anything either. It's not our place to make decisions like that for him."

I let it go, respecting the boundary she'd set, but not liking it.

"Promise me, X."

"I promise I will not say anything." I mimed pulling a zipper closed across my lips.

The other two caught up with us at the elevator, and we all rode up in it together, until it stopped at my floor. I let us into my apartment, and the three of them found various places to settle, Violet perched on a swivel stool at the breakfast bar, Levi and Whip both taking up spots on the couch. Levi leaned over and found the TV remote, flicked it on, and channel surfed until he found a game replay.

I rummaged through the refrigerator, searching for something to make for dinner. I kept the thing pretty well-stocked, because for all my joking, I actually didn't mind cooking. I didn't do it all that often, since it was mostly just me to make meals for, and going to all that effort just to sit at the table alone was pretty fucking pathetic.

But I'd gone shopping just last week with the hope that Violet would be around more, and so I'd bought all sorts of things I thought she might like, just in case. Everything from fruit and meats to Doritos and caviar. I'd also stocked the bathroom with all sorts of girly things. I'd found the same brand of bodywash she kept in her shower and cleared out a drawer to fill with tampons and a spare toothbrush...

I eyed the two guys sitting on the couch and realized that maybe I should have bought a couple more.

I shrugged and pulled some beers out of the fridge instead. Maybe if I got Whip drunk enough, he'd stay.

But I already knew that would be impossible. He was too controlled. And he never would have had more than one when he knew he had to drive later.

My fingers brushed a bundled-up package of oysters

that I'd bought with full intentions of making Violet horny. "Do you guys like oysters?" I handed a bottle each and then went back to the fridge for two more for me and Violet.

"Not for me," Violet replied. "Had them once when Toby and I went to a fancy restaurant for his birthday. Horrible."

Levi cracked open the lid on his beer. "Never had them before but have zero desire to try. They look nasty."

Whip just took a sip of his beer and shook his head. "You two don't know what you're missing. They're the best." He leaned back over the couch, twisting in my direction. "I'm in if you are."

I pointed at him. "That's the spirit!"

I gathered up the oysters and set them on the countertop.

It was only after Violet swiveled on her stool to take in some of the game playing on the TV behind her that I noticed the expiration date on the oysters was two days earlier.

I cringed and went to throw them in the trash can, but then Whip pulled Violet off the stool and onto his lap, and her laughter tinkled around the room.

She smiled happily in his arms, both of them sipping their beers, watching the game, all loved-up.

How could he even think about leaving her when she looked like that? She'd been so sad all day, but now she was smiling and relaxed wrapped around him, the two of them the perfect couple.

He couldn't leave. He couldn't just walk out the door and go have sex with someone else.

I eyed the out-of-date oysters again. And then shrugged.

If getting him drunk wasn't going to keep him here with us, then maybe a minor case of food poisoning would.

14

VIOLET

I sank into the warmth of Whip's body, letting his strong muscles and the slight buzz from the beer soothe away all the sad parts of me that hadn't wanted to say goodbye to my best friend. The football game provided a hum of background noise, though I didn't really pay attention to it. I was more interested in the three humans in the space around me, my heart squeezing at the knowledge they'd all shown up for me today, and that they were still here, keeping me company, making me food, distracting me from the grief that came in fits and starts, sometimes so heavy it felt like it would drown me, and then at others, barely a thought.

This was the only place I wanted to be. With them.

And yet I knew this was limited, because at some point in the next few hours, Whip was going to walk out the door to go have sex with someone who wasn't me.

That thought left me feeling so sick I could barely think about it.

I knew it was his job. Knew if I wanted to be with him

then I would need to get over it.

But I didn't know how.

Every time I thought about him touching another woman, I just felt like I was going to get sucked down into a gaping void of despair and jealousy. Sharing him with Levi felt good. Right.

Sharing him with some random off the street felt like I might take up killing as a hobby right alongside the rest of them.

X's encouragement to tell him rang in my ears, but I couldn't do it. I was terrified of being that whiny girlfriend who laid down rules for her man. I didn't want to be a controlling bitch. What he was doing wasn't cheating. Hell, we weren't even in an official relationship, he had the right to see whoever he wanted. He wasn't even seeing this woman. It was work. A transaction.

So I bit my tongue and tried to just enjoy the moment and not worry about the fact he was going to walk out the door in a few hours, and there was nothing I could do to stop him.

If he stopped, it had to be his decision. Not because I'd forced his hand by being a nagging bitch.

X brought over a tray of oysters, fresh, still in their shells.

I wrinkled my nose at them. "They smell disgusting."

X waved a hand around dismissively. "You just have an untrained palate." He nudged them at Whip. "Eat up."

Whip leaned around me, picking up a shell with a slimy oyster sitting in the middle of it, and tossed it back like he was doing shots at the bar.

X eyed him with a raised brow. "Good?"

He nodded. "What did you put on them? Some sort of

sauce?"

"A combination of soy and Worcestershire sauce and a few other things. A recipe my mom taught me."

Whip reached for another. "It's delicious." He nudged one toward me. "Try it. You'll like it. Barely tastes like oyster at all."

But X quickly shook his head. "Can't waste good oysters on their poor taste buds. Enjoy, friend." He clapped his hand on Whip's shoulder and went back to the kitchen. Pots and pans clattered about, and more ingredients appeared from the depths of the fridge.

X frowned at them. "Shit, I need garlic."

Levi glanced over. "Just leave it out."

"Wash your mouth out. I will do no such thing. Garlic is life." He grabbed his keys from the kitchen counter. "I'm just going to run down to the store and grab some. Sit. Enjoy. More beers in the fridge." He eyed Whip. "Eat all those oysters."

Whip picked up another and swallowed it down. "Not gonna be a problem. Want me to save you some though?"

"Nope, they're all for you!"

X waved as he walked out, and I settled back with my beer.

Happiness washed over me, and I kissed Whip, because he was the closest one to me, knowing that Levi wouldn't mind.

He kissed me back. He tasted of whatever sauce combination X had created in the kitchen, and it was delicious. "Mmm," I murmured on his lips. "You taste good."

He stole another kiss but kept it short and offered me the tray of oysters. "Two left. Go on. Try one. Just because you didn't like the way the restaurant prepared them doesn't mean you actually don't like them. These are really good. The sauce makes them."

Just from the lingering taste on his tongue, I was a whole lot more interested than I had been a few minutes earlier.

I picked one up and downed it in the same way Whip had.

It slid over my tongue, slimy, but the sauce masked any other flavor it might have had. I swallowed it whole, like I knew you were supposed to, and shrugged. "Not awful."

Whip offered the last one to Levi. "Everyone should try them once in their life."

Levi wrinkled his nose but took the last one anyway. "So I'm not supposed to chew it?"

Whip shook his head. "No. Just tip the shell up and let it slide right down your throat." He glanced around the room. "Huh. X isn't here to make an inappropriate blow job joke. What a shame."

I stifled a laugh, both me and Whip watching Levi.

He caved and took the last one, swallowing it down.

We both waited for his reaction.

"Well?" Whip asked.

"I think I like it."

I snuggled down onto Whip's lap farther, loving that I was no longer worried about whether I was cutting the circulation off to his legs. He'd made it abundantly clear for weeks now that my weight was not a problem for him, and because he'd assured me time and time again with such conviction, I was finally believing him. It felt nice to be comfortable with them. To be relaxed and casual, not worrying whether the way I was sitting was giving me fat rolls. Or if they were judging me for eating.

Whip's fingers traced idly over my arm, creating patterns.

I loved the way it felt. He wasn't consciously trying to turn me on, but just the way he wanted to be near me, wanted to touch me, was all it took for me to be thinking about more than just the football game we were supposed to be watching.

I kissed his neck, inhaling the delicious scent of him while my nose was there.

He let out a murmur of approval at what I was doing, and he transferred his beer to the hand that was wrapped around me so he had one free to undo his top button.

The collar loosened, and then some more when I undid the second button to give me better access. I kissed my way all over the side of his neck, the small pecks quickly turning into open-mouth sucks, my tongue flicking over his skin.

He tightened his grip on me. "Don't stop, Violet."

"You've had too many oysters," Levi mock complained from the other couch.

But I didn't miss the way his attention was no longer focused on the game, and instead, was solely concentrated on me and Whip.

I undid a few more buttons and worked my way across his chest and to the other side of his neck, repeating the action there. I brushed my lips over his ear, breathing heavy across it.

He groaned. "Keep doing that, Violet, and you're going to find yourself spread out on this coffee table."

I did it again, letting him know the idea of that threat

was actually very welcome.

He growled in my ear, taking control, and lowering the zipper on the back of my dress. His dick got hard beneath me, and I wiggled on top of it. I knew what I was doing to him.

His fingers found the back clasp of my bra, and he undid it.

I pulled the straps down my arms and dropped it on the floor, leaning back and tilting my head up to look at the ceiling so he had room to kiss his way down my neck, across my chest, and over my breasts.

He gripped one in his hand, flicking his thumb over the tip, tightening the nipple until it was taut and begging for his mouth. He lowered his lips and sucked.

I gasped at the sensation, silently begging him for more. My fingers found the nape of his neck and stroked across it. The short beard that lined his jaw scratched on my skin, but in a way that only increased the pleasure, the sensation of hard against soft so intoxicating I just wanted to feel him all over me.

Levi put his beer down, his gaze fixated on me and Whip and what he was doing to my body.

My gaze held his.

My breath hitched.

Levi dropped to his knees and crawled across the carpet to settle at our feet. He undid my shoes and slipped them off my feet. His fingers held my leg like it was something precious, and he lowered his mouth, kissing the inside of my ankle.

I shivered at the tiny touch, that single touch of his lips somehow so erotic it had a rush of arousal pooling at my core.

His gaze never left mine. He worked his way up the inside of my leg, kissing and stroking and licking at my skin while Whip turned my breasts into his own personal lollipops, devouring each one in turn until I was trembling.

Levi used his shoulders to push my thighs apart. His fingers hooked in the elastic of my panties, and then a tearing sound filled the room.

Seams ripping, Levi shredding my underwear.

Whip and I both stared down at him between my thighs.

Whip raised an eyebrow. "Very caveman."

Levi grinned. "I've always wanted to do that." Then he cringed in my direction. "Hope you weren't attached to those."

"They were my favorites," I whispered.

Levi's mouth dropped open. "Shit." He took the ruined panties off me and held them up, inspecting them. "Maybe I can sew them up? I paid attention during Queenie's sewing lessons."

I couldn't help the slight upturn of my mouth. "I'm joking, Levi."

Whip chuckled beneath me, the vibrations of his amusement humming pleasantly at my back.

Realization washed over Levi's face, and then a wicked glint. He flicked his fingers over my clit. "Just looking to get punished, are you, Violet?"

Why did that sound like a promise on his tongue?

But two could play at that game. I waited until Whip was playing with my nipples again, and Levi had pulled my dress off, leaving me naked between them. I waited until he'd gone back to kissing my inner thighs and driving me mad with the fact he was kissing all around my most intimate area, but not actually putting his tongue where we all knew I most wanted it.

He was teasing me because I'd teased him.

"Levi," I moaned. "I want you to tattoo my pussy."

Both Levi and Whip groaned in unison.

But it had the desired effect. Levi put his mouth right to my clit like he couldn't hold off a second longer.

And I smugly lay back against Whip, letting the two of them pleasure me into an orgasm.

It rose fast and hard, too quick because by now, both of them knew exactly what I liked and how to give it to me for maximum impact. I writhed between them, the orgasm barreling down my spine, spreading across my skin and through my blood. Whip kissed my neck and whispered the dirtiest words in my ear, telling me how he was going to fuck me, how I was going to take his cock, how I was a good girl coming for them.

Levi's mouth and fingers should have been illegal. They worked together in the most perfect harmony, his tongue all over my clit, his fingers thrusting into me, stretching me perfectly, hitting my G-spot until the orgasm took hold.

Neither of them stopped. They pushed me right over the edge, my breaths coming in hot pants, my body clenching around Levi's fingers, back arching into Whip's touch.

The door opened when I was mid-orgasmic scream.

X dropped his shopping bags on the floor. "I was gone ten minutes. TEN MINUTES! And y'all turned my place into Pornhub Premium?" He grinned. "I bought cucumbers but I'm guessing you're good on dick-shaped objects, Violet?"

I couldn't even laugh, though Levi and Whip did.

All I wanted was him.

I reached for him, moaning for him. "Knox."

I didn't miss the way the other two raised their eyebrows at me using his legal name, but somehow, it felt right. At least in this moment.

Something about that name on my lips changed his expression entirely. All jokes he might have been thinking of making evaporated, and he kicked the door shut.

"Make way, boys. Daddy's home, and he brought the chaos kink."

Okay, maybe not all jokes.

Whip cringed like X's words had mortally wounded him. "Did you just refer to yourself as Daddy?"

"Yes, and you're both grounded. Get naked and think about what you've done."

Levi stared down at his crotch. "I don't think my boner has ever shriveled up so quickly. I think it actually just tucked itself right on back up inside my body."

I couldn't help but laugh. It was one thing I loved about X more than anything else. His ability to make me smile with his inappropriate humor. I reached for him, undoing his pants and dragging them down his legs. His dick was hard just from looking at my naked body on Whip's lap with Levi between my legs. I twisted just enough to turn my face toward him, opening my mouth to bring him into this too.

He let out a low, guttural noise as his cock slid past my lips and along my tongue.

I moaned around him, the thickness of his erection stretching my lips wide, the tip of him hitting the back of my throat with every thrust.

It did nothing but turn me on more. He grabbed my hair, fisting it around his fingers, holding it tight in his grasp until my scalp tingled pleasantly, matching the afterglow of the orgasm Whip and Levi had already given me.

I worked X's cock, one hand around his base, as much of it as I could take in my mouth.

Levi dragged me down Whip's legs a little, balancing me more on his thighs than over his dick. Behind me, Whip drew down the zipper on his fly, and from the corner of my eye, with the way my head was twisted to take X, I watched Whip stroke himself.

He was already hard, but watching his fingers wrap his dick and work his length had me moaning around X.

Between my legs, Levi spread my arousal lower, slicking over the area between my opening and my ass, massaging it firmly, until I loosened up even further and his fingers slid back to my asshole.

"He's going to fuck you here." Levi prodded the tight opening, rimming me, working my arousal all over it. "Fuck, Violet, you're soaked."

He didn't say it like it was a bad thing. He said it like the slick juice between my thighs was the hottest thing he'd ever seen. He coated me in it, lubing up my ass, finger-fucking me there until it was me moaning for more.

Whip's fingers found my hips, and he guided me back, helping to lift me just enough to press his cock at my rear entrance. "Slow, sweetheart. Drop down slow."

I listened, because he had more experience than me. Or maybe because I'd turned into a total slut for hearing him call me good girl, and I just wanted him to say it some more.

Either way, I worked myself down on him, inch by inch, my body trying to reject his cock at first, but then relaxing into it when the pleasure overtook everything else. We both groaned once he was fully inside me, both of us breathing hard.

He guided me so my back was against his chest, the two of us joined in such an intimate way I was still shocked I'd given this man so much control over my body.

And yet when Levi brought his cock to my pussy and coated himself in my arousal, I was more than willing to give myself up to him too.

"Fuck," Levi gritted out. "Want your pussy so fucking bad, Vi. Want us both in you."

"Yes," I moaned.

It was all the permission he needed to push his way inside me. I shouted at the intrusion, so damn full of both of them that I instantly wanted to come.

X cut off my shouts with his cock.

He forced it past my lips, and I was grateful for it. It focused me, gave me something else to concentrate on that wasn't just the overwhelming sensation of having Whip and Levi inside me.

I couldn't do much, other than just take what the three of them offered. Whip didn't move much beneath me, but the tiny lifts of his hips were just enough when combined with the full thrusts of Levi into my pussy. I focused on X, sucking and licking him, moaning louder and louder around the thick width of him as Levi really started working between my thighs.

Whip's fingers found my nipples, and pleasure surrounded me. It coursed through every vein, every cell. The orgasm that barreled up from somewhere deep inside carved its way through my system, until I was gasping, spluttering, moaning for them to come with me.

X's grip on my hair tightened. He fucked my mouth faster, shutting me up, me urging him on just as much with eager pulls of my mouth. I moaned around him, more porn star than the meek, timid woman I'd been when the three of them had found me, and loving every minute.

I wanted this.

Wanted them.

Levi's groan of need echoed through the room. "Want to come in your pussy, Vi. Need you to come with me."

"Yes." I needed it just as bad. Needed X and Whip to come as well.

Whip drove up into me, his low murmurs of praise telling me I was perfect and sexy and exactly what he wanted.

Levi's thrusts were deliberate, each one grinding his pubic bone against my clit.

X's precum lit up my taste buds, and I just wanted more. Wanted to watch him fall apart.

Wanted to feel like he owned me just as much as the other two did.

"Come in my mouth," I begged him.

"Fuck," he groaned. "Violet... Fuck. Take it."

I obliged, loving the way he felt inside me.

I knew they were all holding on, waiting for me.

I brought my fingers to my clit, rubbing the little nub, pushing the detonate button on the building pressure inside me.

I fell hard into a spiral of pleasure. My entire body tightened, then relaxed, muscles deep inside me spasming uncontrollably, sending sharp darts of pleasure through every inch.

Levi fucked me faster, harder, and the result was both me and Whip groaning, him clutching at me, fucking up into me until he was taking me as hard as Levi was.

My body welcomed every thrust, so thoroughly gripped with the pleasure they'd created in me.

X stared down at me, our gazes connected, his beautiful lips parted as he watched me through half-mast eyes.

I saw the moment his orgasm hit him. Saw it in his expression, in the jolt of his body, in the way he gripped me, like he needed something to keep him anchored.

His cum spread across my tongue, spurting deep in the back of my throat.

I swallowed him down, licking every inch of him, not minding the taste, not because it was good, but because it was him. All I wanted was to give him the same sort of pleasure the three of them gave me.

He thrust into my mouth at the same time the other two thrust into my body.

I was the center of all of it. The sole focus of their attention.

For a girl who'd grown up hiding away in corners, trying to stay out of view, it felt new.

Good.

Like being loved.

My heart squeezed. I loved them. All three of them. This thing between us was so much more than just sex. So much more than the danger that lurked outside.

There was a connection here that couldn't be denied, and it was the breath in my lungs.

I licked X, keeping him in my mouth until every last shudder had been wrung from his body.

When he was done, he flopped on the couch Levi had vacated, our clothes strewn about the room, all thoughts of the dinner X had been planning to cook abandoned.

Levi pulled out from my pussy, and I knew his cum was dripping from inside me, coating the insides of my thighs, but I was so well-fucked I couldn't fathom cleaning up yet. He lay out on the carpet at my and Whip's feet, his arm slung over his eyes, breathing hard.

"That was...fuck. Good. Really fucking good. I don't think I can move."

"Me neither," I admitted, well aware Whip was still inside me. But I was too boneless to lift off him, and he seemed intent to keep me there, his fingers tracing featherlight patterns over my tits again, like he might have been hoping for a third orgasm out of me.

There was no way. I was so done, so sensitive that even his tiny touches felt like fireworks. I was going to catch fire if he tried wringing another orgasm from me.

But he just seemed intent to lie there in the recliner, with me on his lap.

His breathing deepened, and mine followed, matching the rise and fall of his chest, my eyelids getting heavy.

Levi was quiet on the floor too, clearly just as sleepy as Whip and I were.

X, of course, was anything but tired, his constant need to do something kicking in. He stood, picking up the plate of empty oyster shells. "Back to making dinner!" He tilted the plate a little in my and Whip's direction. "Oysters were good, Whip?"

Whip mumbled sleepily from beneath me. "Excellent. So good Violet and Levi even gave them the thumbs-up."

X froze. "What?" His gaze met mine. "You ate them? You said you didn't like them!"

I frowned at him. "I didn't think I did, but Whip said they were really good, so Levi and I both caved, and I tried them again. Yours were much better than the ones I had at that restaurant."

"No!" X wailed. "Nooooo! You weren't supposed to eat them!"

All three of us lifted our heads to look at him, but it was me who spoke. Something wasn't adding up.

"You made us the oysters but you didn't want us to eat them?"

"Just ignore him," Levi said lazily. "A blow job from Violet would break my brain too."

But X shook his head. "It's not that." Then he glanced at me and added. "Though it was extremely good. Top notch. Can't remember my own name sort of blow job. Do they have a *Guinness Book of World Records* for sexual acts? If so, I'm submitting that one."

I squinted at him, just waiting for his verbal diarrhea to run out.

He eventually sighed. "I have a slight confession to make." He looked between all three of us guiltily. "And I don't think any of you are going to like it."

15

WHIP

The bathroom floor and I were becoming fast friends. I groaned as a bout of crippling stomach pain had me crawling for the toilet. I puked up another round of misery and regret, and then slumped against the bathroom sink, avoiding the tangle of Levi's arms and legs, sprawled out on the other side of the drain.

Violet flapped a limp, sympathetic hand in my direction from where she was curled up in the fetal position in the bathtub.

X peeked his head into the bathroom. "How's everyone feeling?"

I groped around the sink above my head, finding a bar of soap. I hurled it at his head. "I can't believe you fed us out-of-date oysters just to keep me home!"

"I only did it because I love you!"

I searched for another missile to pitch at his head but came up empty-handed, and the effort had me drained.

"This isn't love. It's premeditated intestinal manslaughter."

"It's just a little food poisoning, guys. Come on. Don't be babies."

Levi lifted his head from the floor weakly and glared at him. "This isn't food poisoning. It's chemical warfare. You should be on a fucking watchlist!"

X shrugged. "I probably am. But I swear, I never meant for you or Violet to get sick."

I flipped him the bird. "So glad you only intended to kill me."

"Not kill! Just...maim? I didn't want Violet to be sad that you were going off to have sex with other people!"

Violet glared at him from her makeshift bed in the bathtub. "Nuh-uh, don't bring me into this." Sweat broke out on her forehead. "Oh God, I'm going to be sick again. X, get me that bucket."

X gagged but passed it to her.

She snatched it from his grip and buried her face in it, hurling up the contents of her stomach again.

X held her hair back, but sweat dotted his forehead. "Don't throw up, Knox. Do not throw up," he chanted to himself.

I glared at him. "How's that aversion to vomit working out for you right now, X?"

He smiled weakly at me, his complexion green. "Not great, thanks for asking."

He dry heaved again above Violet's head, but the death look I sent his way had him trying to cover it with a cough.

I was truly going to kill him this time.

Just as soon as I threw up again.

The time ticked by, filled with the moans and groans of the three of us who had been gastrointestinally betrayed, and eventually I had X bring me my phone. I glared at him as I stabbed out a message from the floor tiles, telling my client the threesome he wanted to have with me and his woman wasn't going to happen tonight.

I didn't tell him why.

16

———

X

hip looked worse than either of the other two. I'd gotten them all tucked into my bed, Levi with his arms slung possessively around Violet like she was a stuffed toy. Violet, dead to the world, her lips parted in sleep, had a small smudge of dried vomit still clinging to her hairline. I didn't have the heart to wake her to clean it.

But Whip...

Whip sat on the edge of the mattress, swaying. His skin grayish, eyes dull and glassy.

"You okay?" I handed him the bottle of water I'd been forcing on them every twenty minutes, trying to flush out the plague.

He took a sip, swallowed, and grimaced. "You're lucky I'm too weak to murder you."

I flopped down beside him, my back hitting the headboard, and gently tucked a stray strand of Violet's blond hair behind her ear. "I'm lucky in more ways than that." I jerked my chin toward the lump under the blankets that was Levi. "That one jumped off a cliff for me. Violet's still letting me in her bed. You haven't pissed in my shoes yet. It's been a good day, despite all the vomit."

Whip didn't laugh. He rarely did. But he smiled, just a little. "You're an idiot."

"I prefer 'chaos gremlin,' thank you."

We sat in silence for a long beat, the room full of low breathing and the occasional gurgle from someone's gut. Then I turned toward him, serious and honest. "You know you don't have to keep doing this."

He blinked. "Doing what?"

"Running." I paused to pick at the edge of my blanket. "From us. From her. From...this." I waved vaguely at the bed.

But also at the feelings that existed between the people in it, even when I sort of accidentally, on purpose, poisoned them. "I have a really great family, you know? You haven't met them yet, but they're the best. Great parents. Great brothers. Cute niece and nephew."

"Why do I sense a but coming on?"

I lifted a shoulder and shrugged. "They don't know the real me. I can't show them that. But you..." I gave him a half-smile. "You know me. You might want to kill me all the time, and I know I deserve that. But you're kinda my guy, Whip."

His brow furrowed into a frown. "I thought Scythe was your best friend?"

"Oh, he is," I assured him. "We're like this." I held up my hand, my first two fingers entwined around each other. "But it's you I trust with Violet. It's you who jumped off a cliff for me. It's you who I'd call if I entered a pie-eating competition and needed to be rolled home."

Whip clutched his stomach. "Please don't talk about pie. Or rolling."

I went on like he hadn't said anything because I needed him to understand why I'd poisoned him. "Scythe has a family of his own. But *you're* my family. So when you said you were leaving us tonight..."

Whip's expression finally morphed into one that might have been understanding. "You lost your mind and thought poisoning me was the way to go?"

I grimaced. "In hindsight, after cleaning up vomit for hours, it might not have been my best idea."

"You don't say." Whip's voice was dry as the Sahara.

"I'm sorry." I honestly meant it. I felt like shit over how sick they'd all been.

Whip sighed. "If it's my turn to be honest, part of me was glad I couldn't go tonight." His eyes narrowed. "That part was definitely not my stomach, just for the record. But my heart wasn't in it. I wanted to be here with the three of you."

Something filled with relief unlocked inside me. "So stay. Stop hiding in the beds of strangers when the bed you belong in is right here." I gave a small laugh, feeling awkward about being this vulnerable with someone, and patted the mattress as enticingly as I could.

Whip's voice was quiet when he answered. "It's not that easy."

I pushed the urge to make jokes away and instead focused on the words I knew he needed to hear. The ones I knew I needed to say, not just for him but for me too. "I know it's not that easy right now. But it could be? You belong here. With us. In this madness. In a found-family soap opera of trauma bonding and inappropriate lust..."

Well, I'd tried. It wasn't my fault it was really hard to have a serious moment when you were just naturally hard-wired to be hilarious.

He huffed something that might have been a laugh.

"I'm serious, Whip." I tried again. "You matter to us. To me."

His mouth moved, like he had a thousand replies and didn't know which one was safe to say.

So I saved him.

"Plus, I already added you as my emergency contact. So now you're trapped."

That got a real laugh, small and hoarse, but real.

Whip shook his head, the hint of a smile still curling his lips. "You're a lunatic."

I grinned, reached out, and gently shoved him sideways. "Get under the covers before you collapse and die. I don't want to have to explain to Levi how I had to bury you in Mrs. Sinterro's turnip patch while they were sleeping. He gets all growly and weird about your well-being. It's honestly adorable."

"Goodnight, X."

I tugged the blanket over him. "Goodnight, future husband."

His eyes flew open. "I swear to God—"

I sniggered, enjoying the pure panic on his face. I didn't have any sexual attraction to Whip or Levi. I was a one-Violet man and always would be.

But it was fun to mess with them.

"Shh." I stroked my hand down his cheek. "Rest your pretty face. You're safe here." I switched off the bedside lamp, letting the dark peace settle over us.

I didn't sleep, not that there was room for me in the

bed, even if I'd wanted to, but I didn't leave for the couch either. I listened. Counted their breaths.

And when I was sure they were all out, I whispered into the stillness, "I love you guys. But if you shit yourselves in my bed, I will end you."

17

VIOLET

Somewhere in the middle of a vomit-induced sickness dream, I started thinking about the warehouse of horrors. When I woke with morning sunlight streaming through the windows, and Levi and Whip tangled around me in X's bedroom, the warehouse was still on my mind.

For a long moment, I didn't move. Just stared at the ceiling, playing over every detail of the night Toby died.

But so much of it was a blur. So much of it was dark shadows and fuzzy corners. I knew my brain was trying to protect me from reliving the entire thing out in full, vivid color. I didn't want to see Dickson climbing through that window, only for his lifeless body to fall at my feet. I didn't want to relive that sickening, robotic death count-down, or the way Toby had plunged that knife into his own neck to save me.

Maybe it was the funeral that had forced my brain to let down some of the walls that had been keeping me safe for weeks.

Maybe it was the food poisoning.

But all I knew was I wanted to go back.

Had to go back.

"Omelet? Are you awake? Are you contemplating all the ways you could kill me?"

I jumped at X's voice and twisted, peering over Whip to see X on the floor beside him, surrounded by empty bottles of water, vomit buckets, and towels.

He looked about as wiped-out as I felt, curled up on the floor with no pillow and a towel as a blanket.

"Did you sleep on the floor?"

He sat up and stretched, something in his back cracking audibly. "Not sure I'd call it sleeping. I need new carpet if we're going to make a habit out of staying here. Something way fluffier and preferably with a higher thread count." His gaze flickered over my face. "You seem better. Less... Casper the Friendly Ghost."

I rolled my eyes at him. "Thanks. I think. Good to know vomit-pale isn't my color."

"You feel better though?"

I did a mental sweep of my body and realized I did. "I'm tired but I actually feel quite well. Like all that vomiting detoxed my body or something."

X perked up at that. "So I helped!"

"You most definitely did not help."

His shoulders slumped again, but it was impossible to stay mad at him. His heart had been in the right place and he'd been duly punished, cleaning up after us for hours, which for someone as squeamish as he was, had to have been torture.

"Can you take me back to the warehouse today?" I asked him.

Levi's arm tightened around me, drawing me back into the warmth of his chest. "Not a fucking chance," he mumbled into the back of my shoulder.

I hadn't even realized he was awake. I linked my fingers through his and brought his hand up to my mouth, kissing his knuckles. "I need to, Levi. Please. I don't want to go without you all, but I will if I have to."

He grumbled something else I didn't catch, his arm banding around me again though, so I got the gist he wasn't thrilled by the idea. I couldn't blame him. I'd put myself in danger before, and it hadn't worked out so well. But this seemed relatively low risk. The police had presumably gone through the place and cleared it of anything that could kill us. I doubted whoever had set the trap was going to use the same location twice.

That didn't seem like their style. It was too obvious, and they were too smart.

I'd underestimated them once. I wouldn't make that mistake again.

"I'll take you," Whip said quietly without moving. "As long as I can stand up without the room spinning."

X got up and hovered like Whip might need catching at any minute. The fact Whip didn't complain told me their little conversation last night when they'd thought I was asleep had done them good.

Or that Whip was still seriously ill, but he got himself up with no assistance from X and turned to face me. "I want to look over the place again as well. Then we need to talk about the pile of bodies we found out at the dump site."

"We should talk to Grayson," Levi offered from behind me.

X frowned. "What if Trigger and Ace and Torch are responsible for those bodies though?"

Whip practically growled, "They aren't. They can't be."

X pointed at him. "Times that reaction by a hundred and that's how Gray is going to react. Trigger is his brother. You think he isn't going to automatically want to protect him? He's a biased witness. Or source. What's the difference? I don't know. He's a biased man! But I do know we can't go to Gray. We need to work out if any of the three of them are involved and have solid proof before we go accusing them of anything."

Levi groaned. "I hate when X has a point."

X clapped his hands. "Right then. It's decided. We return to the scene of the crime, check out the warehouse, now that the cops will have quit crawling all over it, and then we go hunting Murder Squad members."

"Not hunting," Whip said dryly. "Researching. Surveilling perhaps. Not hunting. We aren't hoping to have to kill anyone."

X flapped his hand around dismissively. "Potato, pot-ah-to. Same, same. Either way, we have a big day ahead of us. We're going to need breakfast." He grinned. "I think there's some leftover oysters in the fridge..."

The looks Levi, Whip, and I sent in his direction could have peeled his skin right off his bones.

"Or I could just do eggs!" He scuttled out of the bedroom before anything could be thrown at his head.

Whip, Levi, and I all picked at the omelets X set in front of us, none of us quite trusting our tender stomachs. Eventually, we all scraped our plates onto X's, and he happily wolfed down the leftovers.

None of us had clean clothes at X's place, so we did the rounds, stopping so everyone could get fresh clothes, but no one suggested it would be quicker to split up.

I didn't know what had changed, maybe it was the sex, maybe it was the conversation Whip and X had last night, maybe it was just the fact what we were about to do felt a lot like walking back into the lion's den even though the beast had already had a couple of swipes at us. But I wanted to be with them, and they seemed to feel the same, so nobody complained or suggested separating.

It was past midday when we got to the warehouse. Whip parked his car out front, in the same spot he had the night they'd found me inside, covered in Toby's blood.

I hated that I remembered that. But was grateful as well that bits and pieces were coming back to me.

I had to have missed something. There had to be clues my brain wasn't putting together.

Or maybe that was just wishful thinking.

Either way, I wasn't going to get anywhere by sitting in the car, and they were clearly all waiting on me.

I pushed open the door, and without a word, the three of them followed. They flanked me as we walked past industrial businesses, going about their day, working out of the other occupied factories. But a lot of the buildings in the complex were empty, For Lease signs in the windows or taped to the doors.

I couldn't imagine there'd be a rush of businesses wanting to move into the area once they found out the place was a murder scene.

I forced myself to walk confidently, to keep my strides long. I didn't want to give myself a chance to back out.

But the sight of the building where it had all gone down still sent shivers down my spine when it came into view.

We stopped at the door, and Whip took up a sentry position at the end of the row, keeping watch, but it seemed pointless. Nobody cared we were here. The other businesses at the front of the complex, where they had street visibility, were busy doing their own thing, and there was nobody around when Levi pulled tools from his pocket and picked the lock, bright and shiny, like it had been replaced recently.

He pushed the door open, and we all waited for some sort of alarm system, but nothing happened.

Levi put away the pliers he'd brought, ready to cut wires if there had been, and we all stepped inside. Whip put a brick in the way of the door locking, like he knew I wouldn't be able to stand the thought of being completely closed in here again.

Even still, dread filled me. It was brighter than the night I'd been here, sunlight filtering through the high window.

But not enough to ward off the lingering feeling of death and despair.

There was something wrong with this place. The air felt stale. The darkness pervasive.

Everything inside me screamed at me to run.

I stood my ground, refusing.

Even when my gaze caught the faint trace of Toby's blood on the floor. Mostly cleaned off but the stain remained, nonetheless.

X just squeezed my hand and past me, for once in his life silent, his gaze flittering around the space.

The other two did the same, the four of us moving in different directions, wandering around beneath the high ceilings.

But there was nothing much here. Like I remembered from that night, there was no sign of anyone owning or occupying the building. I knew X had Hendrix, his brother, search for ownership records and the building had come back as owned by a huge foreign investment company. Which didn't seem tied to anything relating to me, or the Murder Squad, so the idea of the owner being involved had quickly been dismissed.

But Levi wasn't the only person in Saint View who knew how to pick a lock. Anybody could have broken into this place and quietly laid a trap, just as easily as we'd walked in here today.

"I think this place must have been occupied by a business at some point," Whip called from the front. "There's an old fridge up here and a couple of broken chairs. Might have been used as a break room once upon a time."

I didn't remember seeing that the night we'd been here. Just the dark shadows and evil voice who haunted my dreams.

"Agreed," Levi answered from the other end of the echoing space. His voice bounced off each corrugated metal wall. "There's scrap metal and some other junk back here. If this stuff isn't leftovers from a business, someone has used it as a dumping ground."

I moved slowly to where Levi stood, remembering the same area but dark with shadows. I remembered looking over it that night and dismissing everything there as junk and nothing that could help us.

My heart rate picked up, and I studied it again in the light now. Had I been wrong? Should I have paid more attention? What if there had been something there that could have saved us?

I almost didn't want to look.

But there was nothing.

Just junk like Levi had said. Piles of metal. Some discarded, ripped shirts. Trash.

Relief flushed through me.

X wandered over and kicked at the pile. "Seems like the cops went through it but didn't care enough to take any of it with them. Can't blame them. Look at all this shit." He kicked at a broken crate and then crouched to pick up a grubby teddy bear. "Hi, Violet!" he said, putting on a voice that was supposed to belong to the bear. "I'm Whip's emotional support bear. He cries into my matted fur at night."

Levi snorted on a laugh and swatted it out of his hand. "Don't touch that. It probably has lice."

It landed at my feet, and I jumped out of the way, sure he was probably right. The thing was ugly as hell.

A sudden jolt of recognition splintered through me.

I'd seen a bear that ugly somewhere else.

My stomach twisted. I couldn't stop staring at it. My brain flashing up memories I would have rather forgotten for many reasons except I couldn't, because it had also been the day I'd met X.

"Vi?" Levi asked. "You good?"

X cringed. "Is it another round of the shits? Oh God, not more vomiting! I've done my time, Lord! Have you not punished me enough?"

The rest of us ignored his theatrics.

I slowly raised my head. "I've seen that bear before."

"In a horror movie?" X asked.

I shook my head. "On Paul Jeddersen's bookshelf the day he attacked me. The same day you..." I stared at X. "You know." I ran my finger across my neck.

A dreamy expression spread across X's handsome features. "Ah, yes. Paul Jeddersen on Olympic Drive. Lactose intolerant and wouldn't offer me cheese. Stabbed multiple times until he was barely more than soup." He grinned, focusing on me again. "And you in nothing but your underwear. What a day."

His eyes darkened suddenly, like he'd remembered the rest of the details of that afternoon, the way I'd been in my underwear because Paul Jeddersen had drugged me, cut off my clothes, and was well on his way to raping and killing me when X and Scythe had randomly knocked on his door.

"I'd kill him all over again if I could."

I knew he would, and I would have let him. But it wasn't the point right now. I picked up the ratty teddy bear and held it out to X. "Do you remember this? It's the same one, right? It was on that bookshelf you were hiding behind."

X took it from my fingers but shrugged. "I honestly don't remember. All I saw that day was you."

He said it so seriously and earnestly that if I hadn't been focused on racking my memories for that bear, I might have swooned.

I held it toward Levi and Whip. "I'm one-hundred-percent sure this bear was on Paul Jeddersen's bookshelf."

Levi squinted at it again, though was clearly uninterested in touching it. "Those toys are mass manufactured. There are probably millions of them out there."

He had a point. "I guess so. But what if it's not a coincidence? What if it is his? What does that mean?"

"Definitely not that old farty, rapey, Pauly-boy was here," X piped up. "I killed him good. There was no zombie-style resurrection for him, I promise you that."

Whip reached for the bear. "No, Paul Jeddersen is definitely chopped up into little pieces and disposed of. That was easy enough to do after X went all chop suey on him." He turned the stuffed toy over in his hands and wrinkled his nose. "But it's something." He squeezed the bear, then paused. "Well, fuck me. Anyone got a knife?"

We all looked at X.

He rolled his eyes. "Why would you assume I have one! Geez!" He patted himself down. "Switchblade? Hunting knife? Serrated or just nice smooth steel? Oooh, pocket knife?" He started pulling weapons from various places on his body.

I gaped at him. "How many knives, exactly, do you carry at any one time?"

"On a weekday? Not many. Seven?"

"Only you would think seven knives is not many," Levi muttered, but his gaze was firmly fixed on Whip as he took a blade from X and sliced it through the seams of the bear.

Whip yanked out fluffy bits of stuffing, then a small bundle of wires.

"What's that?" I whispered.

Whip fished around in the bear's belly some more, following the cords, seeing what else was in there. Eventually, his gaze met mine. "It's a nanny cam. I should have realized. We had one when..." He swallowed thickly but then forced himself to continue. "We had one when my daughter was little and my wife went back to work. We were new parents, super overprotective and didn't fully trust anyone."

X squinted at him. "So what? You stuck a bear with a camera in your home and spied on your babysitter?"

Whip lifted one shoulder. "Well, yeah. Essentially."

"Paranoid much?"

Whip glared at him. "When you have a tiny baby who is fully dependent on you to keep them safe, that you love with a depth you've never felt before, come talk to me."

"I love Reginald like that."

Levi sighed. "You do not love your wild park duck like Whip loved his baby, X."

"You don't know the depth of a father's love, Levi!"

Whip rolled his eyes and snapped his fingers between the two of them. "You're missing the point."

X side-eyed him. "The point being Paul Jeddersen's gross nanny cam bear somehow moved from his book-shelf to this creepy warehouse?"

Whip's lips pulled into a thin line. "The point being someone filmed what happened here the night Toby died." He swallowed thickly, eyeing me. "And that if this bear was also on Paul Jeddersen's bookshelf, someone probably filmed everything that happened that day on Olympic Drive too."

My blood ran cold. Him drugging me. Stripping me down to my underwear while I was unconscious. X saving me. Whip cleaning it up.

Someone had seen it all through the glassy eyes of a ratty bear.

18

LEVI

I lowered my binoculars. "I'm not sure watching Ace practice line dances in his living room is really helping us prove anything."

Whip cringed, leaning back in his seat behind the wheel. "He's still doing that? He's been at it for two hours."

"And not getting any better. He's gotta be the most uncoordinated motherfucker I've ever seen in my life."

Violet reached across the back seat and plucked the binoculars from my fingers, holding them up to her eyes again. She watched Ace dance for a bit, a smile playing across her pretty mouth. "I don't know. I think it's really cute he wants to learn."

I tilted my head back and stared at the ceiling of the car. The interior smelled vaguely of grease and salt, courtesy of the McDonald's pit stop we'd made between watching Trigger attend an AA meeting and Torch sitting in his yard with a fire going in a metal drum. Trigger had been serious and solemn, shaking the hands of other members and talking to them quietly. Torch had looked like he was living his best life, watching shit he threw into the bin go up in flames.

Neither had been doing anything that would have made me think they were capable of capturing a bunch of innocent women, torturing them to death, then dumping their bodies without so much as bothering to cover them with anything.

Ace's fumbling, mis-stepping line dances sure as hell weren't giving 'I get off on torturing women' vibes.

I tossed the binoculars down on the seat between me and Violet. "This is a waste of time. We need to go back out to the dump site and check out those bodies ourselves."

"What's the point?" Whip asked. "You searching for some sort of calling card?"

I swallowed thickly. I didn't want to admit that was exactly what I wanted to do.

Ever since I'd realized Lynx was out of jail and Toby's photos had proved he was lurking around with people he shouldn't, a bad feeling had swirled in my gut.

I'd almost wanted to believe that Trigger, Ace, and Torch were responsible for those dead women, and for all the other shit Violet had gone through. I mean, that would have sucked. I'd come to like them all since I'd been dragged into the group, even if I didn't know them as well as Whip and X.

But I'd shared a cell with Lynx for a lot longer than a couple of months. He was my friend in the true sense of the word, not just an acquaintance like Trig, Ace, and Torch were.

I didn't want to think he might be responsible for all the shit that had happened since I'd gotten out.

Since we'd *both* gotten out and he hadn't even said a word.

I knew things about Lynx nobody else knew. Things not even the cops knew, or he wouldn't be walking the street. Things clearly even Grayson and the rest of the Murder Squad didn't know, or Lynx would be on the list too.

If I'd known he was out I would have suggested he join the squad himself. Would have made sure he was turning over a new leaf and putting his skills to use in a way that served the community around us, not hurt it.

But after seeing his face in Toby's photos, I didn't know what to think. Didn't know if the friend I'd made was the real Lynx or if it had all been for show.

If Trig, Ace, and Torch weren't responsible for it all, then Lynx needed to be ruled out.

I just didn't have the guts to put my friend square in the sights of killers without some sort of proof. Sharing years in a cell with him surely meant I owed him at least that much.

If he'd killed those women, there'd be signs.

Four claw marks, ripped into their skin.

I'd seen him draw that mark over and over, etching it into the walls of our cell, drawing it on anything that belonged to him. Everyone in the prison knew if there were four claw marks on something, then it was the property of Lynx.

If he'd killed those women, I would have bet my life he wouldn't have been able to help himself and that his mark would be on them too.

X groaned. "Get it together, Ace! It's left, left, ball change, slap your ass! It's not that hard!" He flung his forearm over his eyes like he couldn't bear watching Ace's fumbling another minute. "Remind me never to go to a honky-tonk with him. How embarrassing."

Whip questioned if there were any honky-tonks in Saint View, but Violet's phone ringing drowned them out.

She made a face at the screen then answered pleasantly, "Hi, Francine. What's up?"

I started to turn away, not interested in Violet's conversation with her boss, but the frown that morphed between her eyes stopped me. I watched her while she listened to the older woman on the phone, her frown deepening with every second that passed.

"No, I haven't heard from her."

"What's wrong?" I whispered.

Violet held a finger up to me, telling me to wait, then answered Francine. "I'm sure she's sick and was maybe just too unwell to call. I can check on her."

She opened her mouth again but then quickly closed it, pressing it into a firm line. She held the phone out from her head just a bit, so even I could hear Francine's ranting down the line.

Violet put it back to her ear. "Like I said, I'll check on her. Can I do that before you fire her, please? She might be really unwell. I can pick up her missed shift so there's no harm done."

Relief spread across Violet's face. "Thank you. Yes. I'll check her roster and make sure the houses she's missed get taken care of."

Whip and X had both fallen quiet, listening to her end of the conversation as well.

She finished the call and cringed. "Nyah didn't show up for her shift today, and she didn't call either. I'm going to make them up tomorrow, and I know we want to go out to where you found the bodies, but can we check on Nyah first?"

Whip put the car into drive. "Of course. Where to?"

"Call her first," I suggested.

Violet nodded, stabbing her phone. "She's probably just avoiding Francine's calls. Can't blame her, she's the last person I would want to talk to if I was unwell."

"Or if you were loved-up and in bed with Dax?" X suggested.

Violet grimaced. "That is also a likely possibility. She's not answering her phone."

I picked up mine and called Dax. He didn't answer either.

Violet's teeth sank into her bottom lip. "Can we go to her house? Hopefully we find the two of them in bed—"

"Oh, you kinky minx! You hoping for a peep show?" X asked.

Violet shot him a look. "Just hoping they're both there and everything is okay."

I squeezed her leg. "They'll be fine, but we can go check." I was suddenly in no hurry to get back out to that pile of bodies. I knew we should go before darkness fell, otherwise I'd have the same problem I'd had when we'd found the bodies, without enough light to properly examine them. But I just didn't want my fears to be confirmed with Lynx's mark I was already half convinced I was going to find.

If I was wrong, that was almost as bad. That would just prove what a shitty friend I was, assuming because the guy had a history, he couldn't turn over a new leaf. Hadn't that been exactly the problem I'd had when I'd first gotten out? That nobody would give me a chance because of who I'd once been? And now here I was, assuming the same of Lynx.

Running around town searching for Nyah was a whole lot more appealing.

Whip pulled the car out onto the road, and X gave Ace a wave as we passed his house, not that Ace would have seen it. He was too busy concentrating on getting his footwork right to notice Whip's car lurking outside.

It wasn't far to Nyah's little house in the shitty back-streets of Saint View. Whip stopped the car in front, and we all piled out, probably unnecessarily, but Violet's worry had permeated the car, and now I was concerned too.

I followed her up the path, X to my left, Whip on my right.

X sniggered. "Wouldn't it be funny if the reason neither of them are answering their phones is because they're naked, tangled up in a sex swing, and that's what we're about to walk in on?"

"Funny for who?" I asked. "I really don't want to see my new boss's balls."

X waved his hand at me. "Yeah, yeah. We all know you only want to see Whip's. You're a one testicle kinda dude."

"That sounds like *I* only have one testicle." I didn't know why I was engaging.

"Want Whip to check for you?"

"Vi," I asked. "Would Francine notice if you borrowed about twenty bottles of bleach?" Then I turned to Whip. "Think that'll be enough to drown him in?"

Whip's lips turned up slightly, but we'd reached Nyah's front door, and all three of us fell silent as Violet wasted no time in rapping her knuckles across the scratched wood.

There was no sound from inside.

X stepped up to the windows. "Dibs on first peeps. If there is a sex show going on inside, you all wait in line behind me." He cupped his hands around his eyes to shield them from the late afternoon glare and peered through the glass. "Damn! Nothing but empty house. How dull. I want a refund."

Violet knocked again, harder this time, her phone to her ear once more, but again, no answer to either the door or her call. She glanced back at me. "Can you pick the lock?"

I eyed it and then nodded. "Easily. But do you really want me to? Bit of an invasion of privacy?"

She stepped back. "You're right. I'm overreacting. But I just don't think she'd go AWOL like this. I'm really worried she might be seriously unwell in there. What if she's passed out or something?"

I was forever a bit of a pessimist. It was hard not to be when you'd been raised in a town where nothing much good ever seemed to happen. Worry niggled in the back of my mind too. She was a single female living in a shitty neighborhood with even shittier security. That lock was flimsy at best. One swift kick would have it flying open, even if I hadn't been able to pick a lock.

I still had the tools in my pocket from the warehouse though, and there was no point in breaking her door when I didn't have to. I had the lock open in less than a minute, and the four of us edged inside.

"Nyah?" Violet crept down the hallway, presumably to where the bedroom was.

X followed closed behind, like her second skin.

Both came back quickly.

"There's nobody here," Violet told me and Whip.

I reached out and rubbed her arm. "Like we said, she's probably with Dax, having a sex marathon."

"Ah, no," a voice said from the doorway.

We all turned in that direction, taking in Dax standing there, staring at all of us. "Is she not here? She was supposed to meet me after work, but when she didn't show I called Francine, who said she hadn't come in at all."

Worry prickled at the back of my neck. "Who else does she know in town? Friends? Family?"

Dax and Violet both shook their heads.

Violet's voice wobbled when she answered. "She moved here to get away from her family. She didn't want to be found. What if...?"

I put an arm around her shoulder. "No need to go there. There's no sign of her purse or phone or keys. She might just be out shopping or maybe she went for a hike and she'll be back soon."

Dax nodded. "True."

A little of Violet's panic ebbed away. "If her family had busted in here in the middle of the night there would have been a broken door, right? And they wouldn't have let her take her phone and keys and purse. Right?"

But my gut churned with the thought of another option. One I didn't want to voice out loud, because if it were true, it would devastate both of them. "Right," I agreed instead. "We just need to give it some time.

There's a reason the cops wait twenty-four hours before filing a missing person's report. It's because people, at least adults, almost always come back within that time."

But the words sounded weak in my ears. "Why don't Whip, X, and I go out for a drive around and see if we can find her. The two of you wait here in case she comes back."

I didn't want to leave Violet alone, but I couldn't take her with us either.

Because a nagging voice in my head said the first place we needed to check for Nyah was that pile of dead women.

19

WHIP

The dump site was hard enough to get to, even in good conditions, but after all the rain we'd had the other night, the track in was almost completely washed away. My car was too low to the ground, and we were forced to abandon it about a mile out and go in on foot.

I was just glad we weren't trying to dump a body. Because dead people were heavy, and I'd barely recovered from X trying to kill us with oysters.

The stench hit before we crested the ridge. Not just rot. Not just the sweet, coppery reek of old blood. This was deeper. Feral. Foul.

Levi moved quietly beside me, his eyes sharper than usual, like being back at a crime scene brought him into focus.

X...not so much.

In the last two minutes alone, he'd tripped over a fallen branch, announced it was a hate crime, and then spent the rest of the walk swatting at invisible flies.

"Remind me again why we're going toward the body pit and not, say, literally anywhere else?" X asked, brushing leaves off his shoulder.

"We need to see if she's here," Levi muttered.

I jerked my head in his direction. "Excuse me?"

He looked at me. "What? Like you aren't thinking the same thing I am? She's been missing for at least eight hours, Whip. You think there's not even a remote chance that's linked to the fucking shitstorm that's surrounded us these last few weeks? You didn't come out here with even the slightest suspicion that we might find her body newly added to the pile we found the other night?"

I didn't want to think about that. I barely knew Nyah.

But Levi was right. We were supposed to be searching the town for any sign of her, and after a single sweep of the main street, this was where I'd driven.

Levi sighed heavily. "Listen. I told you both about my old cellmate, Lynx, being out of prison."

X slapped his own arm, then winced, though I wasn't sure if it was from the sting of the slap or the bug that had bitten him. "Is that the guy who taught you how to give good head? If so, Whip says thank you."

Levi shot him a look. "Lynx had my back. I was in a bad situation, one of my first nights there. Lynx got me out of it. I owe him."

I eyed Levi. "And yet you're bringing him up as we walk toward a pile of dead bodies. All women who died in pretty horrific circumstances, if the sneak peek we got the other night was right."

Levi sighed. "Yes."

I narrowed my eyes. "You think he did it."

Levi shook his head. "No. I don't want to believe that.

He never admitted to hurting a woman. Not to me. But is he capable if the price is right?" He lifted a shoulder. "If Lynx is in town—if he's *working* again—he'd leave a message. He always did. Four claw marks."

"Maybe I should start leaving a calling card on my dead bodies," X mused out loud. "I don't know what though. Maybe a star carved between their eyes. Ooh! Maybe polka dots on their ass cheeks."

I squinted at him. "Just leaving an X for your name is too original?"

X's mouth dropped open, and he pointed at me. "Now you're thinking! The press will know me simply as X!"

"Everyone knows you simply as X," I said dryly.

"Fair point. Maybe I could be X-Man!"

"Pretty sure Marvel has the copyright on that."

"Dammit!"

"You could be X-Ray?" Levi suggested, shaking his booted foot free of the gluggy mud we sloshed through.

X wasn't impressed. "I think we need to workshop this more."

We reached the edge of the site, and I grimaced.

It was even worse in the daylight than it had been the night we'd been here. And after a few days of multiple dead bodies baking in the sun, it smelled twice as bad. The flies that buzzed now weren't the imaginary kind, and I covered my mouth and nose with my arm, taking in the carnage.

Seven bodies. Maybe eight. All women, except for the few we'd tossed in here the other night.

Twisted. Stripped. Broken

Levi swallowed hard. "Jesus. I forgot how bad it was. The darkness hid a lot of this."

X crouched beside the nearest body, his tone unusually sober. "They didn't just kill them. They *enjoyed* it." He glanced back at me. "I know we have some issues, but this..." He shook his head. "This is fucked up."

But my attention was etched on Levi, my gut churning.

I didn't want to find Nyah's body here.

And I didn't want to find a claw-shaped calling card carved into her skin.

Levi's gaze ran over the bodies. He moved around them, coughing at the stench, but getting in close anywhere he could, searching for a sign his friend had done this.

But there was nothing. These women were covered in marks from ropes, cuts from knives, holes from bullets, bruises from who knew what.

But nothing that resembled Lynx's mark.

"They aren't his kills," I said quietly to Levi. "And none of them are Nyah."

Like he'd needed someone to confirm it, even though he could see it with his own two eyes, his shoulders hunched in.

I put a heavy, reassuring hand on his shoulder, letting it rest there, just telling him I was here.

"I feel like a fucking asshole for even thinking it might have been him, you know? He's supposed to be my friend." He shook his head. "Fuck, what does that say about me?"

"It says you've learned to be smart enough not to just blindly trust people. You did that once before, remember? You trusted your old prez, were loyal to a fault, and did everything he asked of you without question. And look where it got you? Six years behind bars." I squeezed his shoulder harder. "Don't beat yourself up because the real world taught you not to be so trusting."

He nodded slowly. "This place is fucking miserable."

He wasn't wrong. "We need to ID those bodies. Find out who they were. Why they were targets. Work out what the fuck they have to do with us." I pulled out my phone and started taking photos. I almost hated that we couldn't call the cops, but we had just as many kills buried out here as whoever had dumped these bodies.

These women weren't going to get a burial.

The least we could do was find out if they had families. Maybe try to get a message to them that would give them some closure. I scrubbed a hand over my face. Fucking hell, this sucked so much.

Levi grimaced and turned away, clearly feeling the same way.

It was one thing to take a life when they were the scum of the earth.

But these women weren't that. They were probably someone's wife. Someone's daughter. Someone's mother.

"Well, well. Seems like someone else decided to take a walk through hell this morning." Trigger's voice cut through the buzz of flies.

Behind him, Ace and Torch stepped into view.

Trigger didn't smile. There was a gun holstered at his hip, his hand hovering over it. "What the fuck are you doing here? This is our site."

I stepped forward, giving him the benefit of the doubt. "Same as you, apparently. Cleaning up a mess we didn't make."

Torch's gaze swept the bodies. His expression didn't

change, but something in his posture shifted. "Those women weren't on the list."

"No shit," Levi muttered.

Trigger's eyes narrowed at his tone. "You accusing us?"

"That depends," I said, immediately having Levi's back. "Are you admitting to something?"

The tension in the air was as thick as the stench of decaying bodies. X, Levi, and I on one side, Trigger, Ace, and Torch on the other. Guns weren't drawn yet, but the crackle between us was the kind that came right before the bloodstains.

Trig's gaze shifted to the last woman I'd taken a photo of. Short blond hair. Staring, faded blue eyes. Tall and solid. "This isn't us."

"And you expect us to believe you?" Levi asked.

"No," he said with a tinge of something that sounded a lot like sadness as he stared down at the women. "We expect you to be smart enough to realize someone's playing all of us."

He was right.

We'd let ourselves get distracted by not trusting each other.

That sentiment passed silently between Trig and me.

He gave a tiny nod.

I returned it, the tension breaking, a silent agreement to believe that neither of us was capable of this sort of carnage.

We weren't good men. I wasn't deluded enough to believe otherwise.

But we weren't this.

"Plot twist!" X piped up. "*We're* the good guys."

Trig pulled a pack from his back pocket and lit a cigarette, dragging deep. "God help us."

But my gaze stayed on the bodies.

No claw marks.

No message.

And no Nyah.

That should've been a relief.

But it didn't feel like one.

20

VIOLET

X met me outside the police station, looking like a treat for my tired, red-rimmed eyes.

He immediately put his arm around me and drew me into the warmth of his chest. "What did they say?"

I shook my head, my nose brushing against the soft fabric of his shirt. "Not much. They've made a missing person's report."

"Did you tell them about her dad having Mafia connections?"

I drew back, my mouth in a straight, unhappy line. "They don't believe that's true."

He frowned. "Why not?"

I shrugged. "They made inquiries into her parents. They're business people in the city. No criminal record."

"So? Doesn't mean they aren't shady as fuck."

"Try telling the Providence Police Department that. They didn't come right out and laugh directly in my face while telling me I watch too much TV, but they weren't far from it. They kept questioning Dax over whether they'd had a—and I quote—'lovers' tiff.'"

"That probably explains him storming out with steam blowing from his ears a few minutes ago. He didn't even stop when I called his name. I was ready to take him off our Christmas card list—you know the one we're sending as a family with Reginald the duck and Harold the ugly cat—but I guess we can still send him one since he's a bit stressed right now." He rubbed his hand over his face. "I really wouldn't want him to miss out on that."

I put my arms around his narrow waist and hugged him harder, breathing in the scent of his cologne. "You are so ridiculous."

"I know," he whispered, pressing his lips down onto the top of my head. "But I hate when you're sad. I don't know how else to help, other than to make you laugh."

I snuggled against him. "It's okay. This is exactly what I need."

"Yeah, this," he agreed. Then pulled back and grinned down at me wickedly. "This, and cat snuggles!"

I widened my eyes. "Did you pick up Harold?"

"Without you? Never. But the shelter did call. He's all up-to-date with all his shots, the vet has checked him over, and we're allowed to go pick him up. You want to come?"

In that moment, with Nyah missing, the police, unsurprisingly, doing nothing, and my nerves a complete and utter mess from everything else, going to pick up an ugly cat with him felt like the easiest thing to say yes to.

I nodded.

X beamed. "Let's go get our son. I've already named him Harold Nigel Meowington the Third. He's a duke.

His royal portrait is being painted in my head as we speak."

"Please tell me you're imagining him in a powdered wig."

"Obviously. With a little waistcoat. And a monocle. Maybe a small sword."

I sniggered, but he held the van door open for me, and I hauled myself up into it. Ten minutes and a drive back across the Providence-Saint View border, we pulled up in front of the shelter. It sat at the end of a cracked asphalt lot behind a discount mattress store, flanked by a crooked chain-link fence. A hand-painted sign that just said Animal Haven in faded, flaking red letters, announced we had the right place.

Someone had attempted to brighten things up with plastic flowers jammed into old soup cans along the path to the door. It didn't help. The building itself seemed like it used to be a dentist's office in the eighties and had been slowly surrendering to mildew and despair ever since.

I pushed through the door, and the woman at the front desk looked up.

"We're here about a cat," I informed her.

"Your names?"

I introduced us and waited as her pink chipped fingernails flew across a keyboard.

She peered at the screen, understanding eventually washing over her pretty features. "Oh. You're here for..." She bit her lip, her gaze flickering to X before coming back to me. "*Harold.*"

She said his name like someone might say *boil*. Or like if she said it too loud, she might summon a demon.

X stepped forward. "Yes. I'm his new dad. This is his

mom. We're a very stable, very responsible family unit. I built him a cardboard castle and put sardines in the moat."

The woman stared at him like she wasn't sure if he was joking.

Honestly, he probably wasn't.

She passed us an invoice, laying out his adoption fees and agreement, and X handed over his credit card without a second of hesitation.

Was it my imagination or did the woman breathe a sigh of relief once everything was signed and the payment had gone through?

"Just a moment," she said cautiously, then disappeared through a back door.

I turned to X. "Do you think he's going to be as ugly as the photos made him look?"

X leaned in conspiratorially. "I saw a video. He hissed at a toddler and then fell off a shelf."

"Oh my God."

X got a dreamy expression on his face, like he was mentally replaying the video. "It was love at first sight."

When the woman came back, she was holding a small, beige-ish bundle of rage wrapped in a towel. It hissed and squirmed in her arms, and the woman fought to keep a hold of it. He lunged his teeth toward her hand, and she squeaked. "I'm just going to put him down here, so he has a bit of room..." She let him go then fled to the perceived safety of her desk, half crouched behind it like she was afraid Harold might come after her in retaliation.

He didn't. He just froze to the spot, glaring at the woman like he might be plotting her demise.

Harold was...a lot. One eye slightly askew, like it had

been damaged at some point and now didn't work properly. A torn ear, half his tail missing, and fur like he'd lost a fight with a lawnmower.

His disgust with the woman waning, he turned his attention in our direction. He blinked at me. Slowly. In the kind of crooked way his dodgy eye allowed for.

Then purred.

I raised an eyebrow.

He stretched out one paw, gently, almost politely, even, toward me.

I'd never had a pet. I'd wanted one for as long as I could remember, but my foster parents had barely kept their human occupants alive. I would have been flogged if I'd dared to bring an animal home. And Toby had been allergic, so once we moved in together, any idea of keeping an animal had slowly faded away.

But now the desire to hold and love one came rushing back. A tiny piece of my ruined childhood mending inside me.

Despite the clear threat to my life, I reached for Harold instinctively. The moment I had him in my arms, he butted his head against my chin and started rumbling like a tractor engine.

X's jaw dropped. "You little liar," he said to Harold. "I watched your YouTube compilation. You drew blood."

The shelter woman beamed. "Wow. He likes you. That's...unusual."

X reached out a finger. "Hey, buddy," he crooned. "You remember me, right? I sent snacks. And a video for you to watch at night before you fell asleep so you'd get to know my voice." He shot a look at the woman. "You played that for him, right?"

The woman cringed and shrugged a shoulder.

X had already lost interest in her response, and his finger was closing the gap between him and the cat in my arms.

Harold's eyes narrowed at X's finger. He hissed. Violently.

X recoiled. "Traitor!"

I burst out laughing as Harold snuggled closer, curling his claws into my sweater like he owned me now.

"He's made his choice," I said, rubbing my face on his head, then instantly regretting it because he smelled horrible up close.

"I'm the one who paid your adoption fee!" X cried at the cat.

Harold bared his teeth.

X's mouth dropped open. "You ungrateful geriatric gremlin!"

Harold snapped his teeth in warning.

X shrieked and backed up so far he bumped into the woman, the two of them cowering behind the desk.

"Take it back!" he yelled, then pointed a finger in Harold's direction. "Reginald would never betray me like this!"

Harold hissed again from my arms but didn't try to jump. He just looked deeply, smugly satisfied with himself.

I scratched behind his one good ear. "You just like drama, don't you?" I eyed X. "Just like someone else I know."

Harold gazed up at me, then closed his eyes, like the head scratches were the best thing he'd ever felt.

My heart cracked open wide. He was so ugly. And so

mean. And I was already in love with him. "You're coming home with me. We're going to get you all the toys your black heart desires. And all the catnip. And you can sleep curled up in a ball at the end of my bed.

X popped up from behind the desk, hair disheveled, and gave me a wounded look. "What about me? Where am I going to sleep when I stay at your place? I draw the line at sharing pillows with something that would eat my eyeballs if I stopped breathing for thirty seconds."

"You're assuming he'd wait thirty seconds."

Harold meowed sweetly.

"Great," X muttered. "He's plotting already."

But as we walked out of the shelter—me cradling Harold like a baby, X keeping a cautious two-feet of distance between them—I realized something:

For a few minutes, I hadn't thought about Nyah. Or the bodies. Or the killer.

Just me, X, and the world's ugliest cat, starting a very weird family.

And somehow, that was everything I needed.

21

LEVI

I both hated and loved that I had to work. Loved that I got to spend the entire day at the shop, surrounded by other artists.

Hated I couldn't be there with Violet when she was upset and needed me.

Though I had a phone full of photos featuring the ugliest cat I'd ever seen, along with Violet looking thrilled and X looking terrified, so I guessed she'd found a way to fill her time and keep her mind off Nyah's sudden disappearance.

I wished I could say the same though. Maybe she had just gone back to her family. Maybe they'd forced her back. I didn't know.

But all I could think about was Dax and how he must be feeling. How out of his mind he had to be, wondering where she was.

It just made me want to put a tracker on Violet, so I knew where she was at every minute of the day.

If someone took her from me, the way they'd taken

Nyah from Dax... My stomach clenched at the very thought of it. I shook my fingers out, realizing they'd clenched into fists. I would burn the fucking world down for Violet. And I didn't mean that in the poetic sense.

I meant it literally.

I was so fucking in love with her, losing her now would destroy me.

King leaned over my shoulder, studying the practice piece I was working on. "Watch those lines. They're shaky."

I nodded, agreeing with him. "I will. Sorry."

"You're good, Levi. But you gotta concentrate. Nobody wants a wonky outline."

"Working on it."

"Good."

We both glanced over as the bell above the shop door tinkled.

Lynx walked in, all broad shoulders beneath a long-sleeved white shirt.

I shouldn't have been surprised. I knew his skin was covered in tats. Some were works of art he'd gotten before we'd been locked up, others the prison variety that looked like trash. I'd refused to let anyone near my skin while we were inside, but I think Lynx had craved the pain.

King nodded at him. "Can we help you with some-thing, bro?"

Lynx's gaze strayed to me. "Wouldn't mind some new ink if you've got time?"

King squinted at the computer on the desk in front of him that held the studio calendar with each artist's time blocked out in various colors. He shook his head. "I've got appointments—"

Lynx nodded at me. "What about you, Reaper? You got any room on your calendar for an old friend?"

King threw a bucket of water on that idea before I could even respond. "He's got a long way to go on his apprenticeship. He's not qualified to be putting a needle in anyone's skin yet."

I knew he was right, but it still kind of smarted. I was new. But I wasn't completely without a clue. The only reason my lines were so shaky today was because my head was full of Violet and Nyah, and memories of those bodies kept playing over and over in my head.

Lynx eyed me. "What if I'm willing to be a test subject?"

I glanced at King. The man might have been ten years younger than me, but while Dax wasn't here, he was in charge. I wasn't stupid enough to fuck up my chances by pretending like I was top dog, just because I was older.

King eyed Lynx. "Gotta warn you, bro, you let a brand-new apprentice ink you, you're brave. You get what you get. He's got talent, but its raw and untrained."

Lynx pulled up his shirt, showing off washboard abs but also a variety of prison tattoos.

King cringed at them.

Lynx chuckled. "I already know he's better than this shit."

King clapped me on the shoulder. "All yours if you want to take it."

I wasn't going to look a gift horse in the mouth. Tattooing something other than these fake skins would be the highlight of my week. I jerked my head at Lynx. "Come on then. Show me what you want."

King wandered away, leaving Lynx to sink into the seat beside mine. He rolled his sleeve up. "Surprise me."

I raised an eyebrow, but when Lynx just grinned back, I couldn't help but smile. I knew him. I'd spent six years in a cell with this man.

I suddenly felt like shit that I'd suspected him at all. Yeah, he was capable of some fucked-up shit, but not the things that had been inflicted on those women. That was some sick son of a bitch, making sure we knew they were watching us, always one step ahead.

Not my good-natured cellmate.

I got my inks out, mentally thinking over what the hell I was going to do with the blank piece of skin he'd offered me. "I still can't believe we're both out."

"Me neither. And you're already all shacked up with a woman and everything." He nudged me with his arm. "She's beautiful, bro."

"I know." I saw Violet's beauty in everything she did and everything she was. Every smile that popped the dimple in her cheek. Every sweet thing she did for other people, always putting her own feelings last. Every wobble of her backside as she walked away, always leaving me wanting more.

I was surprised Lynx had noticed though. Every poster he'd stuck on our cell wall had been of tiny, skinny women with huge fake tits. Beautiful in their own right, for sure, just not what I wanted.

I held the tattoo gun up. "You ready?"

He nodded.

I started working on his arm, freestyling a small

design, noting the way his skin and muscle moved differently than the practice skins I'd been working with up until now.

My heart rate picked up, and I moved the needle across his skin with sure, confident strokes, not a hint of the wobbles I'd had earlier. Something about doing this felt so damn right. It was the same feeling I had whenever I was around Violet. It was the knowledge that this was where I was supposed to be.

Lynx watched me work; his gaze trained on his arm. "You remember your first night inside?"

I paused to meet his gaze, but I didn't really see it. All I saw were men circling me like sharks.

A bag being shoved over my head.

Hands restraining me.

A lack of air. No control.

Fear.

It took me a long time to answer. "Why would you bring that up now?"

Lynx eyed me. "Because you owe me a favor."

The memories flashing behind my eyes changed. Lynx's voice in my ears, telling the men to back the fuck off, that I wasn't fresh meat there for the taking.

That I was his.

The bag disappeared, the claustrophobia and lack of air along with it.

I could breathe again.

But it clearly came with a cost.

I forced myself to nod. In the entire six years that Lynx and I had shared that cell, he'd never brought up that night. Never brought up that he'd saved me, if not my life, he'd at least saved me from men who would have happily held me down and used my body for their own pleasure.

"I owe you," I agreed.

"Good." Lynx tapped his fingers just below the area I was working on, drawing my attention back down to it so I could finish the design.

I bit my lip, forcing my concentration through my arm into my fingers. I didn't want to think about why he was bringing that up again.

I finished the piece quickly, wiping it down, and then allowed him to study my work.

He gave a wry smile at the four claw marks I'd drawn on his skin. The same four claw marks he'd drawn on everything when we'd been inside, making sure everyone knew the property he'd claimed.

He pushed back in his chair, not bothering to let me wrap up the fresh new design. He moved to the mirror, standing in front of it, twisting his arms this way and that, checking out my work from every angle.

King watched on from across the room, and Lynx raised his arm to show him the small design.

"He did good!"

Relief spread across King's face. He nodded and put his head down, going back to work on the massive chest piece he'd been chipping away at most of the day.

So he didn't notice when Lynx clapped me on the shoulder and leaned down, so both of us could see the claw marks, his symbol of ownership. "I love it, Levi." He breathed out slowly, his lips mere inches from the back of my neck and his mouth close enough to my ear that only I would hear. "Maybe you should have tattooed this on yourself."

he rest of my shift was much less eventful. Dax didn't return. I texted him though, and he did reply that he'd found no trace of Nyah anywhere and the cops were fucking useless. I didn't know what else to say to him, so I just said goodnight, packed up my things, hoping I'd get some time to practice at home before my next shift, and then rode back to Violet's place.

X's theatrics filtered down the hallway from behind the closed door, even before I was near enough to knock.

Violet opened the door, her hair an adorable mess, and cat fur all over her sweater. Her eyes widened at the sight of me, but she smiled. "Hey, you. You're a sight for sore eyes."

So was she. I put my hand to the side of her face, cat fur and all, fingertips on the back of her neck, and pulled her into me. "Hey, beautiful."

I dropped my lips down to hers, kissing her pretty mouth. The knowledge I got to do this was the only thing that had gotten me through the afternoon, after Lynx had shown up, reminding me of promises I had never made but would be held to anyway.

I only stepped back when feral hissing caught my attention.

"Omelet! He's doing it again! Harold! Stop it! Love me, damn you! Everyone else does!"

Violet crossed the room, scooping up the most horrifically unfortunate-looking cat I'd ever seen. "Well, what do you expect, X? You just called him a furry hemorrhoid."

"Because he is!"

Violet rolled her eyes and brought the cat over to me. "Harold, this is Levi. Levi, Harold."

I reared back at the sight of it. It was even more horrific up close. "You weren't joking when you said it was ugly, were you?"

Violet and X both glared at me, like I'd just insulted their newborn baby.

"Hey!" I said to X. "You're the one who called it a hemorrhoid!"

X, with his arms full of cat toys, didn't seem to care. "You don't get to call him ugly, Levi. He's been through trauma. Look at that face. He's seen things. Probably your nudes."

I made a face at him but reached for the cat, stroking him beneath his furry chin. "How you doing, Harold? Can I call you Harry for short?"

X made a choking sound from across the room. "You most certainly cannot butcher his name like that. He is a distinguished gentleman! Not one of your football bros you meet down at the bar."

The cat ignored X's righteous speech and closed his eyes, leaning into my touch so I could scratch him. A deep, satisfied purr rumbled from his chest. I smirked at X. "I think old Harry here has spoken."

"Traitorous furball." X shot the feline a dirty look and slumped down on Violet's couch, amongst the cat paraphernalia.

I sank down next to him, and Violet put the cat on my lap. He gave X a half-hearted hiss before curling up into a ball and falling asleep. I ran my fingers through his kinda mangy fur, then thought better of it. Ew. Harry needed a bath.

I didn't want to piss him off by being the one to try to wrangle him into the tub though. I quite liked being one of his chosen humans, especially because it was clearly driving X nuts and tormenting X was always fun.

Violet leaned a hip on the kitchen counter. "Did you hear from Dax?"

I wished I had something better to tell her. "I did, but he hasn't been able to find her anywhere. Guessing you haven't heard from her either?"

Violet shook her head. "No. I called Francine earlier to see if she'd made contact with her or shown up for her shifts today, but nothing. I'm really worried."

I was too, but there was little we could do. We'd checked all the places we thought she might go. But I hated the way Vi nibbled on her nails. Hated the creases between her eyebrows and her forehead furrowed in worry. The police's suggestion to give it some time because Nyah was an adult and most missing people returned on their own within a couple of days didn't sit right with me. I shifted the sleeping cat to the couch and stood so I could pull Violet into my arms.

"This feels like losing Toby all over again," she whispered into my shirt. "Something is wrong, Levi. She didn't just walk out the door of her own accord and not come back. She wouldn't do that to Dax." She peered up at me. "I think she's in love with him."

I slanted my head. "They've barely known each other a few weeks."

"Does that matter?"

"I loved you from the very first moment you threw an egg at my head," X said.

His words were his usual ridiculousness, but his tone was serious.

Violet smiled at him. "I know. You told me. Multiple times."

He nodded proudly and reached for the cat, trying to get a stroke in while it was asleep. Without even opening his eyes, Harold shot out a paw, claws bared, and took a swipe at X's hand.

X muttered something that sounded like a witch's curse and moved back to the side of the couch Harold permitted him to sit on.

But Violet's teeth were still sunk into her bottom lip, and she stared out the glass sliding doors leading to her balcony like the dark night beyond might offer up some sort of explanation as to where Nyah was, and who had taken her.

I needed to do something. This couldn't all be on her shoulders. "We can go find her family."

She looked up at me. "We're willingly going to drive into the city and go knock on the door of people we know are involved in a criminal organization?"

"Is that really any worse than that day you stormed a murder club meeting and demanded to become a member?"

She smiled sheepishly. "But I knew you. We don't know these people. From what Nyah said, they're dangerous."

"What's the alternative?" I asked. "We sit here and wait?"

Her shoulders fell. "I can't do that. She's my friend."

I kissed the top of her head, already knowing that she would agree. "Then we go to the city and find these people and really politely ask if they might have kidnapped their daughter."

X snorted. "I'm sure that'll go down well."

"Tomorrow?" I asked Violet. "It's already too late tonight. But we can take my bike in the morning. Might even be a nice ride." Having Violet wrapped around me for a couple of hours and the wind in my face was exactly what I needed right now.

"Dax will want to come too," Violet said.

"Whip and I will ride with him." X gingerly nudged a tube of cat treats toward Harold, who was still faking sleep. He let X get the tube right up to his nose before getting to his feet and lifting his tail in X's direction.

A second later, X's mouth dropped open. "Did you just deliberately drop a fart at me?" His nose wrinkled, and he waved his hand around. "Oh my God, cat! What is wrong with your bowels?"

The smell reached me. I gagged.

X shot me a look. "Don't you even think of throwing up!"

But my gagging set off his gagging, and Violet's face paled, either from the noises X and I were making, or maybe from the way Harold had stunk up an apartment quicker than a stink bomb could.

The keys to my bike were still in my pocket. "I need to get out of here. Come for a ride with me?" I asked Violet. "I want to make sure you're good on the back of the bike anyway, if we're going to be doing a long trip tomorrow. You haven't been on it much lately."

She quickly followed me toward the door. "Absolutely. Take me anywhere there's fresh air." She glanced back at X. "You want to come with us? Your truck is here, right?"

But X shook his head. "You two go. I need Harold to know that even though he smells like rotten eggs, I will not abandon him."

Harold let out another fart, letting everyone know exactly what he thought about being left in the care of X.

"And if we get back and find you dead on the floor from gas poisoning?" I asked.

X's expression turned grim. "Just take care of Harold."

I could tell he really meant it. I clapped him on the shoulder on my way to the door. "You're an oddly good man, you know that?"

He was still eyeing Harold with wariness, probably just waiting for him to drop another stinker. "He is going to love me. I have declared it, and so it will be." He glanced at me, expression full of worry. "But if you come back and find me facedown, half eaten, I want my obituary to say, 'Beloved local menace dead at thirty. Cause of death? One resentful hairball and a fart so unholy the wallpaper curled in protest.'"

Violet nodded solemnly, though I could tell she was battling back a laugh. "It'll be forever known as The Harold Incident."

X perked up. "I like that."

I shook my head. "Crack a window. We'll see you when the stench clears."

22

VIOLET

resh air greeted me outside my apartment building, the night mild, Levi's bike waiting out front. He took a spare helmet from one of his saddlebags and fit it down over my head.

He kissed the tip of my nose before pulling down the visor and dragging on his own helmet. His long leg swung over the bike, and I followed suit, getting on behind him. Unlike the first time I'd been on his bike, I didn't try to keep any distance from him. I snuggled right up against his back, wrapping my arms around his middle.

He squeezed my thigh once, and then we were off, cruising the streets of Saint View. He didn't go fast, just puttered around, letting me ease into the feel of taking corners again. It was easier this time, when I wasn't desperately trying to keep myself from hyperventilating over being so close to him.

This time, I could touch him all I wanted.

So I did. I slipped my hands beneath his open jacket

and pressed against the ridges of his abs. Even though I couldn't see what I was doing, it was easy enough to find the hem of his T-shirt by feel and slide my fingers beneath it, so I touched his skin.

A tremble ran through his body. Which might have been vibrations from the bike beneath us.

Might have been because of the way I was touching him.

Familiar landmarks of Saint View and Providence flashed by around me, but I didn't pay much attention. All I could think about was where Nyah was and how stressed out Dax had to be right now.

If it was Levi or X or Whip who hadn't come home, I didn't think I'd be functioning.

I'd known them barely days longer than Dax and Nyah had known each other, and yet the way I felt for them had consumed me so wholly that now I couldn't even imagine what I'd do without them.

If they walked away...if they were hurt...if someone took them from me...

My stomach clenched.

I tapped Levi's shoulder and pointed to the side of the road.

He nodded and turned off into the parking lot of the Saint View end of the beach that ran the full length of both towns. It was the one thing Saint View and Providence had in common. Waves crashed beyond the sand, and I pulled off my helmet.

Levi did the same, both of us just sitting there for a moment, watching the ocean.

"I couldn't bear it if it was you missing." Levi's voice cracked.

"I was just thinking the same thing about you." I pressed my lips to the space between his shoulder blades.

He just squeezed my thigh again. "I want to marry you, Violet. I want to grow old with you by my side. I want miniature versions of you running around with pigtails and little versions of me—"

"Running around in leather jackets?"

He snorted on a laugh. "I was going to say barefoot in the grass, fishing poles in hand, and the two of us following them, a dog yapping at our heels."

"I can offer you a stinky cat."

His shoulders shook with laughter. "You're as bad as X, ruining the mood with jokes."

I got off the bike and stood beside him so I could see his face. "Are X and Whip in this vision too?"

He nodded. "Whip is helping the boys tie knots in the line. X is probably still trying to get Harold to love him."

I leaned into him, seeing the vision all too clearly. It was much the same as the one we'd talked about in our letters.

Only now it included two other men.

And somehow, that felt right.

I squeezed his fingers. "Let's go for a walk. It's so nice out."

"There's a towel in one of the saddlebags."

I raised an eyebrow. "In case you feel the need to go skinny-dipping?"

He smirked at me. "Normally I just use it to kneel on when my bike needs attention, or to sit on when I stop somewhere to eat... But hey, if you're offering to get naked..."

I wriggled my eyebrows at him suggestively.

His whole tone changed. "Don't do that, Violet. I will take you hard and fast on the sand if that's what you want."

It hadn't been my intention, but Nyah's disappearance, Toby's death, the constant danger that surrounded us was all so dark and heavy. Any opportunity to forget it and live in the moment felt like it needed to be grabbed with both hands and kept close for as long as possible.

I found the towel in his saddlebag, my fingers brushing over his tattoo kit. "You brought your work home with you."

His gaze had been busily devouring me but switched to the case in my hands. "I just wanted to get some extra practice in while I'm off tomorrow."

I grimaced at it. "But if you take me to the city to look for Nyah, you won't have time."

"Doesn't matter. I can practice later."

I pushed the kit toward him. "Or you could do what I've been asking you for weeks. That thing runs on batteries, doesn't it?"

He stared down at me, fingers wrapped around the tattoo gun. "I'm not tattooing your pussy on the beach, Violet."

I shrugged a shoulder. "Oh well, your loss then." I grabbed the towel and headed into the shadowy darkness beyond the lit parking lot. I didn't get very far before he caught up.

I also didn't miss that he'd brought the tattoo gun with him.

A small smile lifted the corner of my mouth, but I said nothing.

He didn't miss it though. He put his arm around me,

drawing me close, like the beach was full of people and he didn't want anyone to hear, even though there wasn't a person in sight. "When we can't see the parking lot anymore, you're going to take all your clothes off, Violet."

Heat rushed through me, doing pleasant things to my body which was already a little jazzed just from the ride here. "Am I?"

He grabbed a handful of my ass and squeezed it. "You're being a brat. Say, yes, Daddy."

Oh Jesus Christ. I'd never been the sort of girl who thought I would wobble at the knees over something like that, and yet, when Levi said it, I was pretty sure they buckled.

I stopped walking. I was dead serious, breathless, and turned on when I whispered, "Yes, Daddy."

He groaned, dropping the hard-cover case in the sand. "This is far enough."

Excitement lit up inside me, pushing away the thoughts of everything horrible in our lives and leaving room only for the good. For this. For enjoying my man, and living for the way his gaze devoured me, promises held in the depths of his green eyes.

I slowly stripped my clothes. My shoes. My top. My leggings.

He didn't offer to help. Just watched me drop articles of clothing one by one onto the sand, my gaze locked with his, both of us burning.

He spread out the towel in the darkness, but there was enough moonlight to see what we were doing. It glinted off the water, making it sparkle. A breeze blew across my skin, but it did nothing to chase away the heat.

I reached behind me and undid the clasps on my bra,

letting my breasts fall free.

"You worried about someone seeing you?" His voice was like gravel.

I shook my head. "No."

"Good. Because I want to see every fucking inch of you, Violet. Take your panties off."

Wetness pooled at my core, silky and slick. I tucked my fingers into the elastic on either side of my hips and tugged them down over my thighs, not even caring they were dimpled with cellulite.

It was impossible to feel like anything other than the most beautiful woman in the world when a man looked at you the way Levi was looking at me right now.

It was also impossible to deny him anything he wanted.

"Get on your knees."

A small moan slipped from my lips. I knelt on the towel, my knees digging into the soft sand beneath that still held a vague hint of the warm day.

His gaze locked on mine; he undid the button then the zipper on his fly. He dragged his jeans just far enough down his legs to free his cock.

"Fuck me with that bratty mouth."

He'd never spoken to me like this, but something deep inside me, something I knew from how I'd been with Whip and X, knew I liked the submissiveness of it.

I gripped the base of his cock with one hand, the other fitting between his legs to grip his balls. My mouth found the head of him, and I licked his tip, tasting him.

"Need to be in your mouth, Violet." His fingers sank to the back of my head, and he drew me in closer, forcing his cock deeper past my lips.

He slid across my tongue, and then back again, thrusting in and out. He held my head firmly, guiding me, but never in a way that had me feeling like he wouldn't let go the second I made so much as a peep of distress.

He let me breathe. He let me pull off if I needed to. He let me come back to him a willing partner each time.

When his fingers fisted in my hair and my scalp prickled in delight, the moan I let out was one of pleasure, not fear.

I let him have control of me because it turned us both on. Because I trusted him with my body. With my life.

With my heart.

I loved him so damn much. Every side of him, from the sweet and tender, to the way he was now, dominant and strong.

I wanted him inside me.

I sucked him harder, wanting to please him, wanting him to want me as much as I wanted him.

His growl of need told me he did. "Get on your back, Violet."

I lay back, and he followed me down, pushing my legs apart so my heels dug into the sand. I grabbed at his jacket, needing his skin on mine and not the smooth cold of the leather.

He shrugged it off, and I managed to yank his T-shirt up over his head, him dropping it to the sand before lying down on top of me.

God, his weight felt good. He kept a lot of it held in his knees and the strong forearms either side of me, but he was heavy enough that my brain whispered seductive words, telling me I was safe here with him, wrapped up in his arms, sheltered from the world.

His cock inside me was so needed. He drove in like a man on a mission, stretching me, filling me, setting off new pleasure inside me.

He groaned, his mouth trailing up my neck to my ear. "I want my baby in you, Violet."

I stared up at him, at the honesty and raw intensity in his eyes. He'd never had a real family. Neither had I.

I was almost as surprised as he was when I whispered back, "I want that too."

His growl was possessive. Deeply rooted in need. He flipped our positions, so he was on his back, me sitting across him, his cock impaled deep inside me.

He fumbled in the dark. The click of his tattoo kit opening.

And then he was pushing it into my hand.

I stared down at it. "What..."

He turned it on, the electronic buzz mixing with the crash of the water behind me. He drew it down so it touched his skin.

I jerked my hand back instinctively, but he did it again, guiding the nib of the machine down to his chest. "Make your mark on me while I fuck a baby into you, Violet."

Heat rushed me. On instinct, I rocked my hips, chasing down friction for both of us.

He groaned. "Say what I want to hear."

"Yes, Daddy."

He slammed his hips up, and I ground down on the gun. I didn't know what I was drawing. He already had my name and the flowers representing it over his heart, he didn't need me scribbling on him and making a mess.

I tried to keep the wobble out of my hand, but it was

impossible with the way he thrust up into me. I lost myself in the pleasure, grinding down on him when he pushed up, the two of us meeting in the middle to collide against each other.

With barely a few lines on his skin, the tattoo gun fell from my fingers. I needed both hands to brace myself on his chest, so I could tip my head and arch my back, getting myself into the position that had his cock hitting that spot inside me just right.

I moaned, my nipples tight and aching for touch. He drew one of my hands up to them, and together we took a handful. His other hand found my clit, and I dropped my hand over his, not letting him stop.

The orgasm that barreled down on me in the moonlight stole my breath. My lungs hitched, and I gasped. Pleasure exploded inside me, starting low and deep but spreading like fireworks through my blood and across my skin. I pulsed around him, squeezing him tight with internal muscles completely controlled by the orgasm he'd given me.

Our moans mingled in the night breeze, carried away with the crash of waves. I dropped myself down onto him, kissing him hard, breathing against his lips, trying to regulate myself with his body.

He growled and flipped our positions again, laying me out on the towel much more carefully than he had when it had been him in the sand. On his knees, he lifted my hips until my ass rested on his thighs, my legs wide around him, my hips tilted toward the sky.

He was still so hard inside me.

I'd come, but he hadn't.

He reached for the tattoo gun, and I gasped as he

brought it to the place we were joined. His left hand found my clit again, and he rubbed it slowly, half using the buzz as a vibrator against my most sensitive parts.

"You still want me to tattoo your pussy, Violet?"

Oh God. I so did. I didn't know what that said about me, but it was all I'd thought about for weeks. Something about it felt so incredibly intimate and hot that every time I'd thought about it, if one of them hadn't been handy, I'd had to get my vibrator out. I nodded.

"What do I want to hear?'

"Yes, Daddy."

His fingers picked up the pace, just a smidge, rolling my already sensitive clit, sending new ripples of pleasure through my already well-fucked system.

"Don't move."

He didn't try to pull out.

Oh my fucking God. He was going to tattoo me while he was still in me.

There was a swipe of something cold. A disinfectant wipe if I had to guess. I jumped, but he leaned down on me hard, pinning me beneath his forearm on my thigh.

"I said, don't move."

"Yes, Daddy."

He growled like he well approved that unprompted response.

The first touch of the needle shocked me, the tiny stab of pain. But he rubbed my clit at the same time, which made it all go away. He maneuvered the nib over my flesh, his concentration never faltering from the spot just to the side of where we were joined.

I closed my eyes, panting through the pain and plea-sure mingling. I wanted him to move. Wanted that friction. Him inside me, but keeping so still was driving me wild.

I wanted it hard and fast, but I wanted his name on me more.

This was wild and reckless. Some nagging voice in the back of my head said tattooing a man's name anywhere on your body was a stupid idea.

But this man felt different. This man was one who'd already branded himself on my heart. His name on my body just felt like the natural next step.

I clenched around him, my pussy fluttering of its own accord, not with another orgasm but maybe with after-shocks from the first.

Levi's gaze strayed to mine. "Fucking hell, you're killing me."

"I'm not doing it on purpose!"

He tipped his head back and groaned, caving in and thrusting into me just a little, relieving the tension the tiniest bit, except it only lasted for a second before he was peering down at his work and finishing his name.

He reached for his jacket, pulled out his phone, and focused it on his cock inside me, my pussy stretched around him, and the brand-new tattoo he'd inked along one side.

The flash blinded us both. I blinked rapidly, but through my lashes and the bright white spots that danced in front of my eyes, it was him I saw.

He slammed into me, pubic bone hitting the fresh tattoo, pain mixing with the pleasure. His thumb never left my clit, and he drove into me hard and fast, getting me right back to the brink.

"I gave you what you wanted." His voice was low and deep and full of growl.

It was so damn sexy I could have died and gone to Heaven right then and there.

"Now give me what I want. Come for me, Violet."

I moaned, loving being told what to do, loving the response it lit up inside me. I'd been barely hanging on for dear life, so relaxing into the sand, and letting go was the easiest "Yes!" I'd ever uttered.

He came just as hard, his cock kicking inside me, my freshly tattooed pussy clenching him tight, releasing, then doing it all over again. I writhed beneath him until we were both sandy messes, but weak with pleasure and thoroughly exhausted.

He pulled out and lay back next to me, both of us hot and sweaty, the breeze a welcome relief on sticky skin.

He propped himself up on one arm. "How does it feel?"

"A little sore," I admitted. "But zero regrets."

"You haven't even seen it yet."

"I don't need to. You did it. I know it's perfect."

"You have a lot of faith in an apprentice tattooing in the moonlight."

I kissed his mouth. "I have a lot of faith in *you*."

He brushed his lips over mine, then fumbled for his phone sitting on top of his jacket. He opened up the photo he'd taken. "Here. Look."

The close-up photo sent a new flush of heat through my body. My pussy stretched around him.

His name in his perfectly imperfect handwriting that I'd fallen in love with through his letters.

Tears pricked at the backs of my eyes. His handwriting meant something to me. So did the way he'd claimed me.

He took the phone back, and his fingers flew across the screen. Over his shoulder, I watched him pull up his text message chat with Whip and X.

LEVI:

> Change of plans for tomorrow. Violet can't ride. We'll have to take the van or Whip's car.

Whip's response came back almost instantly.

WHIP:

> What? Why can't she ride? Is she hurt?

Levi grinned wickedly and attached the photo to the message.

My breath hitched.

He glanced at me. "Tell me not to send it and I won't."

I should have said no. Should have told him to delete it. Or at the very least, that it was something private, just for him and me.

But I said nothing.

Because the thought of X and Whip seeing that photo only turned me on more.

He hit send, explaining with one image exactly why I wouldn't be comfortable riding for the next couple of weeks.

And then he fucked me again, while his phone exploded with messages from the two men whose names I needed Levi to add when we got home.

23

X

arold yowled from the carrier wedged between the seats, like I'd personally offended his ancestors by forcing him into it. My forearms were covered in fresh scratches, and one of my hoodie strings had been severed in the battle.

He'd peed in the carrier.

All in all, seemed like we were doing quite well. Maybe even on our way to becoming friends.

The hiss Harold gave from his kitty jail like he could read my mind seemed to say otherwise.

I peered through the mesh into his green eyes. "I love you too, and I always will."

"That cat wants you to die so he can eat your eyeballs," Whip said from the front seat.

I squeezed the sides of the soft cat carrier, pushing them in so they muffled Harold's ears. "Would you stop giving him ideas? I'm pretty sure he hissed the word 'die' at me this morning."

Whip sniggered; his gaze concentrated on the long

stretch of boring freeway ahead of us. I put Harold's carrier back down, in the hopes he might go to sleep and stop plotting my demise, and turned my attention to the other bag I'd brought along. "Speaking of eyes, is it time for a road trip game of I Spy? I have snacks, too. Pringles for Levi, Twizzlers for Whip, and Cheetos for Violet."

Violet took her packet from my fingers. "Thank you."

"They aren't going to make your tatted-up vagina feel any better." I rummaged around in the bag. "I did also buy you an icepack for that though."

She laughed. "Um, thanks? But honestly, it's very small. It doesn't hurt that much."

"Are you talking about the tattoo or Levi's cock?"

He flipped me the bird from the front seat without even looking back.

With all the snacks I'd brought for them handed out, I clapped my hands together. "Okay, so I spy—"

Whip groaned. "Do we have to do this?"

"Would you rather I sing ninety-nine bottles?"

He and I had done a road trip once before, helping out Fang and some of the other Slayers to retrieve Rebel's little sister from the cult her parents were raising her in. I still thought it was one of my best performances of the song. Whip had strongly disagreed.

"No! Anything but that song." Whip clenched the steering wheel tighter.

"So you'll play?"

He sighed heavily. "If I must."

"Great! Violet can go first."

She munched on a Cheeto and swallowed before she answered. "I spy, with my little eye...something beginning with S."

"Sadness," I said instantly, pointing at Levi.

"Shut up," Levi muttered. "I'm not sad."

"Sorry, but grumpy didn't start with S."

Whip made an offering. "Sun?"

"Nope." Violet tossed another Cheeto in her mouth.

"Semen," I said. "Because Levi's is probably still in you."

Violet turned around and threw a balled-up napkin at me. "It was street sign, but thanks for giving everyone that visual."

I bounced on the seat. "Ooh! Double S! You get two points for that, you know. Who's going next?"

"You," all three of them said in unison.

"Great! I spy with my little eye, something beginning with B."

Whip looked out the window. "Bridge?"

"Balls. Specifically yours, that are now tragically full since Levi took Violet's pussy out of commission."

Whip glanced back at me in the rearview mirror. "I have others in this car who can help me out with that."

My mouth dropped open, and I snatched up Harold's carrier. "You will not defile my cat, Whip! Do not even THINK about getting the peanut butter out and coating your balls in it so he'll lick them."

Everyone just stared at me.

Violet was the one who choked out a response. "He meant Levi."

"Ohhhh." I grinned, putting Harold's carrier back down. "That makes more sense. I forgot the two of you were butt buddies." I cast a look at Levi. "Is that how you caught Whip? You put peanut butter on your balls?"

"X, I honestly need to know if you have a brain injury. Because it would really explain SO much."

I grinned at Levi. "I spy with my little eye, something beginning with D."

Levi sighed and said, "Dashboard," at the same time Violet said, "Daddy."

Now it was her turn to get stared at.

Her cheeks went pink.

"Who are you calling Daddy?" I choked out, my gaze flitting between Whip and Levi. "It's Whip, isn't it? It's the gray hair?"

Levi cleared his throat uncomfortably.

My gaze snapped to him. "Oh my God, it's you! You filled her up with cum, tattooed your name on her vag, and then had her call you Daddy!"

Levi groaned and rubbed a hand over his face like he was regretting every life choice that had led him to this moment.

Violet squeaked, "It wasn't like that!"

I leaned forward, eyes wide. "It *so* was like that! I can *see* it, Vi. Sand in your crack, Levi all growly, the moonlight reflecting off your freshly inked girl bits while he whispers—"

"X!" Levi barked.

But I was cackling now with my imitations totally on point, even if I did say so myself. "'Say it, Violet. Who's your tattoo artist *and* your daddy?'"

Whip was straight-up wheezing, doubled over in the front seat.

"Are we there yet?" Levi complained.

I sniggered to myself. "We have plenty of time for more of this, Daddy. Eat your Pringles."

24

———

WHIP

I'd lost track of how long we'd been on the road, but it was long enough for five more rounds of I Spy, a painful session of car karaoke, and for X to braid Violet's hair.

He'd only shut up after she fell asleep, her head on his shoulder, apparently only willing to stop running his mouth when he was worried about waking her.

In the rearview mirror I watched them, her sleeping with a slight smile on her lips despite the shitstorm we were potentially about to drive into, but knowing she was safe, surrounded by the three of us.

X, for once in his life, seemed equally settled by her presence. His fingers splayed out on her thigh, and he sat quietly, staring out the window.

I had one arm on the center console and steered with the other.

Levi also rested his arm in the middle, our pinky fingers brushing with each bump of the road.

I wanted to link my finger around his. To hold his hand.

But I couldn't make myself move.

I'd kissed him. Sucked his cock. Had him inside me. And yet, why did I feel like I couldn't just hold my finger around his? Why was that so much harder than anything else?

"You okay?" Levi asked quietly.

I glanced over at him. "Yeah, fine."

"You want me to drive for a bit?"

I shook my head. "I'm good." I swallowed. "Sorry about what I said before."

He frowned. "What did you say?"

I shrugged. "You know, about having someone else to take care of my...needs."

Understanding washed over Levi's face. "Oh. That. It's fine."

"It was presumptuous. We aren't in a relationship..."

I wanted to swear as soon as the words were out. What the fuck was I doing? It felt a lot like testing him, hoping he'd disagree with me.

Which was just a surefire way to hurt my own damn feelings.

A blush rose up Levi's neck. "Yeah, right. Of course. No need to make a big deal out of it and tell everyone our business."

He pulled his hand away and turned to stare out his window, clearly not wanting to talk about it anymore.

I put my hand back on the steering wheel, clenching it with all ten fingers and cursing myself for saying anything. I didn't need Levi to publicly acknowledge what we were doing behind closed doors, both with and without Violet. He was right, it wasn't anyone else's business.

I knew better than anyone that sex was just sex. It didn't have to have meaning behind it. It didn't have to come with the sort of relationship where you held hands across the center console.

Levi was hot. My dick liked him. It didn't have to be more complicated than that.

Then why did I feel so fucking hurt and disappointed?

I knew we'd found the right place before the GPS told us.

The house was huge—wide, white, and symmetrical, with black window frames and a front door that probably weighed more than Levi's bike. A gardener in a beige jumpsuit trimmed rosebushes outside the imposing gates that probably cost more than my entire house and kept out any uninvited guests.

Like the four of us, peering out the windows of the car.

"Holy shit," X muttered. "Are we here to find Nyah or apply to be adopted? This place is massive."

Dax had decided to drive himself, the only other option being the space in the middle back seat between X and Violet. I rolled down my window when he stopped beside us.

He dropped his passenger-side window so we could talk. "This is it?"

I nodded. "According to the records X's brother found, this is their last known address."

Dax nodded, gung-ho determination in his dark-brown eyes. "Let's go then."

I raised a hand. "Let us go first, okay? You follow."

He seemed like he wanted to argue but eventually gave a curt nod when I raised my gun just enough for him to see it over the edge of the window.

We were armed. He wasn't. And walking into a Mafia family home and accusing them of kidnapping their only daughter probably wasn't going to go down well.

I pulled the car into the driveway and pushed the intercom buzzer on the stone pillar.

Levi ducked his head so he could peer up at the top of it. "Video surveillance. At least two cameras. We should probably assume there's more."

I nodded but said nothing, because a clipped, gruff voice came through the speakers. "Yeah?"

"Wyatt DeLeon, here to speak to Jeremiah or Constance Matish."

"Please!" X called from the back seat. "Honestly, Whip, you have no manners."

I shot him a look.

"More than just one of you in that car," the voice came back.

I pressed my lips together, but it was a fair enough statement. "Levi Griffin, Violet Garrisen, and..." I twisted toward X. "What the hell is your real name anyway?"

X rolled his eyes and answered the speaker for me. "Knox Hawthorne."

Levi raised an eyebrow. "You don't look like a Knox."

"What name do I look like then?"

He shrugged. "Peter?"

X's mouth dropped open. "Peter? As in Pan? That's insulting." He crossed his arms over his chest like Levi had mortally wounded his ego.

"I would have gone with Greg, personally," I threw in, just to rub salt in the wound.

X shot me a dirty look. "Why are you both giving me old man names? I can totally pull of Knox! Can't I, Omelet?"

She was much more gracious with his ego than we'd been. "If I can pull off Omelet, you can pull off Knox."

He seemed satisfied that at least Violet thought his name suited him.

Truthfully, I was just messing with him, and I could tell from Levi's smirk that he had been as well.

The security guy eventually came back to us. "You don't have an appointment."

"No, we don't."

"They aren't taking visitors right now."

Mmm. Sure they weren't. "It's important. It's about their daughter. She's missing."

"Mr. and Mrs. Matish are well aware. Miss Matish left town quite some time ago."

Violet rolled her window down. "We aren't talking about her leaving the city. We're friends of hers. She went missing two days ago. Didn't show up for work. Nobody has seen her since."

There was a long pause. "You'll need to make an appointment."

Violet sat back in her seat. "Forget it. They aren't letting us in. Let's just go. Coming here was probably a stupid idea anyway. Nyah hates these people."

But we all knew it wasn't that simple. We needed to speak to Nyah's parents. Either they had her, or they might know who did.

I knew Nyah had run from these people, but my gut instinct said she was a lot better off right now if it was them who'd taken her.

Because the alternative was the sick fuck who'd been messing with us for weeks. And if he had her...

I didn't want to think about finding another of Violet's friends dead in a pool of her own blood.

Violet's fingers shook, and I knew she had to be thinking the same thing. It was why we were here, why we were willing to go to the people Nyah hated.

It was the only hope we had that she was still alive.

She'd been gone forty-eight hours. If *he* had her, then she was probably already dead.

But we weren't getting anywhere just sitting in the driveway. "We'll find another way," I assured Violet.

She nodded but I didn't think she really believed me.

I needed her to have hope.

I just didn't know where to find it. I backed the car out slowly, motioning to Dax parked across the street that it was a no go. I couldn't hear him, but his frustration was clear in the way he slammed the heel of his hand against the steering wheel and his mouth formed a curse word.

Levi's phone rang a second later, and he mumbled into it before ending the call. "Dax is going to find somewhere he can get some new ink. He needs the release before he does something stupid."

I watched him drive off in the opposite direction. "Healthier than getting drunk, I guess."

Levi nodded. "I'll check in on him in a couple of hours when we've worked out what we're doing."

X leaned between the two front seats. "Speaking of, uh, what *are* we doing?"

"Thinking," I shot back.

He tapped his fingers for a moment. "Okay, that's boring. What next?"

"X," Levi warned.

X rolled his eyes and sat back. "Fine. God, I hope I'm not as dull as the two of you when I'm your age. Or is it the fact you're an old married couple now?"

"We aren't married," Levi said with gritted teeth.

"And we aren't a couple, right, Levi?" The passive-aggressive statement was out of my mouth before I even really thought about what I was saying. I could feel Violet's concerned gaze resting on my back and bit down on my lip before I said anything else.

A horn honked behind me, and I glanced in the rearview mirror. "Fucking impatient city assholes." I rolled the window down and stuck my hand out it, waving the guy around. "Just fucking pass if you're in that much of a hurry."

The nondescript white van made no move to go around us. It just honked again, this time with the addition of flashing lights.

Hair stood up on the back of my neck.

Levi took out his gun and checked it, then glanced at the van in the passenger-side mirror. Any talk of what our relationship was or wasn't instantly forgotten.

"Uh, what's going on?" Worry edged into Violet's tone.

X patted her leg as he reached down to pull the knife

he kept strapped to his ankle. "Nothing, my eggggg-stra awesome lady."

She swatted his hand away. "Then why do you all suddenly have weapons?"

I didn't want to scare her, but I wasn't going to keep her in the dark anymore either. "That van honking at us looks an awful lot like the one you said was up on the bluffs that night."

"And the same one from that night when someone threw a brick through your car window after you and Nyah followed us," Levi added.

She twisted around, peering through the back window, before settling back. "Give me a weapon."

"No," all three of us said at once.

I could practically feel the heat from the steam coming out of her ears.

"If that asshole back there is the guy who killed Toby, who also potentially has Nyah, I'm not going to sit here and comb my fucking hair. Somebody give me a gun!"

There was so much wild anger in her voice that I instantly passed mine back to her.

In the rearview mirror, she blinked at me, like she hadn't really expected her little outburst to work. But then she mouthed, "Thank you."

I nodded. "There's a spare in the glove box, Levi."

He reached for the dashboard and found said spare weapon, checked it for me, then passed it over.

I clutched it with one hand, spinning the steering wheel with the heel of the other, turning us down a side street with less traffic. I needed to double-check this guy behind us was actually following us and not just a shit-ass driver.

I glanced over my shoulder, peering through the back window.

The van turned as well.

I slammed my foot on the brake. "Vi, open your door but do not get out."

I didn't wait for her to reply, just trusted she would listen.

Levi and I both opened our doors in unison, sliding out, guns pointed behind us, using the doors Violet and X opened as shields.

The van skidded to a stop in a screech of tires.

A man sat behind the wheel, his eyes huge when he noticed the guns pointed in his direction. He very slowly raised his hands.

"It's the gardener from Nyah's parents' place," Violet called from inside the car.

I glanced at Levi over the top of the car.

He shrugged, then turned his attention back to the guy in the van. "Get out."

The man nodded nervously and very slowly opened his door. I braced myself for sudden gunshots or the back door sliding open and a small army of thugs flowing out.

But none of that happened. The gardener, easily identified now that I was paying attention to his beige overalls and the logo embroidered into his hat, just got out and shut the door, though he eyed me and Levi warily. "You were asking about Nyah. I heard you speaking to the Matishs' security team. They won't take a meeting with you."

"No shit, Sherlock," I muttered. But louder, I said, "Security already made that much clear. What's not is why you're chasing us down."

"I can tell you where you can find Nyah's parents."

I raised an eyebrow but lowered the gun. This guy wasn't going to hurt anyone. "Why would you?"

He shoved his hands in his pockets. "Because she was my friend. She's the best of them, you know? They're horrible people."

"Why work for them then?" Levi asked.

The man raised his shoulder. "Because they pay three times as much as any other job I could get around here. I normally just keep my head down and try to blend in with the bushes."

"So why stick your neck out now?"

"If they've done something to Nyah, I want to help. I was glad when she said she was running. But I knew at some point they'd drag her back. She knew it too."

Violet stepped out of the car, which didn't exactly please me, but even I could admit this situation wasn't as dangerous as I'd first thought it was going to be. "Have you seen any sign that they have her?"

He shook his head. "But they have other properties. Businesses. A hundred places across the city they could have stashed her in." He swallowed thickly. "Your best bet is to try talking to her brother. Unlike her parents, he actually cares about her."

That was worth a shot. "Know where we might find him?"

The man looked me up and down. "Got any clothes suitable for a gay bar?"

LEVI

I stared at myself in the mirror of the changing room and didn't recognize the person staring back at me. "No. Absolutely not. Zero percent."

X ripped open the curtain and hooted. "The cutoff denim shorts are really doing it for me. And hey!" He poked me in the stomach. "You can see your abs in that shirt."

Shirt was being generous. It was so short it barely covered my nipples.

X had found himself a pleated tartan skirt that he was happily prancing around the store in. "Omelet! Do you like this one?" He shook his ass. "Oooh, feel the breeze! I should wear skirts every day, this is delightful!"

He spotted a pair of black thigh-high boots with the chunkiest heel I'd ever seen and bent to pick them up.

I winced at the flash of ass from beneath the skirt. "Underwear, X. While we're here, buy some damn underwear."

"Don't knock it 'til you've tried it. Your balls might like the breeze too."

"My balls are just fine in jeans, thanks." I tugged at the frayed hem of the ridiculous shorts. "And not the cutoff kind."

Whip came out of another changing room, leather pants clinging to his ass and thighs, a black mesh top covering his chest. I supposed I should be grateful X hadn't shoved that shirt in my direction or my nipples actually would be out for everyone to see.

I snorted on a laugh. "You look ridiculous."

"Like you can talk. Nice belly button."

Asshole.

Violet surveyed all three of us with barely concealed laughter. "As great as you all look, I think a nice pair of pants and a button-down shirt might also be acceptable? Not sure we actually have to lean this hard into a stereotype."

X pouted. "But my ass likes the breeze, Violet! Lemme wear the skirt."

"You can wear whatever makes you happy."

"And tell me you'll feel me up underneath it."

She shot a look at the salesclerk who went pink and turned away, trying to cover her laughter. Violet stepped in, pressed up on her toes, and brushed her lips across X's. "If you wear that, I will definitely be taking advantage in a dark corner."

X leaned around her and slammed his credit card down on the clerk's desk. "Sold!"

"I'm finding somewhere to buy a button-down," Whip said. "One that doesn't show off my areolas."

"Fucking hell, why can't Nyah's brother own a restaurant or a laundromat or something? Why a gay bar?" I hated the idea of wearing anything other than the oil-stained jeans and club jacket I pretty much permanently lived in.

Whip shot a tired glance at me. "Why are you resisting this so hard? Wear your jeans. No one is going to care. Or is it more the fact we're going to a gay bar that you have such an issue with?"

"I have no issue with that."

Whip just gave me a look like he was sure that wasn't true.

Oh, fuck him.

I'd spent more than half my life in a biker gang in Saint View. There wasn't exactly a high number of gay bars for me to wander into for an after-work drink. Army, our old prez before War, would have beat the shit out of me if I'd so much as even thought about walking into a place like the one we were going to tonight.

If I was being honest, I was fucking nervous about it. Not just because I was praying we would be able to speak to Nyah's brother, and he might have some information on his sister's whereabouts. I could see the tension radiating through Violet, the stress of not knowing, the constant fear that Nyah's parents had nothing to do with this and Nyah was yet another victim of the killer who taunted us.

I didn't even want to think about that.

Nyah might have hated her parents, and they might have been deep in the criminal underworld, but they weren't the same level of twisted that we'd been dealing with the last few weeks.

But even that wasn't the thing on my mind.

I was going to a gay club and I had no idea what the fuck I was supposed to do about Whip.

I yanked off the ridiculous outfit and jogged across the store to catch up with him at the door. "I'm coming with you to search for shirts without holes."

Violet waved us out the door. "We'll catch up. X wants coffee."

Whip squinted at him. "You really need the caffeine? You've been bouncing off the walls all afternoon."

He rolled his eyes. "Sheesh, I'll get decaf, okay?" Then he grinned. "With a shot of Red Bull!"

"Please don't let him do that," I said to Violet, watching X twerk in the mirror of the store, so his skirt flipped up and down at the back, flashing the entire room with every jerk of his ass.

She hid a smile and tucked her arm into X's. "Come on, let's go find you a nice cup of herbal tea. And some underwear."

"Okay, but I'm only agreeing to a G-string. My ass looks too good in this to cover it up."

"I fear we've released a beast," I muttered to Whip as we walked out onto the street lined with boutique shops.

"Let's just hope there's no stages or platforms for him to dance on."

I wrinkled my nose at the idea of staring up at X's balls beneath a too-short skirt while he danced on a stage. "Is that what this club is going to be like? Psychos but for guys?"

Whip shrugged. "Women can go too. And I doubt anyone will be having full-blown sex in gold cages like there is at Psychos, but I guess its normally a similar sort of vibe."

I side-eyed him. "You've been to clubs like this?"

He shrugged. "Sure. With clients. Not exactly where I'd spend all my weekends, but I've been to a few."

I turned away, wishing I hadn't asked. Because now all I could think about was Whip at a club, surrounded by hot men.

Maybe it wasn't like Psychos where they'd have sex right then and there.

But how long had it taken them to move out into a dark alley where they could be alone? How long had it taken for them to call a taxi to go back to a hotel?

The jealousy that coursed through me was thick and hard and all-consuming. I followed him into another store and grumpily yanked at shirts on a rack, barely noticing the color or size of them, when all I could see in my head was Whip gyrating with other guys, their lips and hands all over him.

Whip's gaze followed me around the store, while I tried to ignore it.

Eventually, he sighed and touched my hand. "You want to talk about what's on your mind, or you just want to tear up one of those shirts right now and get some of that aggression out?"

I yanked my fingers away, irrationally pissed with him because of the visions in my mind.

Whip didn't miss it. The way I'd recoiled from his touch.

He pressed his lips together and nodded, like he understood exactly what my problem was. Anger flashed in his eyes. "Right. I get it now." He grabbed the closest shirt and yanked it off the rack. "Don't worry, I get the message loud and clear."

Unless he could see the parade of made-up images of Whip with other men in my mind, that was driving me insane, I was pretty sure he had no idea what was going on. And it was too fucking embarrassing to admit.

Which only pissed me off all the more. I was mad at him for things he'd done before we'd even met.

I was fucking insane.

He shoved the shirt toward the clerk, but his gaze was on me, his eyes burning. "You don't have to worry. I'm not going to ask you to hold my hand as we walk in so the whole club knows we're together."

I scoffed. "Of course not. Because this is just another opportunity for you, isn't it? Maybe a chance to pick up some new clients? Earn some more money? Go fuck a hot guy in some dark corner and have him shove a hundred in your pocket for the privilege?"

I squeezed my eyes shut the moment the words were out of my mouth. They had my jealousy written all over them.

Because if I was being honest, it was me I wanted him fucking in the corner. It was me I wanted him to choose.

I wanted him to pick me over a job where other people got what was supposed to be mine and Violet's.

But a lifetime of homophobia rang between my ears. Army's and the other guys' sly taunts about fags and cocksuckers. I tried to remind myself I'd already overcome this once. That the club wasn't like that anymore, that War being with Scythe had set the tone for a new era and Whip and I were safe there.

But were we safe here? On the streets of a city we didn't know? Where I knew men were still attacked in broad daylight for holding another man's hand? Where gay clubs were targeted by hate and violence?

My brain was a mess, and I'd always been shit with words. And that tongue-tie only seemed to get worse when my feelings were involved.

Just like the first night I'd laid eyes on Violet, I was royally fucking it all up.

And yet my tongue wouldn't move to say things that made it better.

Whip snatched the bag with his new shirt in it from the woman and then turned to glare at me. "Don't worry, Levi. Your dirty little secret, that you like when a male escort touches you, is safe with me. I won't try to hold your hand tonight. Or to kiss you. Or do any of the other things that have had you moaning my name and begging me for more every night."

His anger speared through me like a flaming arrow.

He leaned in closer. "Tonight when we're in that club, we're nothing to each other. We aren't in a relationship. We aren't fucking. We don't even fucking know each other. How's that? That make you feel better?"

It didn't. I opened my mouth, willing myself to say that to him. To explain that none of that was what I wanted, and all of this was because I was so damn jealous, and that I had these stupid fucking feelings that demanded he only be with us.

But he didn't let me get any of that out.

He just went nose to nose with me, those steel-blue eyes boring straight into my soul, when he whispered, "Tonight I'm just the hooker you think I am."

26

WHIP

I found X, Violet, and Harold at a coffee shop and dropped the car keys onto the table between them. "I'll meet you at the club tonight. Take the car. I need to walk."

They both stared up at me, their smiles fading at my clipped words.

Violet grabbed my hand. "What happened? Where's Levi?"

It was on the tip of my tongue to tell her he was in the fucking closet, being a homophobic asshole, but he was still the man she was in love with. I didn't want to ruin that for her by bad-mouthing him.

Even though he was being a prick and fucking deserved it.

"I don't know. But I've got a few things to do. Just need a couple hours. I'll see you later."

I pressed my lips to the top of her head and breathed in the honeysuckle scent of her hair, using her familiar smell to calm the storm raging inside me Levi had stirred up.

It was on the tip of my tongue to tell her I loved her.

When she looked up at me with those big eyes, rimmed with dark lashes, all I wanted to do was scoop her up in my arms and tell her that everything was going to be okay.

But it wasn't. Nothing was right. Nyah was missing. Someone was hunting us. And Levi was breaking my fucking heart.

That last one was my fault. I was the idiot who'd gone and fallen for an emotionally unavailable straight man, who'd had a few minutes of fun in dark corners with another guy. I should have known falling for him would end in nothing but pain.

Violet and X called after me as I left, but I just couldn't sit there with them while a storm raged inside me. I didn't know what I needed, but I could feel an implosion coming and I didn't want to be around her when it happened.

She didn't deserve the mess of me and Levi detonating whatever relationship we might have been building.

It had been a long time since I'd been in this city, but it wasn't my first rodeo. Memories plagued me.

My wife and I had brought our kids here on vacation. More than once we'd walked these streets as a family of four. She'd loved the ocean and everything in it, so we'd spent hours at the aquarium, staring at brightly colored fish and listening to her talk about documentaries she'd seen on saving the turtles and what we could do to help.

The kids had listened to her every word, and so had I,

not because I cared so much about marine life, but because I'd loved the way she'd lit up when she was passionate about something.

I'd loved the little smile on her lips she'd gotten every time she'd realized I was watching her.

The memories played on in my head. But they felt different than how they had in the past.

I realized with a start that while I would always love the woman I'd married, I wasn't *in* love with her anymore.

I couldn't be.

Because I was so stupidly in love with Violet.

And, if I was being honest with myself, with Levi.

Julia was my past, and those memories of her, Tyler, and Kennedy, the two beautiful children we'd had together, would always be there.

But I'd spent years being angry. Years taking out that frustration with guns and knives and sex.

None of it had ever been enough.

Not until Violet and Levi had come along.

Suddenly, everything felt different. Better. Some of the anger had drifted away, and I didn't want to spend all my time killing or fucking. It had never filled the void the way their arms did.

"Fuck you, Levi," I muttered. "Fuck you for giving me something worth losing."

I didn't know where I was going, walking the streets, clutching my new clothes in a bag so tightly my fingers were losing sensation. I found myself outside a church, a little A-frame out in front advertising that Alcoholics Anonymous was meeting inside.

Without even really thinking about why, I walked along the narrow path and up the old stone steps of the church. I let myself in quietly and took a seat at the back. A few heads turned my way, but nobody said anything, the meeting in full swing and a man at the front speaking to the group.

It wasn't the first meeting I'd been to. I'd never had a problem with alcohol, but after my family had been killed by a drunk driver, I'd started going, hoping this kind of therapy could work for the hate and despair I'd been holding on to so hard.

Hoping it could keep me from taking out my frustrations with a gun or a knife.

My first cold-blooded kill had been a man who I'd met at that group. One who'd claimed to be clean and sober, a ninety-day chip firmly in his fingers at every meeting. But who I'd followed back to a bar every night, where he got so drunk he could barely stand, then got in his car and drove home.

I'd only been able to watch it three times before, one night, he hadn't made it to the bar. Or to his car, ever again.

But I sat at the back of the meeting now and realized that wasn't a life I wanted to go back to. Being alone. Stalking victims at night, trying to fill the hole of my pain with someone else's.

I left before the meeting ended so I didn't have to talk to anyone.

There was nothing here for me anymore.

Not when everything I wanted was out there.

got to the club owned by Nyah's brother, Cedric, less than thirty minutes after it opened, but even so, there was a short line out front. I had a text on my phone from Violet, telling me they would be a little late because they were picking up Dax, but he'd only just gotten back from getting his new tattoo and hadn't had time to change.

I'd just written back a simple, "Okay." I'd wanted to check out the place before they got here anyway, so I wasn't expecting them for another thirty minutes. I probably had more like forty-five now.

The line inched along slowly, but I made it to the front and was eventually let in.

I rolled my eyes in the dim space that had barely any people inside. Clearly the line was a tactic for making the place seem popular. But I was glad to see I didn't stand out like a sore thumb in the outfit I'd haphazardly bought that afternoon. I definitely hadn't packed to be going to a club, but I'd also been so distracted by my argument with Levi that I hadn't really paid attention to what I'd been shoving at the clerk in my rush to get out of there and away from Levi.

At least the shirt fit.

And nobody could see my nipples through it.

I found a free stool at the bar and sank down on it.

The bartender came right over and grinned at me. "How you doing?"

I nodded. "Good. Whiskey neat."

The man raised an eyebrow. "Strong choice. I would

have picked you more as a vodka and lemonade sorta guy."

I chuckled at that. "Oh yeah? Why's that?"

He shrugged. "Guys who look like you generally force themselves to drink whiskey and bourbon when they're at straight bars, then they come in here and realize it's perfectly acceptable for them to order something pink or fruity." He eyed me. "You sure you don't want a cocktail…" He winked at me. "The cock comes free after my shift if you're interested?"

I laughed and shook my head. "Thanks, but honestly, I really do like whiskey."

The rejection didn't bother him any. It slid off him easily, and a moment later I had a whiskey neat in front of me. The bartender waited until I took a sip.

I tried not to grimace. It was cheap and nasty, and clearly not their specialty.

He sniggered. "You sure you don't want a cosmopolitan or something? They're my specialty."

I pushed the whiskey back at him. "I think you just convinced me to try one."

He pumped the air like that was a victory and set to work, pouring various liquids into a shaker filled with ice. I crowd watched while he worked, eyeing people filing in.

I was on my third cosmo when Levi walked in with Violet, Dax, and X. X immediately pulled Violet onto the dance floor, twirling her around, not giving a flying fuck they were the only people on it. They started something though, because a moment later, the dance floor filled up, mostly with men, all moving to the fast-paced beat.

I caught Levi's eye across the room, but I wasn't in the mood to try to work him out tonight. He was painfully stiff and uncomfortable and out of place. Like he wanted to run out the door at any moment and the only reason he wasn't was because Violet was here. His gaze flickered away from mine, and he focused on her.

"How very fucking straight of you, Levi," I muttered into the fruity-smelling pink drink that Kade, the bartender, had been plying me with all evening.

"What was that, Daddy?" he asked with a wink.

He'd been calling me that since my second top-up, but it was with a playful tone and I'd heard him calling the older guy at the other end of the bar the same thing, so I knew it was nothing personal and barely even flirty. We'd already passed that point and established I wasn't interested.

Would have been a whole lot easier if I was. But apparently the only cock I was interested in was Levi's.

And the cocktails I was miserably downing like they were candy. They were surprisingly good and way too easy to drink.

Kade's gaze slid past mine, and he leaned his elbows on the countertop. "You're being checked out, you know?"

"Stupidly attractive prison vibe with a tat on his cheekbone?"

"That's the one."

"Eh."

Kade sniggered. "If you aren't interested, I am."

I raised an eyebrow. "Do you ever go home alone after a shift?"

"Not if I can help it. And the dark and dangerous vibe does it for me."

"That man is never going home with you."

Kade pouted, but he must have seen something in my

expression because his eyes widened, and he leaned in even closer. "Spill the tea. There's history between the two of you, isn't there?"

I shrugged. "Not if you ask him."

He poked his bottom lip out. "Oh, he rejected you? That why you're here tonight, drowning your sorrows?"

I shook my head and figured now was as good a time as any to shoot my shot. "I'm actually looking for the owner, Cedric Matish?"

Kade stepped back a few inches, the easy smile he'd had for me all night suddenly disappearing. "Ah, Daddy, you were so close to snagging me, with those pretty blue eyes and older, experienced vibe you got going on. Now I find out you were just using me to get to my cousin all along? Geez, way to mortally wound a guy. You know he's not gay?"

"That's okay. I'm not here to fuck him."

Apparently I wasn't going to be fucking anyone tonight, not with the way Levi and I were steadfastly ignoring each other, and X was taking up all of Violet's time. I didn't begrudge them some fun. We'd had a long run of shit. They should enjoy themselves. I didn't want Violet anywhere near Nyah's family. If they were as bad as Nyah had told Violet, then the farther she stayed away from them, the better.

"You here to kill him?" Kade asked, wiping down a glass and asking the question as casually as he might have asked someone for the time.

"No. I'm a friend of his sister's."

Kade changed his tune instantly. "You know Nyah?"

I nodded.

"She's been gone for weeks. Ric's been really worried."

My mouth pulled into a grim line, and I studied the man, trying to determine whether I could take his words at face value. "If he honestly cares about her, he should be. She's not safe."

Kade's eyebrows furrowed. "That a threat?"

I shook my head. "No, not at all." I pointed to Violet on the dance floor. There were a handful of other women on it, but men outnumbered them ten to one. "See my girl out there?"

He raised an eyebrow. "Your girl? Thought you were into prison tats over there?"

"Can't a guy be into both?"

Kade sniggered. "Oh, to look like you. Must be nice."

We were getting off track. "She's become really attached to your cousin the last few weeks. They've been working together in a little town a few hours away. But Nyah didn't show up for work two days ago. She's missing."

Kade put the glass down in the sink. "Shit. I think you better go talk to Cedric then. Come on. I'll take you." He called out to the other bartenders to say he was taking a minute and then rounded the bar.

I was still sitting on the stool, debating whether going with him was a good idea or not. I had my gun tucked into the back of my jeans and covered by my shirt, but that wasn't going to be much good if Kade took me into some room surrounded by mob men.

Kade held a hand out to me. "You coming or not?"

"This guy likely to shoot the messenger?"

Kade laughed. "Won't know until you try, right?" He

wiggled his fingers. "Come on. Ric isn't a bad guy, and he loves his sister. He's going to want to hear anything you have to say."

Clearly sick of waiting for me to assess the situation, he grabbed my hand and pulled me off the stool. He didn't let go as he weaved through the crowded club that had filled up considerably while we'd been talking. The alcohol sloshed in my stomach, giving my head a pleasant buzz.

One that was pretty much wiped out completely when my gaze caught on Levi's across the club.

Kade didn't miss the way Levi stiffened, his gaze burning through me and Kade like we were doing something wrong.

Kade tutted. "Uh-oh. Trouble in paradise? Is he going to beat my skull in with his meaty mega fists?"

"No."

"You sure? Because this probably looks a little suspicious, me dragging you down dark hallways, into private rooms..."

I gave Levi one last glance. His expression was unreadable. He was like stone.

It fucking pissed me off. I didn't need him to get all deep and into his feelings, but fucking hell. I was sick of him being so adamant there was nothing between us. He ran hot when we were alone, then cold as ice when we were in public. Maybe I should have been more generous, but he wasn't a scared fifteen-year-old kid, kissing a boy for the first time. An attraction to a man might have been new to him, but he was thirty-fucking-five, and we were in the middle of a gay club. And he still couldn't come over and kiss me?

If he couldn't do it here, he couldn't do it anywhere. I was so sick of being a dirty little secret. I'd spent every waking moment thinking about what the hell I was going to do with my life now because I couldn't stand the thought of fucking anyone but him or Violet ever again. I'd been scouring the newspaper, searching for anything that would make me enough money that I didn't have to go back to being Wyatt DeLeon, the sex worker.

Wyatt was a shell of the man he'd been when his wife and kids were alive. Wyatt was dead on the inside, fucking around for money because it was the only time he'd felt even a spark of being alive.

I wanted to be Whip. With X driving me nuts. With Violet sweet and soft in my arms.

With Levi beneath the sheets, his body hard against mine, his fingers and tongue and cock demanding.

Fuck Levi. Fuck him for making me want that. Fuck him for only giving it to me when we were behind closed doors but never outside them.

"He can think what he wants," I told Kade.

Kade chuckled beneath his breath and pulled me past a roped-off area, giving the bouncer watching it a nod.

"Cedric know his security is somewhat lacking?" I asked. "That guy didn't even look twice at me."

"He thinks we're going down here to fuck. The whole club probably does. But you already know that, don't you? And you're using it to make Jail Bird jealous."

On instinct, I shook my head.

Kade laughed it off. "Come on, we're here." He rapped his knuckles across an unmarked black door. He opened it as he called out, "Ric! Got someone here who has news about Nyah."

I was willing to admit I had been envisioning a scene out of a *Godfather* movie. I'd expected men in expensive dark-colored suits, sitting around a mob boss, his fingers adorned in gold, and beautiful, scantily clad women draped all over him.

The reality was quite different. A slim man with black-rimmed glasses sat behind a desk, peering at a computer screen. The desktop was a mess of papers, pens, and take-out coffee cups. There was no dark, suave suit to be seen. Just a nineties retro T-shirt with the Teenage Mutant Ninja Turtles on it.

Kade cleared his throat. "Ric. This is Whip. He needs to talk to you."

Cedric dragged his gaze away from the screen and blinked up at me. "Is she dead?"

I bit my lip. He'd said it bluntly but not without emotion. He tried to hide it, but his fingers shook as he lowered them beneath the table.

This guy was not at all what I'd expected. "I don't know," I said honestly. "I hope not. She went missing two days ago, and nobody has seen or heard from her since. We were hoping that—"

He let out a sharp laugh. "You were hoping my father had her?" He shook his head. "You'd be better off wishing she was dead. Because that's what she'd prefer if he does have her."

"You sure he doesn't?"

Cedric nodded. "My father barely notices me. I run his books. Keep track of his finances. Our other brothers are his brawn and the outward-facing muscle of his business, but—" He gestured down at himself. "I never exactly fit the mold. So I was put to work in other ways, behind the scenes." He narrowed his eyes at me. "But that doesn't mean I don't know what's going on in my father's house. If he had Nyah picked up, then I would know." He turned back to his computer. "I'm sure she's fine. She probably just got spooked that our dad knew where she was and had to move on."

I shook my head. "I don't think so. She's become really close with my girl and she'd started a relationship with a friend of mine. I don't think she would have just walked out on both of them without a word."

"She walked out on me without so much as a good-bye, and I'm her brother. This is just what she does. I can't even be mad at her for it. If Dad were going to marry me off to one of his ancient, narcissistic, violent friends, then I would run without looking back too."

I still wasn't convinced.

Cedric sighed and sat back in his chair. "I can see you actually care about her, and I appreciate that. But she's run before, and she'll run again. This is her life. If my dad catches up with her, she may as well be in prison for the rest of her days. You can't blame her for just skipping town. If she saw someone we know, that would have been enough to send her running to start over again. She wouldn't risk someone mentioning where she was to our parents." He stood, holding out his hand, clearly ending this impromptu little meeting. "I appreciate you making the trip out here. It's clear my sister made some true friends, and for that, I'm really grateful. She deserves some happiness. I'm just sorry it couldn't last."

I took his hand. "Me too. My girl and her, they were close."

Cedric nodded, and there was true regret in his

expression. "Enjoy yourselves tonight. Kade, give them whatever they want, on the house." He eyed me. "But in the morning, be smart and leave. Go back home before our father gets wind of your presence. He ruins everything he touches. Don't let that be you."

His gaze slid back to his computer, and I realized I was being dismissed.

His warning didn't scare me. But I believed him when he said Nyah wasn't here. It was what I'd suspected all along but just hadn't wanted to believe.

Maybe his suggestion that Nyah had run was true. For all I knew, she'd gotten on a train that morning and was now sunning herself on a beach a few hours up the coast where nobody knew her.

I hoped like hell that was the truth.

But my gut said it wasn't.

My gut said Nyah was as dead as Toby was, murdered by a madman who was always one step ahead.

27

———

NYAH

Two days earlier

The sun shined, the birds chirped, and I was so loved-up that I could have levitated right off the ground. My cheeks actually hurt from smiling so much. How was that even a real thing? It should be illegal for someone to be this happy.

But I was.

Oh God, I was seriously delirious with happiness.

I had turned into one of those women I hated. The kind whose whole lives centered around a man. The kind whose only happiness was derived from sweet words, and him holding your hand in public, and tying you to his bed at night so he could do every wicked thing you'd ever dreamed of.

Dax had done them all.

Plus many I hadn't even had the imagination to conjure up. I blushed every time I thought about it.

I didn't even care we'd spent pretty much every minute together since we'd first met, other than when we were at work. Didn't care that any sane human being would have called us codependent.

I was going to marry that man. And soon, because I was already sure he felt the same way. We'd spent half the night talking about how many kids we'd have—at least four—and we'd already, only half-jokingly, discussed an island wedding, just the two of us, somewhere tropical and warm where we could hide from my family and the rest of the world and just live in a cocoon made up only of the two of us.

The way we talked, it should have sent at least one of us running for the hills, and yet it hadn't. I saw my excitement mirrored in his eyes, and that feeling of it just being *right* never went away, no matter how much we lived in each other's pockets.

So sue me if I skipped to work. That was how he made me feel.

It was only as I approached my first job, my cleaning caddy clenched in one hand, that I truly registered the address.

I cringed up at the building, but it looked a lot different in the daylight. In Toby's photo, the house appeared dark and ominous, long shadows falling across the yard, hiding secrets in the corners.

In the daylight, it could have been any other house. Just a regular suburban home. It wasn't even in the worst part of town.

An odd feeling skated down my spine, but I brushed it off, embarrassed for getting carried away.

My father would have been mortified if he knew his daughter was balking at the sight of a house, just because it was in the background of a photo where a couple of ex-con thugs had been dealing drugs or whatever the fuck it was Lynx and his friends had been up to in Toby's photos.

I could practically hear the insults my father would have hurled in my direction.

Soft. Pathetic. Scared of your own shadow, Nyah? Didn't I raise you to be better?

I ground my molars.

I hated that he was always so in my head, even when he was miles away and I hadn't seen or spoken to him in months.

But my father wasn't the sort of person you forgot easily.

Unfortunately.

But in this case, his taunts would have been warranted. I'd already cleaned this house once. The owners hadn't been home at the time, and they'd left a key for me beneath the mat. It had been a simple, straightforward clean, bathrooms, kitchen, vacuum, mop, out the door and on my way to the next house.

I wasn't the weak little princess my father accused me of being. He *had* raised me to be stronger than that.

A few weeks wrapped up in the arms of a man who was sweet and kind and gentle hadn't turned me soft.

I pulled my shoulders back and strode to the door, tapping my knuckles against it. There was no answer, so I checked beneath the doormat for the key, and just like last time, one waited for me. I fit it to the lock and got the door open, before struggling inside with my caddy.

The door closed behind me with a bang loud enough

to make me jump. I spun around, staring at it, but there was no one there.

The wind was picking up. I didn't need to get all twitchy just because slamming doors sounded a lot like gunshots.

I wasn't back in the city. I didn't need to worry about people shooting at me. Nobody knew who I was here. Nobody had painted a target on my back, just because of who my father was.

I put the caddy down and shoved my hands on my hips. "Right. Where to start..."

Bathrooms were always my go-to first stop, so I fell into my regular routine, spraying cleaning liquids around, wrinkling my nose at their fake lemon scents. As I moved into the kitchen, I hummed beneath my breath, any stress I'd had melting away with the repetitive work.

My father would have said it was beneath me to be cleaning other people's shit stains and dirty kitchens. But I didn't have a problem with it. It felt like good, honest work, and when you'd spent your entire life doing anything but, surrounded by people who had never worked an honest day in their lives, it was nice.

I found a mop in the bathroom cupboard and got busy with it. The floorboards creaked beneath my feet, but I took great pleasure in shining them up, washing away the thin layer of dust and grime that had built up since the last time I'd been here.

> *"Just another day, just another chore,*
> *Just another girl scrubbing at the floor."*

I jumped a mile, spinning around at the voice.

There was nobody there.

My heart rate picked up. "Hello?"

Nobody answered. I squinted, and inched toward the stairs, calling up them, "Anyone up there?"

When nobody answered, I slowly looked around the room. Gaze falling on a Bluetooth speaker on the kitchen counter. A green light indicated it was on.

"A friend once came and left just fine.
But second guests run out of time."

That definitely came from the speaker.

I stared at it for a long moment, trying to comprehend what it had said. I didn't get it. But the whole thing was creepy as hell. My Spidey senses tingled, and I wasn't the sort of woman to ignore them twice.

"Yeah, fuck this." I didn't care what my father would have thought of me gathering up my things in a rush, eyeing a cheap plastic speaker like it had the ability to hurt me.

He would have laughed and accused me of being scared of badly delivered poetry.

But he wasn't the one here listening to it, alone in a creepy house.

My purse falling off my shoulder, my cleaning supplies tipping over in the caddy because I hadn't taken the time to stack them properly, I rushed for the door.

I had the distinct feeling of being watched, even though there was no one in sight. It was so strong, I paused before I left and flipped the empty room the bird. "See ya later, weirdo."

I reached for the doorknob.

Twisted it.
It didn't give.

"Sweep the floor and mind the grime. You've walked into the perfect crime."

I searched for a lock I could flip, but there was nothing.

"Sweep the floor and mind the grime. You've walked into the perfect crime."

Panic skated across my skin. I dropped the caddy, not caring that the contents spilled everywhere. With both hands, I grappled with the door, my fear disabling my brain so all I could do was act on pure instinct.

"Sweep the floor and mind the grime. You've walked into the perfect crime."

A whirring mechanical noise started up.
I spun, trying to work out where it was coming from.

"Your hands are swift; your steps are light. But not all stains wash out at night."

I stared at the speaker in horror.
The mechanical noise came again.
The floor fell away from my feet.
I didn't even have a chance to scream.
I hit something hard, my ankles twisting painfully beneath me. I cried out, pain shooting through my legs as

I crumpled into a ball, the floor I'd just been cleaning now somehow above my head.

The trapdoor slid shut again, enclosing me in a box beneath the floor of the house.

"Perfect crime,"

the speaker taunted as the darkness sealed me in.

28

LEVI

The club bass pounded through my skull. We'd spent some time asking around after Nyah and her brother and had met with nothing but tight-lipped scowls and denials. If the bouncers here knew anything, they certainly weren't talking, at least not to us. I'd watched Dax's and Violet's desperation grow with every shutdown, until X had dragged her out on the dance floor and spun her around and around until she'd started smiling again. They'd eventually convinced Dax to join them too, and I was glad for it because sitting at a table with him, watching him drown his sorrows, watching the pain he was in at not knowing where Nyah was, had been killing me.

I hated seeing him like this.

Could only imagine what I would be feeling if it was Violet missing.

I shoved the thought away just as quickly as it came because it hurt too much. Losing her would just be swapping one prison for another. Losing her would mean my heart and soul and everything I was would be locked up, the key thrown away.

She was it for me.

I'd known it long before I'd ever laid eyes on her.

But she'd brought Whip into my life, and now I was so fucking confused I felt like I was back in that ocean, the waves smacking me in the face, invisible forces trying to drag me under.

I wanted Whip. I'd done things with him I'd never considered doing with another man, and yet they'd come easily with him. I stood in the middle of the club, watching men kiss other men, watching them dance and gyrate on each other. Watching them find dark corners to do more than anyone should be doing in public but unable to stop themselves because they wanted each other so bad.

It was exactly how I felt watching Whip walk away with a bartender twenty years younger than him.

My stomach twisted in knots as they'd moved past the bouncer, their fingers entwined around each other's.

I wanted to rip the bartender's hand off and throw it into the cocktail blender. I wanted to tear his eyes out with the spoon he used to scoop maraschino cherries into his drinks.

All because Whip had looked at him.

I stared at that hallway without blinking, the seconds ticking by in my head like a bomb, ready to explode.

I could imagine what they were doing back there, in some private back room of the club.

Their lips joining, opening, tongues stroking together in hot, dirty kisses. His hands running beneath Whip's shirt, fingers finding the fly on his jeans.

Opening it. Pulling out his cock.

The bartender dropping to his knees to take him in his mouth. Whip pulling him to his feet, spinning him around and fucking him hard and fast against the wall.

I clenched the table so hard my knuckles went white. "Sit your ass in this fucking seat, Levi. Do not fucking move," I reminded myself through gritted teeth, knowing well that nobody would hear me because I could barely hear myself. I repeated it over and over, reminding myself I could not leave this seat. I could not storm down there and kick down that fucking door and beat the shit out of that bartender for touching him.

But the minute the door opened, I was on my feet. Storming through the club. Pushing past the bouncer who glanced at me but made no attempts to stop me.

The bartender blinked at me in surprise and held his hands up. "Nothing—"

I didn't give a shit what he had to say. I barreled past him and straight into Whip, pushing him farther down the hallway.

The bouncer said something to the bartender, but I didn't hear it. My attention was too taken up with Whip. I slammed him up against the wall, not even giving a fuck when his head hit the drywall too hard.

His eyes turned from wide with surprise to narrowed with anger. He shoved me off him. "What the fuck, Levi? That hurt." He rubbed the back of his head.

I didn't give a shit. I moved right back in, crowding him against the wall, taking up space so he couldn't get away from me again, not that he was trying to. "Did you fuck him?"

Whip rolled his eyes. "So what if I did? We aren't together, are we? You made that pretty clear."

I pushed him against the wall again. "Did. You. Fuck. Him?"

"No, asshole. I didn't fuck him. He introduced me to Nyah's—"

I didn't care. I slammed my mouth onto his, kissing him hard and fast and with anger that was fueled by jealousy and confusion but also by something so much more.

"I fucking love you." I breathed across his lips.

The words shocked me just as much as they shocked him.

"What?" he asked.

"Don't make me repeat it." Heat bloomed across the back of my neck, but I ignored it. I knew that embarrassment was made up of a lifetime of homophobic remarks from men in my life who I'd loved and respected. But they had been so fucking wrong about this and what it felt like.

The way I felt about him was all-consuming. It chewed up every part of me and then spat me back out then asked for more.

A tiny smile flickered at Whip's lips. "Nah, I want to hear you say it again."

I rolled my eyes. "I fucking love you, okay? I don't want you chatting up random strangers in clubs. I don't want you holding their hands. I don't want you sneaking off to back rooms to fuck them."

"I don't want that either. But I'm not going to be some secret that you're ashamed of either. I've spent years hiding who I am. I bury every urge. I work after dark. I've never been anyone's first choice."

I mumbled over his lips. "I won't give up Violet—"

"I won't either."

I sucked in a breath and knew it had to be me who made this right. I had been the hold-out in this relationship the entire time. But I never wanted to feel the way I'd just felt watching him walk away with another man. It made me sick to my stomach. "It's you and me and her."

Out of the corner of my eye I caught sight of X, his arms in the air doing the YMCA.

He was slightly out of time, his hair mussed up with sweat, a grin almost too wide for his face plastered all over it.

But Violet laughed up at him like he'd hung the fucking moon.

"You, me, her, and X," I conceded, realizing she loved him. I was never going to take anything away from a woman who had already lost so much.

Whip fit his fingers to the back of my neck and dragged my head down the inch or two to meet his lips. With his forehead against mine, he mumbled, "You, me, her, and X. No one else."

I nodded. "Family."

Something flickered in his eyes, and I knew he was thinking about the one he'd lost. About the years of being alone. My fingers found the back of his neck too, pressing him close.

"No more running. No more hiding." I wanted to kiss him so fucking bad it was like a tidal wave inside me, drawing him in. But I fought it, grabbing his hand and pulling him out into the middle of the club. Onto the dance floor.

"No hiding," I whispered, then kissed him hard, not

giving a fuck if the entire club saw. I plastered my body to his, not an inch of space between us, and deepened the kiss, tongues meeting. I needed him. Wanted him. For more than just sex.

Fang had been my best friend once, but things had changed. He had a family.

Now I did too.

Arms encircled me, but they weren't Whip's. Violet and X joined our embrace. Whip and I both instinctively opened our arms to Violet.

X was too busy doing his best impression of a jumping bean for us to really hug him properly. "Aw, Mommy and Daddy kissed and made up!" He grinned. "Are you two going to go have dirty hot sex on the kitchen counter now?"

I would have been lying if I'd said I didn't want to. My dick was hard just from kissing. Or maybe it was the jealousy.

Fuck, maybe it was the realization I was just as in love with him as I was with Violet.

"I spoke to Nyah's brother," Whip told X and Violet.

Violet looked up at him hopefully, but it just as quickly faded at his expression. "He doesn't know where she is either, does he?"

He shook his head.

"Her dad—"

Whip shut down that scrap of hope before she could get carried away on it. "He was pretty adamant that he would know if their parents had her. And I believe him. I don't think she's here, sweetheart."

Violet's face crumpled. "Then..."

She didn't need to finish that sentence for us to know what came next.

We all knew.

The psychopath we'd been dodging for weeks had claimed another victim.

29

VIOLET

"We should go back to Saint View." My voice sounded as broken as my heart felt.

Whip pulled me into his arms and held me tight. "We can't go anywhere tonight. I've been drinking, and it's too late. Come back to the hotel. We'll leave first thing in the morning."

All I could think about was where Nyah was.

If she was alive or dead.

That while I'd been here, having fun, she was probably lying somewhere, bleeding out. Or worse, still alive, and being psychologically and physically tortured by the psychopath who'd killed Toby and Dickson. The one who'd set up a fucking nanny cam so he could watch it all with sick satisfaction. The one who tried to push me over the edge of a cliff and who had failed but had nearly cost X his life instead.

Nyah was no match for him. She was bright and sharp and smart, but she was one person.

And he'd had her for days.

Deep down, we'd all known it was a possibility. But we'd come on this wild goose chase because the psycho messing with us had always been one step ahead. We didn't know how to find him. We didn't know where to look.

Praying Nyah's sadistic, Mafia family had her had been the easy route.

But now I realized we'd made a vital mistake.

I let the three of them guide me out of the club and into the back of Whip's car. I didn't know who drove. I was too numb to pay attention and safe in the knowledge Whip would have never let one of them get behind the wheel if they'd had too much to drink.

I didn't know where Dax was, and I couldn't bring myself to ask. Just trusted one of them would have made sure he got back to his hotel safely.

My head was right back in the past, reliving every trauma. The attack at the house on Olympic Drive when all I'd wanted to do was my job.

Being locked in a warehouse, excited to meet the man I already knew I was in love with, only to lose the best friend I'd ever had.

That night up on the bluffs, standing in the pouring rain, explosions ringing in my ear and watching the three men I loved go over the edge of the cliff into the swirling void below.

"He's never going to stop, is he? He doesn't even want us dead. He just wants us scared. He's the cat and we're the mice."

Nobody could assure me otherwise, and I was glad they didn't try.

We pulled up outside the hotel X and Levi and I had

dropped our bags and the cat at earlier in the night when Whip had needed to be alone. We made our way straight up to our room without stopping at reception.

Harold snored from his carrier in the corner of the room. We'd left it open for him, but clearly he was protesting even being here at all by refusing to move out of it.

Two king-size beds filled the room, leaving plenty of space for all four of us to sleep. And that's exactly what we should have been doing. It was already after midnight, and we needed to leave as early as possible.

To do what exactly, I didn't know. I just needed to get back to Saint View. To storm the police station and demand they do something more. To knock on every door of every house and find out where Nyah was.

It was my fault she was missing.

My fault Toby had died.

My fault this guy kept coming after us.

I couldn't say exactly why, but my gut knew that everything that had happened was because of me and that night on Olympic Drive.

"Violet," Whip urged. "Get into bed, sweetheart. You need to sleep."

But I shook my head. I was tired, but I knew as soon as I closed my eyes, I was going to see blood. Tears. The face of Paul Jeddersen as he'd loomed over me, as he'd cut off my clothes and touched me.

I was going to see that bear watching it all, someone on the other side getting sick pleasure out of my pain and fear.

"Touch me," I whispered. "I don't want to sleep."

Whip looked at the other two, as if checking they

thought it was okay to give me what I was asking for when I was clearly in a state.

"Please," I whispered. "I don't want to sleep. I can't. Not until I know she's okay."

Whip stopped hesitating. He stepped in behind me and drew down the zipper on the back of the dress I'd bought with X at a thrift shop that afternoon. It was sparkly blue and covered from neckline to hem in glittery sequins. It was slightly too small and clung to my curves, but it had been so fun I hadn't been able to resist buying it.

I knew I'd never wear it again. It would be a constant reminder that I never got a night off. I never got to have any fun.

He wouldn't let me.

He always found a way in. A way to ruin everything, even when he wasn't there.

He'd found a way to live in my head, and that was the biggest betrayal of all.

The dress pooled on the floor at my feet, and I kicked it away to the corner, never wanting to see it again.

I turned in my underwear and unbuttoned Whip's shirt. Then Levi's. Then X's. They all watched me carefully, taking their cues from me, moving slowly. Levi undid my bra, and I pulled it off.

None of us had bothered to turn on the lights. We were high up, and the city lights from outside shone in, giving us more than enough light to see. There were buildings just as tall as ours across the street, and I idly wondered if the occupants of them could see us.

Then decided I didn't care. What did any of it matter?

How long would it be before I was dead and buried and nobody would ever see me again?

Either this guy was going to find me and kill me himself. Or he was going to torture me into a grave by taking out the people I loved one by one.

All three of these men were in danger, and I was suddenly sure, despite who they were and what they did, it was all because of me.

It was me the killer wanted to torture.

They were just collateral damage.

I dragged my panties off and crawled onto the nearest bed. I lay down, head sinking into a soft pillow I was sure I didn't deserve when Nyah had been out there somewhere in the cold for days.

I squeezed my eyes shut tight, not wanting to think about it but unable to get it out of my head.

The mattress dipped beneath me, but I didn't open my eyes. I didn't need to. I already knew it was X in front of me, his warm fingers finding mine, his gentle hands guiding me out of the defensive ball I'd curled myself into. He draped my arms around his neck and fit his thigh between mine. Our bodies connected, his naked skin against mine, him burying his face in the crook of my neck and whispering I didn't need to worry about anything because he had me.

Oh, how I wished I could fully believe that. How I wished I could just let myself off the hook that easily and place all the stress and worry on someone else.

But it didn't work like that.

Levi fit himself behind me, Whip behind him. With all four of us on our sides, we could fit on the bed. Barely, but nobody moved for the spare, and I was grateful for it.

I needed them close. Needed their bodies to remind mine to keep breathing, to keep functioning, even when it felt like everything else around me was on fire and I was in Hell.

X's lips found mine, like he knew my brain was whirring a million miles a minute. He kissed me, quieting the blame inside my skull.

I tightened my arms around him, kissing him back with everything I had, loving the way everything about him was familiar now.

Was this seriously the man I'd been so scared of? I'd run from him, more than once. I'd screamed at the sight of him. Been so damn sure that with his fingers around my neck, he was going to kill me.

He was now everything that represented safety. I dragged his hand up to my throat, needing the touch of him there, trusting him with everything I had.

He squeezed my throat lightly as we kissed, and the slight lack of oxygen made my head spin pleasurably. I wriggled closer to him, moving my leg up his thigh until it hooked over his hip.

"Fuck me," I whispered to him, not missing the hint of desperation in my tone.

He was already there, dick hard and waiting at my entrance.

I didn't need foreplay. Didn't want it. Hell, I wanted the burn. The stretch. The distraction with the way he could make my body feel.

He wouldn't give it to me. He teased my entrance with the tip of his cock, giving me just the tiniest bit and reaching between us to rub my clit.

Despite me trying to punish myself, my body

responded to his, loosening up, muscles relaxing. He didn't stop until arousal pooled at my core, and when his dick slid inside me, it wasn't a punishment.

It was with sweet words and gentle movements, him refusing to hurt me even though I wanted him to.

Why this man had ever been scared of killing me was beyond my comprehension. He couldn't even hurt me when I was begging him to.

Levi kissed my neck from behind, while X thrust into me. His lips were warm and soft, and his fingertips wandered all over my skin, lighting up little trails of fire wherever he touched.

He moaned, but I knew it was nothing I was doing, so it had to be what Whip was doing to him.

I waited until X pulled out, and then I twisted, rolling over so I could kiss Levi too.

Whip had his hand over Levi's hip and was stroking him, jerking his cock.

Levi desperately sought out my mouth, needing that contact, and I gave it up to him without hesitation. He gripped my face, kissing me hard, panting into my mouth. I lifted my leg to rest on top of his, opening myself up for him.

But it was Whip who guided his cock to my entrance.

Levi slid in easily, my pussy already well prepared by X.

I reached back, finding X's wet cock and drawing it between my ass cheeks, letting him know exactly what I wanted.

He nudged open my rear hole, toyed with it, adding pressure to Levi's deep thrusts and hitting every pleasure point my body stored there. X slid in inch by inch until I was taking both of them.

They sandwiched me, and my body came alive, my breathing too fast, but only because of the pleasure. The panic ebbed away, no place for that here when they were touching me like they were.

Levi's pubic bone hit my clit so perfectly it was impossible to keep from crying out. When they both pushed inside me at the same time, the feeling of fullness splintered my brain. It traveled down my neck, taking hold of my pulse, my nipples, my pussy. I spasmed around them both, crying out into the quiet room, unable to keep in my release another moment.

I bit down on Levi's shoulder, not wanting to wake the entire hotel floor, or the cat, with my shouts, but my body was on fire, electric, joined so perfectly with the two of them that nothing had ever felt like this.

X came with a shout no quieter than mine. His lips drew patterns on the back of my neck, and he alternated between whispering how good I was, how much he wanted me, how my body was perfect for his in every way, and that he loved me.

I couldn't say any of it back. I was too breathless. Too full. Too consumed by them to make any coherent sense.

But I hoped he knew it too, in the way my body moved with his, the way I reached back for him, holding him tight against me, and the way I twisted my head back, needing to claim his lips.

His hips slowed, but he didn't pull out. His dick stayed warm inside me, the occasional kick and pulse of my body sending shivers of pleasure through his.

Levi fucked me slow and steady, every press of his

hips deliberate and sweet.

He was holding back. My pussy fluttered around him on every thrust, aftershocks from the orgasm I couldn't control.

"Whip," Levi groaned, reaching back for the other man. "Need you inside me."

I moaned, just the words, the thought of them fucking while Levi was still in me so hot I couldn't keep the thought to myself.

Whip hesitated though. "You sure? We don't have any lube."

Levi pulled out of me and guided Whip's hand over his hip to my pussy. "Feel her. She's drenched."

Whip slipped two fingers inside me.

Levi got greedy and pushed his cock inside as well.

"Oh!" I shouted, stretched in a new way, but one that was so deliciously perfect.

Whip's fingers all up on my G-spot, hitting it in a way Levi's dick alone couldn't. I grabbed Whip's hand, me suddenly the greedy one who wanted him for herself. I held him there, riding the combination of his hand and Levi's dick, writhing, searching out that perfect place that would send me over the edge again.

I came hard, my clit so incredibly sensitive but the orgasm building somewhere deeper than that, milked out of me by the combination of the two of them.

I jerked, crying out their names, begging them for more and less all at once because it was too much but so right.

It wasn't until I was limp and only hanging on because I was so tightly wedged between Levi and X that Whip removed his fingers.

I mourned the loss of him, but my body quickly adjusted, and Levi was still buried deep inside me, just grinding on me, breathing hard, waiting for Whip.

"Fuck, Levi," Whip groaned. "You're so tight. You need to relax. Kiss her."

He didn't need to be told twice. Levi stole my lips, licking inside my mouth, devouring me.

I grabbed his hip, holding him to me, vaguely aware of Whip working his body from behind.

Levi froze, but then slowly began to move again. His breaths changed, until they were moans.

"Fuck." He twisted back to Whip. "What are you doing to me?"

Whip chuckled. "Feel good?"

Levi's answering moan and the way he rolled his hips to take more of Whip's slick fingers was all the answer he needed.

"Want you," Levi whispered.

My heart squeezed, watching the two of them together. Watching them open up to each other and being vulnerable. It was sweet and sexy all at once.

X had pulled out of me, completely spent, and Levi took the opportunity to roll me onto my back. I opened my legs wide for him, and he kissed me again, my lips, my cheeks, my throat.

His knees sank into the mattress, and he braced his weight on his forearms.

Whip fit himself in behind Levi, hooking an arm around his midsection and dragging his lips down his spine.

I reached up a hand from beneath Levis arm, and

Whip linked his fingers through mine, his gaze holding mine, Levi between us.

It was me he watched when he pushed inside Levi. But it was Levi we both listened for. Whip held still, letting his body adjust, but Levi buried his face in my neck, breathing heavily.

"Fuck." His pleasure was evident in the tremors that shook his body. "I need to come."

I met his thrusts. Whip matched him, both of us centered on Levi and making this as good for him as possible.

But it was good for me too. So freaking good. My entire body felt alive, every nerve ending sparking, their noises of pleasure only fueling me on. Whip picked up the pace, his weight driving Levi down onto me, but it wasn't too much. It was just right, the feel of them moving together, knowing all three of us were joined.

Whip squeezed my fingers and shouted my name. He came hard, and Levi followed right after.

I'd already come so many times and was so full of sensation I was lost to whether I had a third orgasm or not. It didn't matter, every second was pleasure, every moment was perfect.

Whip eventually flopped over onto the other side of the mattress.

Levi collapsed down on top of me and whispered sweet but dirty things in my ear, promising he was going to do this every night for the rest of our lives if I would only let him.

I imagined at some point, when we were old and married, I might not want to do this every night.

But right now, with the way the three of them had

made me feel, I wanted to quit my job and do this all day and all night for eternity. I had no experience, outside the three of them. But I couldn't see how any other man could love me or touch me the way they did. There was no better than this. There was nothing more than the three of them and the way I loved them all.

They were the family I'd never had but always wanted.

They were the love and the care I'd craved but never received.

They were men who saw me for who I was, fat lumps and imperfections, and still loved and desired me anyway.

The realization took my breath away.

"Whip," I whispered, twisting my head to the side so I could see him.

Levi's head was buried on the other side of my neck, and I wasn't sure if he was asleep or just so exhausted his body had slowed right down to look like it. From the bathroom came the sound of running water, and I knew X had to be in there cleaning up.

Whip opened an eye. "Yeah, sweetheart?"

I shifted just enough beneath Levi that I could kiss Whip's mouth. "I love you."

"I love you too." He responded so quickly, with no fanfare, it was like the words had been sitting on his lips for the longest time, he'd just been waiting for me to realize.

I smiled softly at that.

And finally let sleep pull me under, safe and surrounded by three men I had no idea how I'd ever existed without.

30

X

"**I**'ve been thinking about it, and I think I can be gay for you two."

Whip raised his head from the other bed that he and Levi had moved to once Violet had fallen into an exhausted sleep. She hadn't even stirred when they'd switched and I'd gotten back into the sex scented sheets.

I hadn't minded. I had her, and that was all I had cared about.

Whip frowned. "What exactly do you mean by that?"

I cuddled Violet closer, my head propped up on two pillows so I could see Whip over her shoulder. "I've been thinking about it for a while, and I think I can be gay for the two of you."

Levi shifted so he was up on one forearm. "I don't think that's how it works..."

I frowned at him. "You don't think I can be gay for you?"

"I don't think I have any idea what you mean by that."

Levi's brow was pinched. "I haven't had coffee yet, so I think you should probably explain."

I shrugged. "The four of us are a thing, right? We all mess around with Violet. You two mess around with each other. Seems unfair that I'm also not a part of that."

Whip eyed me. "So you're saying you want me to kiss you?"

I wrinkled my nose on instinct, then deliberately tried to smooth it out before they noticed. "Yes. Sure. I love kissing."

Whip seemed skeptical.

Levi picked up the line of questioning. "Okay, kissing is one thing, but are you saying you want us to blow you?"

The idea of Whip or Levi down on their knees in front of me did absolutely nothing but shrivel my morning erection. But hey, they seemed to like when they did it to each other, and getting your dick wet was getting your dick wet, right?

I nodded. "Blow jobs are great. Love those."

Laughter flickered at the corner of Whip's mouth. "Come over here then."

I faltered. "Uh, like, right now?"

Levi nodded. "Sure. Come over here and get in the middle of us." He reached down between him and Whip. I couldn't see him gripping his cock, but it was pretty obvious that was what he was doing. None of us had put on clothes, there were no barriers between us. Levi scooched back and patted the space he'd made.

Now I very much could see his cock, hard just like Whip and I were.

At least, I had been. My morning erection had been happy as Larry nestled up against Violet's curvy ass. At the idea of swapping beds, it wanted to run away screaming.

But hey, maybe I'd like it once I tried it? My mother had always said that to me about vegetables. "How will you know you don't like it if you never try it?"

And I didn't like the challenging look on Levi's face.

He thought I was going to back out.

So I untangled myself from around Violet and got up, crossing the room.

Crawling in between two big, very naked men was about as comfortable as a root canal.

I settled down in the middle of them, lying on my back with my arms crossed over my chest like I was in a coffin.

Because that's kinda what this felt like.

Death.

How the hell could I be so into Violet and so...not into the two of them? But she liked them. They liked each other. Maybe Levi had super-tasting spunk and it was the secret to eternal youth. There had to be something good about it. I'd watched Violet and Whip suck him off enough, and they both seemed into it.

And Whip was all right, I supposed. If the whole silver fox thing did it for you and you didn't think of him as a father figure...

I closed my eyes. Maybe I could just pretend they were Violet. That would work. At the very thought of her my dick got hard again, and my brain started screaming that I was very much on the wrong side of the room and needed to get my ass—and my dick—back to her immediately.

But I'd committed to this, and now it was going to happen.

I was going to have sex with men.

Yep.

That was definitely happening. And I was definitely one-hundred-percent happy about it.

Or maybe like. Ninety percent.

I mean, definitely at least thirty percent.

"Let the blow jobs commence!" I raised my hands like I was a music conductor at a symphony.

Whip trailed a finger down my chest.

I fought the urge to punch him.

He circled my belly button. "Why bother with blow jobs? Let's go right to the good stuff. Roll over."

Oh fuck. I had bitten off way more than I could chew. But I wasn't going to admit that to them.

I rolled over and clenched my ass cheeks so tight it would have taken a crowbar to get them open.

I thought I heard Levi laugh, but I was so fixated on my buns of steel that I couldn't be sure.

"Relax, X," Whip soothed in a voice I'd never heard from him before but absolutely did not like the sound of. "We'll warm you up. Fingers only at first."

Oh, that was so much better than them just diving in dick first.

Not.

"Breathe," Levi coached.

That was a good idea. I panted like I was in a birthing class. Short, sharp breaths.

Someone's finger touched my asshole.

I jumped a mile and leaped off the bed. "Not gay!

Definitely not gay!" I clutched my behind like it was on fire.

Whip, Violet, and Levi all dissolved into hysterical laughter.

It was Whip who practically drawled, "Yeah, you don't say?"

I glared at him. "You knew I wasn't gay for you?"

"You're about as straight as an arrow, but who am I to tell you you can't explore?"

My butt cheeks were so clenched they could have snapped a pencil in two. "I explored. Lost my map. Maybe got eaten by a lion. Which, by the way, would be preferable to either of you ever touching my ass again."

Levi had tears of laughter watering his eyes. "Noted. But fuck, that was funny."

I scowled at him, but I was saved by the bell when message tones started going off on our phones.

Levi, Whip, and I all went quiet.

Whip swore under his breath. "They're the group phones, aren't they?"

I was the closest to our bags, so I pulled mine out and read the message, my blood running cold. "We need to go back." I looked up at them, my lips pressed into a thin line, all traces of laughter gone. "Another letter has been delivered."

31

VIOLET

By the time we got back to Saint View, the clubhouse was chaos. Kids ran riot, in and out of the doorways, laughing and full of excitement about all being together.

But the vibe amongst the adults was very different.

Rebel sat surrounded by a pile of suitcases, scowling at Fang who didn't appear any happier. Bliss had baby Ridge on her hip, trying to distract him with a teething toy, but she seemed distracted herself. Kara walked over to her and took the baby, plonking him down in a playpen with her youngest daughter, Wren, and Rebel's little one as well.

The room was full of big men in motorcycle jackets, all of them as worried as the three men who stood behind me.

I waited on War to say something, seeing as he was the president, but it was Grayson who spoke up. "As you all know, some members of my support group—"

"You mean, Murder Squad," X interjected.

Grayson sighed. "X, haven't we talked about not calling it that?"

X shrugged.

Grayson continued like he hadn't spoken. "As you all know, some members of my support group have been receiving threats for some time now. We had hoped it was limited to the group and wouldn't extend to the rest of you—"

Scythe held up a piece of paper. "I got one yesterday."

X held out a fist for him to bump. "One of us! One of us!"

He was the only one who found it funny. His chanting died off. "You have been coming to meetings a bit. Maybe they thought you were a fully-fledged member, out hunting down targets at night."

Bliss looked at him sharply. "Have you been killing again?"

He shook his head. "No. Just...watching."

Bliss, War, and Nash all stared at him.

"I swear! I haven't stabbed anyone!' His voice lowered. "Today."

War scrubbed a hand over his face. "That's all well and good, but we've still got one of those fucked up rhyming letters. To our house. Hence why we're all here. And why we won't be leaving until this is sorted out."

I grimaced. No wonder Bliss and Rebel were so unhappy. Kara didn't seem as bothered, but she lived here on the MC grounds in a home they'd built within the safety of the fences but away from the clubhouse.

Bliss and Rebel were stuck here in this communal building with their kids, not enough space, very little privacy, and a group of bikers watching their every move. I couldn't blame them for being pissed off. This sucked.

But I couldn't blame the guys for wanting them here, where there was twenty-four seven protection.

I knew the alternative. Knew what we were up against. Now that we had ruled out Nyah's family as a suspect, I had to believe she had been lured into some sort of trap, the way Toby and I had that night at the warehouse.

I didn't believe for a second she would just leave without even saying goodbye. If it had just been me, maybe.

But she was in love with Dax. They might not have said it to each other, but I'd seen it in the way they were together. Seen it in the complete and utter state of devastation he was in now.

As much as Bliss and Rebel might hate being in lockdown, it hadn't been called for no reason.

But how long could that last? The kids needed to go to school. Everyone would go stir-crazy locked inside these gates with no release date in mind.

All I could think about was that this whole thing was my fault.

"I don't get why we're suddenly getting letters," War said. "Why now?"

I swallowed thickly, hating that I could answer that. "It's because of me."

All three of my guys were quick to jump in and disagree, but I shut them up with a look that clearly said: Let me speak.

"We found a nanny cam teddy bear at the scene of Toby's murder. I saw the same one in the home of the man who attacked me." I turned to Scythe. "That was the night I met you."

Scythe's forehead furrowed into lines. "That ugly bear that was on the bookshelf?"

Relief rushed me. "You remember it too?" I'd almost thought my traumatized brain had made it up.

"Yeah, I do. I remember thinking it weird 'cause the guy clearly had no kids. There were no photos of him with any children, no kid-sized shoes at the door or coats on the racks or Lego lying in wait for someone to step on in the middle of the night." He winced, like he was remembering that pain. "I know what a house with kids looks like, and that wasn't it. So that bear stuck out to me." He shrugged. "But then you and X were throwing knives and eggs and fuck knows what else at each other, and I didn't give it another thought."

"I didn't either. Until we found that same bear, or at least one that looked exactly like it in that warehouse where Toby died." I bit down on my lip, not wanting to scare anyone when we probably should have had this conversation in private first, but it was a bit late not to drag Bliss and my sister-in-law into this now. "I think someone watched what Paul Jeddersen did to me that night. And I think someone saw what you and X did to him afterward."

Grayson swore under his breath. "And watched me, Whip, and the others all arrive to dispose of his body. Shit, that would explain all the letters. We were all there that night."

Levi cleared his throat. "Only one problem with that theory. I wasn't there that night. Some of those letters felt like they were addressed to me."

"I've been thinking about that, and my gut instinct is they used you to get to me. And when I didn't die in that warehouse, like I was supposed to, their anger extended to you. Or maybe it's just that hurting anyone in my life will hurt me. Maybe that's why Fang's family has been dragged into it. Maybe that's why Toby is dead and Nyah is missing." My voice broke. "It's me they want, isn't it? Everyone else is just collateral damage."

X pulled me into his arms. "I'm the one who killed him. This could be just as much about me as it is about you. If it's anyone's fault, it's mine. I should have waited to kill him. Should have done it somewhere else. I was hyped up and distracted and sloppy. It shouldn't have gone down like that at all."

Bliss shook her head angrily and held up her hand, silencing us all. "Stop it. It's neither of your faults. That man lured you to his home, drugged you, attacked you, would have raped and killed you if X and Scythe hadn't been there that day."

Bile rose in my throat at the memories she was dragging up. I didn't want to think about that night where I'd lain helpless and tied up, stripped of my dignity, praying for someone to help me. My entire world had changed that night, for the better in so many ways, but it had come at a cost.

A steep one, and it wasn't just me paying it.

"So let's assume Paul Jeddersen was working with someone." I wasn't really talking to anyone in particular, just thinking out loud.

"He might have just been filming your attack so he could rewatch it himself later," Whip said quietly, smartly poking a hole in my theory.

My shoulders slumped. "That's true."

"And sick." Rebel wrapped her arms around herself.

I hated that this was probably triggering old traumas for her too.

Whip held up a hand. "But just because that's a possibility, doesn't mean it's the most likely scenario. I agree with you, Vi. I do think he was working with someone else, and that someone else knows what happened that night and has been trying to punish us for it ever since."

X shook his head. "We researched Paul Jeddersen though. He had nobody in his life except a set of elderly parents, who weren't even in the country when old farty Paul got a knife through his lactose-intolerant guts for touching something that wasn't his."

His eyes flashed with anger, and he edged closer to me, until his warmth permeated through my shirt. I knew he was reminding himself that I was here, and I was okay, and that Paul Jeddersen was dead, probably chopped up into little pieces and left for the fish to eat.

X circled his arm around my middle, pulling me back against his chest. "I don't even think they realize he's dead. I drive past the house regularly on my ice cream route and I've never seen anyone there. The lawn is overgrown, and there's a pileup of mail on the doorstep. If they know he's dead or missing, they haven't bothered to stop by and sort out anything with his house."

"If Paul Jeddersen was my son, I wouldn't visit him regularly either," I muttered.

But my gut still screamed that Paul did have someone in his life. Some sort of sick accomplice who had been out to get us ever since that night.

"It could be Lynx," Levi said quietly, stiffly, like he was

forcing the words out but desperately didn't want them to be true. "He got out around the same time I did."

Whip shook his head. "But not before you, and Violet was attacked before you got out. That gives Lynx a pretty good alibi."

The frown between Levi's eyebrows eased a little at that, his relief evident. I reached over and squeezed his fingers. Lynx might have been loitering in some dodgy places since he had been released, and hanging out with some undesirable people, if Toby's photos were anything to go by, but my gut said that whoever Paul Jeddersen was working with had been a thing before I came onto the scene.

I couldn't have been their first attack. "I went to Paul's house that night to do a job. He'd booked a cleaner."

X cocked his head. "Are we sure it was Paul who booked you? Maybe his partner did? Would Francine have a record of that?"

Everyone looked at me. "I have no idea, but we could ask her."

I gazed around at the grim faces of the men I loved and the friends I'd made. They all stared back at me, concern in their gazes.

I'd never had so many people actually give a shit about me. It was almost unsettling. I'd spent so much of my life only ever worrying about myself. Toby was added on later, the only person I'd ever cared about. But now... Now I had an entire room full of people I didn't want to see hurt.

And the only way I could make sure that happened was to find out who was working with Paul Jeddersen that night.

And let the Murder Squad deal with him from there.

I went to Clean Sweep HQ that afternoon, not even sure if Francine would be there. Without Nyah, and with me in the city, she had to be short-staffed. It was entirely possible she would be out on a job herself.

Unless she'd already hired a replacement for Nyah.

The thought left me so freaking cold I rubbed my arms briskly, trying to ward off the chill, and made my way up the steps. Whip and Levi hovered on the street, but X had refused to let me go in alone.

Apparently, they were back to babysitting me twenty-four seven. I had to be in sight of at least one of them at all times.

This time, I hadn't argued about it though. I no longer found it stifling.

I felt safe. Protected.

And it felt necessary.

I put my hand on X's before we walked in. "Let me talk to her, okay?"

X pouted. "You don't want me to interrogate her?"

I shook my head. "Your interrogations usually involve weapons."

"And bad jokes. Don't forget the bad jokes."

"I'm not sure which is scarier."

He made a face and leaned around me to hold open the door. "Go on. I'll behave."

Francine glanced up from behind her desk when we entered.

X was good for exactly three seconds before he

slammed his palm down on Francine's desk. "Tell us who he's working with!"

Francine jumped a mile, papers spilling over the edge of the desk onto the floor. She glanced between me and X in confusion, eventually settling on me. "Violet? What is this?"

I closed my eyes and grimaced, linking my arm through X's and pinching his forearm hard.

He yelped like an injured puppy, but I elbowed him, and he shut up. "Please excuse my friend. He has a head injury and apparently thinks he's in some sort of *Dirty Harry* movie."

X mumbled something about it being more James Bond, and I glared at him silently until he sheepishly pretended to button his lips.

If only it was that easy to keep X quiet.

Francine edged her chair away from him and closer to me. And the door.

I laid the charm on thick. "What we actually wanted to know was if you could have a look at your records for us. Please."

Francine settled in her seat, some of the fear filtering out of her expression now X wasn't being psychotic. She adjusted her glasses on her nose and turned to her computer. "What do you want to know?"

"Do you keep a record of who books a job? Like, when they call for the first time, do you record the caller's name?"

Francine shrugged. "I might ask them their name, or they might offer it when I first take a call. I need someone's name to put the booking under."

I nodded. "Paul Jeddersen on Olympic Drive—"

Francine scowled. "You mean the job you lost me after just one clean."

I wanted to roll my eyes that she was still holding on to that grudge. "Yes. That one. Can you tell us who booked that job?"

She squinted at us. "Why?"

X slammed his palm down again. "Just give us the intel, woman!"

Both of us stared at him.

His expression grew sheepish. "I did it again, didn't I?"

"Do you literally need to go stand in the corner and have a time out?" I asked.

"I think I might. I'm overexcited." He slunk off to the hard plastic chairs beneath the window and sank into one.

I smiled at Francine apologetically, and she just shook her head as she pushed her glasses back up on her nose and peered at the computer.

"He must be really good in bed for you to put up with that level of crazy," she muttered.

She probably wasn't wrong. Or maybe I was just as crazy as he was. Because he looked kind of cute just sitting over there in disgrace.

I couldn't help but smile at him.

He was like a wounded dog who'd just been tossed a juicy bone. He lit up as if my smile of forgiveness was all he'd ever dreamed of.

"It's a bit more than that," I said softly. "But if you could have a peep at your records, it would help us out a lot."

Francine scrolled a little, typed a few words, and

peered at the screen again. "So why exactly am I doing this?"

I opened my mouth to lie. But the words that came out were the truth. "A man at that house hurt me. And I think he was working with someone else. I need to know who."

Francine's gaze snapped up to meet mine. "He...he hurt you while you were on the job?"

I nodded.

Francine's hands shook. "Violet, I'm so sorry. I had no idea. Why didn't you report it?"

I reached across the desk and squeezed her fingers. "I know. It's okay. I'm all right."

"He was a new client. If I'd known..."

I shook my head. "You couldn't have known. It's not your fault."

She nodded grimly, then peered up at me and said, "You aren't going to sue me or something, are you?"

I fought the urge to roll my eyes. There she was. The Francine I knew, always a bit self-centered. "No, I'm not suing. I just want to know who made that booking. If there's nothing under Paul Jeddersen, try Claire. Or Clara. I remember that being a contact name on the job form and thinking it was his wife, but it was weird because he kept using them interchangeably. Like he had no idea what his own wife's name was."

In hindsight, I wished I'd paid more attention to that little slipup.

Francine focused again, clearly reassured now that I wasn't trying to take her to court. She scrolled on her mouse until she found what she was looking for. "Okay, here it is. Booking was made a week before, and Claire was listed as a contact person for that address. But there's no other details…"

"Oh," I said, deflated. "Well, thanks for trying."

She went on like I hadn't spoken. "It was an email booking. Let me just find that and see if I can find a phone number I might have missed adding to the system."

"Thank you."

"Happy to help." She smiled up at me. "As long as you don't sue."

This time I couldn't stop the eye roll.

She clearly took that as her sign to get back to work. Her fingers pecked at the keyboard, and her frown grew deeper.

"What's wrong?" X asked

"I can't find an email from a Paul or Claire Jeddersen. Odd, because I never delete emails." Her frown smoothed out. "Oh, wait. Their names do come up when I search it, just not as the sender. Let me just…"

She clicked something on her screen then sat back, her gaze lifting to mine. "You're right. Neither Paul or Claire Jeddersen made the booking. Someone made it on their behalf."

"Is that normal?" X asked.

Francine nodded at him. "Happens all the time when people are elderly or sick. A relative or caregiver will often make a booking on behalf of someone else."

"Paul Jeddersen wasn't either of those things," X said quietly. "And we all know Claire Jeddersen isn't a real person."

But they were both missing the point. There was only

one thing I wanted to know. "Who sent that email, Francine?"

She peered at the screen again and then up at me. "A Travis Brumley."

My blood ran cold at the sound of my foster brother's name on her lips. Something Paul had said that night rang through my head. He'd taunted Toby, calling him my "gay boyfriend."

Paul Jeddersen wouldn't have known anything about Toby. But Travis would have.

I'd assumed Paul had been stalking me. But maybe he'd just been fed the information.

"That name mean something to you?" Francine asked.

I so desperately wished it didn't.

32

VIOLET

I walked out of Francine's office like I was in a daze. I barely saw the late afternoon sun sinking behind Psychos across the road. Barely felt its warmth.

All I felt was cold shock and sickness swirling inside me.

Travis's name repeated over and over in my head.

Whip caught me on the sidewalk, his hands gripping both my arms. "Violet? What happened in there?"

I shook my head, burying it in his chest and inhaling his warm, masculine, familiar scent that always calmed my nervous system.

X answered for me, his tone grim. "It's her foster brother. He's been threatening her for weeks. I thought it was harmless, but Francine just told us he was the one who booked her for that job at Paul Jeddersen's house."

Levi swore under his breath. "Her own brother sent her to that creep? What the fuck?"

"He is NOT my brother," I snapped at him. "Fang is

my brother. Travis is a piece of shit. Always was. Always will be." I shook my head. "He's been threatening me, demanding I get money from Fang to give to him. Saying I owe him."

"Why would he think that?" Whip asked.

I shook my head. "I always hated him. I would catch him watching me in the shower, through the crack in the door. He would always make sexual comments about me and the other girls in our home. I started barricading our door at night, scared he would try to get in while I was sleeping. And there were rumors. Toby told me one of the girls at school accused him of touching them, but rumors like that aren't exactly uncommon at Saint View High, and nobody ever did anything about it. It all just got swept under the rug, nobody gave a shit when a girl from a trailer park tried to say that someone had abused her." I breathed out a wobbly breath. "There was one night, when he was seventeen and I was sixteen, he and his friends had a party at our foster parents' house when he knew they would be down at the bar getting drunk. The party got wild. I had our two younger foster siblings locked in a room with me. Travis and his friends were all drunk. There was so much noise. Music and laughter and screaming and shouting. It all mixed together. Them banging on the door, trying to get in. Me pushing anything I could in front of it and assuring the kids they were just mucking around and they weren't really going to hurt us. I think I was trying to convince myself even more than them."

I remembered it all too clearly. Like it was playing out in front of me again, as crisp and clear as that night fifteen years ago when I'd been a terrified teenager with no power, no agency, no life skills to know how to help.

Screams in the night were all too common in my world.

"The next day, the police came to our house," I practically whispered. "Someone had made a report, saying Travis and his friends had indecently assaulted her. Our foster parents told them to get fucked, that they were here all night and nothing had happened. That the girl was a well-known slut and a liar. They didn't even ask Travis about it. They just knew if they admitted they'd both been off drinking at the pub and had allowed an underage party and rape to happen in their home, they would have lost their foster license. That was the only income either of them had. Neither of them could ever hold down a job long. They lived solely off what they got paid for taking in kids."

X's fingers clenched into fists. "I'm going to take a lot of pleasure in ending their pathetic lives."

I wouldn't stop him.

"I was so mad. I'd spent all night with two crying kids, terrified Travis or his friends would get into the room. I was so sick of feeling helpless and small. So I snuck out the back door and stopped the cops on their way out. Told them our foster parents were lying. Told them whatever that girl had said was true, even though I hadn't actually seen it with my own eyes. I believed her."

"Let me guess," Whip ground out through gritted teeth. "They didn't believe you."

"Actually, they did. The girl was the daughter of a cop, so they really wanted to nail Travis and his friends to the wall. They were so close to eighteen, they tried them as adults. They got ten years each, but I don't know how much of it they served." I swallowed thickly. "I don't even know that he really did hurt that girl. I was scared of him and just wanted him out of the house. I didn't know he even knew about my role in it, but obviously he did."

All three of them looked at me.

Levi gripped me tighter. "What he did to you was more than enough to warrant talking to the cops. If they put your complaint together with that other girl's then he got what he deserved."

"That explains why he's on the list then," Whip said. "Grayson must suspect him of reoffending since he's been released."

I should have felt good that my suspicions about Travis were being backed up by someone else. But instead I just felt stupid and brainwashed. My foster parents had spent the next two years bitching about him being put in jail. He suddenly became the golden child who had never done any wrong, even though they'd beat the shit out of him as much as they had the rest of us when he'd actually been in the house. But they swore to CPS that Travis had been wrongly accused. That he was innocent, and because nobody gave a shit about poor kids in the foster system, we'd been left there with them. Somewhere along the line, I think I'd started to believe Travis wasn't that bad either. That he wasn't dangerous.

Or maybe that was just what my brain had tried to convince me when he'd walked back into my life a few months ago.

I'd been numb. I'd convinced myself he was a pest but that he wasn't the biggest danger in my life, so he wasn't worth wasting thought on.

How wrong I'd been.

"He knows what I did," I whispered to them. "I should have just gotten him the money when he asked for it. Maybe none of this would have happened."

Whip shook his head. "This was happening before he wanted money, Vi. Paying him off wouldn't have gotten rid of him."

"Why didn't he just kill me in that warehouse? He could have. Many times."

Levi cleared his throat. "He's getting off on tormenting you. It's a game in his mind, pushing you just far enough that you're close to breaking only to back off so he can do it all again. Sending us all letters. Heightening the panic of everyone around you so you never get a break from it."

"It's working. God, I feel so stupid!" Another long-forgotten memory rose to the surface, and I felt so sick I had to clutch my stomach. "He used to make traps. I saw him and his friends one day out in the woods, digging a hole and sharpening sticks to make a pit for someone or something to fall into. I ran back home before they could see me, and they came back pretty soon after, so I think I convinced myself they lost interest and gave up. But I never went back into the woods to check. I was too scared I would accidentally fall into their trap myself." I squeezed my eyes shut. "I had nightmares for weeks after, of being forced into the woods and falling into a black hole of nothingness where I just fell and fell, the antici-pation of landing on those sharpened sticks always there but never actually happening." I stared at them in horror. "I'd forgotten so much of this."

"You hadn't forgotten," Whip said quietly. "You'd repressed it. Compartmentalized it, and who could blame you? You were barely more than a child and not equipped to deal with anything like this. You had no one to protect you." He rubbed my arm. "I'm no Grayson, but maybe it's only now you feel safe enough to let it out."

Which seemed crazy because I was hardly safe with Travis out there, clearly still wanting my head on a spike. And yet there was truth in his words.

For the first time in my life, I had a family. Not just one friend who served as my crutch, but a real support system. Three men who loved me and proved it every single day in the way they touched me, cared for me, protected me. A brother who had already proven once he would kill even his best friend for me if I asked him to. A sister-in-law. Nieces and nephews. Friends in Bliss and Nyah.

I wasn't the girl who sat scared in her apartment every night, living vicariously through doctors on a TV show. I wasn't the woman clinging to her one and only friend, knowing that at some point, he was going to meet someone and leave her.

Toby had never held me back, but the way I'd clung to him had. I'd trauma bonded to him in high school and then spent ten years holding on to that, too scared to walk alone because I'd spent my childhood with no one and I didn't want to go back.

I still didn't. Nobody wanted to be alone.

I still had a long way to go, but where I was felt healthy.

Whip and Levi and X all clung to me in the same way I held on to them. I wasn't dragging them down.

We were all holding each other afloat. Supporting each other.

"So, what now?" X asked. "Other than killing Violet's foster parents, killing the CPS workers who left you with them, killing Travis..." He cracked his knuckles. "It's a good thing I put my lucky killing socks on this morning!"

Levi glanced at him. "Do you really—" He shook his head. "You know what? Never mind."

Whip ignored them and focused on me. "Do you have any idea where he's staying?"

"No. None. Probably nowhere nice, if he truly is broke."

"Maybe at a friend's place?" Levi asked.

I shrugged. "If he still has any. I can't even remember the names of the boys he was friends with in high school. They were older. One might have been Andrew or Andy or something." I screwed up my face. "Sorry, that's really not much to go on, is it?"

X squeezed my hand. "Don't worry. We'll find him."

I had no doubt he would. The only question in my mind was whether Nyah would still be alive when they did. Realization dawned on me, and I covered my mouth, bile rising up my throat. "Oh God." I rushed back up the path without a word of explanation to the guys.

I didn't need to. I knew they would follow.

I banged my way back inside Francine's office.

She jumped a mile again then scowled at me. "Violet! Dammit, you have got to stop doing that! My heart can't handle it. Just knock like a normal person!"

I ignored her reprimands. "The jobs Nyah was supposed to do the day she went missing, did Travis Brumley book any of those?"

Francine pressed her lips together. "I already gave the police a list—"

"Yeah, a list of the house addresses and the owners' names. I got all that from the roster too. But who booked those jobs, Francine?"

She squinted at the screen again and her fingers hovered over the keyboard.

I wanted to reach across the desk and force her hands to move faster.

"Ain't got all day, lady!" X shouted, straight back into his *Dirty Harry* role. "You type slower than my grandma!" He turned to me. "Which actually is not really an insult because she's pretty fast. You know Silas has apparently been teaching her 'digital skills?'"

Levi glanced at him. "Silas is that guy you went to school with who's now banging your grandmother, right?"

X went pale. "Why remind me?"

Levi shrugged. "You sure when he said digital skills, he didn't mean digit skills? You know a digit in some places is the term they use for fingers."

X frowned, Francine's slow-ass click-clacking on the keyboard the only sound in the room until X put together what Levi was getting at.

His mouth dropped open. "What are you saying? That Silas isn't teaching my grandmother how to touch type but he's using his fingers to..."

Levi shrugged one shoulder. "Get all up in her hot pocket?"

Whip grimaced. "For fuck's sake, Levi. What is wrong with you? You've been hanging out with X too much."

I couldn't have agreed more. But I'd seen Silas and X's grandmother together...and they'd definitely seemed like they were more into Silas's 'digit' skills, rather than learning about emails and the World Wide Web.

X was positively green. He glared at Levi. "You are so lucky my digits are only interested in Violet's hot pocket. Or I would *so* be tracking down your granny right now and offering her a little digital relief!"

"Please stop talking, both of you," I said weakly. "Please never say the words hot pocket or digit ever again."

Francine gave them both a stern look from behind the desk. "I agree with Violet. Just because women get older, doesn't mean they don't have needs too. We were all once twenty and thirty like all of you. Our hot pockets don't stop needing to be filled just because we hit our forties and fifties and beyond."

Christ. I did not want to have a conversation about who or what was filling my aging boss's hot pocket. "Please, Francine," I begged. "Just tell us if Travis booked any of Nyah's jobs that day."

She muttered something but must have finally found whatever she was looking for because she nodded slowly. "Yes. He booked her first job of the day. 1705 Fire Ridge Way."

Any glimmer of hope that Nyah had just upped and left Saint View of her own accord vanished.

She'd gone to that house.

I knew it in my bones.

And now a madman had her.

33

VIOLET

*T*he guys talked me out of going with them to check out the address Francine had given us and left me in the safety of the clubhouse to wait. They'd convinced me it was highly unlikely anyone would be there, and if they found a body, I wouldn't want to see that.

I hated that my last memory of Toby was of him bleeding to death on my lap.

When they came back barely thirty minutes later, I knew they'd found nothing. Apparently, there had been no signs of a struggle. Just a perfectly cleaned home. The owners' names didn't ring any bells, and the guys had determined the house was probably unoccupied, since they hadn't found food in the fridge or clothes in any of the upstairs rooms.

None of us had been surprised.

Whip rubbed my arm. "We knew it was a long shot. I wouldn't hang around the scene of the crime either. It doesn't mean she's dead. Most kidnappers try to get their victims to a second location."

I'd heard that in self-defense videos.

I'd also heard that if you were taken to a second location, your chances of survival drastically plummeted.

Levi shoved his hands in his pockets. "So we go to plan B. We have his email address."

It didn't feel like a great plan. Emails could go to spam. Maybe he wouldn't check his inbox. Even if he did, there was no guarantee an email from me wouldn't make him suspicious and that he wouldn't just ignore it.

But at least it was proactive. It was better than just sitting and waiting for him to make contact with us again. Which was plan C.

I sent the email, hoping he wouldn't question where I'd gotten the address, and stating a time and place for him to meet me. I told him I had the money he wanted from Fang, hoping that would be enough to sweeten the deal and lure him out.

Then I waited, part of me hoping he wouldn't show. But the rest of me knowing that he would. Because he had never been able to pass up the opportunity to torment me. Not back when we were kids. And not now.

Just like that night up on the bluffs, I sat alone, this time on a park bench in the backstreets of Saint View. We weren't far from Psychos and Clean Sweep, the trailer park just across the road. But unlike that night, this time, the shadows felt loaded.

Quiet.

Brutal.

I wasn't really alone. X, Whip, and Levi lurked. I couldn't see them, but I could feel them. It was the only thing holding me together, the weight of everything I'd realized too heavy to bear. I didn't want to be here. Didn't want to come face-to-face with the monster who'd trapped me in that warehouse and messed with our heads until Toby had sacrificed himself for me. Nerves rattled my entire body. Travis had always been sneaky. A narcissist and a manipulator, twisting words until you were so confused and back to front that you honestly believed it was you who'd done something wrong, and not him.

He was smart. Wily and ruthless. I'd already underestimated Travis once, and it had nearly cost X his life.

I wouldn't make that mistake again. Even though X and Whip and Levi had assured me they would never be farther than a few feet away, and they would get to me before Travis could do anything, my stomach still swirled with nerves.

Beneath my purse, perched primly on my lap, I clutched the knife I'd once told X I didn't want.

I still wasn't sure I would be able to use it, but the feel of it between my fingers no longer terrified me, like it had that night in my bedroom. Now I clutched it like it was a lifeline.

Whip's voice came quietly from the darkness. "Vi. Trigger just reported a white van approaching, same as the one we've seen before. Get ready."

I couldn't say anything. My mouth was too dry. I knew Trig and his crew were spread out, farther away than the three men who hid in the darkness around me. They were there as backup, but this show was mine.

The white van parked across the road. And for the longest moment, Travis and I just stared at each other. I couldn't see him through the van's dark tint, but I didn't need to. It was just like the days I'd felt him watching me while I was showering. I knew before I saw him that he was there, in the darkness, watching me, ready to make his move but not before I was scared and shaking.

Travis was a man who got off on fear.

He'd shown me that when we were kids, him and his friends taunting me as we walked home from school. The way he'd made up stories so our foster parents would punish me.

And he'd shown it again as adults. Trapping me and Toby in that warehouse. Rigging traps on the bluff. Sending rhyming notes that threatened everything and everyone I cared about.

All of it had been about fear. About control.

About revenge for the fact I'd cost him years of his life, when I'd backed up the claims of a girl he'd abused.

When he got out of the van, his smile was smug. Like he didn't have a fucking care in the world because he had a gun clutched in his hand. He sauntered over to me and took up the seat beside me.

I stiffened at being so close to him.

If he noticed, he didn't show it. "Hey, fellas?" he called into the darkness, then chuckled when there was no reply. "Levi, right? Come on, man, come out and say hi. You and I have so much in common. Shame we weren't in the same prison. We could have been friends."

I wanted to spit out that Levi would have never been friends with a sniveling weasel like Travis but I bit my tongue, knowing I needed to keep my cool and my head clear, no matter what he said.

"Who else is out there? Wyatt DeLeon, am I right?"

He finally glanced over at me. "How does it feel to be so fucking fat and ugly that you have to settle for a man who's been between the thighs of a thousand women?"

He didn't bother waiting on my reply. "And Knox. I think we all know you don't go anywhere without your guard dog, do you, Violet? Excuse me if I don't call them by your little code names. I like to be more personal than that. I did my research. I know all about Knox's brothers and his parents and his sweet niece."

There was a rumble of a growl from the darkness that I knew without a doubt belonged to X.

Travis didn't look bothered. He just pointed the gun at me and kept running his mouth. "I know all about how Levi fell on his sword for a club who doesn't give a shit about him. And I know all about how Wyatt killed his own family with his shitty driving."

Red-hot rage coursed through me.

Travis let out a low whistle. "You seriously know how to pick 'em, little sis. What a fucked-up, pathetic group of men you've surrounded yourself with. Though I use the term 'men' loosely. They're just boys, aren't they? Little lost boys who couldn't save their kids, who got screwed over by a biker gang, who have spent their entire lives pretending to be one thing because they know their family would never accept the truth. You ever wonder why they picked you? You ever stop and think it's 'cause they're so fucking broken themselves that nobody wants them?"

He finally focused on me, and the depth of his hate and revulsion hit me full force in the chest.

"And you're just as scared and pathetic, aren't you?"

"I'm not scared of you," I muttered.

Travis moved fast, knocking the purse off my lap, unveiling the knife in my fingers before I could even react.

"No?" he asked. "If you're not scared, why haven't you plunged that knife into my neck yet?"

I wanted to. My fingers shook with the need to use it. "Where's Nyah?"

He leaned in close, not bothering to answer my question. "Pathetic," he whispered in my ear. Then he stood, scooping the purse up from the grass and opening it, checking inside. He raised an eyebrow, then closed the zipper again. "Not going to lie, I was pretty sure I wasn't going to get a cent out of you, but I'm pleasantly surprised that you've proved me wrong." He shrugged. "So you get a free pass tonight. You can go home to that shitty apartment and sleep soundly, knowing all your friends are safe in their beds at the MC compound. And for tonight at least, I'll leave them alone."

He went to walk away.

I couldn't just let him leave. "And Nyah?"

He twisted and grinned, his voice dropping to a chilling tone that almost perfectly matched the monotone, robotic one of the voice changer he'd used at both the warehouse and that night up on the bluffs.

"You followed the rhyme, you followed the thread—But you're far too late, your girl is dead."

They didn't sound like the words of the boy I'd known. He'd been mean and angry. But this version of him was sharp and cruel. His laughter echoed as he walked away from me. I forced my feet not to move. Forced my entire body to stay still and not budge an inch.

He was still laughing when he got back in his van and drove away.

One by one, all three men emerged from the darkness. Levi sat beside me on the bench, and X took the knife from my hand. Whip stood, staring after Travis like he might come back at any second.

"Did you do it?" I asked, trying to ward off the violent shaking I couldn't seem to control.

Whip turned back around and bent to brush his lips over my forehead. "You did great. Tracker is on his van." He pulled out his phone and brought up an app. He flashed it in our direction, showing us a green dot traveling a map of the streets of Saint View.

I breathed a sigh of relief. "Maybe we should have just killed him now and been done with it?"

Levi shook his head. "No. That would have been sloppy. He had the upper hand."

Whip's lips flickered at the corner, though he didn't look up. "First rule of Murder Squad, patience."

X let out a whine. "I thought it was no witnesses? And no innocents? You guys have got to stop making up new rules! It's very confusing!" His eyes brightened. "But hey! You called it Murder Squad! You know what we need? A symbol. A calling card. So the cops know it was us. We could brand our kills. Ooh—maybe a duck. For Reginald."

No one replied.

"I'm serious," he said. "Or a cat. For Harold. Or both! We leave a feather and a furball on the body. BAM! Case closed. The Murder Squad strikes again."

Levi squinted at him. "My killer calling card is definitely not going to be an image of your ugly cat, X."

X side-eyed him. "Do you have a better idea?" He held up a finger. "And do not say an image of Whip's cock. You're the only one who wants to see that."

"Definitely not what I was going to say..." Levi muttered.

Whip flapped a hand at the two of them to shut up. "No calling cards. That's...so...try-hard. Makes you look like a pick-me girl. Like you're only doing it for the fame."

I wasn't sure at what point in my life conversations like this had become the norm and acceptable, but pretty much nothing surprised me anymore. "Oh, right. Heaven forbid you kill for the fame. How unclassy."

All three of them stared at me.

I raised an eyebrow in challenge.

None of them went there. I folded my arms across my chest and focused on Whip. "Where is he going anyway? Can we get this over with?"

But Whip frowned at the screen on his phone. "I think he's stopped. Seems to be a residential house a few blocks away."

I held my hand out for the phone. "Let me see."

Whip handed it over, and I peered down at the address displayed on the screen.

I felt the blood drain out of my face. It was as if I'd been on the receiving end of a cold bucket of water.

"Vi?" Levi twisted to catch a glimpse of my face. "Why did you just go all stiff?"

I stared down at the blinking green dot, willing it to move. Willing it to be anywhere but there.

But it didn't budge.

I looked up at them. "It's the house we lived in as kids. Our foster parents' home."

34

VIOLET

We sat in Whip's car in front of a house I thought I would never see again. The last time I'd walked out of it, my shoulders had hunched, arms wrapped around myself, eye swelling from a backhand I'd received for no apparent reason, other than my foster father had been in a mood. Losing income because I'd aged out of the system would do that to a guy, I guessed.

I'd been a broken shell of a girl, my foster mother's *sweet* reminders echoing in my head. I could hear them again now, clear as day.

What do you mean you're leaving? You're just going to walk out? We need the money from your job! What the hell are we supposed to do?

You're a fat, ugly bitch, Violet. Your heart is as ugly as your face.

You ungrateful piece of shit, you aren't even going to thank us for everything we've done for you? You owe us.

She'd always had the sharpest, most vile tongue. I'd

preferred my foster father's blows. Physical bruises had always been easier to heal from than the constant torment of my foster mother's cruelness.

"Vi?" Whip said quietly from behind the steering wheel. "You don't have to do this, you know? We can take care of it."

The thought was tempting. It would have been so easy to just let them take me back to the clubhouse. So easy to curl up in Levi's bed and be lulled to sleep by the knowledge I was safe.

But the girl who'd lived in this house once upon a time, all those years ago, screamed I would never be safe until I faced down the demons that had haunted me my entire life.

That just like Travis popping up again, so would every other monster from my past, until I slayed them all.

I couldn't just sit back and let them take care of this for me. I could let them back me up and support me, but I had to face it myself, or I would never be truly free from the shackles my shitty past held me in.

"I'm fine. Let's do this."

Whip didn't seem terribly happy about it, and I knew all three of them would have preferred to tuck me up somewhere safe. But none of them argued with me.

They just silently got out of the car, and one by one surrounded me, the four of us moving as a group on near silent feet.

The house wasn't big. It was a shitty three-bedroom place, practically falling down in ruin. It reeked of rot and despair. A junky, rusted-out car sat on the overgrown lawn, a new addition since the last time I'd been here. Weeds grew up around and beneath it. There was a dim glow from behind the ratty curtains covering the windows, and the sound of a TV beyond. The front porch, where I'd copped one of my worst beatings ever, looked like it hadn't had any maintenance in the entire time I'd been gone. It had squeaked something fierce fifteen years ago. I pointed at it and shook my head at the others.

They got my meaning. We crouched in the darkness. All three of them turned to me.

Despite the situation, despite the fact my heart hammered and my palms sweated just from being back here, the fact they valued my opinion meant everything.

"There's a living room at the front of the house, and a kitchen and dining area at the back. Bedrooms upstairs. My guess is they'll be in the living room, watching TV." I eyed the living room windows. "Front porch will be a dead giveaway we're here. We'll be better off going through the back."

Levi nodded. "We need to split up. The two around the back enter first. Two of us stay here and come in through the front after."

"How many people do I get to stab?" There was no laughter in X's question. None of his usual hyperactivity or humor. His eyes held an expression I'd really only seen once before.

When I'd watched him stab a man to death in cold blood.

This was the side of him I should have been scared of. I had been, in the beginning.

But things had changed. The only people X was going to hurt were the ones who truly deserved it.

And the people in this house truly did. They'd lived

in my nightmares for years. It was no wonder Travis had run back to them. No wonder they'd happily welcomed him back with open arms.

Travis had come from a fucked-up family home, and they'd only made it worse.

They'd created the monster he was today. Nurtured it with their neglect and hate.

But it was me paying the price. Me. Toby. Nyah.

I swallowed thickly, refusing to believe Nyah was dead. Travis was a liar. Through and through. A narcissistic son of a bitch who would have said anything to hurt me.

Maybe I couldn't blame him for that. Hadn't I done the same thing to him? Hadn't I told the police he'd hurt that girl, just so I could be free of him?

I squeezed my eyes shut tight, forcing out the past, focusing on the now. Because anything else would get us killed.

"I'm going through the back," I whispered.

Levi squeezed my fingers. "I'm coming with you."

For once, X and Whip didn't argue. They knew each other well. They might have fought like cats and dogs the majority of the time, but they moved in unison, like a well-oiled machine through the darkness, each of them taking up a spot either side of the porch steps, crouched in the darkness, and just waiting for all hell to break loose.

I drank in the sight of them as I followed Levi around the back of the house, dodging rusting car parts and broken toys.

We reached the back door, and he leaned in, pressing his mouth against mine. "I love you."

God, I loved him too. I kissed him back hard, making sure he knew.

"I'm going first," he whispered, gun pulled out of the waistband of his jeans and clutched in strong fingers.

I wasn't stupid enough to argue with him. I needed to be here, but he and Whip and X had done this a million times. While I had exactly no experience and wasn't even sure which way to hold the knife.

Was there a right way? I had no idea.

But now wasn't the time to ask. I lurked behind Levi, my heart thumping when he reached up and turned the handle.

It gave easily, clearly unlocked. It squeaked a little as he pulled it open, but when no gunshots or shouts rang out, we both breathed again and crept inside.

The TV blared from the front room, light flickering around a shadowy corner.

But the kitchen, where we stood, was in darkness.

The smell hit me hard. I wrinkled my nose, covering it with my arm. Flies buzzed somewhere around us, though it was too dark to see them. Rotting food sat out on the counters and the tabletop, dirty dishes and pots and pans stacked up in the sink.

The house was as disgusting as I remembered it.

But the smell. I fought back the urge to gag and was glad I hadn't come in here with X because he and his weak stomach wouldn't have stood a chance.

I did not remember that smell. It had never smelled good, but this was next-level revolting. We crept toward the living room, me sticking close to Levi, the rustle of chip packets and the clinking of beer bottles giving away exactly where Travis was, even if his shouts at the football game hadn't.

Levi reached the corner first and peeped around it.

He recoiled so fast fear jumped into my throat. I waited for gunshots to ring out, Travis realizing we were here.

I gave Levi a questioning look, but he just shook his head, motioning for the back door.

I frowned at him, trying to understand what he meant.

There was no time. A shotgun cocked in the darkness. "Come out and say hello to Mommy and Daddy, Violet."

There was no chance to run. He knew we were here.

I flipped the light on.

Travis sat on the couch, football on the TV, beer in one hand, shotgun in the other.

And two dead bodies sitting either side of him on the couch.

I gasped, horror clawing its way up my throat, a sick realization that the smell in the house wasn't just moldy food and unwashed clothes.

It was the decaying bodies of my foster parents, with bullet holes in their foreheads.

There was dried blood everywhere. More of it than I'd ever seen in my life. Sprays of it across the walls behind them. Pooled on the floor where they'd dripped blood until they'd bled out. Seeped into the couch where Travis sat like he'd just dropped by to have tea and a chat.

The scene was so bitterly gruesome and horrific that it took me a good minute to even register that he now had that shotgun trained on me.

"Well?" He barked out a bitter laugh. "Don't be so fucking rude, girl. Say hello to your parents."

I couldn't speak. Couldn't move. Couldn't stop staring at the bodies of the two people who'd haunted my childhood and teenage years.

They hadn't been good people. I would cry no tears over their deaths. I wouldn't mourn them.

But the way Travis sat between them on the couch, despite the stench and the flies, the way he'd killed them then left their bodies there as some sort of sick decoration while he continued to live around them...

All of that was too much for my brain to process. Too much for anyone to comprehend.

He'd completely lost his mind.

"Say hello to your parents, Violet!" he screamed.

I whimpered, cringing away from the shotgun aimed at me. "Hello," I whispered, giving him what he wanted.

I gave myself another long moment to feel the fear. To feel the disgust and the shock and the horror.

And then I let it go.

This house wanted me to be that scared teenage girl who'd had to lock and barricade her door at night to keep out the monsters living beneath this roof.

And now one of them was staring at me again.

But I'd defeated him once.

I could do it again.

"What did you do, Travis?" I asked softly.

He laughed bitterly. "Sorry I didn't invite you to the family reunion. It didn't last long."

"Have you just been living here with dead bodies?"

Travis glanced over at them, like it was the first time he'd really even considered the question. When he turned back to me, his eyes were hard. "Where else was I going to go?"

In another life, maybe I would have felt sorry for him. He was just as broken as I was, ruined by two people who should have never been parents and a system that didn't work.

But it was impossible to feel anything but thick, stabbing hate. "You're sick," I whispered.

He laughed like the maniac he was. He'd kept it hidden well while we were in public, but now, surrounded by the evil that lingered in this house, it was all out on display. "I am what you made me."

But I wasn't taking that. Maybe once upon a time I would have. I would have let a narcissist blame me for their poor choices. Blame me for the shitty hand they'd been dealt. But I wasn't taking that anymore. "You are who you *chose* to be," I seethed.

"I never had a fucking chance." Spit frothed at the corners of his mouth that he didn't bother to wipe away. "You know what they fucking did to me? They kept me in a fucking box beneath the floor. Shoved me in there for hours at a time, in the dark and in the cold. You were the fucking lucky one, Violet! You think you had it bad? You should have seen what they did to me!"

I didn't doubt it. Didn't doubt his claims of abuse and neglect.

But that didn't mean I could forgive him.

"Where's Nyah?"

He laughed bitterly. "You've known that bitch for two fucking minutes and she's all you talk about." He stood and crossed the room, pointing the shotgun at my head.

"What about me, Violet? What about your brother?" He shoved the gun between my eyes.

I didn't fucking flinch.

I couldn't look away from the pain and torture in his expression.

Levi growled behind me in warning, and I was vaguely aware of X and Whip storming in, weapons drawn.

I held my hand up, stopping all three of them from going farther.

This was my fight.

Mine and Travis's.

"You killed my best friend," I whispered.

He barked out a laugh, his fingers trembling over the trigger. "Who, Toby? He killed himself. Watched it with my own two eyes." His eyes narrowed at me. "And yet you still came up golden, didn't you, Violet? Still came up with a family who loves you. A best friend to laugh with." His voice turned into a snarl. "What the fuck do I have? I thought I had a woman who loved me too, but you fucking ruined that as well, didn't you?"

I didn't know what woman he was talking about. Nyah? Maybe the girl he'd attacked and gone to prison for? I didn't care.

One thing was clear.

Travis had made his own bed. And now he was going to have to lie in it.

"Where's Nyah?" I whispered again.

"Dead, bitch! How many times I gotta tell you! She's as dead as you are!"

His finger didn't even get a chance to squeeze the trigger. Levi's gun exploded, his bullet catching Travis in the shoulder.

He jerked, the gun slipping from my forehead and pointing up at the air.

Someone grabbed me.

I was barely aware of it in the tussle of arms and legs and gunshots.

Each one splintered through my brain, bringing with it the pain of everything this man had taken from me. Safety. Toby. Nyah. Any sense of worth.

A scream ripped from my mouth, and I charged forward, staring down the man I'd hated for as long as I could remember.

Levi and X held him, waiting for me for a decision on what to do. Travis howled indignantly, his shoulder bleeding, the wound nasty but unlikely to be life-threatening if treated.

"What do you want to do, Vi?" Levi asked, his eyes ablaze.

X practically vibrated with the scent of an impending kill in the air but held himself in check. Barely.

Blood seeped from Travis's gunshot, a mesmerizing spread of red across his dirty T-shirt. I stepped in close, and without any forethought or planning, I brought the tip of my knife to his wound and pressed it.

Hard.

His scream of pain would probably be heard blocks away, and for once in my life, I was glad that Saint View was the sort of place where screams in the night were common and people were smart enough to mind their own business.

I dragged the knife across his shoulder, cutting

through flesh and tendons, blood spilling beneath my blade like it was an extension of my body.

"That's my girl," X encouraged, almost panting at the sight of me with his knife in my hand, drawing another man's blood.

I was his girl.

His and Whip's and Levi's.

And Travis was never going to take another person from me.

I plunged the knife into his jugular.

X crowed in victory as Travis slumped between him and Levi. He hit his knees, the knife sticking out of his neck.

Levi and X dropped him to the floor.

But I wasn't done.

Something stirred inside me. Something strong and rich and...powerful.

Like I wasn't even in control of my body, I drew the blade out, letting blood spurt like a fountain.

Then slashed the knife across his neck, slitting his throat.

More blood.

I did it again and again. Opening him up. Making him bleed. Making him pay for the fear I'd lived with my entire life. Making him pay for the lives he'd taken from me. Making him pay for every shitty thing our foster parents had done, because he'd taken away the opportunity to confront them myself when he'd killed them.

Maybe he'd been owed those kills.

But so had I.

The darkness that had opened up in me demanded them.

I turned, facing the three men who'd brought me here.

I knew what they saw. A woman covered in blood. A woman with crazed eyes.

A woman who'd taken her first life and suddenly realized why they liked it.

Whip's forehead furrowed. His gaze skipped from X to Levi, and then back to me. "Vi, sweetheart. Give me the knife."

I didn't want to. Couldn't.

I stepped over Travis's bleeding body and slammed it blade first into my foster mother's chest. Over and over. Until it was a pulpy, disgusting mess.

And then I did the same to the man slumped beside her.

It didn't matter to me that they were dead long before.

"I hate you," I whispered while I stabbed them. Travis's blood smeared my face. The stench in the room was overwhelmingly vile, but I couldn't stop. "I hate you for what you did to me. Always making me feel like shit. Always making me scared." I glanced down at Travis, his dead, unseeing eyes. "And I hate you for what you did to him. None of us deserved this. None of us deserved *you*."

All the fight went out of me.

And I stared in horror at what I'd done.

"Please don't hurt us," the tiniest whisper came from the doorway.

I spun. The knife clattered to the floorboards as my knees crumpled.

And all four of us stared in horror at the two little faces peering up at us.

35

WHIP

"Well, shit." X shoved his hands on his hips and stared down at the two children. "Guess I'll go google 'how to explain murder to minors.'"

I shot him a look, and he pressed his lips together but didn't make a move toward the kids.

Levi was so frozen it was like his feet were cemented to the floor. "What the fuck do we do now?"

Wasn't that the million-dollar question?

Violet stood in the middle of the carnage, soaked in blood and shaking, her hand still twitching like it missed the weight of the knife she'd just used to carve open the man who used to be her brother.

She stared up at me helplessly. "I didn't... What do we...?"

All five of them seemed to be waiting on me for answers. The two kids included.

It had been years since I'd had anything to do with a child. I'd actively avoided them after I'd lost mine, the hurt of seeing other dads with their kids too much for my broken heart to bear. Even now, my stomach rolled at the sight of the boy and girl, who were much too close to the ages my children had been when they'd died.

But where my kids had been blond and blue-eyed, these two were dark-haired with the biggest brown eyes I'd ever seen.

I found myself down on my knees in front of them, using a voice I hadn't used since I'd gotten in a car with my family. and I'd been the only one to walk away from it.

"Hi." My voice cracked, and I had to swallow hard. "My name is Wyatt. Sometimes people call me Whip though. What are your names?"

They were dirty, hair matted and unbrushed. Despite the late hour, they didn't wear pajamas. They both had on oversized T-shirts that fell around their knees, and grimy sweatpants that clearly hadn't been washed in a very long time.

I suspected the kids probably didn't smell very good, but it was hard to tell with the stench of rotting bodies and blood in the air so thick that it drowned out everything else.

They were roughly the same height, and when they didn't offer their names, I tried a different question. "Are you guys twins?"

The boy nodded.

I smiled at him. "Let me guess. You're the oldest, right?"

The girl shook her head sharply. "I'm older! By two minutes!"

I widened my eyes like that was quite the feat. "Wow. You were faster than him, huh?"

The boy frowned at me. "But she's not faster anymore! I can beat her in a running race."

"Only if you cheat!" she shot back at him.

My heart squeezed at their bickering. It took me right back to being in that little house with my family around me, the scent of coffee in the air, my wife humming along with the radio playing in the kitchen, the kids running around our feet, arguing with each other while they got ready for school, and I got dressed for work.

Those were the things I'd missed most.

The silence in my house had been deafening ever since.

"You know who else is really fast?" I pointed at X. "His name is Knox."

The kids both peered up at him. The boy cocked his head to one side. "I could beat you."

X looked him up and down. "I dunno, kid. Your legs are pretty short." He sat himself down on the edge of an armchair, so he was more eye height with the boy. "Want to know a secret? These guys don't call me Knox. They call me X."

The boy's eyes widened. "Are you a superhero? Like X-Men? Is that why you're fast and you have a special name?"

Levi snorted.

X shot him a glare then turned back to the kids. "You know what? I kind of am a superhero."

"Explains your love of tight pants," Levi muttered.

"Hey!" X scowled at him. "I wore Hendrix's suit like, two times! It's not my fault he has chicken legs and I work out!"

I squeezed my eyes shut, wondering if there would ever be a time in my life where things weren't chaos.

But then I would take X and Levi bickering any day over the silence in my house.

I tried again to get the kids' names. "So my superhero name is Whip, he's X. That big guy over there with the drawing on his face? His superhero name is Reaper. And this beautiful lady here is—"

"Omelet," X filled in.

The kids both squinted at him.

"Violetta," I corrected. "But you can call her Violet."

They both seemed less confused by that.

A tiny bit of the tension in the boy's shoulders dropped away, despite the fact we were still standing in the middle of a murder scene. "Her name is Arianna, but I call her Ari."

I held my hand out to her. "Nice to meet you, Arianna. Can I call you Ari too?"

She looked a little hesitant but took my fingers and nodded. "He's Will."

I raised an eyebrow. "Short for William?"

He nodded.

I grinned at him. "So we all have superhero names. That's pretty cool."

The little boy kept glancing over at Violet, and then back to me. "Is she okay?" he whispered.

I glanced up at Violet. She hadn't moved. It was clear to me she was in shock, and we needed to get her out of here so Grayson could check her over.

But we couldn't just leave these kids here either.

I smiled at Will. "She's okay...she just..."

I had no idea how to explain to a child what Violet had just done.

X bent to murmur in my ear, "You're really wishing you'd let me google it right now, aren't you?"

He wasn't wrong.

Ari's big eyes took in every inch of Violet's blood-spattered body. "She's a super hero too, isn't she? That's why she killed the bad guys?"

Violet flinched, but the girl's question had gotten through. She knelt beside me, so she was at their eye height. "Is that what these people were to you? Bad guys?"

Ari's eyes darkened. "Yes."

Will picked up her hand, facing off against us in a way that made me think it wasn't the first time the two of them had only had each other.

Violet's voice trembled, and she pointed to Travis, dead on the floor. "Is he your father?"

Will shook his head. "No. He is." He pointed at the dead body on the couch.

Ari sniffed, but she wasn't crying. She just stared down at Travis's body on the floor. "We thought he was going to be a superhero too...but..."

My jaw clenched. "But he wasn't a good guy either, was he?"

Will and Ari both shook their heads, but it was Will who spoke. "We hid upstairs when he was here. He was mean. He did bad things..."

"That was smart of you," Violet told him gently. "To hide."

Ari's eyes had suddenly lost all of their innocence.

She stared down at Travis's dead body, then she leaned down, so her face was mere inches from his.

She screamed.

She screamed her little lungs out, inches from his dead, unseeing eyes. Then did the same to both of her parents.

None of us moved to stop her or silence her.

When she finally looked up, tears ran down her cheeks. But when Violet opened her arms, Ari walked right into them without hesitation.

She crumpled into Violet's embrace and let the tears come, her sobs mixing with Violet's as the two of them cried together, the bodies of their shared enemies dead around them.

We didn't ask if they wanted to come with us. When Violet scooped up Ari and carried her out the door, Will followed without hesitation. Violet's free hand fell to the back of his head, keeping him by her side.

Violet Garrisen might have been someone's monster tonight.

But just like that, she'd also become someone's hero.

---

*I*n the darkness, the six of us piled into my five-seater car, the two kids squished into the middle back seat between X and Violet. X made them play I Spy the entire way back to my place, and I parked the car in the driveway to excited shouts of "Traffic lights! Street sign! Rat!" and "You didn't see a rat! That doesn't count!"

Rat was the only one that had actually started with R, which was the letter X had given them.

We all got out of the car, shushing the kids, trying not to wake my entire neighborhood since it was the middle of the night, and we didn't need any extra eyes watching us.

Once we were inside, I went about doing all the things that needed doing. "Right. Everyone needs a shower. And food."

"I don't want a shower," Ari said quickly.

Levi's eyes flashed at her response. "I'm going to go back there and kill those motherfuckers all over again."

He would have to get behind me.

Violet squeezed her fingers. "You don't have to do anything you don't want to do. But I know that Whip has a nice shower here and the bathroom door has a lock on it. You can go in there and you will be absolutely safe, and nobody else will come in."

Her voice was small when she said, "Will you stand at the door and make sure?"

"Of course I will."

Ari nodded, but then she looked Violet up and down and grimaced. "Maybe you should go first though. You've got that bad guy's blood all over you."

Violet glanced down at herself in surprise, like in caring for the kids and keeping them distracted, she'd almost forgotten about the state she was in herself. She forced a laugh, like it was no big deal. "You're right. I'll go first."

Ari nodded fiercely. "I'll stand at the door and protect you."

I could practically see Violet's heart melting. But she

knelt so she was at Ari's eye height and said seriously, "You don't need to protect me, sweet girl. There's nothing here to be afraid of. You see all these men? Including your brother? They're the good guys."

I wasn't sure she was one-hundred-percent convinced, but then X, with his head in the back of one of my cupboards, let out a shout of glee. "Pop-Tarts! I knew I left some here that day we tortured—"

I coughed loudly.

X, for once in his life, got the subtlety. He grinned apologetically and waved the box of sugary treats in front of the kids' faces. "Who wants one?"

Will stared at the box with clear hunger in his eyes but also a healthy amount of distrust. "What do we have to do to get one?"

I frowned. "What do you have to..."

It dawned on me that someone had forced them to do things in order to be given food. My fingers clenched into fists. I looked to Levi, knowing I needed someone to ground me before I flew out the doors and resurrected the dead, just so I could abuse them the way they'd abused these kids. "I can't—"

My brain knew these kids weren't the ones I'd lost. But it didn't matter.

Levi caught my gaze. His eyes burned with the same intensity. "Breathe," he murmured.

Our gazes locked on each other. We both inhaled audibly, and I forced air down my lungs, hoping it quelled the rage inside me. I didn't understand how people could abuse their own children the way Violet's foster parents had.

How did they get to keep their kids? I'd done everything for mine, loved them, cared for them, went without so they would have everything they needed.

And yet I'd lost them.

While people like Violet's foster parents just got to keep theirs? How was any of that fair on any of us?

I needed another three deep breaths before I even felt remotely in control of my emotions.

By the time Levi and I had finished deep breathing, X had the kids' hands washed and them sitting up at the kitchen counter, Pop-Tarts in the toaster, plates in front of them, waiting for them to be ready.

X tapped a knife on the edge of the countertop, battling back his amusement. "If you two want me to lead you in some yoga, just say the word." He sniggered. "Gray is going to be so happy you're using his calming techniques."

I rolled my eyes, pulling out a stool next to Will. "Speaking of Grayson, is he coming over?"

"Should be here any minute. Trig and the others are taking care of..." Levi eyed the kids. "You know."

"You mean the dead bodies?" Will piped up.

Levi grimaced. "Well, yeah."

Will nodded, but then X put a Pop-Tart in front of him, and the kid wolfed it down like he hadn't been fed in weeks.

It made me sick to my stomach that there was a good possibility he hadn't ever had a regular supply of food. He was tiny. All skin and bones. I'd thought him maybe six, judging by his size, but after speaking to him, I suspected he was actually a good few years older. Maybe eight or nine.

"How old are you guys?" I put my Pop-Tart on Will's plate.

Will glanced at his sister.

She shrugged; chocolate filling smeared across her mouth. "I don't know."

X frowned at them. "Do you know your birthday? Or what year you were born?"

They shook their heads.

I tried a different line of questioning. "What about school? What grade are you in?" At least that would give us the general idea of how old they were.

"We've never been," Ari mumbled with her mouth full. Her eyes lit up. "Could we go?"

I didn't even bother asking them if their parents had homeschooled them. I knew there was no chance that would have happened.

I gave her a tight smile. "I think it's safe to say you're definitely going to go to school now."

She shook her brother's arm in excitement. "Did you hear that? Will, did you hear him? This is the best day ever."

And that was possibly the saddest thing I'd ever heard.

From down the hallway, the water running in the bathroom stopped. A quiet knock came from the front of the house, and I slid off the stool.

The others went back to their conversation, and I went to the door. Grayson stood on the other side, looking haggard.

I stepped aside so he could come in, and checked the street, making sure nothing was out of place before I closed the door.

He didn't make a move to go any farther into the house. He just jerked his head toward the living room. "Kids in there?"

I nodded, crossing my arms over my chest and leaning back against the wall. "You been over to the scene?"

He grimaced. "It's a lot. But the others are over there, dealing with it. They said to tell you, you now owe them multiple cleanups."

That was great and a tiny weight off my mind. I didn't even care that at some point, I'd have to pay back the favor and get my hands dirty, cleaning up a mess Trig and his guys had made. That's what we did for each other. We always had.

But what we'd left for them tonight was a mess of epic proportions.

And we'd brought two of the biggest problems home with us.

"Did you find anything out about the kids?" I asked him.

He made a face. "Not really. I had a quick search around while the guys were dealing with the bodies. Found a creepy as hell trapdoor that led to a coffin-sized box beneath the floor. But there were no signs of birth certificates or anything with their legal names on it. I know some people at DCFS, and in the morning, I'll subtly ask them to look up any kids who might have been staying at that address. You said Violet had been fostered there when she was younger, right? So it's possible they're foster kids."

I nodded. "They said they were their parents, but

maybe they're too young to remember if they came there from another family. I don't know."

"We'll know more tomorrow when I can get my friend to look into it." He glanced past me at the kids sitting at the kitchen counter. "Question is, what are we going to do with them in the meantime?" Grayson frowned. "I guess I could take them with me—"

Ari's head jerked up, and she twisted to stare at us.

She'd clearly been listening. That fear was back in her eyes again. The one we'd only just removed through reassurances and food and stupid I Spy games.

Her eyes begged me not to give her away.

"No," I told Grayson, but my words were for the little girl sitting in my home with sugar on her face. "They stay here with us."

36

VIOLET

In Whip's bathroom, I stood beneath the shower spray for a long time, mentally trying to process what we were going to do with two kids who'd watched me murder someone. I got the impression they were well used to keeping secrets, but I didn't want to be another adult who asked them to do that.

And yet, what was the alternative?

I still had no answers when I wrapped myself in a towel, and started searching the drawers for a hairbrush. I felt bad for going through Whip's things, and I really didn't want to snoop, but he hadn't had any conditioner in his shower. So although I had spent a long time scrubbing the blood out of my hair, and it was now clean, it was a matted, tangled mess that finger combing wasn't going to fix.

Each drawer held all of Whip's things. Cologne. Toothbrush and paste. Deodorant. A facial cleanser that I mentally high-fived him for because even I, as a woman, was pretty slack about skincare.

No hairbrush. I supposed he didn't have much need for one when his hair was only a few inches long.

I'd almost given up hope when I pulled open the bottom drawer.

The contents were very different from all the other ones. It was filled with bright colors, unlike the grays and blacks with the odd splash of red that branded all the items Whip used regularly. A lady's hairbrush sat among a packet of pads, a box of tampons, makeup removing wipes, old, unused pregnancy tests, and an eyelash curler. My fingers brushed over a headband, some ponytail ties, and a necklace with a J hanging from the end of it.

Whip's wife's things. I was sure. Things that had at some point probably littered the countertop, in use every day. They'd probably gotten ready for work, side by side in this bathroom, brushed their teeth, and loved each other in it.

And then someone had taken her away from him.

I could feel her ghost in the room with me.

Could practically see their life together, playing out around me.

Yet there was no jealousy. For maybe the first time that night, there was a calmness in the air. He'd loved her. I knew that. They'd had a family together, a life. That was a part of him I would never want to take away.

Something about being in this home felt right. Seeing her things in that drawer reminded me this had once been a happy house, filled with love and laughter. And my heart whispered that it could be like that again.

I could see myself here, with Whip stepping out of the shower behind me, dripping wet, wrapping a towel around his trim waist and then his arms around me. Placing a good morning kiss to the side of my neck.

I could hear kids' voices outside the door, and my heart squeezed at the thought of raising a family with him. Not replacing the one he'd lost. But finding solace in the people who were in his life now.

I plucked the brush from the drawer, but my attention caught on the period supplies.

I couldn't remember the last time I'd used them.

I racked my brain, thinking back through the weeks and months. Had I even had a period since I'd met Whip? Since Levi had gotten out of jail? Since X had murdered Paul Jedderesen at that house on Olympic Drive?

I didn't think I had. The days were a blur of grief and fear, of happiness and laughter…

And the nights were a whirlwind of hot sex.

Hot, mostly very unprotected, sex.

We'd been so careless, but I hadn't really even thought it would matter. The voice of my doctor, the one I tried really hard to never go see, was always in the back of my mind. Every time I went there, he reminded me I needed to lose weight. That I was considered obese. That I would never be able to get pregnant at the weight I was.

I'd gotten so sick of hearing it, I had basically stopped going to the doctor altogether. I would be dying on the couch, and Toby would beg me to go find a new doctor, but I knew they would all say the same thing, and I couldn't bear to hear it from someone else's mouth. I'd spent my entire childhood hearing people tell me I was too big, too fat, too unhealthy. Too *everything*.

I didn't have to hear it as an adult. Didn't have to subject myself to that sort of shit.

So I just never went.

But my period had always been regular.

And now it wasn't.

"Stress," I told my reflection in the mirror, raking the brush through the tangled lengths of my hair with a vicious stroke. "You're stressed. Nothing more."

Except my gaze kept straying to that bottom drawer. To the pregnancy tests just sitting there, right next to the tampons.

I forced my gaze back to the mirror. Forced myself to brush my hair until it was smooth and straight. "You have no pregnancy signs..."

I had thrown up a few days ago, but that had been food poisoning, not morning sickness.

Yet that pregnancy test felt like it had been left there for me. A little gift from Whip's wife, rather than a left-over from when they'd been trying.

I gave in to temptation and picked up the box, flipping it over. It was definitely out-of-date.

Clearly not a sign from a dead woman that I might be pregnant.

And yet I couldn't put it down. My fingers shook and clenched around the box.

My other hand came to my belly, resting there, like my heart already knew if I took that test it would be positive.

Tears pricked the backs of my eyes. Part of me knew, that deep down, the reason I hadn't been at all careful when we'd had sex was because I desperately wanted a family of my own. That despite what doctors had told me, I still had belief in my body. That if just given the chance, it could bring me the family I'd always dreamed of.

Guilt plagued me. What I'd done wasn't fair to any of those three men out there in the kitchen.

And yet none of them had brought up contraception as more than a passing thought either.

"This is stupid," I whispered to myself in the mirror. "You don't even know you're pregnant."

I tried to force myself to put the test back down. To walk out of the bathroom and deal with everything that had happened tonight. I had to be in shock. I'd murdered a man tonight, and there were two very traumatized children out there who'd watched me do it, who I needed to deal with. Yet here I was, standing in a bathroom, daydreaming about babies I probably couldn't even have.

I ripped the packaging off the test. Read the instructions three times before my brain comprehended the words and worked out what I was supposed to do.

I peed where I was supposed to pee. Then set the test down on the counter and stared at it, counting seconds in my head because I didn't have a watch or my phone and didn't dare stick my head out of the bathroom door and ask for one.

The test said it would take up to five minutes for a result to show.

Mine showed up positive in under sixty seconds.

I stared at the two pink lines until my vision blurred. And then I blinked a few times fast to clear them and stared at it some more.

But there was no mistaking the bright-pink lines that said I was very definitely pregnant.

"Don't get your hopes up," I whispered. The test was years out-of-date. It could very well be a false positive.

Yet my heart whispered that it wasn't. My head

screamed in excitement, and my entire body trembled with the adrenaline that coursed through my system, wiping away the memory that I'd done a horrible thing tonight and taken a man's life.

I should have cared more about that, but I couldn't. Not when I was standing here, holding a test that told me I was going to be a mom.

<hr>

I'd never had the full tour of Whip's house. It was nothing fancy. A master where he obviously slept. A second room had nothing in it except the unpleasant smell of bleach.

Whip had closed that door, saying no one was to go in there. He'd exchanged a look with X as he'd said it, and my gut instinct knew that room had seen things I probably didn't want to know about.

The last bedroom had a set of bunk beds, a closet full of kids' clothes, and a chest full of toys.

I'd gasped when Whip opened the door. Ari and Will ran in like someone had just opened the gates of Disney for them.

Whip and I stood in the doorway, his arms wrapped around me from behind, the exact same way I'd imagined him doing in the bathroom. The pregnancy test burned a hole in the pocket of the sweats I'd borrowed from him.

Despite it being the middle of the night, and the fact they'd both had a warm shower which I'd thought might settle them down, Ari and Will tore through the toy chest, pulling out everything and exclaiming over each toy with excitement.

"Is this okay?" I asked Whip quietly.

All I could think was this room hadn't seen children since the day he'd lost them. Someone had clearly come in here afterward and tidied up, but Whip had never gotten rid of their things. Not their toys or their clothes or their beds.

I couldn't blame him. My hand hovered over my belly. I'd known about my child for literally less than an hour and I already couldn't imagine the pain of losing him or her. How Whip had gone on after having his babies in his life for years, and then just not...I couldn't even imagine.

I twisted back to look at him.

He let out a deep breath and then nodded. "Yeah. It really is. I never really knew why I couldn't get rid of their things when I moved my wife's clothes." He rested his chin on my shoulder. "But maybe this is why."

When the kids finally tired of the toys, they explored the clothes hanging in the closet and then finally moved on to the beds.

"I get the top bunk!" Will shouted.

Ari couldn't stop stroking the soft fabric of the quilt covering the mattress. She stared up at us. "I sleep here?"

I nodded. "Sure. At least for now, until we work out if you have family to go to."

Her shoulders slumped. "Oh."

She looked so disappointed, my heart shattered into a million pieces. How awful had this girl's life been that she would want to stay here with strangers, ones she'd watched do violent things no person should ever see another doing?

Except I knew how horrible it was. I knew she had probably endured beatings and sexual assault. Knew she had probably been starved and withheld basic life necessities by parents who were sick and cruel.

I moved to pull back the covers and knelt beside the bed as I tucked her in. Her hair was still a matted mess. That was going to take scissors and was a job for another day. But her skin smelled clean and fresh, the dirt and grime streaks washed away from her tiny body.

She was so young. But her eyes held the horrors she'd been subjected to, and the fear this safe place was going to be taken away from her.

Maybe it was the pregnancy hormones.

Maybe it was just that I'd once been this little girl. Neglected and scared and just wishing someone would care enough about me to give me even a tiny scrap of what I needed. At least I'd had DCFS checking in on us from time to time.

But these two kids looked as if they'd been left to rot away in that house, with no intervention. Had no one known they were there? I couldn't remember family or friends ever coming to the house when I'd lived there. If either of my foster parents had people other than each other in their lives, I never saw them. They were often out, drinking at the bar, but their friends had never come to our place.

Hadn't the neighbors seen the kids in the yard and made a call? Hadn't anyone cared they were being kept like prisoners?

Something Travis had said echoed in my head. That he'd been locked in a box underneath the house.

It was on the tip of my tongue to ask the kids if they knew about this box, but I didn't want either of them to ever have to think about that horrible house ever again.

So I just tucked them both in, murmuring that they were safe here, and we would be just in the other room, all night, if they needed us.

Whip picked up two stuffed animals. One a dragon with blue-and-green scales. The other a princess with a felt crown. He smiled down at them fondly and then tucked them beneath the arms of the quiet children. "My kids liked these two the best. Maybe you will too."

"Thank you," Ari and Will said in almost perfect unison.

Whip's eyes were soft, and his fingers hovered over both kids, like he wanted to rub their backs or stroke their hair but knew they didn't have that level of trust with any of us.

At least not yet.

I stepped out of the way, and Whip closed the door.

I stared up at him, the two of us there in the hallway, stealing a moment alone. "Are you okay?" I asked him.

He shook his head. Then nodded. "I don't know. I feel like I shouldn't be and yet..." He glanced back at the closed bedroom door. "I am. Tucking those kids into bed felt as normal and natural as when I'd done it with my kids. The clothes are going to be too big. My two were taller..."

I took his fingers, threading them through mine. "It doesn't matter. They're clean. And we can get them new things."

He stared down at me. "You're talking like they're already ours."

I dared to say the words I knew were in my heart. "Aren't they?"

Whip blew out a long breath and leaned in, pressing

his lips to my forehead. "I don't want you to get hurt. If we find their family, or if DCFS…"

"DCFS can go to hell," I seethed. "Those kids are not going into the system."

He held me tighter, wrapping his arms around me. "I know. I know. Shh. It's okay. We'll work it out."

I didn't sleep a wink that night. I lay in Whip's bed, his warm body beside me but neither of our breaths falling into that slow, relaxed state of deep sleep.

I just kept listening for the kids to call out.

I was convinced they were having nightmares with me covered in blood and wielding a knife at the center of them. I got up at least a dozen times and poked my head into their room, but each time was the same, both of them completely dead to the world, snuggled up and cozy, their expressions gentle and soft in the dim glow of the night-light.

X and Levi slept in the living room, X sprawled out on the couch, one arm dangling down to the floor. Levi in a recliner. They opened their eyes every time I tiptoed around them, and their fingertips reached for me each time I passed by.

By the time the sun rose, the kids seemed to be the only ones well-rested. Whatever hesitations they'd had the night before had disappeared, and they played together noisily, dragging X into every game and using Levi as target practice for a Nerf gun war.

I was pretty sure it was X who caught Levi with a dart right between his eyebrows, but X swore blindly it was Ari with a hella accurate aim.

Trigger, Ace, and Torch came to the door midmorning, and Whip, Levi, and I stepped outside to talk to them while X moderated the Nerf gun war that raged inside.

Trig folded his arms across his broad chest. "We just wanted to check in and make sure you were all okay."

Whip put his arm around my shoulders. "We are. Thanks for last night."

Trig nodded. "Don't mention it."

Will's happy shout of surprise as X or Ari caught him echoed out from inside.

Trig turned toward the sound then back to us. "We went through the entire house. Found these." He pulled some folded papers from the back pocket of his jeans and handed them to me.

I unfolded them gingerly and stared down at them. "The kids' birth certificates."

"They really were the biological kids of those two assholes in that house. Gray's friend got back to him, and he asked us to let you know that they've had no record of foster kids living in that house in the last decade. They removed their license."

My fingers shook as I gripped the paper. "And yet they did nothing about the two biological children the two of them had. Unbelievable."

"So, what do we do now?" Levi asked. "There's two kids in there who witnessed Violet kill a man last night."

And yet this morning Ari had woken up and shyly walked up to me and hugged my legs. It hadn't lasted long, but it was clear to me that her watching me kill Travis hadn't made her fear me.

It had made her love me.

It was a trauma bond, no doubt. I'd killed a man who'd hurt her. Taken her out of a house where she and her brother had been neglected. Forming a real relationship with her would be hard and filled with ups and downs, but in my mind, I had already decided what we were doing with those two kids inside that house.

"We keep them," Whip and I said in almost perfect unison.

A smile spread across his lips that was so contagious I could feel it on mine as well.

We both looked to Levi.

My heart pounded; I was scared he was going to say no. That pregnancy test I'd taken felt like a fever dream, but it was wrapped up in tissues in my purse. We had written each other ridiculous letters for over a year, letters where we'd confessed every hope and dream we had for the future. We'd talked about kids being a part of it.

But neither of us had considered a ready-made family falling in our laps.

Or finding out I was pregnant the very same day.

I needed him to respond well. Needed him to tell me it would all be okay because I was spiraling on the inside. Sure of what I wanted, no doubt, but terrified he or X wouldn't want what Whip and I so clearly did.

The front door swung open, and Will barreled out of it, Nerf gun in hand, bellowing out a war cry. Ari and X followed a moment later, Nerf darts shooting in every direction, the three of them chasing each other around the yard.

A slow smile spread across Levi's face as he caught a dart to the shoulder and clutched it dramatically. "I'm shot! I'm going down!"

His knees hit the dirt, and the kids ran over, laughing

hysterically, attacking him with more rounds until he lifted his hands zombie-style to tickle their bellies.

He winked at me when they ran off laughing and he rolled to his feet to chase them. His lips landed on my cheek, just below my ear as he said, "Of course they're ours."

X spun around. "What? Who? Who's ours? Are we keeping them? Do Harold and Reginald have a big brother and sister?"

He said it so loudly the kids both stopped and stared at me too.

My gaze caught X's. A moment of silence passed between us, where words didn't need to be said, because the connection between us was already there.

I needed him to confirm it before I said anything to the kids. There were four of us in this relationship. We all needed to agree.

But God, my heart so wanted him to say yes.

I'd never seen a more genuine smile on his face. He stormed across the yard, picked me up, and spun me in a circle. "Hell. Fucking. Yes."

Giddy joy spread through me.

He set me down, checking I was steady before he held his arms out to Whip. "Your turn for a spin!"

Whip opened his mouth, no doubt to threaten X with deadly violence, but X held up one finger. "Uh! No threatening to kill me in front of our children!"

The kids stared between the four of us with huge eyes. But it was Ari, actually the older twin by minutes according to her birth certificate, who asked the question I knew they were both thinking.

"We're your kids now?"

Oh God. I didn't know what to say. It couldn't be that easy. I doubted we could just adopt them legally. We would need to somehow get paperwork that would be good enough to pass if their guardianship was ever questioned. But we knew many men who had...questionable skills...and I would have bet money at least one of them would know how to get that done.

We would need to learn how to be parents. We'd need to work out where we could all live. Not only were we committing to these kids, to give them the stable home they'd never had, but we were committing to each other.

To a real, permanent bond.

One I knew was already there, cemented in the tiny baby growing in my belly that linked us all, no matter who had fathered it.

X nodded. Levi and Whip did too.

I stared down at Will and Ari. "Would you like that? To stay here with us and for us to take care of you? For us to be your parents?"

Will cocked his head to one side. "What do I call you though?"

Whip laughed. "Whatever you want. Whip. Or Wyatt."

Ari's voice was quiet. "But if you're going to be our parents, shouldn't we call you Dad?"

My heart stopped at the expression on Whip's face.

But he very quietly got to his knees, so he and Ari were the same height. "If the day ever comes when you want to call me Dad, then I will be honored."

That was too much for my hormones and for my heart. A tear slipped down my face.

Ari turned away, not committing to calling Whip Dad but not saying she wouldn't either.

That was more than enough for right now. What they called us didn't matter. They would find what suited them best, and we would let them call us whatever they wanted.

All that mattered was in that moment, the six of us, or seven if you counted the baby I hadn't told anyone about, became a family.

37

VIOLET

I couldn't stop staring at the twins' birth certificates. More specifically, the names of their parents, written in little black, nonthreatening letters that gave away no sign of the cruel, horrible people they were.

How they had created the two children who currently sat on the floor at my feet, X in the middle of them, reading from a stack of books he'd brought over earlier in the day, was baffling to me.

"Again!" Ari shouted when X finished the fifth picture book for the second time. Then she quickly added, "Please."

X didn't complain. He just nodded. "Yes, ma'am. You got it. Which one first? *Giraffe Attack* or *My Daddy Snores?*"

"All of them." Will inched closer to X, though he was practically already on top of him.

X looked like he wanted to pull the kids onto his lap and give them the affection they so clearly had never felt before, but we were all trying to take things slowly with them, moving at their pace, letting them know affection and touch were there if they wanted it but only on their terms, never ours.

It had been the hardest week of my life. All I wanted to do was scoop them up and smother them in love. I saw so much of myself in them, shared all the same traumas they had, and I just wanted to make it better for them.

I would. I had made that vow in my heart the moment I'd seen them there, covered in filth and too skinny to be healthy. But it would take time, and I had to be patient.

A wave of nausea swept over me, hot and thick, taking me by surprise.

X caught sight of my expression and stopped mid-sentence. "You okay?"

I still hadn't told anyone about the baby. I kept trying to. Every day I had woken up, convinced that today was the day I would tell them.

Then the day slipped away, turning into night, and my mouth still couldn't find the words.

I knew why.

I was living in a dream. One I hadn't even acknowledged until I was in it. I was surrounded by these men I loved and two children, who had come out of their shells a little more each day. Watching them realize they were safe and loved, watching them begin to heal, did the same for the wounded child inside me who had lived her own horror in that house.

But this one, this tiny shack in Saint View that was too small for this many people, was a bubble I never wanted to leave.

I didn't go to work, because work was out there, in the

real world, where bad things happened. I soaked up every second of being inside these walls where it felt like nothing could touch me.

Not Toby's death. Not the fact Nyah was gone, probably dead, and the only person who knew where her body was now slept six feet under himself. Out there were the police and the prison and the reminder I had taken a life and should be in jail for that crime.

If I thought about it for too long, my hands shook and sweat beaded on my forehead.

But then Ari laughed, or Will smiled, and the guilt fell away.

I'd spent my whole life trying to be good.

Letting go of that and realizing that life wasn't that black and white and living in the gray was new. I wasn't scared for my soul. I wasn't worried that killing Travis would scar me for life.

I was only scared the police would find out and I'd be taken from this bubble, where everything felt right.

But that knock on the door didn't come, and day by day, I put my faith in the men I'd chosen to keep me safe.

"I'm fine," I promised X. "Just need a bit of air, I think."

He nodded. "Okay, but if you're sick, I take no responsibility for it this time." He elbowed the twins in unison. "It was probably these two gremlins, picking up bugs at school and bringing them home."

Ari dropped her mouth in indignation. "My school has no bugs, X!"

I hid a smile. They'd only started at the school a few days ago, both of them incredibly eager to go. Though they were a bit older, they'd been put into the kindergarten class so they could catch up on what they'd missed. They didn't realize they should have been in the grade above, and they were in the same class as my brother's twins. Madden and Will had become fast friends, both of them a little hyper and talkative. Remi and Ari had been more standoffish, but I'd smiled when I'd picked them up yesterday, and the two girls, now cousins, had walked out holding hands.

Ari and Will were like sponges, their brains never stimulated in any way until now, and Ari in particular had talked at length about every detail of her classroom and teacher, and there was a spark in her eyes that hadn't been there when we'd found them in that house.

It didn't surprise me that she wouldn't hear X talk bad of a place she clearly loved.

"No?" he asked. "No bugs? What's this then?" He wriggled his fingers at her, imitating a spider about to tickle her belly.

She shrieked with laughter and ran away, her annoyance with him bad-mouthing her school clearly forgotten.

I got up. "No bugs or oysters. I just need some air. I've got my meeting at work in thirty minutes anyway, so maybe I'll walk there."

X stopped mid-step, pausing their game of chase. "I'll drive you, especially if you don't feel well."

I waved him off. "I'll be fine. The walk will do me good."

He crossed the room as the kids whined for him to keep playing, but his gaze was all for me. He brushed his lips over mine. "If you change your mind, you'll call one of us?"

I kissed him back. "I promise. But I already feel better." It wasn't a lie. The nausea came and went in waves, and so far I hadn't even thrown up, so I was feeling pretty lucky overall, apart from the nagging worry that I would be arrested and lose it all.

But I wasn't going to confess that to X. I said goodbye to the kids and let myself out of the front door. Levi and Whip leaned against the ice cream truck, standing so close their arms touched, despite there being more than enough room to stand apart.

Levi held his phone out, the call on speaker so they could both hear it.

They looked up as I approached, and I caught the end of their conversation.

Dax's familiar voice was on the other end. "I don't know when I'll be back. But it might be a while. King is going to continue your apprenticeship in the meantime."

Levi caught my hand but continued his conversation. "I understand. I really fucking do, and don't think this is about me. I'll be fine with King. But, Dax, fuck, man. What are you going to do?"

Dax heaved a sigh and shrugged. "I can't just sit here, hoping she'll return. I need to know what happened. I need to go search for her or something."

Levi bit his lip, and when he didn't say anything, Dax went on. "I love her, man. What the hell else am I supposed to do? What would you do if it were Violet?"

"Burn the world down until I found her," Levi agreed without a second of hesitation. He squeezed my fingers, like he was reassuring himself I was still there. "Go. Don't worry about the shop. We'll do whatever needs doing until you return."

He ended the call.

Tears pricked the backs of my eyes. "He still doesn't believe she's dead."

Levi shook his head. "We have no proof she is. No body."

"Travis said…" We all knew what Travis had said.

Whip sighed. "I hate seeing Dax like this. I think we should go out to the dump site again and make sure Nyah's body wasn't added since the last time we were out there. If Travis killed her in the days before we killed him, he still could have had time to add her body to his and Paul's collection."

Levi shook his head. "I reckon they were storing bodies somewhere else first. And Travis moved them when he realized it would fuck with us."

Whip screwed up his face. "You're probably right. But those women out there, unidentified… It doesn't sit right. We need to bury them properly at the very least. What's left of them."

I shuddered at the knowledge those women's bodies were still there, with nothing we could do to give their families closure. Alerting the police to their whereabouts would mean pointing them at evidence of crimes we'd committed too. We could move them, but they would all be in various stages of decomposition.

My stomach rolled again at the thought of the horrifically messy job, and I doubled over, clutching my belly.

Both guys lurched for me.

"Vi?" Levi asked, panic in his voice. "What's going on?"

I told myself to tell them. But I was clammy and going to be late for work if I didn't get a move on. So I waved them off and forced myself to straighten. "Nothing. Just a bit of heartburn or reflux or something. Nothing to worry about."

Neither seemed convinced.

I ignored them. "I've gotta get to work."

"I'll drive you," Whip said instantly.

"Or I can take you on my bike," Levi offered. Then grimaced. "Though taking corners on a bike if you aren't feeling great might not be the best idea. Whip, you take her."

I tried to argue with them, that I really wanted the walk, but the nausea didn't pass as quickly as it had earlier, and suddenly the ride to work felt like a great idea. Especially since I was going to be on my feet for the rest of the day.

I kissed Levi goodbye, and Whip opened the door of his car for me. I climbed in, instantly rolling down the window so I had air.

We drove in silence, my stomach too queasy for me to make conversation. Of course I had to feel the worst I had yet on the day I had to go back to work. But I couldn't delay it any longer. Francine was going to fire me if she had to cover my shifts for another week. She'd been very understanding about my abrupt need to take a week of personal leave, but when I'd called her it had sounded like the sort of forced polite you had to be, rather than true concern for whatever was going on in my life.

By the time we got to Clean Sweep and Whip stopped the car, I was really pretty sure I was going to vomit at some point today. Whip got out, and despite my trying to shoo him away, he insisted on walking me inside, clutching my arm like I was eighty and might fall and break a hip if he didn't hang on to me.

"You're babying me," I told him as we reached the doors.

"I'm not. You're sick and insisting on going to work. If I was babying you, I would hoist you up into my arms and carry you to the car and back to bed." He paused and looked at me funny.

My heart tripped over itself at the expression on his face.

"You're sick. And you've been feeling off every day for a few days now."

Shit. I thought I'd hidden the bouts of nausea better than that. Maybe I'd done enough to keep it from X and Levi, because they had no experience with pregnancy.

But Whip had watched his wife do this twice. He knew the signs.

"Violet," he practically whispered. "Are you pregnant?"

I felt everything all at once. Joy and excitement. Fear and nerves. Embarrassment to have kept it from him, even though in my heart I knew I'd been in shock and just needed time to process everything.

A slow smile crept across my face, and I nodded.

He said nothing but swept me into his arms, holding me so tight I could hear every beat of his too-fast heart. "God, I love you," he murmured.

There were no questions about whether the baby was his or not. No questions on whether all four of us would raise it together. Those questions had already been answered when we took in two kids who needed a home.

They'd been answered when three men let me love all of them and hadn't made me choose.

Telling Whip he was going to be a dad again was the sweetest moment I could have imagined for him.

Apart from the fact I really needed to vomit.

It rose up my throat, and the last thing I wanted to do was puke on the man right after I'd confessed we were having a baby. I shoved inside the Clean Sweep doors and sprinted for the bathroom on the other side of the office.

Francine squeaked out something, but I slammed the door shut behind me, only just making the toilet bowl.

Once my stomach was empty, I almost instantly felt good again. I cleaned up and pushed open the door to find Whip and Francine on the other side, hovering nervously.

Francine handed me a tissue and patted me awkwardly on the arm.

"Feel better?" Whip brushed my hair back off my face and tucked it behind my ear. "I'm going to go get you some saltines. Unless you want to come home?"

I glanced at Francine, who tried to fix her scowl into something more friendly.

I almost laughed at her. At least she was trying to act like she cared, but I could tell the last thing she wanted was for me to go home and have to cover my shifts for a sixth day.

I knew I'd pushed my luck with her as far as I could. "I'm fine," I assured them. "I feel much better, I promise. I'm here, I might as well work."

Whip seemed like he wanted to argue, but Francine beamed at me. "Thank you, Violet! This is exactly why I'm making you employee of the month. Look."

She pointed at the wall, and to my surprise, I found a photo of myself on it. It was the headshot I'd had taken on my first day for my ID badge, and it wasn't exactly flattering, but she'd taken the time to frame it, and there was a sticker beneath it saying: *Employee of the Month*.

Nyah's photo was on the wall next to mine. I hadn't even noticed the last time I'd been in here. I pointed at it. "You gave Nyah employee of the month too?"

Francine rolled her eyes. "Well, yes, but that was before she up and disappeared without even giving me two weeks' notice, like her contract stated. So in hindsight that was a little premature of me. I've been listening to business podcasts, and I keep hearing that keeping good staff happy is the key to a successful business."

Nyah's photo sat next to the last employee of the month, who was the woman who'd trained me. She'd left barely days after I'd started. And there were no employees of the month in between. So clearly this initiative hadn't exactly been high on Francine's priority list.

But it was the thought that counted, and I could tell she was trying to make an effort to improve morale and her business practices.

Anything so she didn't have to clean toilets herself, I guessed.

Whip studied the wall and then pulled out his phone. "Stand next to it."

"What?" I laughed. "Like I'm one of the kids with their school awards?"

"Exactly like that! We'd take a photo of the kids if they won something. Why wouldn't we do it for you too?"

I glanced at Francine, and she also had her phone out and was shooing me toward the wall.

"Go on, Violet. I'll put it on the Facebook page. My podcasts say social media marketing is also very important for small businesses."

I couldn't deny both of them, so I shuffled over to it and gave them a cheesy smile.

Francine's flash went off, but it was the honest pride on Whip's face that really got to me. I'd never had anyone love me so much they thought I was all that just because my employer had stuck a photo of me up on an outdated wall of honor.

But I knew that if it was him, I would have done exactly the same.

Francine moved back to her desk, muttering curses about technology and why she couldn't find the upload button on her app, and I took the opportunity to step into Whip, who was still grinning up at the stupid photo like I'd just won a Nobel Prize or something.

I dragged him away and pushed him toward the door. "I'd kiss you for being so sweet if I hadn't just puked."

He chuckled and stepped out, his fingers grazing my belly that had absolutely no outward signs of the baby growing inside it. "Have you told the others yet?"

I shook my head.

He nodded, but I could see the pleased uptilt of his lips that he was the first. "I won't say anything. But, Vi, you gotta tell them soon. What are you waiting for?"

I no longer knew. Suddenly I wanted to run home and shout it from the rooftops to every person I knew. I wanted to call my brother and Rebel and Bliss. I wanted to tell old Mrs. Sinterro, who I cleaned for every week. I wanted to get Harold a little shirt that announced he was going to be a big brother.

I couldn't spend my life living in the shadow of the things I'd done to Travis. That would be a life half lived, and I'd already been kept small for too much of this one lifetime I was getting. I couldn't live in the grief of losing Toby, or in the ache that existed without Nyah here to celebrate with.

I wanted to live for the people I did still have. They deserved that.

I deserved it.

I deserved to be happy. "Tonight," I promised him. "I'll tell them all tonight. It's time we had something good to celebrate."

"Violet!" Francine called from inside. "Meeting is starting!"

Whip kissed me quick, his eyes crinkling at the corners with how happy he was. "We're having a baby, Violet."

Yes, we really were.

38

WHIP

I whistled the entire way home, like I was in some sort of Hallmark movie. I couldn't wipe the cheesy grin off my face, and I did a little shoulder shake shimmy as I pulled into my driveway that was very unlike me, but I needed somewhere for the excitement to go.

Levi looked up from where he sat on the front steps and caught the end of it. "What was that?"

"I'm dancing."

"Looked more like you had a mini seizure."

"Fuck you."

He cracked a grin and reached an arm for me. "Come here."

I flipped him the bird and tried to get past him, but he grabbed me and dragged me down on the step next to him.

It didn't take much convincing.

He leaned in, kissing the side of my neck. "You mad at me now?"

"I'm not a teenager. I'm not going to hold a grudge because you don't recognize great dancing when you see it."

Levi sniggered. "No? I figured if you were mad, then I would have to take you inside and blow you until you forgave me."

I raised an eyebrow. "I think I am mad, actually."

Levi pushed to his feet and offered me his hand. "Funny that. Come on, X took the kids to school. We have the house to ourselves for at least five minutes." He glanced over his shoulder at me. "That's all you need, right?"

"You're really trying to pick a fight so we can have make-up sex, huh?" I muttered, though not really insulted because I was pretty sure I had more than proven to him I could get him off in less time than that, even if I did only have five minutes in me.

I'd drag it out today, tease him until he was begging. Just for being a smart-ass.

He was on me as soon as we shut the door. His hands in my hair, his tongue in my mouth, lips on my neck, my face, my chest.

Fingers found zippers, mostly his finding mine, and then he was on his knees, my cock in his mouth, taking every inch.

I leaned back against the wall, groaning at the feel of his warm, wet heat wrapped around me. It felt so freaking good, and yet I found my mind wandering.

I needed to babyproof the kitchen. I didn't one-hundred-percent trust the twins not to get into the chemicals.

I needed a more secure gun safe. Or shit, maybe I

should move it out of the house entirely? With kids here now, things had to change.

Did I even need a gun anymore? I'd never had one when my family was alive. I'd only picked one up the night I'd been so wrecked and filled with grief and loneliness. It had taken me another two days of no sleep and pure, gut-wrenching pain to follow the drunk driver who'd killed my family.

And put a bullet through his head.

Just like that, some of the pain had lifted. It was like I'd passed it onto someone else.

So I'd kept doing it, craving that release with every life I ended, until years had passed and my body count was higher than I cared to think about.

The sex work had been more of the same. With good things in my life again, how toxic my behavior had been really started to sink in. I'd explained it all away with expensive suits and claims I was helping people. When really, all I'd been doing was helping myself.

Going back to killing felt the same as going back to sleeping with random people for money.

I was pretty sure I didn't want to do either anymore.

Unlike X, who I doubted would ever give up his knife, I'd known a life where I didn't need more than the family who lived under this roof.

I had that again.

I had two kids who had needed someone to step up and take care of them, and I had done it without a second thought. I had X and Levi and Violet, all of us under this one roof, nobody complaining it was too small, even though it definitely was. But I was providing that for them. None of us wanted to leave the kids, and so this house that had felt so cold and lonely for the best part of a decade, now felt warm and cozy again.

Levi paused and looked up at me. "You okay?"

I'd almost forgotten what we were doing. "Shit. Yeah, sorry. Fine."

He pushed to his feet. "You aren't into it."

I shook my head, drawing his hand to wrap around my cock. "No, that's not it. I'm just distracted."

He stroked me a few times. "By what?"

A stupid grin spread across my face before I could stop it. I tried to force it down, but I couldn't.

Levi's fingers stopped moving. "Okay, what the fuck is going on? First you're seizing in the driveway—"

"Dancing," I corrected.

"Debatable, but whatever. And now you're off in la-la land. I'm pretty sure you're not thinking about what I was planning to do to you once we're naked and in bed." He squinted at me. "That grin is starting to freak me out."

I couldn't hold it in another second. "Violet's pregnant."

He froze. Not just his hand or his mouth, but a literal full-body freeze, muscles locked tight, eyes not blinking.

X chose that minute to crash through the back door. "Hi, Levi. Hi, Whip." His gaze dipped. "Hi, Whip's cock."

He moved through the kitchen like catching me and Levi in the middle of a blow-hand-job combo was an everyday occurrence. He grabbed a banana from the kitchen counter and peeled it, tossing the skin into the garbage and munching down on the soft fruit.

He frowned, pointing what was left of it at Levi. "What's wrong with him? Levi, you're supposed to stroke his cock. Not just hold it like a dead fish." His nose wrinkled. "I'd show you how but I think we've established I'm not for the butt stuff."

I removed Levi's fingers from around my junk and tucked it back in my underwear.

Levi still didn't move.

I snorted on a laugh and clicked my fingers in front of his face. "Levi. Blink once if you're okay. Blink twice if I need to get medical intervention."

He snapped out of it, but he still stared at me like X wasn't even in the room. "Are you serious?" he whispered.

"Serious about giving you some dick?" X asked around a mouthful of banana. "I think we all know the answer to that."

Levi twisted to look at X like he'd only just realized he was there. "Violet's pregnant."

X's fingers loosened on the banana so much it slipped and landed on the floor. He didn't even try to pick it up. But then he shook his head and laughed. "I'm sorry, I thought you said Violet was pregnant."

Harold meowed from the corner of the room and then darted out from his hiding place between the wall and the couch to pounce on X's dropped food.

"He did," I answered. "She just told me."

X's whoop of glee was the complete and utter opposite of Levi's quiet shock. His shout sent Harold screaming back to his hiding hole, and X chased after him. "Harold! You're going to be a big brother! Again!"

Harold didn't seem to care. He hissed at X and swiped a paw at him in indignation.

X gave up and grinned at us. "This is the best week ever. Two kids. A baby. And a murder!" He sighed dreamily, like those three things were all he'd ever wanted and someone had handed them all to him on a silver platter. "And bonus, I got to see Whip's cock."

I rolled my eyes at him, but it was hard to be a downer when all I could think about was a tiny baby growing in Violet's belly.

And that maybe, just maybe, it was mine.

I squeezed Levi's fingers as X pulled out his phone, claiming he needed to start a new Pinterest board for our baby shower and that he would send a link to us all so we could add to it.

"You okay?" I asked Levi.

He nodded, a little numbly. "It's a lot."

It was. Especially for someone like him who had never really been around kids, nor had expressed any desire to have them. At least he hadn't to me. I didn't know what him and Violet had discussed. "Nobody would blame you if you were freaking out a bit. You had no kids a week ago, and now we have three."

Levi shook his head. "No, it's not that. The idea of Violet pregnant..." He grinned at me. "I was shocked at first, but fuck yes."

I chuckled. "What then?"

He glanced at X. "I'm just trying to work out what a Pinterest board is and what I'm supposed to add to one?"

X busily pinned baby things to his virtual board, with Levi and I both watching on over his shoulder, adding our own suggestions. The three-way debate over strollers was getting heated when a knock came from the front door.

I dragged myself away from our ridiculously overexcited baby planning session and opened it. Dax stood on the other side.

My heart fucking broke for him. He looked completely and utterly destroyed. "Fuck, man. We thought you were out of town, still searching. Come in."

He shook his head.

Levi and X abandoned the laptop and came to join us.

We all just waited for Dax to say something.

"She's dead, isn't she?" he asked. "I've searched everywhere I can think of. I don't know where else to go."

I sighed. "We don't know that for sure."

Anger radiated from him. "Don't bullshit me, Whip!"

Just as quickly as the anger had come, it disappeared. His voice dropped to something barely above a whisper. "Please. Just tell me she's dead so this fucking pain can stop. I can't keep doing this. I need to let her go."

Levi's mouth pulled into a grim line, and he said the kindest words he could have to a man in Dax's situation. "She's dead, Dax."

I winced at the finality in his tone, but I knew what he was doing. Dax was clearly running himself into the ground, searching for the woman he loved. Even though Levi had nothing to go on, other than Travis's word that he'd killed her, he was trying to give Dax some closure.

Dax shook his head miserably, and we all knew Levi's words weren't enough. "I need to see her body."

I opened my mouth to say something, maybe try to convince him that he might never get that. Thousands of people went missing every year, and their loved ones never got that sort of closure.

But Levi was nodding at him. "I know, brother." He glanced at me.

I didn't need his words to know what we needed to do.

We'd already checked the dump site once, when we'd made sure Lynx hadn't left his calling card on those bodies. But there was a gap in the timeline. A couple of days where we'd been in the city, and Travis could have dragged Nyah's body out there. None of us had been there since then, even though we'd talked about it.

But looking at those bodies, and the things he'd done to them, wasn't easy, even for those of us who could take a life without blinking. It had been easy to talk ourselves into doing it later. We had the kids to settle. New jobs to go to. Cooking and shopping and exercise and anything else we could think of to avoid it.

X frowned, clearly also following the silent conversation between me and Levi. "It's not smart to keep going out there. The cops could be watching it."

It was another of our excuses, but one that also rang true. We didn't know who Travis had told about the spot. He had to have followed one of us out there, so others could have too. He could have anonymously reported it to the cops, and they could be biding their time there, just waiting for us to come back and add to the body count. I knew Trig, Ace, and Torch had gotten rid of Travis and Violet's foster parents' bodies at a new site, one well away from where those poor women lay, exposed and decomposing in the elements.

We'd gotten lucky twice. My gut said we may not be as lucky a third time.

But the agony on Dax's face ate away at me. And all I could think was how I would feel if it were Violet.

I picked up my keys. "Come on then. We've only got a few hours until school pickup. We need to go now if we're going."

Levi put his hand to the back of my neck and squeezed it, a silent thank you. X didn't seem as keen, but in typical X fashion, he shrugged it off quickly. "I call shotgun."

Levi and Dax sat in the back of my car, and X filled the silence by yammering about the pros and cons of baby-led weaning, a new term we'd all learned today, courtesy of his Pinterest surfing.

But I didn't miss the worried tapping of his fingers on the center console, and I knew none of us were very happy about where we were going. It felt like beating a dead horse. Like we'd been here, done that. We were all only here for Dax.

Otherwise, I was pretty sure we would have avoided this place forever. Always saying we should, but finding an excuse.

Seeing dead bodies of people who were inherently evil was entirely different from seeing the dead bodies of women who had been beaten and abused and mutilated. But if Nyah had been a late addition to the pile of women Travis had left here, then Dax needed to know, even if it hurt.

Travis had said she was dead.

My gut said he wasn't lying.

We got there as the sun was high. The flies buzzed, and birds and other small animals scattered as we approached.

Dax choked on the horrific stench, but it was nowhere near as bad as that house we'd pulled Ari and Will from. The dead body smell had permeated the walls and the carpets there, and I doubted that would ever be removed. At least out here, there was a breeze to carry the scent of death away.

"Fucking hell." Dax turned away to puke.

He retched, and we let him, knowing he needed it. Even X, with his hate of all bodily functions, didn't complain. Just patted Dax gingerly on the back.

"You okay?" Levi asked eventually.

Dax straightened and nodded, a determination coming over his eyes. "I need to know."

I led the way to the pile of bodies, but nothing seemed different from the last time we'd been here.

"Sick fucking bastard." Levi clenched his fists, staring at the horrific acts these women had endured.

We'd seen it before, but it didn't get any easier to bear.

Last time, I'd looked at their bodies, searching for Lynx's mark. This time, I concentrated on their faces. Their unseeing eyes, their noses, cheeks, mouths. Anything that would identify one of them as Nyah.

I stepped away from the main pile, and my stomach turned. "Fuck."

Levi's head snapped up. His gaze met mine, a silent question hanging in the air between us.

Nyah?

"It's not her. But I know this woman."

Levi and X moved to flank me, and all of us stared down at the body. Her hair had probably been blonde once, but now it was dark, matted with dry blood and dirt. Her dark eyes stared up at the sky, her skin ravaged by the sun and birds and decay.

But I still recognized her face.

X shook his head. "I don't know her."

"Me neither," Levi added.

I couldn't place how I knew her either. But I was sure I did.

Dax picked his way over to us and covered his mouth. "Fuck," he moaned, like he was in physical pain. "I know her too. Her photo is on the wall at Clean Sweep. She was employee of the month. I saw the photos one day when I was early picking Nyah up and she wasn't back from a job yet. Francine let me wait for her."

The jolt of recognition hit me hard. "I saw that photo this morning." My voice dropped to a whisper. "Right next to Nyah's and Violet's."

Levi looked at me sharply. "What the fuck are you talking about?"

My brain couldn't quite catch on quick enough to put the pieces together. "It's their Employee of the Month wall. This woman was on it. Then Nyah's. Then Violet's..."

A sick, churning feeling that was maybe more instinct than anything else clawed its way up my spine. It wrapped around my heart, squeezing it so tight I couldn't breathe.

"This woman. Nyah. Violet. What do they all have in common?" Levi asked quietly.

I swallowed hard. "They all worked for Clean Sweep."

X stared at me. "Where is Violet right now?"

But he already knew the answer. We all did.

"She's with Francine."

39

VIOLET

It was surprising how much better I felt after vomiting. The nausea cleared, and I almost felt like a normal person again. I figured it would come back, if not today, then most definitely tomorrow morning, but the reprieve was nice. I wanted to work. Francine had been so accommodating in letting me have some time off to deal with settling the twins into school and into our lives. The least I could do was make sure I was working when I was feeling good.

She smiled at me from behind her desk. "So, you're pregnant?"

I gave a small laugh. "That obvious, huh?"

"The vomiting and hovering man kind of gave it away."

"It's really new, so we haven't told anyone yet."

Francine nodded like she understood. And I realized I'd never even asked her if she had children of her own.

"Do you have kids, Francine?"

"No. I was never blessed with any. You're a lucky

woman, Violet. Two kids practically delivered to your doorstep. A third growing inside you. You're clearly someone's favorite."

I found myself bristling at the odd description. After everything I'd been through with Toby and Nyah, and my foster parents and Travis, the idea I was one of God's favorites felt ludicrous. And yet I could see how someone might think that, if she was a middle-aged woman with no life partner and had never had the opportunity to have kids.

There was definitely a hint of bitterness in Francine's tone, but I had sympathy for her.

I looked at her and saw the path I could have so easily walked, if X and Levi and Whip hadn't come into my life when they had. They'd changed me. Changed my future. And though I knew that family wasn't everything for a lot of women, and that thousands of them were happily single and childless by choice, that wasn't what I wanted.

Judging from the expression of jealousy on Francine's face, it wasn't what she had wanted either.

The joy of my life wasn't ever going to be my shitty paying cleaning job.

It was in the people waiting at home for me after a shift.

My heart broke for Francine that she didn't have what she so clearly needed.

I tried to be friendly. "How's your new boyfriend going?"

Francine shook her head. "It didn't work out. He didn't want kids."

I grimaced on the inside, wishing I could pull my big

foot out of my mouth. I shouldn't have said anything, I was clearly just making her feel worse.

I was surprised Francine still wanted children though. Maybe she wasn't as old as I'd thought. I'd assumed her to be in her fifties, but maybe she was late forties? I supposed that wasn't too late to adopt. Whip was mid-forties, and it hadn't even crossed my mind that he was too old.

But Francine seemed much older than Whip, even if his hair was completely silver.

"Are the others coming in for the meeting this morning?" I asked, trying to change the subject to anything but our personal lives.

"No. I already sent them out to their jobs." She plucked her keys from the desk. "Come on, I'll drive you to yours."

"Oh!" I peered at her. "I thought we were having a meeting?"

She pointed at my employee photo on the wall, next to Nyah's and the woman who trained me, Elizabeth. "No, I just wanted you to see your photo up there."

"I really appreciate you choosing me. That means a lot. I take so much pride in my work, so it's lovely to be recognized." I did feel a bit bad for the guys though. They had worked for Francine longer than either me or Nyah had, and neither of them had their photos up there.

But I wasn't going to question it. That would seem ungrateful.

"You really don't need to drive me though. I'm fine to walk or hop on the bus if you give me the address."

Francine collected her purse and shooed me toward the door. "Nonsense. You're pregnant now, Violet. You need to take better care of yourself. The house I have you scheduled for is big and I'll need to help you with it. I would have scheduled someone else to go with you if I'd known about your condition—"

There it was again, the hint of bitterness.

Awkward embarrassment crept up my neck. "I can handle it."

But she just picked up her cleaning caddy and nudged me out the door so she could lock it behind us.

Well, this was going to be a fun day.

We piled into her white hatchback that smelled vaguely of cigarette smoke. I rolled the window down a little, claiming fresh air helped the nausea.

And then wanted to punch myself in the face again when the space between Francine's eyes pinched.

I'd clearly been hanging out with X too long. I'd officially stuck my foot in it way too many times, and I needed to give up speaking altogether.

Francine seemed to appreciate that. The silence in the car would have been unbearable if it hadn't been for the hum of the engine and the mindless chatter of the radio DJ. I stared out the window, watching the streets of Saint View pass by, not really paying attention to where we were since Francine was navigating and seemed to know exactly where to go without turning on the car's GPS.

She was right. This pregnancy probably would slow me down and limit the sorts of jobs I could take on, especially as I came into the final months. I would need to get a car somehow. I couldn't drag two children and a baby around on buses for the rest of my life.

A car like Francine's might be good. I gazed around it, considering how much room there was in the back seat.

"What are you looking for?" Francine's tone was sharp, her fingers white-knuckling the steering wheel.

I glanced at her tense jaw and knew exactly what I wasn't going to tell her. Saying I was checking out her car to see if there was room for my family was definitely off the table.

I tittered out a laugh. "Just making sure I picked up new sponges for my caddy."

Francine said nothing, and I had a feeling she knew I was lying.

Why was this drive taking so long?

As soon as she stopped the car in front of a house somewhere on the border of Saint View and Providence, I got out, grabbing my things from the back seat and piling them up into my arms before Francine could tell me not to.

I hurried toward the front door, rapping my knuckles across the wood while Francine followed more slowly behind me.

There was no noise from within, and I peered back at Francine coming up the path with a mop in her hand. "Did the owners say they wouldn't be home?"

She nodded. "There's a key beneath the mat."

I bent and lifted it, finding the single silver key beneath and fitting it to the lock. Juggling my supplies and purse in one hand, I pushed through the doorway, calling out loudly, "Cleaning!" just in case someone was actually home and just hadn't heard my knock.

A noise came back, and I stopped, just inside the large living area. "Hello?"

The noise came again.

Not a person calling back from the kitchen or one of the upstairs bedrooms. It was a weak moan.

One filled with pain and terror.

Hairs on the back of my neck stood up. My fingers trembled. My body reacting to the situation before my brain could even comprehend what I'd walked into.

A teddy bear sitting on the bookshelf caught my eye.

I spun around.

Francine stood in the doorway; a gun pointed right at my belly.

I shook my head, backing up a step. "Francine?"

Her eyes were dull. Her mouth twisted in a line. "Three..." She whispered. "Two..."

My entire body screamed *no*. My brain shut down.

I was back in that warehouse. Back on the bluffs.

Back at the mercy of a madman.

Or a madwoman.

I clutched my arms around my belly, like that might save my baby from a bullet. On instinct, I stepped back, away from the gun.

The mechanical whirr was all I heard before I fell, my body hitting a cold, hard floor beneath. Pain registered for only the briefest of seconds, then my head met stone and the entire world went peacefully black.

"Vi! Violet!"

My head splintered, my brain rattling from side to side. I winced at the sound of my name, even though the person saying it was clearly trying to be quiet.

I blinked my eyes open groggily and did a double take at the woman kneeling over me.

A sob rose up my throat so quick I had no chance of holding it back.

Tears poured down my face, and I shook my head, even though it only made it hurt more. "No," I moaned miserably. "No."

"Violet!" Nyah whisper-shouted again, her voice hoarse.

I clutched her fingers. They were cold, but she squeezed me back tight.

Why did she feel so real? Was it me who was dead? Confusing thoughts fluttered around my brain, none of them sticking long enough to become clear in the fog. "You're dead," I whispered.

She brought her face closer to mine. So close I could smell her, though she didn't smell like the Nyah I knew. The Nyah I'd known had smelled of pretty, delicate perfumes that had always reminded me of fruit and summer.

This version of Nyah smelled like dirt and sweat and worse.

My nausea came back full force, and it seemed cruel that if I was dead, I was still suffering with morning sickness.

"Not dead," she practically whispered. "Though I have wished I was, more than once." Her voice caught on a sob, and she pulled my head onto her lap. "I'm so scared."

I couldn't keep up. I had no idea where we were or why she was shaking so bad. All I knew was I wanted to comfort her, and that I'd missed her, and if she wasn't dead then maybe neither was I. I turned onto my side and hugged her around her middle, my face pressing into her belly.

And the tiny bump there.

I glanced up at her. "Nyah? Are you pregnant?"

A tear spilled down her cheek, and she covered her belly with her hand, hiccupping on a sob. She shook her head sadly. "I don't know. I was...I missed two periods, so I did a test the morning I came here." She wrapped her fingers around mine and squeezed them. "But I'm bleeding."

"Oh God, Nyah." I squeezed my eyes shut and clutched my stomach. "I'm pregnant too."

She stared down at me, her bottom lip trembling as she stroked my damp hair back away from my face. "Oh, Vi. That's wonderful."

I struggled to sit up. It was only wonderful if we were alive.

I blinked in the darkness, trying to adjust my eyes, but the only slivers of light that came were from little splinters of sun piercing through the wooden floorboards above our heads.

I stared at them, completely unable to make sense of any of it. "Where are we?"

Nyah bit her lip and opened her mouth to answer, but the floor, the one over our heads, slid open.

Francine stared down at us.

All of it came rushing back. Francine bringing me here. The gun at my back. Falling...

I tried to stand, but pain kept me down. It wouldn't have mattered anyway. Francine was at least ten feet above us, and even at almost six feet myself, I knew I would have never been able to pull myself up and out, even if she'd stood there and let me.

We were completely at her mercy.

"Why?" I whispered to her.

She squatted on the edge of the hole and cocked her head to one side. "Didn't your mama ever teach you to keep your man happy?"

I blinked, those words not at all what I had expected her to say. "I didn't have a mother."

She snorted and leaned the tip of her gun to the floorboards beneath her feet as she stared down at us at the bottom of the trap she'd laid. "You're lucky. I unfortunately did." Her voice turned high-pitched and mocking. "You'll never keep a man with your hair like that, Francine. Francine, why don't you put some more makeup on, cover up some of that ugly? Francine, if you just lost some weight, you'd be so much more attractive to men."

I flinched at the familiar words. I might not have had a mother, but I'd had a foster mom who had said much the same things. "I know what—"

Francine cut me off with a sharp laugh. "Don't tell me you know what that feels like, Violet. You have so many men falling all over you, you can't even keep up."

I nodded, not stupid enough to argue with the woman with the gun, who clearly didn't want to hear the truth. "Skinny girls are what men want, Francine," she mocked. "Not girls who look like they could eat a man whole."

If I hadn't been lying at the bottom of an oversized coffin, I might have felt sorry for her. Her mother sounded like a piece of work. "She shouldn't have said that to you. It's not true."

But Francine laughed bitterly. "But it is true, Violet. You don't know it yet, but they'll leave. Those men, they'll leave you. No matter what you do." Her eyes darkened. "I did everything. Everything he wanted. And he still left."

I glanced at Nyah.

Her mouth pulled into a grim line; her gaze trained on that gun in Francine's hands.

I didn't know what to do, other than to keep her talking. To give the guys time to find me.

Because unlike whoever Francine was talking about, I knew my guys were never leaving. The realization, the strength of that knowledge, fueled me, pushing away some of the fear.

I wasn't that girl back in Paul Jeddersen's house on Olympic Drive. I wasn't the girl in the warehouse. I wasn't the girl on the bluffs.

I wasn't alone.

They would come.

"Who left, Francine?" I asked, voice clear and strong.

She stared at me. "Paul. I sent him girls. Watched him have sex with them. Watched him…" She shook her head. "I did everything he wanted, and he still left."

My blood ran cold. "You sent me to Paul Jeddersen's house, knowing he was going to rape and kill me?"

Francine shrugged. "You. Elizabeth. The women before. I kept their bodies for him. But it was never enough, was it? He always wanted more." She sniffed. "I just wanted him."

Bile rose in my throat, anger stirring up from deep inside me. That same anger I'd felt the night I'd killed

Travis. "He didn't leave you," I hissed. "We murdered him."

In reality, it had been X's kill, but in the moment, it didn't feel like it mattered.

Francine pointed the gun at me. "You think I didn't know that? You think I didn't watch the entire thing happen? You took him from me, Violet!" She laughed bitterly. "So I took something from you."

"Toby," I supplied for her.

Francine nodded. "With a bit of help. I wanted to go after all of you. Everyone who was there that night. Everyone who helped cover up Paul's murder. Everyone who had ever meant anything to you. I knew all about your men and their little murder squad. They laid it all out for me, all the details of the list. I have it all on the fucking nanny cam Paul made me watch through."

My stomach twisted at the thought of someone having video of X killing a man in cold blood in the most violently brutal way. "Why not just go to the police and have him arrested?"

"Because you were all to blame!" She pointed the gun at me again. "You most of all, you slut. But if I'd taken that footage to the cops, they would have said, oh poor Violet. Wouldn't they? And you would have walked away, scot-free!"

I didn't understand her twisted ramblings. The lies she'd let herself believe.

"I was a victim, Francine." I cleared my throat. "Maybe you were too."

"No, don't try to make me feel sorry for you. You were a slut, with your pretty blond hair and big blue eyes. I saw the way he stared at you. Saw the way he stripped your clothes and touched your body."

My skin crawled at the memory. "He attacked me. I didn't want him."

"But I did," she said miserably. "I wanted him, and you took him from me. So I have to take everything away from you. I zoomed in on the footage of your little list, made out as many names on it as I could, and then tracked them all down. Offered them all a bribe to take you all out, one by one. Not that I had to incentivize them much, considering they weren't too happy to hear they were targets themselves. They were more than happy to turn the tables and come for you. I just added some theatrics to the game, writing rhymes, making sure you knew you were being hunted."

I let my anger get the better of me, remembering the men who'd stalked X in the darkness. He'd avoided death only because he was skilled and because Levi and Whip had his back. We'd known someone was paying people on the list to come after us.

But I never would have expected it to be the woman perched above us now, staring down at us with hate and malice in her eyes. "That's how you met Travis, isn't it?" I asked. "Travis never made the booking for Paul Jeddersen's place or for Nyah to come to this house, did he? That was you. You just threw him under the bus when you realized we were getting close to working it out." I shook my head. "And we killed him for it." Not that I felt an ounce of regret over it. He might not have made those bookings and lured Nyah and me into houses where danger lurked on the other side of the front door, but he was hardly innocent. There was no guilt. I'd seen the haunted look in my daughter's eyes after she'd been left alone with that man for days.

The world was a better place with Travis dead.

Francine's mouth flattened into an angry line. "Don't say his name."

I raised an eyebrow. "Why not? You don't want me to speak ill of the dead?"

"Vi!" Nyah clutched my arm.

I knew I was being wild and reckless, antagonizing the woman. And yet I was so angry. So deeply, bitterly hurt. So fucking over people underestimating me because I was the fat, ugly, gentle girl who never made a fuss and never wanted to be seen.

Levi, Whip, and X had seen me anyway.

Will and Ari had seen the good in me, even when I'd stabbed and killed a man right in front of them.

This baby growing inside me would never hear me call it fat or ugly or useless.

I wasn't going to stand here and let Francine walk all over me. If she was going to kill me then she would, but I wouldn't go down being scared.

I wouldn't go down without a fight.

"Travis was a piece-of-shit rapist and murderer, Francine. But you already knew that when you tracked him down, didn't you? You knew that's why he was on the list." It wasn't really a question. More of an accusation.

"He was a genius," she hissed.

"He was a high-school dropout who killed cats for fun."

She shook her head. "He rigged that warehouse perfectly, just like I asked him to. He planted those explosives on the cliffs. He created this trap for you to fucking rot in, you stupid bitch! Is it familiar? He said it's just like the one your foster parents kept him in when you were kids. The one you never let him out of."

I'd known nothing about that until Travis had mentioned it the night we'd killed him. Though I didn't doubt it.

I also knew, if I had known I wouldn't have let him out, only for him to peep on me in the shower, torment me, hurt me.

The gun in Francine's fingers shook, but something in her words clicked puzzle pieces together in my head.

She might have delivered me on a silver platter to Paul and Travis. She might have watched it all through the nanny cams.

But the kills weren't hers.

She had helped facilitate them. She'd written the rhymes. The one he'd uttered that night in the park before we'd followed him back to our childhood home had never sat right with me. I remembered thinking at the time that they hadn't sounded like his words.

Francine had blood on her hands, no doubt, but she'd never actually pulled the trigger herself.

Judging from the way her entire body shook right now, she knew she couldn't.

"You took Travis from me too," she whispered. "We were supposed to be together. We were a team."

Oh, that was rich. "You don't really believe that, do you? He strung you along, let you write your letters, made you think he needed you when all he really wanted was for you to supply him with girls to rape and kill. Just like Paul did. I bet he got real excited when he realized it was me whose life you wanted to ruin. I'll give you that, you had that in common. Is that what you bonded over?" I curled my lip at her in disgust. "But your mother was right, Francine. Men like Paul and Travis will never love you. Men like them don't know how to love anyone. That's really why you're mad right now, isn't it? It's not at me, or Levi or Whip or X. You hate yourself for believing their lies when really you knew better."

I knew I was right when a tear dripped from her eye, splattering on the dirt floor beneath me. She swiped at her face with rough, jerky motions to prevent it happening again.

"What's your plan here, Francine?" I asked. "If you'd been able to kill, you would have already killed Nyah a week ago, am I right? Clearly you were happy to drug her because otherwise the guys would have found her when they checked this house out after you gave us the address. But this is a much nicer neighborhood than Saint View. The neighbors would have called the cops if they'd heard shouting. You would have had to keep her quiet while you were at work somehow."

Nyah's exhausted, raspy voice lent itself to my theory. "My brain is so foggy," she whispered. "But how... She never came down here. I don't think..."

I remembered the lovely case of food poisoning X had given us. Whatever Francine had given Nyah to keep her quiet, she'd probably put it in her food.

It only deepened the theory that Francine could be an accomplice but not a murderer. I stared up at her. "I know you aren't going to pull that trigger."

She laid the gun down on the edge of the trapdoor. "You're right. I can't kill you."

I nodded. "So just let us go." I reached a hand toward

her. "Just grab my hand and help us out, and this will all be over."

For a split second, I thought she was going to agree.

But then the hurt and anger disappeared from her features, and she was no longer the broken shell of a woman Travis and Paul and her mother had turned her into.

She was something far more dangerous. She blinked and then laughed. "Oh, Violet. Sweet, sweet Violet. You misunderstand. I can't kill you now. You or Nyah. Hasn't she told you all about the nice food and drinks I've been giving her? Hasn't she told you about all the prenatal vitamins?"

I couldn't tear my eyes away from Francine to look in Nyah's direction to confirm if any of that was true.

Francine's voice was practically a snarl when she leaned down once more, her beady eyes staring into mine. "I don't care about Paul or Travis or any man. Not anymore. I gave up on that when Travis said he was done with me." She cocked her head to one side, her gaze dropping to my belly. "All I want now is a family, Violet. Children. And you and Nyah are going to give me yours."

40

———

LEVI

I leaned forward in the passenger seat, my foot pressed hard to the floor like there was an accelerator there, or like the tilt of my body would somehow make Whip's car move faster.

"We're too far away." Anxious anticipation raced around in my blood, my heart beating too fast. "She's been there for hours."

Whip, ever the voice of reason, kept his voice calm and low. "And she's been with Francine many other times and nothing has happened."

"Yeah, but her face wasn't on the creepy wall of death before either," X said bluntly from the back seat.

I shot X a pointed look.

At least we had hope Violet was still alive.

I was fairly sure Dax's hope had completely run out.

X cringed and patted his shoulder awkwardly. "Uh, not wall of death. Just a regular old run-of-the-mill Employee of the Month wall. Definitely has no bearing on who Francine the Freak decides to kill that day..."

I sighed heavily.

"What?" X asked. "I'm being comforting."

"You're making it worse."

"I use humor as a coping mechanism, Levi. If you prefer, I could do Whip's cold and grumpy thing." He put on his best wise old man voice. "Listen here, sonny. I've been doing rescues since before you were born, and I'll be doing them long after you're dead. Now pass me my orthopedic sneakers."

Whip glanced back at X. "When have I *ever* sounded like that?"

He shrugged. "Or how about I do Levi's snarly angry prison-man thing?"

"This'll be fun," I muttered, willing the car to go faster, not just because I wanted to get to Violet, but because X was making me want to murder something.

He ignored me. His voice turned gruff, apparently in imitation of mine. "Here's the plan! Kick in every door, glare at everyone until they wet themselves, and then maybe punch a few walls for dramatic effect. That's how we *communicate*." He tapped me on the shoulder. "How'd I do? I think I really committed to the part at the end there."

I couldn't listen to it anymore. I pulled out my phone and jabbed my finger against the screen so hard it hurt. "I'm calling Fang and War and Hawk and anyone else fucking close enough to do something." I stabbed the screen again, anger spearing through me when the stupid thing did nothing. "Fuck! Open, you bastard!"

"Ah yes," X said like he was David fucking Attenborough. "Here we see the male of the angry prison-man species, attempting to make a phone call while in full rage mode. As you can see, he is not a very smart animal. If only he knew if he just calmed his tits and unlocked the phone gently, it would allow him to make contact with others of his species."

I finally got my pin code in correctly and hit call on Fang's number. I turned around and hissed at X, "If she's dead—"

"She's not fucking dead," X warned in a voice that sent chills down my spine, with eyes suddenly so dark it was like he was possessed.

I was instantly reminded that although he was an idiot ninety-five percent of the time, he was also capable of snapping a man's neck with no remorse.

And that was something to be respected.

I pressed my lips together and nodded. "She's not dead."

He went back to golden retriever mode and grinned like we were just out on a Sunday drive and not speeding toward Saint View on a rescue mission. "Do you think we'll be able to get Violet back before school pickup? I promised the kids donuts."

I left Whip to answer that question because Fang's voice was saying hello in my ear.

"Fang. I need you to go to Clean Sweep and see if Violet or her boss, Francine, are there."

To Fang's credit, or maybe to the credit of the friendship that had existed between us for fifteen years, he didn't question me. He stayed on the phone until a moment later, I heard the roar of his bike, and then the call cut out.

I called War next, then Hawk, then dropped the

phone onto the floor at my feet and buried my face in my hands.

Whip's fingers found the back of my neck and squeezed it. "Just breathe, okay? Fang will call back in a minute."

But a minute could be too long, when every second felt like it lasted a year, and every tick of the clock could mean the difference between Violet walking away from this alive or us finding her dead and bleeding out somewhere.

I looked over at Whip miserably. "She's fucking pregnant."

Whip's fingers tightened in the tense muscles in the back of my neck. "I know. It'll be okay."

But he didn't know that. Couldn't promise that by the time we found her she'd still be breathing.

All I could see in my mind was the night we'd found her covered in blood.

I was so fucking scared this time, it would be hers.

My phone rang, and I jumped like it had electrocuted me. I scooped it up from the floor with trembling fingers and answered. "Fang. Tell me you have her."

Fang's voice was grim on the other end. "There's nobody here. The Clean Sweep car is gone too. We sent the prospects over to Violet's apartment, but nothing there either."

Whip's calm voice pierced through the screaming in my head. "Ask him if he can see a roster there anywhere. They might just be at a job. We need to check the obvious first before we jump to the—"

Fang interrupted him. "I heard him. We already checked the roster hanging on the wall, but all the jobs on today have a red cross through them. War is calling around to the owners of the houses that were scheduled, but so far, all of them have said Francine cancelled the jobs."

Well, that blew any ideas that Francine hadn't planned this all out perfectly. I put Fang on speaker so everyone in the car could hear. "What the fuck do we do now?"

Fang was silent. Whip's foot lifted on the accelerator, and the car slowed.

I wanted to scream at him to keep going. That we had to get to her.

But none of us knew where the hell to look.

"Hey, Siri? Take us to 1705 Fire Ridge Way," X called from the back seat, then he swore under his breath. "Damn, there's a really good burger bar just down the road. I hope we have time to stop there on the way home. Did you know they have the world record for the most barbecued pork ribs consumed in an hour? Says it right here on their web—"

"X!" Whip snapped. "Why the fuck are we going to Fire Ridge Way? We already checked that house. There was nothing there."

X blinked like that had been a dumb question. He held up his phone and spoke in his David Attenborough voice again. "When the male of the species has calm breasts, he can navigate thought quite well. When he is filled with an impeccable sense of humor and model good looks, as well as brains for days, he can make many a deduction." He dropped his fake accent and picked up his regular one. "They're not at Clean Sweep or their cleaning jobs or Violet's apartment or Francine's house. I figured if that house was good enough to lure Nyah in, then she might do the same with Violet. Where the hell else would she go to murder someone in the middle of the day? She's not going to do it out in broad daylight. What other stomping grounds does she have? The bluffs are crowded with hikers and families at this time of day. She wouldn't be able to lure Violet to the warehouse again, or to the house on Olympic Drive. The only place Francine has that Violet hasn't been to is that house on Fire Ridge Way."

"The only other house we *know* of," Whip muttered.

He was right. Maybe Francine had other places she could go. But we had to check all the obvious places first.

We were only a few streets away from the address, according to the GPS on the dash. Our little green dot moved faster as he put his foot down on the accelerator again.

Whip turned the corner, into the barely familiar street the three of us had checked no more than a week ago. Had we missed something? The place had been spotless, not a speck of dust out of place.

My stomach twisted in knots at the sight of Francine's car sitting outside the house. That had definitely not been there the last time we'd visited. It was in a nicer part of Saint View, where the houses were old but bigger than the shit shacks the government put up as low-income housing. We were closer to the Providence border than the center of town where the Clean Sweep offices were. It would take Fang and the others fifteen minutes to get over here.

I wasn't waiting that long.

Whip drove past the house and parked a few doors

down. I yanked on the door handle the second he stopped the car.

X was out just as quick, Whip and Dax a second later.

X led the way back down the street but stopped suddenly well before the house, lifting his arm at a right angle, his fist clenched.

I ran smack into his back. "Ow, Jesus, X! What the hell are you doing?"

"That's the sign to stop! Haven't you ever watched a cop show? The SWAT leader puts his hand up like this, and his men all freeze behind him until he says it's safe to go on."

"Well, maybe you should have told me that before I practically bowled you over!"

"As your captain, I object to your tone, Soldier!"

I rolled my eyes. "So sorry, Captain Crunch."

X grinned. "I like that. You can be Sargeant Sassy Pants, and Whip, you can be Drill Sargeant Daddy." He winked. "But if I hear Levi say, 'Drill me, Daddy,' there will be consequences. Dax, you can be...actually, I don't know you well enough to give you a code name, sorry. You're just Dax."

Dax looked completely baffled.

Clearly, he hadn't been around X long enough to know this was completely typical X behavior, and I suspected his verbal diarrhea was a very real reaction to stress. But he could unpack that with Grayson later.

"Drill Sargeant Daddy—" I shook my head and sighed. "I mean *Whip* and Dax can cover the rear."

"That's what he said." X sniggered.

I sighed heavily. "And you and I can create a distraction at the front. That work for a plan?"

It was as good as any. I just needed to get in there. If this woman had hurt Violet, she was dead. I'd wring her scrawny neck, twisting it like one of Grayson's balloon animals if she had so much as touched one hair on Violet's head.

I blinked at the thought.

X might have had a point about my angry prison-man persona.

Whip and Dax jogged through the neighbor's yard, and I hoped they didn't find dogs once they jumped the fence. And the owners were at work or something and not perfecting their tans in their backyards.

X looked at me. "If she watched the whole thing that happened at Paul Jeddersen's house, she's going to know my pizza delivery act. That won't work. Got any other ideas we can use as a distraction?"

I didn't know and I didn't care. I couldn't wait another second to get in that house. The anticipation was killing me.

X trotted up the path after me, and I forced myself not to slam my fist against the door. Instead I knocked politely, and X raised an eyebrow at me, a silent, "You went in without a plan, so you better come up with something quick," expression in his eyes. Knowing he was right, I screwed my face up and called, "Hello? We'd like to talk to you about your car's extended warranty..."

I was pretty sure I would be hearing X's laughter in my nightmares.

41

VIOLET

Francine had dropped her bomb about taking our babies and then locked us back in the darkness. It pressed in like it had weight, the air down here already stale and sour.

I clutched Nyah's fingers, still trying to convince myself she was alive and not just a figment of my imagination. The daylight barely filtered through the cracks in the floorboards, but it was enough to see the dullness in her dark eyes.

I rubbed my thumb across the back of her hand. "Have you been down here this entire time?"

"Yes." Her whisper barely carried over the sound of my heartbeat. She wrinkled her nose, and when she spoke again, her voice was a tiny bit louder. "As you can probably smell. She brings food and water. Changes the piss bucket occasionally. But it's not exactly a five-star stay." She sniffed and tried to laugh at herself. "I'll be leaving a very poor one-star Yelp review."

I would have laughed if the sadness hadn't been breaking my damn heart.

I put my arm around her shoulders and drew her close, feeling her shudder as she hugged me back. I didn't care how bad she smelled. Only that she was alive. "We've been searching for you," I swore to her. "Me, Whip, X, and Levi. And Dax."

She lifted her head, her tears shining in her eyes. "Dax? I figured he would have just assumed I ghosted him."

I shook my head and laughed, just a little. "I think he might be in love with you."

She breathed out a long, slow breath. "I hope he isn't."

"Why would you say that? I know you love him too. I'm pretty sure you told me you were in love with him the very first day you met him."

"And look at the hurt and danger I've already brought into his life in just a few weeks. I should have listened to my father when he told me I could run but never hide from him for long."

She wasn't being fair to herself.

"None of this has anything to do with your family," I assured her.

"Maybe not. But if it hadn't been Francine hunting me down and locking me away, it would have been one of my father's enemies. And if it hadn't been them, then it would have been my father himself. I was free on borrowed time only, and I knew it. I had no business starting something up with a man like Dax." She sighed heavily. "He's so good and sweet and kind. He has a regular, run-of-the-mill job and comes from a normal family. His life and mine are worlds apart, and I was kidding myself, hoping I could live in his, even for a little while."

I hated the sadness in her tone. "I don't think you get to choose who you fall in love with."

She shrugged. "I guess. But it doesn't really matter, does it? It ends with a broken heart, either way."

The helplessness and despair radiated from her, and I couldn't blame her. How many days had she been down here? How many weeks? I couldn't remember, everything since she'd gone missing had become a blur.

But I needed her to rally. Needed her to have hope. We weren't dying in this goddamn hole. We were getting out.

My eyes adjusted enough to make out the shapes in the gloom—our knees drawn up, the jagged seams of floorboards above us, and the cleaning caddy that had been in my hand when I'd walked inside. It had come down into the hole with me. The handle was cracked, one side bent out of shape. Supplies spilled across the compacted dirt floor, rags and spray bottles and scrubbers.

"Bleach," I breathed, nodding toward the white bottle tipped on its side.

Nyah's face turned toward me, teeth flashing faintly. "You want to do some cleaning while you're down here? I think that red warning label would advise not to use in enclosed spaces." She poked the bottle with her foot. "I know the piss bucket smells grim, but pretty sure this does not count as a well-ventilated area."

"If we could get her close enough, we could spray her in the face with it though. You said she brings you food and changes the bucket. So she has to get close at least once a day, right?"

Nyah peered up at the floorboards, a good distance above our heads. "She lowers everything down on a rope."

But I wasn't going to be deterred that easily. The pit was deep beneath the house, there was no doubt about that. It had clearly been dug with the intention of keeping grown adults in. The walls seemed to have been reinforced with whatever they'd been able to find—bits of wood and steel, all things easily found on any construction site.

"Did I ever tell you I did cheerleading in high school?"

She raised an eyebrow. "You don't strike me as a pom-pom, fake-smile sorta girl."

I half smiled at that. "Toby made me do it. But point is, I could boost you up." I studied the mechanical bits and pieces someone had rigged up beneath the floor. "We'd just have to time it right so you go up right as she opens it."

Nyah looked doubtful. "And if she's not bending down?"

I could admit that was a fault in the plan. "Then I guess she'll get bleach spots on her socks."

Nyah snort-laughed at that. "That'll teach her!"

I dissolved into giggles as well. Despite the situation, I was so damn glad to have her back. "I've missed you."

She bit her bottom lip, and her eyes filled with tears again. "I missed you too. So much."

I wasn't willing to die down here and lose the first female friend I'd ever truly made. I'd loved Toby with every beat of my heart. He'd been my person. But he'd also been my crutch. I'd clung to him in a way that wasn't healthy because I'd had nobody else.

This friendship with Nyah felt different. It felt like something I wanted to hang on to and cherish. Something that would last, if only given a chance. She might have fallen in love with Dax at first sight, but I think a part of me had recognized her as a soul mate at first sight as well. I didn't love her the way I loved Whip and X and Levi, but there was a connection there that felt important.

"Okay, we need a plan B then." I leaned forward, groping around in the dirt, sorting through the things that had been in my cleaning caddy. Why the hell hadn't I packed a pocket knife in there? Or better yet, a gun. Maybe a ladder to climb out of this freaking prison hole.

My fingers closed around a stiff piece of plastic from the broken handle. "Plastic can get sharp," I whispered, scared Francine had her ear to the floor above us, listening to every word.

Nyah offered up a suggestion of her own. "There's a big rock over here. Maybe we could dig it out and throw it at her."

I grinned at her, not hopeful in the plan, but happy there was a little fight in her expression again. "Or we could try breaking this plastic up against it. Maybe seeing if we can sharpen it on the rock."

Nyah nodded and scuttled onto her knees.

I pressed the broken plastic to the rock until it gave with a brittle *crack*. Shock punched through me when I came away with a jagged spear, crude and barely longer than my palm but perhaps sharp enough to do some damage if it caught a person somewhere soft or vital.

Excitement replaced some of the fear circling around inside me.

The same feeling I'd had when I'd taken Travis's life.

If Nyah noticed I was having a psychotic daydream, she didn't comment on it.

She took the plastic weapon, turning it over in her hands, then looked up at me, clearly just as shocked as I was. "That tip is really kind of sharp. This could actually work."

She went to give it to me, but I pushed it back into her palm. "Hold on to it. I'm going to try—"

A banging on the front door cut me off. "We'd like to talk to you about your car's extended warranty!"

I frowned.

Nyah widened her eyes. "Is that X?"

But I knew my guys, and even though that was a very X thing to say, I'd recognize Levi's voice anywhere. "Levi!" I screamed. "Help!"

Nyah instantly joined me, her voice much weaker but screaming Levi's name, even though her voice was hoarse. "Please! We're down here!"

I had no idea if they could hear us. There were gaps in the floorboards, so I wasn't worried about running out of air, but I had no idea if our shouts would carry far enough for Levi to hear while he was standing outside the door.

I opened my mouth to scream that we were beneath the house, when a darkly taunting voice filtered through the gaps.

"Come through my door and you'll dance with the dead,
The floor's full of teeth and they're hungry for red.
Stay where you stand if you value your skin,

One wrong little step and you'll see I win."

Nyah froze, clutching my arm with trembling fingers.

But I'd heard that voice before. Heard the robotic, distorted sound of its threats.

And this time, I heard Francine speaking into the voice changer as well.

Travis might have been the brawn. He might have been the one who'd built this prison, who'd rigged explosives and traps.

But Francine was the brain. It was her twisted mind who'd come up with these games to torture us for taking away the man she'd loved.

Were we really so different? Wouldn't I have completely lost my mind if someone had murdered Whip or X or Levi? Wouldn't I have hunted them down and made them pay?

I could have so easily walked in Francine's shoes.

Except I would have never sent young women to a predator's home so he could rape and murder them. And Levi, X, and Whip would have never asked me to.

We were not the same.

Francine repeated the message, and I heard it in both places, from her, standing somewhere above our heads, and through speakers I was sure Levi, X, and Whip could hear from outside.

"Come through my door and you'll dance with the dead,
The floor's full of teeth and they're hungry for red.
Stay where you stand if you value your skin,
One wrong little step and I win, I win."

"What does that mean?" Nyah asked in a whisper.

"It means she knew this would happen. She knew they'd come. And she wants them dead." My shouts for help turned into warnings. "Don't come in here! This place is trapped!"

But it was too late for them to hear me. Somewhere above me, something exploded, the crack like a hundred tiny bullets whizzing through the air and finding a resting place somewhere vital

Whip's scream of pain echoed back to me, and my blood ran cold.

I clutched Nyah's arm, probably hurting her with my fingernails digging into her skin, but I couldn't breathe.

Thumps of footsteps on the steps confused me, shouts and swearing, and above it all, more howls of pain.

And that robotic voice, that warning that played on a loop, threatening and ominous.

I knew what came next. How long would it be before a countdown started?

"Francine!" I screamed. "Francine!"

The hatch above our heads slid open. "What!" she snapped. "Quit yelling. They can't get to you. The entire house is surrounded by traps. Ones that clearly work as intended if your man's hollering was anything to go by."

Her eyes were wild, unfocused.

Nyah clutched the sharpened piece of plastic, but what the hell were we going to do with that when she was nowhere near us? In the same vein, I held the bottle of bleach.

Francine's gaze strayed to it, and a cruel smile twisted her mouth. She gave a bitter laugh. "What are you going to do with that, Violet? Spray me in the face?" She snorted a derisive laugh. "Terrible plan, but I like the gumption. This is exactly why we let you go, that night in the warehouse." She shook her head. "Travis didn't want to. He said we should just kill you then and there, but a deal is a deal, right? And I liked your spark. You remind me of myself."

Despite the fact I'd been grappling with the same idea, hearing it on her lips cemented it wasn't true. "I'm nothing like you," I snarled back. "You used your business to feed young women to predators. How many women did you do it to, Francine? It was more than just me and Nyah and Elizabeth, wasn't it? How many women did you help Paul Jeddersen murder? How many did you help Travis murder? How much blood is on your hands?"

Francine sat on the edge of the hatch, legs dangling down into the hole, though still far enough above our heads that we couldn't touch her. "I can't remember all their names."

"But you remember their faces, don't you? Because you watched Paul Jeddersen kill them on that nanny cam."

More shots pierced the air, more screams. My heart thudded against my chest.

My guys were out there, fighting a war I couldn't see to get to me. And there was literally nothing I could do about it.

Nothing other than keep Francine talking. And keep Nyah and myself alive.

Francine's eyes narrowed, and she shifted, waving her hand around, as if my question had agitated her.

She had the gun in her hand again, but it clearly wasn't the one being used to shoot at my men.

"I remember every single one of their faces," Francine

admitted. "And I remember the way he touched them like he loved them. Remember the way he made me keep their bodies so he could look at them whenever he wanted to."

"Oh God. I'm going to be sick," Nyah whispered.

I couldn't blame her. My stomach twisted into painful knots. "How could you?"

Her eyes narrowed. "He loved me! That's what you do for someone you love, Violet! You do things to make them happy! To make sure they stay!" A tear dripped down her face, and her voice softened just a little. "I just wanted him to stay."

I would have felt sorry for her if the things she'd done hadn't been so horrific. I understood what it felt like to be unloved. To feel like you had nobody in your life who cared. Nobody who wanted to stick around and stand by your side.

But Francine was sick and twisted and just as much to blame for the deaths of countless women as the men she'd claimed to love were.

"You took them from me. Paul. Then Travis. You took them both," Francine whispered. "You owe me, Violet. You owe me a family."

"I owe you nothing."

She laughed. "And yet your men are out there, dying one by one trying to save you. I warned them not to try to come in here, but they didn't listen. That's the universe, Violet. That's the universe punishing you because you stole what was mine."

Bile rose in my throat. I could hear the shouts and the thumps and the pain all around but could see none of it.

Their voices drifted in and out between the red-hot rage building inside me.

"Stop this," I said in a voice that shocked even me. It was low. Sharp. Deadly.

There were none of the insecurities that normally plagued me. None of the quiet timidness that had characterized my entire life and every conversation I'd ever had.

I was a fully grown woman with children who needed her, and three men I would fight to the death for.

Because that's exactly what they were doing for me right now.

I cracked open the lid on the bleach. "Stop the games. Stop the traps. Stop it all."

The voice sounded like it didn't come from me at all. Even Nyah let go of me and took half a step backward.

But my gaze was only for Francine. She and I locked eyes and didn't turn away.

"Or what, Violet? What the hell are you going to do down there with your bottle of bleach? You aren't going to reach me from your hole." Her smile was so evil it chilled my bones. "A hole where you'll stay until I have a baby of my own."

I lifted the bleach to hover just over my lips. "I can't reach you. But I don't need to. What you want is inside me. But if I'm dead from swallowing down a bottle of bleach, then the baby is too."

I didn't want to do it. I didn't want to end my life or that of the baby I so desperately wanted.

But no baby of mine was going to be raised by the woman sitting above me. A woman who would kill me the moment she got what she wanted.

So it wasn't a bluff, and she knew it. I would rather die

in this hole and take my baby with me than live and watch her snatch it from my arms.

I'd already lost too many people. I wouldn't lose any more.

I tilted the bottle up.

Francine threw herself over the edge and into the hole with us.

Nyah screamed as we broke Francine's fall. Pain jolted through my neck and shoulders, the sharpness of it loosening my fingers. The bottle of bleach hit the dirt, splashing over our legs and rolling away, the acrid stench burning my nostrils.

It took a good few seconds for me to even register what had happened and to think through the pain that radiated through my body from having a fully grown person land on top of me when I was already injured. The chemical smell clogged the air, making it hard to breathe.

Nyah's shouts, my name a short, sharp blast from her lips, jolted me out of it. "Violet!"

She grabbed for Francine's gun, the two of them fighting for control, Francine taller and stronger, Nyah weakened from so long in the hole.

The gun went off with an ear-splitting explosion that rang in my ears, only adding to the pain in my body.

Nyah and Francine both stared at me with wide eyes.

And for a moment, I had no idea why.

It wasn't me who'd pulled the trigger.

And yet it was Francine who crumpled to her knees.

A plastic shiv sticking out of her neck.

Nyah took the gun from Francine's fingers and turned it on her.

"Are you shot?" I whispered.

She shook her head, both of us staring at Francine, slumped at our feet. She fumbled at her neck, and I didn't stop her when she yanked the shiv out, making the bleeding so much worse.

I watched in morbid fascination while the blood flowed from her neck across the dirt.

"You moved so fast," Nyah whispered. "I barely even saw you pick it up after I dropped it."

I had literally no recollection of doing it.

All I remembered was the red haze of anger and a blinding need to protect what was mine. My friend. My baby.

Myself.

Francine spluttered and choked on her own blood. She clawed at our legs, her mouth opening and closing silently, and I knew in my heart she was begging us to save her.

Neither of us made a move to help her. I let the dark part of me take hold and just stood there, watching a woman die.

It didn't take long. The wound in her neck had clearly caught something vital, and the blood pumped hard and fast, emptying from her body until she stopped fighting at all.

Nyah didn't lower the gun until Francine's chest stopped rising. But once she did, she looked up at me with a new fear in her eyes. "What do we do now? What if they can't get in here, Vi? What if she's..."

I filled in the blanks.

What if Francine's traps had killed them all and nobody else knew we were here?

42

X

"**We** are under fire! Drill Sargeant Daddy went down! And not in the good way!"

Whip groaned and pointed his gun at me. "I'm literally going to add to our bullet count if you do not speak like a normal person!"

I rolled my eyes and translated down the line to Scythe. "Violet's psycho boss has a house of horrors that shoots lovely sharp bits of shrapnel every time we try to get close to it, and Whip got hit in the leg. Went down like Levi was on his knees with his mouth open. Or so legend says. Dax was the one who dragged him out."

Scythe was silent on the line for a second, then eventually said, "I... Don't have words. Is this what my family feels like when they have to deal with me? I need to buy them all flowers or something. We're two minutes out. Just sit tight until we get there."

Yeah, there was no way any of us were doing that.

Levi breathed heavily, maybe from the short dive off the porch we'd both done when the fucking house started shooting at us. Maybe from the jagged wound on Whip's leg that was bleeding profusely as Dax tried to wrap strips from his shirt around it.

Levi seemed torn in two, his gaze dragging from the house that held Violet prisoner, and Whip bleeding, though definitely not dying, on the ground.

"We need to get in there," Levi muttered, finally making a decision.

"No shit, Sargeant Sassy Pants. Got any ideas on how?" I mused on that for a second. "Maybe I should call my new friends at the hockey rink and ask to borrow some pads? Then we could just storm in, deflecting shrapnel like its pucks. Kiii-ya!" I straightened my fingers and threw a wobbly roundhouse kick at the air.

"Are you doing karate or playing hockey?" Levi stared at the house that kept trying to kill us. "Violet!" He edged closer again, even though every time he did a new round of tiny sharp bits of metal went flying through the air.

I dragged him back, and we both crouched, trying to come up with a plan. "We go through the roof," I suggested eventually. "Climb the tree, shimmy along that branch, drop onto the roof, remove a few shingles, and burst in through the ceiling."

Levi glanced at me. "I weigh two hundred and fifty pounds. I'm gonna snap that tree branch like it's a matchstick."

I rolled my eyes. "Well, you should have laid off the steroids in prison, then, shouldn't you!" I huffed a sigh and headed for the tree. "Don't worry. I can climb. I had plenty of practice climbing into Violet's apartment before she liked me."

Levi stared at me. "You did what?"

I cringed. "Nothing. Give me a boost."

Whip looked like he was going to have a coronary. "Hurry the fuck up! She could be dying in there, X!"

Did he really think he had to tell me that? Did he really think I wasn't playing it over and over again in my mind like a waking nightmare, dredged up from my own personal pit of hell? Did he think I wasn't scared out of my fucking mind that I was going to get into that house and find out we were too late?

All I had to calm me down was bad jokes. Otherwise I'd be self-combusting on the sidewalk like he and Levi were.

And where the fuck was that going to get us? If Whip was injured and Levi was out of his mind, and I was just flapping around with them.

Someone had to be the hero.

And it was definitely going to be me.

I scaled that tree like I was part koala, clawing and scratching my round little booty up the branches, clinging to it for dear life once I got high enough for the fall to kill me. I eyed the branch overhanging the second-story roof and debated whether it really could hold my weight or not.

The ground suddenly seemed really far away, and climbing this tree was a lot harder than climbing the balconies of Violet's building. I was getting splinters in my fingers, and twigs and leaves were poking me in the eyes.

"Go, X!" Levi shouted from beneath me. "She needs you!"

He was right. The branch had looked thick enough to hold my weight from the ground. Just because when I got up here it was about as sturdy as a toothpick didn't mean anything.

I needed to do this for my Omelet.

I lay down on the branch and inched my way along. I wrapped my legs around it, squeezing my thighs. Splinters stabbed me in the belly, but I kept going, reminding myself the branch would hold, that I would land safely on the roof, and I'd sweep inside like a knight in shining armor, pluck Violet up from wherever she was bound and gagged, and carry her out to cheers and applause.

That was the image I kept in my head, and not the ground that was so far away I could barely see it.

I might as well have been on a plane.

I was nearly there, my stomach threatening to erupt, when Levi's phone rang.

I stared down at him and watched him pull it out of his pocket.

My mouth dropped open. "Not the time to be taking a call, bro! I need some support here!"

Or this freaking tree branch did. It protested my weight with a violent-sounding creak.

"Violet!" Levi shouted.

I froze, dread filling me.

His head jerked up. "It's Violet! She's in a pit beneath the house. Francine is dead, but they're both okay. Francine had her phone on her when she fell into the pit with them."

"What do you mean Francine is dead but they're *both* okay? Who's them?" Whip asked.

Levi looked over at Dax. "Nyah is there too. She's okay."

Even from up in the tree, I could see the color drain

from Dax's face. He sat down hard next to Whip and buried his face in his hands, his shoulders silently shaking.

Whip slung an arm around his shoulders, and Levi crouched, awkwardly patting him on the back.

Which was all fine and good, but hello? I was up in a tree on a branch that was about to snap. "So, uh, Violet doesn't need rescuing?"

Levi shook his head. "No, she's okay. She said she doesn't want any of us trying to go in there because she thinks there could be more traps set. I'm calling the cops, and they can get the bomb squad or whatever the hell department down here to check the place out first and get them out. You can come down."

"Uh..." I stared down at the ground beneath me that spun in dizzying circles and clenched the branch a little tighter.

Levi squinted up at me. "What do you mean 'uh'? Get down."

"I can't."

"You got *up* there!"

"Yeah, well, that was when I was fueled by adrenaline and the belief I was going to rescue my girlfriend from certain death! Now I know she's fine, and my heroic purpose has been stolen from me, and I'm just some fat raccoon in a tree!"

Whip groaned. "You're not fat, but you *are* a raccoon."

"Thank you. That's the nicest thing you've ever said to me."

Levi pinched the bridge of his nose. "Just climb down."

"I would love to, Sergeant Sass, but I have a medical condition."

"What condition?"

"Severe and sudden onset of Don't-Wanna-Die-itis."

They ignored me and went back to talking about bomb squads and trap layouts like I wasn't clinging to bark and my dignity in equal measure.

The police arrived with lights and sirens, men and women in uniforms convening at a safe distance, a few of them peering up at me curiously.

"Nothing to see here, fellas." I lowered my voice so only I could hear it. "Just your regular old, completely average psychopath, trying not to piss his pants."

Although it could be funny to watch urine drip down onto Levi's and Whip's heads, since they were doing literally nothing to help me out of this tree. But I really did hate the smell of piss, even my own, so I clung on.

Ten minutes later, the rumble of a fire truck echoed down the street.

"Oh, you didn't." I glared down at Levi as two firefighters in full gear hopped out.

"We can't leave you up there," he said flatly. "You'll either fall and break your neck, or I'll let my intrusive thoughts win and start shaking the tree to speed things up."

"I will land on you out of spite. I swear I will, Levi!"

The firefighters positioned a ladder, clearly fighting to keep straight faces.

One of them called up, "Just swing a leg over and come toward me."

"I don't swing my leg over for just anyone, pal."

"X," Levi warned.

I sighed theatrically, inching toward the ladder. "If I die, tell Violet I fought bravely. And if she asks why my hands are bleeding, say it's from combat. Do *not* tell her it's from a particularly aggressive pine cone."

43

VIOLET

Nyah and I sat huddled in our pit, as far away from Francine's dead body as we could.

Despite assuring Levi I was fine and not to come in here, all I wanted was to see his face. I wanted Whip's strong, reassuring arms around me. I wanted X's bad jokes in public, and then his fingers around my throat in private.

The worst part was, I could hear their shouts from outside and I couldn't get to them.

It took what felt like a lifetime for the bomb squad to clear the house of the shrapnel-shooting devices Travis and Francine had set up. There were so many of them, it was a miracle Whip had been the only one injured. But I was also aware I'd lost all concept of time, and every second felt like a year, when all I wanted was to get out and check that the people I loved were okay.

Eventually, a round-faced cop, perhaps in his mid-twenties, peered over the top of the pit. He did a double take at Francine's body and then focused on us. "You two okay?"

We nodded.

"You armed?"

I pointed at the gun Nyah had laid down on the dirt. "Francine fell in here with it. We have touched it, but I don't know if it's loaded."

"Anything else?"

"A mostly empty bottle of bleach and a few scrubbers," Nyah called up.

He gave us a small smile. "I'll report that." He disappeared for a second to speak to someone else. A moment later he was back, this time with a ladder. "Ready to get out?"

A sob burst from Nyah's mouth as we both got slowly to our knees. I guided her to the ladder first and let her climb up ahead of me, sticking close behind her in case in her weakened state, she fell.

I tried not to notice the dried blood on her legs.

But a new wave of anger flushed through me, all of it directed at Francine. I wanted to jump back down there and pummel her with fists and feet for what she'd done to Nyah. To me. To everyone I loved and cared about.

But I didn't look back. I only wanted to look forward from now on.

At the top of the hole, the officer escorted us from the house and out the front door.

Nyah blinked in the harsh, afternoon sunlight, and I caught her arm, steadying her while she got her bearings.

"Nyah!"

My heart splintered into a million pieces at Dax

sprinting across the yard, his voice hoarse, tears shamelessly streaming down his face.

Nyah took one step forward, and they collided, Dax cradling her head to his chest to stop her from taking the impact, her arms wrapping around him, and sobs falling from her lips freely. Her fingers twisted in his T-shirt, her face in his neck, and within seconds, he had her up in his arms, carrying her across the lawn to where paramedics waited beside an ambulance.

They moved toward me, but Levi pushed past them.

The fear and worry and love in his eyes told me everything I needed to know. He hugged me tight and then drew back, cupping my face with both hands and tilting it up to stare down at me.

He closed his eyes and pressed his forehead to mine, and for a second, we just breathed together. He didn't need to say anything. It was all there, in the trembling of his fingers, in the connection between us. I knew him. I knew his heart, his words, his love.

"I'm okay," I whispered to him.

"And the baby?"

I smiled a little. "I thought Whip could keep a secret better than that."

He shook his head, his forehead rubbing against mine. "I think he was home five minutes before he blabbed. You probably would have had better luck keeping it a secret if you'd told X."

"I don't want any secrets," I whispered. "I just needed a minute to believe it was real."

He kissed my mouth, and I felt the tension slipping away, my heart beating with his, both of them slowing down, calmed by us being in each other's arms.

"Is Whip okay?" I asked.

Levi had already told me he was injured but it wasn't severe.

I caught sight of him sitting on the grass, surrounded by paramedics, and my mouth dropped open. I brushed past Levi and ran to Whip's side, my fingers hovering uselessly over his bleeding leg that the paramedics were trying to inspect.

I winced at the spray of gashes up his leg. "You guys told me it wasn't serious!"

Whip put his hand to the back of my neck. "Hey. I'm fine."

"You most certainly are not fine! Your leg..." I could barely look at it. The skin and muscle were torn to pieces, jagged bits of metal still embedded in his flesh.

If that had hit him in the chest, or the face or any other vital organ...

I couldn't even think about the sort of damage it could have done. Tears slid down my face. "You could have died."

His thumb stroked over my skin, and he stared into my eyes, pure reassurance and determination in them. "I'm not going anywhere, Violet."

"Except to the hospital," the paramedic interrupted. "We need to get you loaded, sir."

"Not until I kiss my woman and tell her I love her."

"Well, if you could do that fast—"

The man didn't need to tell him twice. Whip dragged me in, pressing his lips on mine and kissing me until my head spun. I clung to him, inhaling his scent, reminding myself I would get to do this for the rest of my life.

"I love you," I whispered to him.

"I love you too, sweetheart. See you at the hospital."

I nodded fiercely. "I'll be in the next ambulance. I just need to see X…" I frowned, glancing around. "Where is he? Did he go to pick the kids up from school or something?"

Whip chuckled. "No, Kara picked them up. They're at the clubhouse. But if you want to see X, you're probably going to have to look up."

I frowned but did as he said.

My mouth dropped open.

"Hey, Omelet!" X called from up in the tree. He waved at me with one hand, but that caused him to wobble so hard his eyes went wide and he clutched at the branch again.

A very patient firefighter sighed heavily. "Sir, you really are *right* there. Like, if you just scoot back an inch—"

"Scoot back an inch and DIE, I think you mean."

The firefighter squinted at him. "You really aren't going to die, sir. I can promise you that. I mean, even if you fell onto the ground—"

X shot him a horrified look, and the firefighter lifted his hands in mock surrender.

"Which you won't because we have an air pillow down there for you, just in case. But it really isn't that far."

"I might as well be on the moon, sir! I'll beg you not to downplay the seriousness of this situation!"

It really wasn't that high, especially compared to my third-floor balcony, but I guessed he'd felt a bit more stable clinging to metal rather than the branch that groaned beneath his weight.

"X?" I called. "I need to go to the hospital and get them to check on the baby. I really want you to be there for that."

His expression changed in an instant. Gone was any fear, either the fake kind for a laugh or the real kind. In its place was the man I loved. The one I saw beneath the jokes he used as armor to hide the insecurities about who he was and how his brain worked. He might have never felt like he fit in with society. But he fit here, with me. With the family we were creating together.

"I need you," I told him.

He moved down the ladder like it was as easy as strolling down a footpath. And then I was in his arms, him holding me tight, his lips pressing kisses to my hair.

"I thought I was going to lose you," he whispered in my ear. "I was all set to come through that roof and save you. But you didn't need me. You saved yourself."

I shook my head. "I always need you."

He didn't say anything, but his answer was in the way he held me, like I was something tiny and precious, something he was never going to give up.

It was X who loaded me into an ambulance, and ours followed the one Levi and Whip had gone in. The paramedics asked me all sorts of questions, and I wasn't sure if I answered them well, because all I wanted to do was curl up in X's arms and have someone reassure me that Whip was okay.

Saint View Hospital was a hive of activity, and a bunch of staff came out to meet Whip's ambulance, a handful of them whisking him away on a gurney. Levi jogged after them until they refused to allow him to go any farther.

Worry creased his brow when he returned to us, but he assured me the paramedics had said all of Whip's injuries were superficial, but they would probably take him into surgery to remove the pieces of shrapnel from his skin and stitch him up, since there were so many of them.

Once I was inside the emergency department and settled in a bed, a nurse came over and smiled at me warmly. "Hi, Violet. I'm Willa. I'm a friend of Kara and Hawk's. They called to tell me I needed to give you the VIP treatment."

I shook my head, not wanting to make a fuss. "You really don't need to do that. I'm fine apart from a sprained ankle and some cuts and bruises." I didn't mention the mental trauma and the unsettling realization that I'd killed two people without regret. But they were things I could unpack with Grayson later. I needed the hospital only for one thing. "It's just, I'm pregnant."

She smiled softly. She had pretty horrific scarring on her neck that disappeared beneath the collar of her shirt, and I wondered how much time she'd spent in a hospital bed just like this one having that treated.

"Do you know how far along?" she asked.

I shook my head. "We only just found out. So not far, probably?"

She grabbed a stool and a portable ultrasound machine from across the hall, pulling both over to my bedside. "That's okay. We can have a quick look to set your mind at ease while we wait for the doctors to come see you."

I put my hand up, motioning for her to stop. "Can I ask you something first? If the baby was hurt when I fell, and I'm miscarrying, is there anything you can do to stop it?"

Willa pressed her lips together. "Assuming you're as early as you think you are? No, probably not. Are you having cramping or any other sort of pain?"

Her words confirmed my suspicions. "No, nothing like that," I assured her. I bit my lip. "This is going to sound really odd, but I don't want to do the ultrasound until Whip—I mean, Wyatt—is here."

Willa smiled at me. "Oh, he's the father? That's totally understandable." She glanced at X and Levi. "You two are her friends, then?"

I had no idea how to tell someone that no, they weren't my friends. And Levi had already started nodding, clearly not wanting to start an uncomfortable conversation.

But something inside me needed this woman to know that no, these men weren't my friends. They were my family. "No," I shook my head. "They're the baby's fathers too."

I knew I didn't have to explain myself to a complete stranger, but something in me wanted her to understand. "I love them." I shrugged. "All three of them."

Willa patted my hand. "Oh, I'm very familiar with unconventional relationships, sweetie. You don't need to explain. My son, Colt, has been in a relationship with a woman and two other men since he was in high school." She smiled proudly. "My two grandchildren are a result of that love, so you'll get no judgment from me." She put the ultrasound wand back in the machine. "You all just sit tight until your partner is cleaned up, and then we'll have a search around and see if we can find a little heartbeat for you all to hear."

*L*ater that night, Whip sat in a wheelchair on my left, his leg covered in strips of fresh white bandage. X sat to my right, holding my hand so tight I thought I might end up needing an ultrasound on that to check for internal damage. Levi was next to him, his hand resting on my thigh buried beneath hospital blankets. His leg bounced nervously, and all three of them were fixated on Willa as she nudged Whip's chair over a little so she could get the ultrasound machine where it needed to be.

Despite the three men around me, all twitching and barely breathing, it was me Willa turned to. "You ready?"

My heart thumped against my rib cage. My brain whispered threats that I wasn't ready at all.

But I hadn't been ready for Will and Ari to walk into my life either, and yet I hadn't hesitated in saying yes to giving them a home. I hadn't been ready for three men to love me, and yet opening myself up to them and a lifestyle that society wouldn't accept had been the best thing I'd ever done.

So I nodded at Willa.

I was ready to be pregnant. To grow a baby we'd made with love and to raise it.

After everything else we'd been through, this seemed like the most natural, easiest thing in the world.

I closed my eyes and squeezed X's hand.

"Please be okay. Please be okay," he murmured.

My heart freaking shattered for him. He wanted this so much.

Willa pressed the gooped-up wand to my belly, and for an agonizingly long minute, nothing happened. I stared at the screen, not having any clue what I was seeing. Willa moved the wand around, poking and prodding me, her poker face better than anything I'd ever seen, her expression giving away absolutely nothing.

Until she glanced over at me and smiled. "Want to hear the heartbeat now?"

I widened my eyes. "There is one?"

She nodded. She flicked something on her machine, and the most glorious sound filled the little curtained-off cubicle.

The tiny thumping heartbeat of our baby.

X elbowed Levi. "You gonna cry?"

I waited for Levi to come back with a smart-ass response, but his voice was choked and gruff when he replied, "There's a good chance I might. Fucking hell. Listen to that."

"Is it weird if I make this my ringtone?" X grinned and took out his phone. "Too late, I'm doing it."

I had to hold in a laugh at that. I glanced over at Whip, knowing this had to be painful for him. He was the only one out of the four of us who had done this before. He had to be remembering the times he'd sat in a seat at his wife's side and listened to his child's heartbeat. Only to lose them before they'd even truly begun to live.

"Are you okay?" I reached for him, and his fingers gripped mine tightly. "It's totally fine if you're not."

But he smiled over at me. "I feel more at peace today than I have any day since I lost them." He leaned over the armrest of his chair and brought my fingers up to his lips to kiss. "Thank you."

I didn't know what exactly he was thanking me for, but all I cared about was that he was happy.

I really hoped that somewhere in the hospital, Nyah was getting the same sort of news. "Willa? My friend, Nyah, would have been brought in a few minutes before our ambulances got here. She went ahead with her partner, Dax. Do you know where they are? Can I see her?"

Willa frowned and pulled a device from a pocket on the ultrasound cart. "How do you spell her name?"

I spelled it out, and she typed it in, but the frown didn't lift from between her eyebrows. "There's nobody here by that name."

I squinted at her. "Are you sure? They were right ahead of us."

But Willa shook her head. "We've only had two ambulances in so far today. Yours and the one Wyatt came in. Maybe they took your friend to a different hospital."

That didn't sound right. "Is that something they commonly do?"

"No, not unless her injuries were life-threatening."

Worry trickled down my spine, but I was fairly confident Nyah had been in decent shape. She'd been walking and talking. She was probably dehydrated and would need to be treated for her miscarriage. But none of that should have equaled an emergency.

Levi squeezed my leg. "She'll be okay, wherever they've taken her. She has Dax with her." He grinned. "I don't think he's going to be letting her out of his sight ever again."

I smiled at that too, remembering the way she'd flung herself at him and how he'd melted around her. His relief that she was alive and the love he had for her so evident in the way he'd scooped her right off her feet and cradled her close like she was the most precious thing in the world to him.

Levi was right. Dax was never going to let her go again. Francine was dead. Nyah was safe, and so was I. I guessed we both no longer had jobs at Clean Sweep, but that seemed insignificant in the scheme of things.

Jobs would come and go. But I had a lot more than a job waiting for me outside these hospital doors. I gazed around at my men. "Take me home."

44

VIOLET

The clubhouse erupted in cheers when the four of us limped our way through the doors. My ankle had swollen up to grapefruit size, courtesy of the fall I'd taken into Francine's pit of hell. Whip was on crutches, completely unable to put weight on his bad leg.

Fang stood at the front of the crowd, holding his youngest daughter in one arm. But that didn't stop him from striding forward and wrapping his other arm around my head and holding me tight. The hug was almost more of a headlock and felt so naturally brotherly that it made me laugh into his shirt.

"You're hurt," he complained.

"Sprained ankle. Nothing more." Though that wasn't quite true. I pulled out of his embrace and looked up at him. "I know you suddenly gained a niece and nephew just recently, but I was wondering if you maybe wanted one more?"

His eyes widened. "What does that mean? You... you're..."

"Pregnant," I filled in for him.

His mouth opened and closed a few times, and then his gaze slid to Levi. "You knocked my little sister up?"

"Hey now, why are we assuming Levi did? Could have been me." X folded his arms across his chest.

Fang switched his glare in X's direction, and X suddenly saw the error of his ways.

He pointed at Whip. "He slept with her first!"

And that was about enough of that conversation.

Fang looked pained, but he kissed the top of my head affectionately. "I'm just going to tell myself it was a miracle conception."

Rebel snorted from behind him. "That how our babies were conceived too, babe? It wasn't that dirty hot foursome where I had your dick—"

Fang circled his arm around her and fit his hand over her mouth.

Her muffled laughter filled the room, and she winked at me.

I searched for the only two little faces I really wanted to see. "Where are Will and Ari?"

Rebel dragged Fang's hand down off her mouth. "Down at Kara's place, playing with Hayley Jade and my older two. Little Jax is helping to watch them."

Little Jax was Rebel and Kara's youngest sister, who at around fourteen, was the very cool young aunt all the kids adored.

I didn't need to tell anyone I wanted to go see them. The guys led me toward the door, Rebel and my brother close behind.

War called after us. "Slayers family night tonight! We'll put on the food and drink. I think we all need it."

I was exhausted, but he was right. Being surrounded by safety and these people who had opened their doors for us time and time again, was exactly what I needed.

I wanted to live in this bubble for just a bit longer.

It was the comedown from the adrenaline high. Tomorrow, or next week, we'd find our groove again with the kids and with pregnancy, and I'd be asking Bliss for more hours at Psychos or searching for another day job. Whip probably would be too. But tonight, I just wanted this. Family. Friends. A fence around us only to keep out the wildlife, instead of people who wanted to kill us.

The baby in my belly. The two kids we'd opened our home to. And the three men who'd stolen my heart.

---

*W*ill scrunched his nose up at the ultrasound photo we showed him. "That's not a baby."

I chuckled and pointed at the bean-shaped object on the printout. "I know it doesn't look like one right now, but I promise you, it's growing every day, and the next time we get to see it, it will definitely be baby shaped."

Will looked at me like I might be lying to him, and I ruffled his hair.

What I really wanted to do was pull him onto my lap and hug and kiss him to pieces, but we were still letting them come to us in their own way and in their own time. I'd been worried that as soon as they started school, they would say something about the night we'd taken them from that house.

But neither had said a word. Whip thought they were

probably smart enough to realize what might happen to me if they said anything, and both were already very attached to me.

I suspected both of them would rather think about anything other than that night. Their childhoods were full of trauma they would need to unpack with therapists at some point. But for now, it seemed to me like they'd blocked it out entirely. I saw it in little things they did, so I knew it was there, buried deep, but I was no longer worried they would bring it up at school.

Will ran off with Madden, and I couldn't help but smile at the new cousins who had become fast friends. Madden was a boy's boy through and through, and Will had been happily coerced into games of trucks and Nerf guns and footballs.

I glanced over at Ari. She hadn't said a word.

I bit my lip. "Did you want to look at the photo of the baby?"

"No."

"That's okay," I said quickly. "You don't have to."

X and Levi looked worried, but neither said anything. I wasn't exactly sure what to do either. I'd had no training in dealing with the grief and trauma of a child who'd watched her parents die right in front of her. Even if they hadn't been good people, they'd been the only parents she'd known. While things seemed to roll off Will's back, Ari took them deep, internalizing them, thinking them over in a way that made me feel like she was so much older than her years.

I hated that she'd had to grow up. Hated her parents hadn't protected her and allowed her to be an innocent child who openly trusted the world was a good place.

Whip inched forward on the couch, wincing as he moved his leg awkwardly but the dad in him needing to get closer to her. "You're allowed to be mad about the baby. Or sad. Or happy. Or whatever else you want to feel."

Ari shook her head.

X plonked down next to her. "Personally, I'm scared." He leaned in and stage whispered to her. "Scared of the poopy diapers!" He held his nose theatrically, clearly trying to make her laugh.

And to his credit, her lips did flicker up into a half-smile, but it faded quickly, her gaze coming back to me. Her bottom lip trembled.

My heart shattered into a million pieces. This little girl might have only been in my life a couple of weeks, but I was already so in love with her. It was impossible not to be when I had been her. I related to her so easily and just wanted to fix every horrible memory so all she had left was good ones. I couldn't do that, but I had already committed to trying, so one day, when she was older, she could at least say she had more good memories than bad ones.

I didn't want this to be one of the bad ones.

I picked up her hand and just quietly gave her the space to talk in her own time.

Eventually, with her eyes full of tears, and her voice barely more than a whisper, she asked, "When do I have to go back?"

Levi's forehead furrowed. "Go back where, sweet girl?"

"To my real parents' house."

I smoothed back the hair from her face. Her forehead was sticky with sweat, but it wasn't even hot, and it broke my heart that the sweat was probably a stress reaction. I kept my voice gentle. "You're never going back there."

Her face crumpled. "Then where will I go?"

"You'll stay with us," I assured her.

"But where will I go when your baby comes?"

I suddenly realized what she meant.

I couldn't help myself. I scooped her up in my arms and tucked her onto my lap, holding her close. "Ari, you'll go nowhere when this baby comes. This baby isn't replacing you."

She peered up at me through big eyes. "But it doesn't have a bed to sleep in."

I laughed a little at that. "We'll buy it one."

I could see the idea starting to sink in, the thoughts processing through her mind, one by one. "Can she sleep next to me?"

I nodded. "Absolutely, if you want her to."

"Him," X corrected. "It could be a boy."

Ari wrinkled her nose at that.

Whip ruffled her hair. "Hey, I'm a boy. And so are X and Levi and Will. We're all right, aren't we?"

She shrugged. "I guess so. But I still hope it's a girl." She looked up at me. "Can I go play now, Mommy?"

I froze at that word on her lips, but Whip gently nudged me, startling me into a fast nod. "Of course. Go."

The moment she disappeared into Hayley Jade's bedroom to play with her and Remi, I burst into tears.

Levi pulled me into his arms and held me while I got myself under control. His lips brushed over the top of my head. "That was the sweetest thing I've ever heard," he whispered to me. "Her calling you Mommy. Fuck, I can't wait for the day she calls me Dad."

I couldn't wait for that either.

* * *

*L*ynx showed up at the club gates as discussions about what needed to be prepared for dinner commenced. Levi told the prospects to let him in, and he and I stood among the bikes and cars and an ice cream truck in the parking lot, waiting for Lynx to make his way down the hill on foot.

Expression pinched, Levi watched his old cellmate stroll down the dirt road.

I squeezed Levi's fingers. "Lynx wasn't involved with Francine or Travis. So why are you looking like the Grim Reaper is walking toward us right now?"

He kept his voice low. "Last time I saw Lynx, he said I owed him. I'm pretty sure this—him turning up here unannounced—is him claiming that debt."

Nerves flittered around my belly, but if that was true, how bad could it be? Lynx would have to have a death wish to walk in the Slayers' gates and start something with a member. The entire club was here, rubbernecking while they got ready to barbecue.

We fell silent as he drew closer, and eventually Lynx stopped in front of us.

He shook Levi's hand and then turned to me. "Hey, Violet."

I offered him a smile, trying to break the tension, while also trying to subtly remind him that Levi had people here. "You picked a good night for a visit. We're having a full club barbecue. All the members and their families are here."

I could feel the gazes of Whip and X from across the yard. Fang and War and Hawk all hovered around, keeping an eye on the newcomer since he was an unknown in their territory.

Lynx nodded. "I can see that." He glanced at Levi. "Hope I'm not in the way."

Levi's fingers strangled the neck of his beer bottle. "You aren't. But if we're being honest, I am wondering what you're doing here."

Pink tinged Lynx's cheeks, and he shoved his hands deep in the pockets of his jeans. "Yeah, I get that." He squinted at Levi, the blush deepening. "You know that favor you owe me?"

My stomach sank. Even though nothing about Lynx's posture screamed a warning, him bringing up the debt that Levi owed him made me feel sick.

Clearly, it had a similar effect on Levi. He picked his words carefully. "I haven't forgotten."

"Was hoping I could call it in," Lynx said.

Levi just waited.

I wanted to vomit, but I couldn't tell if it was the anticipation or a sudden bout of morning sickness.

Lynx glanced around the yard full of bikers and their families and then back at Levi. "I was hoping for an introduction. Or maybe even a good word with your prez?"

Levi blinked. "Sorry, what?"

The pink in Lynx's cheeks deepened. "I know I'd have to start at the bottom. I don't expect no special treatment..." He ran his hand through his hair. "It's just fucking shit out there, man. I'm couch surfing. Job prospects are bleak. You know how it is, right? I just thought maybe the club..." He shook his head. "Sorry. This is fucking embarrassing. I shouldn't have come and interrupted your dinner." He took a step backward.

Levi's fast-spreading grin stopped him. "Hold up. You want to join the Slayers?"

Lynx shrugged. "Thought I'd start with an introduction first, but I mean, yeah? Or, I don't know, maybe? If I'm stepping all over your territory—"

Levi slung his arm around Lynx's shoulder, and Lynx barely missed the beer that sloshed over the lip of the bottle.

"Is that seriously all you want? An introduction and a good word put in for you?"

Lynx nodded. "I ain't got nowhere else to go, honestly."

Levi's relief was palpable. He laughed; the sound filled with relief. "War! Come over here for a second, would you?"

War walked over, carrying his baby son in his arms.

I smiled as Levi introduced his old cellmate to his president. The two men shook hands, and Lynx gave baby Ridge a tiny fist bump, even though the little boy was really too young to understand what was going on.

All three men talked for a minute, Levi explaining that Lynx was interested in joining the club. War seemed open to potentially taking on a new prospect, and they set up a time for further discussions when War wasn't needed for family duties as he was tonight.

Levi couldn't stop smiling. To the point that both Lynx and War noticed.

War frowned at him. "Any reason you're all Cheshire

cat right now? You that excited by the idea of a new prospect to boss around?"

Levi snorted on a laugh. "No. It's just..." He shook his head then said to Lynx, "I thought you mass murdered a bunch of innocent women. And that when you said I owed you, you were going to..." He shrugged. "You know."

Lynx's eyes got big. "Going to what? Ask you to kill a few more with me just for shits and giggles?"

"Or worse." Levi's grin returned. "Glad I was wrong though. For the record."

Lynx glanced at War. "I don't make a habit out of killing innocent women. Just so you know. Despite whatever this idiot thought."

The corner of War's mouth lifted. "Good to know. We don't approve of that."

Lynx nodded and then gave War a sheepish look. "Any problem with killing dumbass over here though, for thinking I'd ask him to do something like that?"

War glanced at me and Levi. "I think Violet might have some objections to that somehow."

"Violet does indeed," I agreed.

But it was clear to me Lynx was just as lost as Levi had been when he'd first gotten out of prison. Levi had found his way back here, to the family that lived beyond the Slayers' gates. And now it seemed like we'd be opening them again for Lynx.

Levi elbowed him as War walked away to join his family again. "So we're good? Debt cleared?"

Lynx jerked his head toward the ice bucket filled with drinks. "Get me a beer and we'll call it even."

The police came somewhere in between steaks, a text from Nyah saying she was okay and she'd see us later, and the prospects' rowdy rendition of "Take me Home, Country Roads" that X had joined with off-key warbling.

The officer who Hawk scowled at through the wrought-iron gates was the same one who'd found me at the bottom of the hole.

Fang stood on my other side and lowered his voice so only I would hear. "You don't want to talk to them yet, you don't have to. In fact, you shouldn't. I'll call Liam, our lawyer."

But clearly he hadn't spoken softly enough, or maybe the officer had just dealt with my brother and his club enough times that he probably knew the gist of what Fang was whispering in my ear. "Please don't call Liam." He grimaced in a way that told me he'd dealt with Liam before and didn't particularly want the displeasure of doing it again. "All I wanted to tell you was that you can come down to the station whenever you're feeling up to it, but we aren't wanting to press any charges against you. The woman's death was clearly self-defense, and you aren't in any trouble. We had a tip come through the call line about other bodies we've connected to her and Clean Sweep."

My brother nodded. "Fair enough then. But when she comes down, we'll bring Liam anyway."

The police officer grimaced at that but nodded. "As is your right."

I waited until he'd driven away before I turned to Whip, Levi, and X who'd followed us up to the gates when Hawk had come to tell me the cops were up here, wanting to talk to me. "They had a tip about the other bodies?" I raised an eyebrow.

Whip shoved his hands in his pockets. "We couldn't just leave them there. Their families deserve closure."

I didn't disagree, but my heartbeat sped up, knowing they weren't the only bodies out there. Trig and X and all the guys had left evidence that could be tied back to them.

But Whip clearly saw all of that flashing like a warning light in my expression. He chuckled. "We've been doing this a long time, sweetheart. Don't worry, nothing is blowing back on us, or on you. We had the place scrubbed."

We walked back toward the clubhouse slowly, but my questions played on a silent loop in my head. I wanted to know everything about how they'd done it. How they'd covered it up. How they'd gotten rid of the bodies.

Maybe I'd watched too many true crime documentaries and needed that closure.

Maybe the part of me who had found pleasure in taking the life of people who'd hurt me was storing information for the next time I needed it.

That thought was so terrifying it stopped me dead in my tracks. "Do I need to join the Murder Squad for real?"

All three of them stared at me.

Whip raised an eyebrow. "Sweetheart. Really?"

I nodded. "What if I just start randomly killing people?"

X snorted on a laugh. "Well, that would be hot, and hey, if you need a partner, I'm your guy."

"X!" I wailed, truly concerned I could see a future

where he and I were like Batman and Robin, running around the city in bad costumes, unaliving people who had done wrong.

I might have learned to love my body a little more, since seeing it through the eyes of three men who loved me, but I wasn't sure I was ready for full-body spandex.

Clearly, I was spiraling.

Levi took my hand and threaded his fingers through mine. "Vi, you are not a psychopath. You are just a woman who loves hard. You protected yourself. The little girl you were. Us. Nyah. I have zero concerns that we'll need to lock you in X's bedroom because you're about to go on a bender."

X shrugged. "If you want to join me when I'm going on one though, I would love the company."

That unsettled part of me came to rest at their reassurances. "So you aren't scared I'm going to start stabbing people?"

Whip shrugged and grinned. "I wouldn't get between you and a boy who pulls Ari's hair, but I think the general population is probably pretty safe."

I elbowed him and muttered something about making sure Ari knew to kick anyone who pulled her hair, but he just chuckled like I was being cute.

We strolled back to the club, Hawk and my brother a few paces ahead of us. Drinks and food flowed inside, and we were instantly the center of attention once more. Word of my pregnancy had gotten around like wildfire, and more than one biker asked if I would name the baby after them.

But I kept glancing over at Whip and remembering the children he'd lost. And all I could think about was naming this baby after them. It's big brother and sister, gone but never forgotten, deserved that honor.

It wasn't my choice to make alone, of course, but it sent a warmth through me nonetheless. Beers were passed around, and I declined them all. Will and Ari played happily, and when they came running over at some point before midnight, with their eyes drooping but happy smiles on their faces, asking if they could sleep at Hayley Jade's place, I glanced at Kara, and she nodded.

"We'd love to have them for the night."

I wasn't sure at all about letting them be away from us. But they were so insistent that I found myself nodding and saying, "We'll be right here in Levi's room. So if you need us in the night, just tell someone and we can come get you right away, okay?"

I really wanted them to understand that we were absolutely not abandoning them. And if they needed us, we would be there in a heartbeat.

The fact that Kara's house was literally just a one-minute walk through the trees helped.

Ari and Will both cheered, and it looked like Kara had drawn the short straw, with half of Rebel's and Bliss's kids all filing out after her, their laughter and chatter trailing away as she took them all down to her place to sleep. Grayson, Hayden, and Hawk all followed her, scooping up trailing kids.

Bliss and Rebel were left with their youngest children, and one by one they retired to their rooms here at the club. Prospects paired up with the club girls and disappeared into bedrooms of their own. Some of the guys moved outside and talked shit quietly in the moonlight, beers clutched in their meaty fingers.

When the club around us was finally quiet, Levi eventually reached a hand out for me. "Bed."

I nodded, letting him pull me up.

X laid himself out on the couch. "I'll be here if anyone needs me."

I hated the idea of him sleeping out in the common room. But me, Whip, and Levi were going to struggle to fit in Levi's bed as it was. There was zero chance X would fit as well.

But Levi offered X his hand. "Come on. Get up. You aren't sleeping out here."

X squinted at him sleepily. "No offense, but I don't really want to sleep on your floor either. I've already got splinters from that tree. Don't need any extras from your ancient floorboards."

Levi rolled his eyes. "Just come."

X took his hand and let Levi help him up off the couch. We all followed him into his room, but nothing was any different than the last time we'd been here.

"Levi, I—" X started to complain.

Levi bent down and peered beneath his bed.

For the first time, I noticed that there was no longer the dusty, empty space beneath the frame. He dragged out a rolling mattress, already neatly made up with sheets and blankets.

X's eyes widened. "You bought me a bed?"

Levi pulled a spare pillow from the top of his closet, his cheeks a bit pink with embarrassment. "I bought you a mattress on wheels, but sure, if you want to call it a bed, then so be it."

"So we can have sleepovers and braid each other's hair? YES! Except yours is getting a little thin on top—"

Levi shot him a look.

X grinned, already plonked down on his bed and taking off his shoes. His expression turned serious, and he glanced up at Levi. "Thank you."

Levi just nodded.

I fell in love with Levi just a little more. It was one thing for him to make room for Whip when there was an attraction between the two of them, just as strong as the one between me and Levi.

But it was next-level sweet for him to recognize X's place in our relationship and for him to make room for it.

X's honest thank you told me he felt it too.

We all stripped off layers, and my body ached as I crawled beneath the covers, gratefully flanked either side by Whip and Levi, not minding I had no room because there was nowhere else I wanted to be.

Silence settled over us almost immediately, and I was practically asleep when a thought splintered through my brain and my eyes flew open. "Francine offered a reward to anyone on the list who took one of you out." My body that had been on the verge of complete and total relaxation suddenly went into hyperdrive, muscles tensing, a sense of doom and despair floating down around me, invading the bliss bubble I'd found myself in. My body shook at the sudden, very real notion that there were a hundred or more ex-crims out there somewhere, still all thinking they were going to get some sort of reward for hunting down the men I loved.

But X waved me off from his nest on the floor.

"We'll make sure word gets around that the newest member of Murder Squad ended Francine. And that with her dead, there's no reward for coming after us. That should take care of it."

I lay back down among the blankets. I couldn't help smiling at the ludicrous idea that men like that would be scared of someone like me. Except, hadn't I earned that respect? Hadn't I done things I never thought I was capable of, all of them fueled not by hate, but by the love I had for the men surrounding me?

"You're a badass, Violet Garrisen," Whip whispered sleepily.

For the first time in my life, I believed it. Not because I'd killed Travis and Francine. But because I'd finally stepped out of my own way. I'd let go of the girl who'd been abandoned, overlooked, unloved. And I was finally walking in the shoes of the woman I was always meant to be.

Out of ruin and into the sun, surrounded not by the family I'd been born into, but by the one I'd created for myself.

EPILOGUE

Nyah

I rubbed my hands together briskly and stomped my feet on the hockey rink flooring. "Let's go, X!"

Beside me, Violet's eyes were bright and shiny, excitement and pride shining as her breath misted in front of her lips. "I'm so nervous for him."

Her phone rang, and she took it out, blinking at the display then answering it quickly. "X?" She listened for a second, then sighed and said, "Okay. When I hang up, I'll do it. Good luck. I love you."

She ended the call, and I raised an eyebrow.

"Did he need a last-minute pep talk?"

She shook her head and leaned down to pull something from beneath her seat. "No. That would be too normal."

It took me a second, and an almightily pissed-off hiss,

to realize the thing that had been beneath the seat was a cat carrier with a very angry feline inside. "What the...?"

Violet shook her head and held it up so the cat could see the ice through the mesh of its enclosure. "X insisted Harold needed to come and that he would feel like he wasn't part of the family if he didn't. Look, Harold. Daddy is going to come out of those doors any minute now."

I hid a laugh.

Dax leaned over from my other side, offering everyone some of his fries, though quickly removing his hand when Harold tried to take a swipe at him through the mesh of his prison. "I can't wait for this. The team here is terrible. X's show is going to be the best part of the game. If anyone is well-suited to being a club mascot, it's him." He shoved another fry into his mouth. "What's his costume like?"

Violet grimaced. "It was supposed to be a python but—"

"Ladies and gentlemen!" the announcer said with fake enthusiasm over the loudspeaker, cutting her off. "Please put your hands together for the newest member of the Saint View Vipers, team mascot, Vicious the Viper!"

The lights in the rink went out for dramatic effect, the spotlight shining down on the doors at the far end of the rink.

X, dressed in his homemade, sparkly snake costume, stood there proudly.

I tried to hold in a laugh. "I can see where you were going with the snake...but does it kinda look like a..."

"Big black sparkly dildo?" Whip asked.

Violet hushed him. "Don't say that in front of the cat! He has a cape! Dildos don't have capes!"

The crowd went wild anyway. From down the row, far away from the dildo talk, Violet's kids stood and whooped and hollered at their father.

Beneath more sequins than I'd ever seen in my life, X waved and did a little shimmy. In gold skates, he moved slowly across the rubber-matted floor to get to the ice.

Violet stood and cheered and shouted, and the rest of us followed suit, screaming in the dark.

The people around us laughed at X's dance moves, and he fist pumped the air, hyping them up, clapping his hands together above his head, encouraging the crowd to do the same.

We joined in, big grins all around. I couldn't deny the mood was infectious. The claps got faster and faster as he approached the ice.

"He's doing so good!" I said to Violet. "He's made for this!"

She couldn't hold in her laughter, or her pride. "Isn't he? I think he's found his calling. The crowd is loving it!"

Loving it was an understatement. There was something ridiculously perfect about the way X flashed his sparkly cape and danced his way to the ice, and the crowd around us lapped it up.

"I really had my doubts about this," Violet leaned in to say to me. "But I take them all back. He's—"

X stepped onto the ice for the first time.

His arms pin-wheeled. His feet kicked, trying to keep him upright.

None of it was to any avail. He went down like a sack of potatoes, crashing hard.

The entire stadium winced all at once. You could hear it in the collective "ooh" that reverberated around the circle.

X lay on the ice for a second, doing his best stunned mullet imitation. He lay there for so long and so still, I wasn't fully sure if he was just trying to get his bearings or if he'd hit his head and knocked himself out.

But then his arms and legs started air flailing, and suddenly he looked more like a turtle stuck on his back, trying desperately to flip over but unable to, due to the weight distribution of his massive shell. Or in X's case, his massive mascot head.

Violet clutched my hand. "Oh, this is bad, isn't it?" She clapped her free hand against her leg. "Come on, X! I mean, Vicious the Viper! You got this!"

Whip, on the other side of Violet, sank lower in his chair. "This secondhand embarrassment burns worse than an STD."

I snorted on a laugh, and even Violet was trying to keep herself in check.

It was so bad. It was clear to me that if X could normally skate, he definitely couldn't in that suit, with a snake head five times the size of his own. "Didn't he practice in costume?" I asked, wincing as he finally found his hands and knees and crawled around the ice, trying to find the railing.

"We only finished putting the final touches on it last night. There was no time." She gripped the cat carrier and covered the mesh with her hand. "Don't watch this, Harold. It's not pretty."

X managed to get back up, only to crash again. The

crowd erupted into laughter, like it was all part of the show.

Eventually, two of the players skated out onto the ice and helped him up.

X hung between them while they hauled him off the ice, and we all politely clapped.

Violet bit her lip. "That'll probably be on the news tonight, won't it?"

I tucked my arm through the crook of her elbow. "Oh, one-hundred-percent. But for now, let's just watch the game. Hopefully the players can skate better than X can."

She nodded, and I left her to wrangle her two overexcited kids, her men, and a very angry and probably slightly chilly cat. Though part of me did wonder if Harold had rage to keep him warm.

I settled back in my seat and leaned into Dax.

"French fry?" he asked me, offering me the paper bowl full of deep-fried goodness.

I grinned at him and kissed his salty lips instead. "No, thanks."

He kissed me back. "You feeling okay? You should eat."

"You worried about my lack of desire for a heart attack?"

"No, just worried that coming out here today was too much, too soon. I still think you need to go to the hospital and get checked out."

I sighed. It wasn't the first time we'd had this argument since I'd run into his arms outside Francine's house. He'd been nagging me for days.

But I shook my head. "I can't afford it. I have no health insurance. Unless I want to go running back to my father, which I do not, I can't afford to be going to the hospital for no reason."

Dax picked up my hand and threaded his fingers through mine. "Having a miscarriage is not no reason. Being held captive for over a week is not no reason."

I knew that. But I also felt fine. At least, mostly fine. I was weak and tired, but it was nothing rest and watching X crawl around the ice wouldn't fix. I'd stopped bleeding. Being here was good for me.

"I promise, I'm okay. You can take me home straight after this and pamper me for the rest of the night if you want."

Dax nodded at that. "Exactly what I plan on doing for the rest of my life."

My stomach sank at the easy way words like that fell off his tongue. "Don't say things like that."

He glanced over at me, his eyebrows furrowing. It took him a long moment of silence to say, "Why not, Nyah? I know what I want."

I breathed out a long shaky breath, a smile forming on my lips. I turned away so he wouldn't see. "Let's just watch the game."

He didn't push me. Just like I'd requested, he gave me space. I shoved the thoughts away, and we watched the game, cringing every time the other team scored.

Which was a lot. Our team sucked as bad as X's skating.

During the third period, my phone rang. It was just a string of numbers, but instantly, my blood ran cold.

I quickly cancelled it and shoved it in my purse.

It rang again, and my gut knew that until I picked it up, it would just keep going.

If I didn't answer, it would be worse.

Dax was distracted, shouting at the players on the ice. I slipped the phone from my bag and answered it quietly, turning to face Violet, so Dax would be less likely to hear. "Dad?"

Violet looked at me sharply.

I'd had his number memorized since I was old enough to know what numbers were. His voice on the other end of the line was no surprise.

"Hello, my princess. Long time no speak. How are you?"

I fought to stiffen my spine. To not let his smooth tone and fake care get to me. "I'm not even going to ask how you got this number. What do you want?"

There was a moment of silence on the other end, where I could practically feel the crackle of his annoyance that I'd dared to speak to him like that.

It was not how I'd been raised. I'd been brought up to speak to him only with the respect my mother had claimed he deserved, as head of our family. It hadn't taken me long to disagree with her. But I'd mostly kept my true opinion of the man to myself, never wanting to rock the boat, knowing that whenever I acted out, it was my mother he took his anger and frustration out on.

But I'd left. I'd gotten out. And I'd realized I couldn't live my life for her. She'd made her choices. I had to make mine.

"I think it's time you came home, princess."

"No."

This time, there was no hesitation. "I wasn't asking."

I closed my eyes. He never was.

I'd been waiting for this day. Known it was coming. "No," I said again.

My father sighed. "Nyah Louise, I have been incredibly patient with you. I allowed you to run off and spread your wings because your mother wanted you to have that freedom. But playtime is over. I need you home."

This man had never needed a woman for anything in his life, apart from to fuck or raise his children. Since I wouldn't be doing either of those, there was only one other reason he would be summoning me home.

And I didn't even have to wait for him to say it. "Your marriage has been arranged."

I tried to breathe. But suddenly, I was back in that pit in Francine's house, with the walls closing in on me, the air stale, no light or hope. "No."

It was all I could whisper.

My father went on like I hadn't even spoken. Like what I wanted didn't even matter. It never had. This shouldn't have been a surprise.

"You'll leave now. Stand up and meet me in the parking lot. Everything has already been taken care of. Your things have all been packed and are already on their way back here."

I jerked. "What? No."

I was like a broken record, just repeating the same thing over and over. But nobody was coming to repair the scratch. I was about to be tossed in the garbage.

"You can't make me." I knew I sounded like a stubborn two-year-old, but I had no idea what else to say.

Violet kept shooting me little looks of worry in between watching the game, and I knew it was only a matter of time before Dax noticed too.

Dax.

I clutched his hand. He was everything that was good and sweet. Everything I wanted. When he talked about forever, in my heart, I was right there with him.

But my head knew that sort of future had never been possible. And now my father was on the other end of the line, reminding me of my place.

"Turn to your left, Nyah."

My stomach sank, but I did as he said.

My father's second-in-command sat barely ten seats away, in the row in front, staring up at me instead of at the game in front of him.

"Now to your right."

I already knew who I'd see. My uncle raised one hand in greeting, like his presence there was no big deal.

And to most people it wasn't. But to me, it might as well have been my death warrant.

"Look around you and you'll see at least a dozen more of my men, princess."

The hopelessness flooded in. Even with Whip and Levi just feet away, and knowing what they were capable of, I knew they were no match for my father and his men. If he'd brought them all, there would be no fighting back. Violet had her kids here. There were families all around us.

That wouldn't matter to my father's men. If they had to slaughter an entire arena to bring me home, that's what they would do, and they wouldn't lose a wink of sleep over it.

But I would.

I'd already felt the pain of losing a baby. I wouldn't be the reason another mother lost hers.

"Say goodbye to your friends. Put on the show of your life, princess, because if they follow us, you will not like what happens."

I found myself nodding, resigned, knowing there was nothing more I could do.

I'd left knowing this day would come.

I tried to memorize Dax's features, the warmth of his skin, the kindness in his eyes. And I wished so much that my life could have been different.

He glanced over at me and did a double take when he noticed the expression on my face. "Hey, what's wrong?"

"He's dead if he follows you, Nyah. Thank him and your friends for leading me back to you, but know I only let them live because of that. They come for you again, I will not be as lenient."

I didn't push back. Didn't argue. I knew his threats weren't bluffs.

My father never bluffed.

"Just let me have ten minutes," I whispered to him.

"I'm not an unreasonable man, Nyah." He paused on the other end of the line. "Ten minutes. Not a second more."

If my heart hadn't just been ripped from my body in the most painful of ways, I might have laughed. But there was no humor in this situation.

I turned to Violet. "I have to go home."

Violet's eyebrows drew together sharply. "Your father—"

I forced myself to shake my head and to lie to the best friend I'd ever had. "No, it's not that. My mother is ill. I need to go back and be there for her."

Violet bit her lip. "Okay, but you'll be back when she's well, right?"

Lying to her was the hardest thing I'd ever done in my life. "Sure."

She hugged me quickly, and I stood, pulling Dax to his feet with me.

"What's going on?" he asked.

I knew my uncle and my father's men would follow us, but I didn't care. I moved past him, and he followed me up the stairs, cheering hockey fans sitting either side of us. The landing where the food and bathrooms were was much quieter, most people saving their snacking and restroom trips for between periods.

I wished that was why I was up here. Wished all we were doing was getting Dax a refill of his fries.

I tugged him to a stop, facing him, staring up at the eyes I'd so easily come to love. "I'm leaving."

He didn't hesitate. "You're tired? I knew this was too much. Come on, let's get you to the car."

I shook my head. "No. I'm leaving town."

He froze. "What do you mean? For the weekend?"

He already knew. I could see it in his eyes.

"No. I'm going home."

"Your family—"

Again, I knew I had to lie. Because he would come for me if I didn't. He would never stop coming if he thought I wasn't there of my own free will. This man would burn the world down for me if I asked him to, and I knew it.

The only problem was, if he tried, he'd only be setting himself alight.

I couldn't let him do that. I loved him more than that. More than he would ever love me.

His forehead pinched. "If this is about what I said... about forever... If I'm moving too fast..."

I squeezed his fingers. "It's not about you. It's about me. I'm broken, Dax. I don't feel safe here."

"We'll go somewhere else!"

I shook my head. "I can't. It hurts too much. I need to go home. My mom is sick. I need to be there with her."

He pulled me into his arms, holding me tight, his desperation thick in the choke of his voice. "Okay, but she'll get better, and you'll come home."

I couldn't give him the false hope I'd given Violet. Violet's heart wouldn't break when I didn't return.

But Dax's had to. It was the only way he would ever be able to move on. I couldn't string this out, just hoping he'd forget. "I'm not coming back. And I don't want you to come with me."

It was like every word was a hot dagger of pain right to his stomach. Each one drawing out blood and vital organs he needed to live. I could see it in his expression.

He shook his head. "Don't do this."

But I had to. Out of the corner of my eye, my uncle lurked, watching, making sure I was the good little princess my father had always expected me to be.

I pressed up on my toes and kissed Dax's mouth. Then delivered the death blow. The one I was hoping I wouldn't have to use, because it would hurt so much. "Every time I see you, all I think about is the baby I lost. I can't Dax. I just can't. Please let me go."

And because that man would always give me whatever I wanted, he did.

He let go of my fingers, despite the agony written all over his face.

He let go of me, despite the fact I wanted to fall straight back into his arms and tell him it was all lies.

He let me go because it was what I'd asked him for, even though I knew I would regret it for the rest of my life.

I walked away before I couldn't. My legs shook, my fingers trembled. My father's men fell into step beside me as we rounded the corner, out of Dax's sight.

That was when I finally let the tears fall silently down my cheeks. Mourning him. Mourning the baby we'd lost. Mourning the future we could have had together if I had been someone else.

I let my uncle lead me to a blacked-out car. He put me in the back seat.

I didn't even acknowledge my father sitting on the other side, waiting for me with slicked-back hair and an expensive suit.

He didn't try to touch me. Just nodded, like I was a good dog and he was pleased by my obedience.

It took me a long moment to even realize there was anyone else in the car.

But when I noticed the man sitting on the opposite-facing seats, my blood ran cold. "Why is he here?"

My father settled back in his seat, crossing his arms over his chest. "Your fiancé wanted to meet you in person." He glanced over at the man. "See? She is just as I said. Worth every penny, is she not?"

The man's dark gaze rolled over every inch of my body, my skin crawling beneath every sweep of his beady eyes. "Indeed, she is. For once, we agree on something."

I shook my head at my father. "What are you doing? I'm not—"

His palm smacked across my face so hard blood spurted in my mouth.

I clapped my hand to my stinging cheek and stared at him in shock. He had never been a warm man, never loving or kind. But he'd never laid a finger on me.

Apparently, that reprieve was over. I was no longer something sacred.

I was just another one of the women he beat up on.

I stared at him with feral anger raging inside me. "This is who you've chosen for me? This is who you want me to marry? A fucking Guerra?"

The man sitting across the car smiled like a serpent, all teeth and hiss and venom.

My father was marrying me off to his enemy.

The End.

Want to read the scene where Violet has her baby and they find out who the daddy is? Grab the free bonus epilogue at www.ellethorpe.com.

There's more to come from Saint View! Nyah's story, Saint View Blood and Ink is coming in 2026! Get it here

If this is your first trip to Saint View, check out the Also By pages at the end of this book for stories about Bliss, War, Scythe, Rebel, Fang, Grayson, Kara and more of the characters you met in Murder Squad.

ACKNOWLEDGMENTS

I can't believe we're saying goodbye to another Saint View trilogy. If you'd told me back in early 2020 when I wrote Saint View High that I'd still be writing in this world almost 6 years later I would have been so shocked. I think this year's trilogy was a little bit different, with a strong lean into dark rom com that has been insanely well received. I'm so glad you guys loved X like I do, as well as his dynamic with Whip and Levi. I can't wait to give you more of that sort of humor in future books.

There's an ever growing group of people who make these books possible and they all deserve the hugest thank you.

Thank you to the Drama Llamas. You guys make my days fun. If you aren't already a member, it's a free reader group on Facebook where I share all sorts of stuff. Come join us, everyone is welcome. www.facebook.com/groups/ellethorpesdramallamas

Thank you to Montana Ash/Darcy Halifax for writing with me every day and being the best office buddy/work wife ever.

Thank you to Sara Massery, Jolie Vines, and Zoe Ashwood for the constant support, friendship, and book advice.

Thank you to the cover team:

Wander Aguiar and his team for the photography.

Thank you to my editing team:

Emmy at Studio ENP and Karen at Barren Acres Editing

Dana and Louise for beta reading. Shianne, Jessica and Annie for beta listening. Plus my ARC and street team for the early reviews.

Thank you to the audio team:

Denise and Marnye at Audio Sorceress for producing this series. Thank you to Kelsey, Gregory, Sean and Theo for being the voices of The Saint View Murder Squad Series.

And of course, thank you to the team who organize me on the home front:

To Donna for taking on all the jobs I don't have time for. Best admin manager ever.

To my mum, for working for us one day a week, and always being willing to have our kids when we go to signings.

To Jira, for running the online store, doing all the accounting, and dealing with all the 'people-ing.' Not to mention, being the best stay at home dad ever.

To Flick and Heidi, for helping pack swag, and to

Thomas, who refuses to work for us, but will proudly tell everyone he knows that his mum is an author.

From the bottom of my heart, thank you.

Elle x

ALSO BY ELLE THORPE

Saint View High series (Reverse harem, Bully Romance. Complete)

*Devious Little Liars (Saint View High, #1)

*Dangerous Little Secrets (Saint View High, #2)

*Twisted Little Truths (Saint View High, #3)

Saint View Prison series (Reverse harem, romantic suspense. Complete.)

*Locked Up Liars (Saint View Prison, #1)

*Solitary Sinners (Saint View Prison, #2)

*Fatal Felons (Saint View Prison, #3)

Saint View Psychos series (Reverse harem, romantic suspense. Complete.)

*Start a War (Saint View Psychos, #1)

*Half the Battle (Saint View Psychos, #2)

*It Ends With Violence (Saint View Psychos, #3)

Saint View Rebels (Reverse harem, romantic suspense. Complete)

*Rebel Revenge (Saint View Rebels, #1)

*Rebel Obsession (Saint View Rebels, #2)

*Rebel Heart (Saint View Rebels, #3)

Saint View Slayers Vs. Sinners (Reverse harem, romantic suspense.Complete)

*Wife Number One (Saint View Slayers Vs. Sinners, #1)

*Torn in Two (Saint View Slayers Vs. Sinners, #2)

*Three to Fall (Saint View Slayers Vs. Sinners, #3)

Saint View Murder Squad (Reverse harem, romantic suspense. Complete)

* X's and O's (Saint View Murder Squad, #1)

*Whips and Chains (Saint View Murder Squad, #2)

*Reaper and Ruin (Saint View Murder Squad, #3)

Saint View Strip (Male/Female, romantic suspense standalones. Complete.)

*Evil Enemy (Saint View Strip, #1)

*Unholy Sins (Saint View Strip, #2)

*Killer Kiss (Saint View Strip, #3)

* Caged Bird (Saint View Strip, #4)

Dirty Cowboy series (complete)

*Talk Dirty, Cowboy (Dirty Cowboy, #1)

*Ride Dirty, Cowboy (Dirty Cowboy, #2)

*Sexy Dirty Cowboy (Dirty Cowboy, #3)

*Dirty Cowboy boxset (books 1-3)

*25 Reasons to Hate Christmas and Cowboys (a Dirty Cowboy bonus novella, set before Talk Dirty, Cowboy but can be read as a standalone, holiday romance)

Buck Cowboys series (Spin off from the Dirty Cowboy series. Complete.)

*Buck Cowboys (Buck Cowboys, #1)

*Buck You!(Buck Cowboys, #2)

*Can't Bucking Wait (Buck Cowboys, #3)

*Mother Bucker (Buck Cowboys, #4)

The Only You series (Contemporary romance. Complete)

*Only the Positive (Only You, #1) - Reese and Low.

*Only the Perfect (Only You, #2) - Jamison.

*Only the Truth - (Only You, bonus novella) - Bree.

*Only the Negatives (Only You, #3) - Gemma.

*Only the Beginning (Only You, #4) - Bianca and Riley.

*Only You boxset

Add your email address here to be the first to know when new books are available!

www.ellethorpe.com/newsletter

Join Elle Thorpe's readers group on Facebook!

www.facebook.com/groups/ellethorpesdramallamas

ABOUT THE AUTHOR

Elle Thorpe lives in a small regional town of NSW, Australia. When she's not writing stories full of kissing, she's wife to Mr Thorpe who unexpectedly turned out to be a great plotting partner, and mummy to three tiny humans. She's also official ball thrower to one slobbery dog named Rollo.

When she's not at the office writing, she's probably out on the family alpaca farm, trying not to get spit on.

You can find her on Facebook or Instagram(@ellethorpebooks or hit the links below!) or at her website www.ellethorpe.com. If you love Elle's work, please consider joining her Facebook fan group, Elle Thorpe's Drama Llamas or joining her newsletter here. www.ellethorpe.com/newsletter

www.ingramcontent.com/pod-product-compliance
Lightning Source LLC
Chambersburg PA
CBHW050603170726
48283CB00001B/80